THE PRICE OF RETRIBUTION

AN AMERICAN TRAGEDY

JOHN ANDERSON

In memory of Papa Gene, Grandma Tillie, and Grandma Christina—
Heroes of love and mercy.

To request permissions, contact
andersonbookworks@gmail.com

Paperback: - 979-8-9988492-0-6
Hardback: - 979-8-9988492-1-3

Printed and bound in the USA
Book Design | Kexa

A Warning from the Author

To my average believer readers,

Beware: here, there be monsters.

The journey ahead is dark, graphic, violent, and *scary*. For this story to be told appropriately, many mature elements were necessary to convey the crucial message and themes it explores. Due to its graphic nature, the wicked men who reside within, and the horrors that await, it is necessary that I encourage you to proceed with wisdom and warning.

Guard your mind. Be careful with your heart. Turn away if you must.

The villains and heroes in this tale extend beyond the page, having the potential to reach into your mind to your *detriment* if you are not careful. If you feel the journey becomes too graphic, terrifying, or challenging for your spirit, turn away *immediately*.

Live to revisit this tale another day.

Though my work is intended to challenge believers and non-believers alike, this is no venture to be taken lightly. In stark contrast to the first novel, which is a tale of hope and light, this is a story of desolation and darkness.

I will always be appreciative of your love and support for my work, but the last thing I want is for you to be stumbled by it. If the monsters in this story become too scary, *be cautious*.

Read if you can, but if you cannot, *run*.

This world is hungry for *you*.

~ John Anderson

CONTENTS

But in the middle of a time,
in a world much like our own...

CHAPTER 1

Upon His Rock, He Proudly Stood

ind brutally cut through the Arizona trees as the snow whipped mercilessly across Michelangelo's face. The winter had been long and harrowing, and its ending was as unexpected as its beginning. Snow had grown increasingly thick over the past four months, the blizzard beating relentlessly against the face of the Northern Arizona Territory. Michelangelo rode his horse along the vague outlines of a trail, visible only by the faint horseshoe indents that headed in one direction. His mare heavily trod over the same territory, the snow solidifying around her hooves, giving out loud crunches. The snow was packed to thin ice, old and hardened, only occasionally taking on a soft and powdery texture when snowstorms like this one gave it a fresh coat. The two were surrounded by a thick forest of long-stretching pines that rose dozens of feet into the midnight sky, the moon shedding its light upon the snow-covered forest. The trunks had piles of tufted snow at their base, similar to the branches that occasionally let their clumps loose when gusts of wind violently hit them. The forest was vast, with miles

ind brutally cut through the Arizona trees as the snow whipped mercilessly across Michelangelo's face. The winter had been long and harrowing, and its ending was as unexpected as its beginning. Snow had grown increasingly thick over the past four months, the blizzard beating relentlessly against the face of the Northern Arizona Territory. Michelangelo rode his horse along the vague outlines of a trail, visible only by the faint horseshoe indents that headed in one direction. His mare heavily trod over the same territory, the snow solidifying around her hooves, giving out loud crunches. The snow was packed to thin ice, old and hardened, only occasionally taking on a soft and powdery texture when snowstorms like this one gave it a fresh coat. The two were surrounded by a thick forest of long-stretching pines that rose dozens of feet into the midnight sky, the moon shedding its light upon the snow-covered forest. The trunks had piles of tufted snow at their base, similar to the branches that occasionally let their clumps loose when gusts of wind violently hit them. The forest was vast, with miles of darkness surrounding it; the only sign of life came from a lantern-lit saloon twenty feet away from his current position.

It was a cold and deadly time, and the snow that fell upon this land was as cold as the killers who traversed it. February 1902 marked the end of the outlaw era; this land was no longer home to outlaws, but a land of men and monsters.

Michelangelo rode slouched, his head down and his hips firmly placed upon his mare. She was a beast of pure muscle, with dark brown fur covering her body and a long black mane and tail whipping in the wind. Her nose was black, leading to a black diamond on her forehead, her eyes scanning her surroundings amid the dark brown of her irises. Her hooves and ankles were black, matching her mane and tail. Everyone knew what she was—she was easy to identify when she marched. Michelangelo, on the other hand, could not be said to be the same.

He was a different creature.

Michelangelo wore a blue Navy man's hat with a broad, round brim covering his head. A thick yellow string wrapped around the base of the headwear, tied firmly together, led to the knots that closed off both ends at the front of the headpiece. They were frozen solid and were held among the collected snow that weighed the hat down. It had been heavily stacked against his shoulders, lap, forearms, and steed's mane. She bowed her head and took the same stance as the soldier. The bottom of his locks sprouted from under the headpiece's shielding, the flakes freezing. His hair had grown long and wavy, ending just below his ears near the middle of his neck. It was as brown as his beard, which had grown long enough to cover his mouth, chin, and neck. A bushy, curly, and untamed monstrosity stretched down to meet the uppermost part of his collar. His eyes were a deep green, and his skin had an olive complexion, with wrinkles stretching from his eyelids. The overgrowth of his facial hair covered his mouth, the puffs of oxygen occasionally flowing through as he breathed the freezing air from his lungs. Slightly frozen droplets built up on the bottom of his mustache, adding to the light ice that coated his beard.

He wore a large, navy blue winter jacket that covered his body and stretched to just above his knees, the collar surrounding his neck. The jacket had white, puffy fur that fluffed out slightly, particularly around his neck. Large black buttons held the coat together, each holding the loops sewn into the right side of the jacket. Large black winter gloves were at the end of his sleeves, helping him fight against the cold of the hour, much like his black boots, which were frozen just the same. They were black rider's boots with two leather straps around the calf, held together by buckles that complemented another strap and buckle, firmly around his ankles. They were a worn and scraped pair, each caked with miles of mud and snow. His pants were tucked into the top of the boots, tied tightly just below his knees. It was a slender look that major generals had, identifying their role in the United States Military, ideally, from head to toe.

The rounded tips of his footwear rested firmly in his mare's silver stirrups, his toes freezing solid through the socks and leather. Michelangelo's pants were navy blue and featured two yellow stripes running straight down the outer sides. His hips were adorned with a gun belt holding two holsters, each containing a navy revolver. It was a faded, brown leather, frozen firm. The navy revolvers had silver metal with golden inlay etched in. The inlay was wavy and trickled down like a growing stream from the barrel. The wooden handles were stained a blended yellow and brown color, with the grizzly bear's design carved into each innermost grip. Right behind his right-hand revolver was a large hunter's knife that measured approximately six inches in length. The blade was made of black steel; the handle was darkened brown wood. The knife seemed to have flakes of a dark red substance caked in between the wood and the metal—an uncleaned residue from Michelangelo's previous hunt.

Michelangelo wore a button-up underneath his navy blue jacket, silver metal buttons lining the center of his chest in two rows. It was a long-sleeve shirt that fell to his wrists, tucked into his blackened gloves. The sides of his shoulders had two rectangular patches with two yellow stars sewn into the middle. These stars were complemented by a dozen tiny golden stars sewn into each patch's borders. Despite being made for a large man, his outfit fit him snugly, neither too tight nor too loose, given his beastly and athletic build.

He towered over the average man at a whopping six feet tall and two and a half feet wide. Even at thirty-three, he intimidated those who looked upon him. In most cases, those who saw him never looked into his eyes for fear of what they might have seen, which worked in his favor, given that his eyes had a tired, weighted look. His mission had been exhaustive, plagued by an unforeseen and mysterious snowstorm that had been there from the start.

He looked at the Navy-issued saddle, which was made of material consistent with that of a blanket, noticing a leather strap coming loose. He reached down and gripped the frozen, hardened material and pulled it down firmly, anchoring it to his beast's belly. The loose and wavy blanket was scrunched under the torque. Michelangelo looked over at the patch of leather on the other side of the saddle. It, too, was worn, and though it was designed for Union soldiers to rest their legs, these had been worn so much that they might as well not have been on at all. White stripes followed along the border of the blanketed saddle, creating a prestigious design.

A rugged leather canteen with a silver steel coating on the bottom was near the stirrup. The cap was made of the same metallic material and was easily removed due to the grips that quickly spun under the lid, allowing the owner to drink with ease. Behind him, upon the saddle, a large sleeping bag was strapped to the back of the seat. A one-man canvas tent was found tied beside it, the slight rips and tears revealing the tent's old age and constant use. The sleeping bag was a dirty white color, just like the canvas tent, with the only difference being the size of the tent compared to the sleeping bag. Strapped beside his horse's front leg, on the right side of the saddle, was a double-barrel shotgun that aimed past her, loaded and ready for use, with a shoulder strap attached to it at the end of the barrel and stock. The strap hung loosely below the saddle holster, lightly tapping against her as the wind tapped it. On the left side of the saddle was a major general's saber, out of sight and out of mind, hidden within a navy blue casing with a faded, yellow, metallic gold handle. The hilt was molded in a perfectly rounded "C" shape, only made more apparent by the broad golden grip that attached to it. The handle and hilt protruded from the navy casing, ready for use.

However, this sword was nothing more than a second thought to Michelangelo, for the mission he acquired needed far more than sabers and swordplay. He needed bullets and blunderbuses that were fit for the savagery of Man's state.

Behind him hung two large saddlebags that flopped heftily on each saddle side. They bounced against his mare's hips, the frozen snow-topped lids stationary. They were worn in the shape of a "U", with tiny leather strings hanging down the front of the lids. Inside the bag on the left side were a small number of supplies needed to make a campfire, including a flint and steel that had been chipped away due to constant usage. A lit lantern hung strapped beside the bag, for there was no light in the blizzard's late-night hours, as the moon could not shine through the thickness of the stormy sky.

The right saddlebag was filled with ammunition boxes, a small collection of munitions that Michelangelo had acquired that could destroy a small army. As he approached the saloon, which shone with a drunken glow, he slowly reached down and felt the bag, checking its weight to estimate the remaining contents, then leaned over to the other side and put out his lantern with a gentle and quiet twist of the lantern knob. His face hardened into a deepened, angry frown, the flesh below his eyes darkening from an unrelenting fire that overcame his exhaustion.

It was this that would enable him to complete his mission.

His mare heftily made her way to the outside of the saloon, noting the lot in front of the building, which was filled with slightly less-deepened snow as the faint, muddy remains of hooves and footprints slowly filled with snow. This saloon was a rest stop, the halfway point between the surrounding towns. In front of the saloon were many wooden posts built to tie your horse to the infrastructure. The posts took the shape of a wide lowercase "n" and were made of wood, tied together by thick straps of light brown leather. Seven horses were around the side of the saloon, settled underneath the horse keep, and in front of it, there were only three. Michelangelo eyed the last post up front, just off to the right of the front swinging saloon doors. As he arrived, he hopped off, hitting the ground with a weighty thud, the snow shifting, smashing, and crunching beneath his weight. He led his mare and tied her to the post, then looked up into her eyes and petted her, doing his best to warm her freezing neck in the wintertime cold.

"Won't be long, Bleu," he comforted.

He looked back at the saloon, the orangy white light shining upon his face, then quickly took in his surroundings. The pine trees encased the entire building, standing high in the back and on the side, only being stopped by the trails that were cut for the many travelers who traversed this trade route. He grimaced and breathed one deep breath in and out, then made his way to the three steps that led to the porch. It was a light brown wood put together in a pleasant and presentable fashion. The roof paired perfectly with the porch and was supported by four posts. The guardrails were built into the bottom half of these posts and bordered the entire front of the porch.

Michelangelo looked up at the sign just above the roof, now moving out of his view. The sign read 'Saloon,' but from what he had discovered, the spot was more accurately and formally referred to as 'Alcy's Point.' He looked forward at the saloon doors again, gently and barely waving in the winter wind, making his way up the stairs, then at the windows on each side of the doors, noticing the snow piled in the corners of its old, aged wooden border. He focused on what was inside: on the left, three men sat quietly before the window, smoking their cigars and staring at the table before them, lost in a resting emptiness that all had come familiar with. On the right, a room full of men. All of them, save the bartender, had a particular attire. It was intentional and agreed upon, taking the form of black winter jackets and jeans, paired with black boots to match. Their clothing was worn from miles of travel, and underneath, they wore buttoned-up shirts that were a range of simple, poor man's clothes, sharing the look of faded whites and greys that even a simple farmer might wear. Their bandanas and hats were black, the same.

He looked back at the bar with its single bartender serving drinks. He wore a clean white button-up shirt and some black slacks to contrast. He wore a white apron and shiny black shoes that would make a churchgoer moderately jealous. His hair was combed and parted down the middle, black and slicked, just like his mustache, which was pointed at the ends and curled upward for a fancy presentation, actively portraying the bartender as a man of prestige. Glasses were stacked high behind him, all made of different colors, sizes, and, most importantly, alcohol choices. The bar was complemented by a round, closed-front counter with an exit, featuring a slim lifting frame on the right side, towards the back of the building. The bar counter was shiny, letting the dark brown top glisten despite its dingy habitat. Two men sat drinking whiskey at the bar, hunched over and staring through the wooden counter beneath them as though they stared into their souls' abyss. They cupped their empty glasses in their hands, with only slight signs of brown liquid coating the rims of the cups. Those who still had drinks drank them from similar dishes, holding that yellowish-brown liquid that sloshed and warmed when it hit their gullets.

Michelangelo looked over the saloon doors and saw inside, noticing the five tables within, all of which were kept just as clean as the bar's counter. Their dark wood reflected the fire within the establishment's fireplace, similar to how it did off of the four chairs at each table. At the table, near the right-side window, two men were playing cards and smoking cigarettes. The table behind them had three men wildly and uncontrollably eating their meals with more food in their beards than in their mouths. Then, he saw it. He saw them: two men, one large and bulky and the other skinny and weasel-like. Michelangelo clenched his jaw but forced himself to focus. He looked just beyond the two and saw the stairs that led to the second-story floor wrapped around the interior of the building, creating a balcony that let one overlook the whole scene. Regardless of its glory, it was still somewhat under construction. Thus, the top had not yet completed adding rooms meant to be 'stayed' in.

Michelangelo figured no one would be up there, given that no normal man would need to be. He refocused on the first floor once again, noticing the large stone and mortar fireplace rising through the middle of the stairs. The light brown wooden stairs wrapped around each side, connecting like water that flows around a rock in a stream. This made the room hot, negating all wintry weather that might flow in, even from the self-opening and shutting saloon doors. The fire seemed to crackle and pop louder than the whistling winter storm, keeping the place aglow with its radiating, flickering, bright, and beautiful glow, which made it comfortable. It lit the room with a red and orange light, like the lanterns on the walls and some of the tables, pairing well with the faint glow of the burning cigarettes in the men's mouths as they inhaled. Plumes would flow from their mouths, choking the oxygen in the atmosphere and sinking deep into the lungs and nostrils. Michelangelo looked back at the rock chimney that led out of the roof, blew out a bit of air from his nose, and shook his head gently as he pondered the irony.

He rotated his shoulders, then slowly tilted his head side to side as he clenched his teeth with an angry, slow bite. Then, like a phantom stepping from the shadows, he walked in, gently pushing the saloon doors in, a brisk gust entering with him. The men's attention in the room started to shift toward the soldier. The chatter slowed and silenced as more eyes began to look at him. They were fixed, tense, and, for some, horrified. Michelangelo looked back at them under the brim of his hat, making eye contact with each other as the deafening silence became apparent. Each of his heavy steps ended in a booted thud against the wooden floor, followed by a creak of the wood. The wind howled outside, now heard through the window, as the fire crackled, almost quivering now that the soldier had entered. The flakes on his hat's rim and jacket started melting, flaking, and plopping onto the ground as he approached the back.

He took note of their filth, their low upkeep—the faces of devils that hid themselves underneath the flesh of men. Two dozen eyes targeted the soldier, the smoke flowing from their cigarettes to the ceiling, each man inside the saloon not moving a muscle. They were tense due to his invasion of their privacy, which, to those who knew, was a surefire sign that something was wrong. Those eating soup had food dripping from their mustaches and raggedy-hair-ridden chins; those playing cards lifted their eyes just above the decks as their cigar smoke climbed from the tips' embers. The men who sat alone with their thoughts lifted their heads and leaned back in their chairs as their arms dropped slightly nearer to their revolvers. Knowing he was good and noticed, Michelangelo focused on one man in the back, sitting as stiff as a board and as pale as snow.

It was as though he had seen a ghost, and worse than this, that the specter had seen him.

A big man sat before the weasely one. He stared at Michelangelo, grimacing and presuming what his business purpose was. He waited for the soldier to make a move, not knowing how he would do it, but his only job was to protect his weasely boss's life at all costs. On the other hand, the weasel stiffened with fear, to the point you'd think he was a corpse that hadn't realized it yet. With a casual change of direction, Michelangelo noticed this, faced the bartender, and made his way to his bar. He, too, was frozen in place, having stopped cleaning the drinking glass in his hand as he quietly looked at the soldier standing before him. The two at the bar paid him no mind and took two more drinks of whiskey, which were a bit larger than the last. They did their best to ignore the hulking man beside them, who was looking, waiting for them to look at him. Instead, they focused on the buzz of the liquid, hoping it would numb whatever happened next.

The tension became thicker than the wooden bar Michelangelo now leaned against. As he considered the men in the room, with their worn revolvers at their sides and their mutual dislike for him, he smiled and eased the tension in his shoulders.

"I take it you're Howard, the legendary bartender of Grizzly Pines," he said calmly with his southern, aristocratic accent. "I am," Howard replied. Michelangelo nodded. "So what's a man gotta do for a drink around here?"

Howard released a half-cheeked smile of relief as a thin layer of peace coated the room again. The bartender put down the glass he was working on as Michelangelo pulled out a dollar coin from his jacket pocket and placed it face down in front of the bartender. He began to undo his jacket, letting the fireplace warmth in, disconnecting the loops from their buttons, and pulling it fully open. As he did, he knew that though the room was a bit eased, there was still one ear and eye from every man permanently glued onto his position. He gently slid the bottom ends of his jacket behind his navy revolvers and hunter's knife. He raised one eyebrow and shifted his chin to the left, sharing a nonchalant and off-putting smirk with the gentlemen beside him, who were now staring. They looked back at their drinks slowly. The bartender took the coin; the soldier rested his weight on both elbows upon the fancy counter.

"The rumor is you like whiskey," the bartender checked. "That's the rumor," Michelangelo confirmed.

The bartender grabbed an empty drinking glass from the wall behind him, placed it before the soldier, and grabbed the whiskey bottle. He popped the cork off it and poured the golden-brown liquid into the glass. Michelangelo fixed his gaze on the liquid and thought about the appeal of drinking the entire bottle, but knew he could not do so now. He needed a clear head. The bartender slid the glass toward Michelangelo, who lifted the glass to his lips and, with a slow tilt of the head backward, drank and swallowed the burning juice with one unfazed gulp. It burned down his throat, but only slightly, warming his belly and body as its numbing started to take hold. He bit down on the flavor, placed his glass on the counter, clicked his tongue, and let out a small exhale.

"Much obliged, 'tender," he thanked tensely. "Of course," he replied with a hint of concern. Michelangelo turned to his right and made his way toward the weasel that was still cowering. His put-on smirk faded.

"Hello, Winston," Michelangelo greeted.

Winston gulped, then slowly turned to face the approaching predator. As the soldier neared him, his eyes looked higher, then higher still. Winston was a short and scrawny man. His large, black winter jacket was far too oversized for him. Like the rest, he wore a white button-up shirt and black jeans, but paired them with brown winter boots for contrast. His clothes were torn and tattered from the miles of travel he had seen, given that he hadn't changed his clothes much in the many years of life Winston had been given. Winston was about thirty-three years old and had a white complexion. His hair was short, messy, and black as coal, while his eyes were dark brown and twitched occasionally. He gulped, then pulled himself together. "Michael the Merciful!" he greeted back, with a friendly excitement. "Been a while, hasn't it?" Michelangelo replied with an empty smile. He turned the corner of the table and approached the wooden chair across from Winston's, sitting beside where the muscle was as well. He looked at the barn-sidered man who was looking up at him, then at Winston. "You gonna tell Goliath to move, or should I?"

The large man let out a huffy growl as he stood from his chair. Michelangelo followed the giant's head with his eyes, looking up at his six-foot-five glory. "It's all right,

Henry. He's an old friend," Winston eased. Henry walked away, not saying a word, creaking upon the wood far greater than Michelangelo did, bending the beams to their limit as he made his way to the table ten feet behind Winston.

He sat, crossed his arms, and watched.

Michelangelo clicked his tongue, pulled out the wooden chair, and took a seat as he gestured to Henry. "He come with a beanstalk?" Winston forced a chuckle. "I see you still got the jokes."

Michelangelo's smile began to fade. Winston gulped. "Henry's a good friend of mine. A member of the team, really. Where he goes, I go."

Michelangelo stared at the weasel in silence as he continued to ramble. Then, he took his whiskey glass from his left hand and rested it on the table. This startled Winston, causing him to stutter and go silent. Michelangelo looked at the glass and then began to rotate it counterclockwise on the wooden countertop.

"How long has it been since we last met, Winston? Fifteen years?" he looked up. "Or do you not remember?"

Winston stared silently, his smile fading. Michelangelo noted the change.

"In fairness, it wouldn't surprise me if you didn't. Remember, I mean," he lifted the glass and positioned it between a lamplight and his eyes, then turned it to examine its distortion. "You seem to be doing a lot of 'forgetting' these days." his eyes suddenly shifted to Winston's. "Now, I may be a war-torn soldier who's getting riper in his age by the day, but my memory still serves." He put the glass down on the table and leaned forward. "It's hard to forget some things, you know. Those things we had to do back then to make this country what it is today. To survive." He leaned back slightly, letting his weight rest upon his forearms again. "Or at least, that's what they told us, what they keep saying. The funny thing is, the more I keep getting told about the laws of survival, the fewer people I see surviving."

"Your definition of funny is a lot different than mine," Winston joked nervously.

Michelangelo didn't laugh.

"You know, some things are so horrid that not even a joke will lessen their impact. Some things are so coated in death and blood that you can't see anything but red. That's the only way I've seen the world. Through that shade of red, and while I looked through that tint, I had a message being driven into my head that it was all done in the name of 'good conquest.'" He chuckled and shook his head. "I wonder if there is ever such a thing." He looked back at Winston, just under the brim of his hat. "You never forget the first moment you're welcomed to the new world, that moment that taught you how cruel it *really* is—how cruel it can be." He gently tilted his head to the side. "Do you remember, Winston? Do you remember that moment? Do you know how cruel it can be?"

Michelangelo leaned in slowly, placing his left hand on his left thigh.

"Whenever you're ready," Michelangelo urged with an angry smile, his eyes straightening.

Sweat dripped down Winston's face as his heart pounded, thinking of the best way to explain the situation. "Michael," he shakily pleaded. "Listen, you got it all wrong—" Michelangelo leaned back in his chair and raised his left hand, stopping Winston's yammering. The men in the bar tensed slightly, some looking at Michael once again. "Cut the lies, Winston. You know that won't do anything for you here. Not with me." He rested his hand on his thigh again. "Last chance."

Winston's mouth was sealed with fear. "Fine," Michelangelo started again. "Why don't I remind you, and then you can tell me if you hear any bells ringing? The year was 1887. You were eighteen years old, the same as I, and I was sent down with a small batch of fresh bloods to a town of civilians just outside the reach of Fort Hollow. There were twenty-eight people in that town, one of whom was a sheriff. It was a small area—Colorado. The Great Mount Gang had slaughtered the people there," he paused. "You remember them, don't you?" Winston nodded quickly and quietly, sweat dripping from his forehead. Michelangelo smiled. "'Course you do. Yeah, they were wild boys, taking and doing as they pleased, anywhere, anytime. 'Bunch of arsonists and violators, especially of the women, who, if you recall, often ended up killing, too. After, of course."

Slight tears began to form in Winston's eyes as the memories came flooding back. Michelangelo continued, a painfully small smile forming. "Anyway, we rode up, and with the full force of the United States backing us up, we saw, we killed, and left little to no trace of those Great Mount gang members." He stopped and tilted his head again. "But little to none is not to be mistaken for none, right?" He nodded and rested his head again. "Yeah. As I recall, one member of the Great Mount Gang left alive... some young, weaselly little man who, then, went by the name of Winston Riverbottom." He leaned forward slowly and weightily. "Those bells of yours ringing yet?"

Winston's heart raced as his left hand shook, his right one reaching up to subtly stop it as best he could. Michelangelo noticed this, and although he didn't say so, he undoubtedly enjoyed moments like these.

He took pleasure in striking fear into the hearts of the wicked.

He leaned back again, a little quicker now. "Naturally, we found Mr. Riverbottom, and honestly, he was in such a *pitiful* state. Just a small, slimy, weak little weasel in a barrel he had managed to stuff himself into." Michelangelo chuckled. "We pulled him out, and before we could even get in one word, he told us how he was nothing more than a manipulated victim who was just trying to get away from a band of outlaws, but couldn't because they gripped his life. And honestly, after looking at that ratty little figure, I couldn't help but sympathize. I couldn't even blame him. After all, I was a young man, and Mr. Riverbottom was a young one just like me: a fellow caught up in a bad situation. His rulers made him feel too afraid to turn his back on those who saved him, afraid to do anything that might jeopardize his survival. Additionally, I figured a man of his size couldn't overpower even the smallest woman or kill the weakest man. So, I offered him a deal."

Michelangelo paused momentarily, remembering not to break eye contact with Winston. "Do you remember that deal?" The tear-made frown on Winston's lips began to tremble. With a deep growl, the soldier leaned forward and reminded, "As long as you don't fall in with outlaws again, you may keep your life." He leaned back and, with a tone a bit more aggressive, continued, "Now, as I'm sure you already know, Mr. Riverbottom did go free, but the ironic thing of it was that I came to find out later that he was *just* as *guilty* as the rest of the Great Mount Gang." He smiled, lifting his arms out to the side. "From the mouths of babes, it's said." He dropped his arms, his left hand sternly gripping his thigh. "The children of the town had hidden themselves far better than Mr. Riverbottom ever had, and they told us every *bit* of the vile atrocities you had done. The ones they were forced to watch as they hid in the places only their mothers knew. Some of the things they said... I couldn't believe it."

He crossed his arms and shook his head. " *'That weasel?'* I thought. *'That slimy, little weasel?'* Couldn't be him." His eyes darted to Winston's. "But then I remembered." He leaned forward, putting his right arm on the table and his left arm on his thigh. "There was a condition to the deal I gave Mr. Riverbottom for his deal, and it was that in his failure to uphold his end, I would hunt him down and kill him just like I did his brothers."

The men in the saloon were all watching now, waiting and listening for the other boot to drop. Their hearts pounded, but nowhere near as much as Winston's, whose body shook just as severely as his hand.

"Fate truly is a cruel and betraying mistress, isn't she, Mr. Riverbottom?" Michelangelo teased.

"Michael, please," he cried. "I-I don't know what you heard, what you know, but it's not true—"

"Ah, save your words, weasel." He swatted the air in Winston's direction with his right hand. "If I wanted to kill you, you'd be having a conversation with the Devil himself about your misdeeds rather than me." He rested his shoulders. "I'm here to offer you a new deal: information for salvation. How does that sound?"

Winston released a heavy breath of relief, a smile frantically spreading across his face as he dried the tears. "What, uh— what kind of information?" Winston opened up gladly. The soldier's eyes tightened. "The kind that gives me the location and name of the man you've been working for. The man who's been giving you your murderous marching orders for about six months now."

A series of twelve revolver hammers clicked, echoing through the bar. Winston's relief and smile slowly faded from his face. Michelangelo continued to stare him down.

"You remember who you work for, Riverbottom?" the man at the bar piped up.

"Well, we certainly hope so," Michelangelo quickly replied, turning to the man.

"Otherwise, I'll have to go to the next best man, which, judging by your mouth, that's as big as you are, just might be you."

"You ain't getting a peep out of me, out of any of us."

"What makes you think I want a peep, not a piece?"

"You couldn't get a bit of either."

"You're right, I'd get a lot. Big man, big target, big mouth. You're easily my next go-to."

"Michael," Winston interrupted. "Winston," Michelangelo interrupted back, re-directing his attention. "Though I did not ask for Porky's input, I agree with what he said: it would be good to remember whom you work for, Mr. Riverbottom."

Winston sighed, letting out a nervous smile. "Though I understand what you're saying," he started, gesturing to the other men with his head. "Look around... do you see where you're s-sitting? Twelve fully armed men are here, w-waiting to fill you with lead. Do you really think *any* of us will give you his location, much less a name?"

"So it's a he."

The men growled at Winston. His breathing began to be labored. "N-no! No! That's not—" he composed himself. "This is just a small group of men, Mike... what you're up against is an army. There are still hundreds of men all over th-this countryside. We also know you ain't got no cavalry coming with you or after—"

"Half an army," Michelangelo interrupted.

Winston stuttered to silence. "I beg your pardon?"

"There is *half* an army of men all over this countryside, if not less." He tilted his head slightly to the side. "Do you know why that is?"

The tension heightened, and some of the men's hands in the room shook as they gripped their revolvers. Michelangelo looked back at the bartender, standing completely still, frozen in a cleaning formation. "He knows," Michelangelo clarified, looking back at Winston. "He knows about 'Major General St. Hart, the man of justice.' " He looked back at Winston. " 'Judge, jury and executioner, all in one man.' That's why the cavalry isn't coming. The U.S. Government won't attach itself to it. Not in these 'prosperous' hours."

He leaned forward slowly as his chair creaked, his arms crossed on the table, sliding the glass cup across the wood just before Winston. His eyes widened, the two only mere inches away, and Michelangelo's shadow was overtaking Winston almost entirely.

"Certainly, you know the stories of men like you piled high across the state of Arizona, of men like you who've been lying low but know a little more than they should about the man I've been trying to find. Men like you who have watched me single-handedly take his leader in every one of his occupied towns, only to find *men like you* stashed away in bars, shacks, or wherever else you *rats* manage to hide out. Men like you, who may not give me a name but will always give me a location, leading me to more *men* like *you*." He paused for a second to let the comments sink in. "In some capacity," he continued, "Men like you must register somewhere in that tiny little mind of yours that every single one of those dead men led me right here, and they were all *men like you*."

He turned to the group. "Every one of you." He looked back at Winston. "Everywhere I go, a trail of blood follows behind me, sending a message to every wicked man who hears my name that they, too, will bleed. I am the nightmare that haunts you in your sleep, only so you awaken to a hellish grave; I am the wrath of God come to pass judgment upon monsters and destroy all who are found to be villainous." His voice lowered to an

27

angry growl. "You may have heard of me and know my name, but you have not *seen* my vengeance. So, as you ponder your next words, I suggest you choose them *very* carefully, for they may be your last."

Winston breathed shakily. "Mike, I— I hate to go here, but why do you care? Now, all of a sudden. I can't help but think that it's because your brother died."

All reason and thought began to drain from Michelangelo's mind slowly.

"We read the story. 'Outlaw Saves Believers Holding Last Remaining Bible,' so it read—a touching tale. What happened to him to make that story happen was a shame, but what would b-be the bigger shame is *this*.

Is this how you honor his memory? Continue his story? Or are you just trying to change what happened? To right the wrongs?"

Michelangelo didn't answer.

"I mean, I get it, Mike, I d-do. Grief is a horrible thing, but your brother owed the same retribution you're giving to us. How is that fair? Why are we the only ones who have to pay?" Winston got more comfortable, confusing Michelangelo's silence with an agreement. "Look, you've heard t-tales like this, tales of vengeance. But what about ones of mercy, Mike?" He touched Michelangelo's sleeve gently, his eyes darting down to Winston's unwelcome hand. "You showed mercy to me once. That's the Michael I remember. A man who was merciful to even the most wicked, who would show mercy to his brother of wickedness if the opportunity presented, and would not do to him what you have done to us." He released, resting his hands on the table again. "I mean, are w-we not all brothers as the sons of Man? As your brother, allow me to take the first steps of mercy by telling you to stop this while y-you still can. This 'justice' i-isn't worth the bloodshed."

Michelangelo looked down at the glass cup in his hands, gripping it tightly. "See, that's where you missed it, Winston." He looked up into Winston's eyes abruptly, the fire within them burning redder than the hottest flame. "The story was never his. It was always mine." Michelangelo's muscles enlarged slightly as he tensed. "I've spilled blood in the name of justice that amounted to nothing… but *this* blood? *Your* blood… every last drop will amount to *everything.*"

He slammed the glass across Winston's face, the tiny, sharp pieces shredding Winston's left cheek and forehead as Michelangelo grabbed Winston's crossed wrists with his left hand. Blood seeped through Winston's skin as he let out a frightened yell, the glass only slightly tearing Michelangelo's black glove. He wasted no time and furiously unsheathed his hunter's knife with his right hand, stabbing it through the center of Winston's hands straight into the table. He threw his head back and screamed, the men in the bar standing from their seats clumsily, fearfully, pulling their revolvers out and aiming them at the soldier. Winston looked down at the handle stuck out half an inch from the top of his hand, the blood immediately seeping through both openings as tears flowed from his eyes. Henry stood, alarmed but not unwilling to rip into Michelangelo with his bare hands.

"You better get your boys. It looks like they're just about ready to fill you with more bullets than blood," Michelangelo said, holding the knife with his left hand as he pulled his navy revolver from his right holster.

"*No! Don't shoot him!* The entire U.S. Government will be on this bar in a week! I don't *need* that; I don't *want* that! Please!" The bartender pleaded, throwing his hands in the air. Michelangelo loaded a round in his revolver's chamber, aiming it directly at the center of Winston's forehead.

"No, they won't, bartender. He's a problem just the same as the rest of us," one of the men piped up.

"Besides, unless one of us is a rat, they ain't gonna know," another one said.

"Who's gonna tell? I ain't gonna tell," another one agreed.

"If you kill a Major General, you will give them *every* reason to come down here! That's all they've been waiting for, all they need! I'm not sure who he is, but I'm sure he wouldn't want that," the bartender pleaded again.

"They won't find his body out here in this blizzard," a neighboring man agreed.

"Then let's end him. He's just a man after all... right?" another man with a cigar concluded.

"You're running out of time," Michelangelo urged Winston.

"*Wait! Wait*, okay, *please! Don't shoot!*" Winston begged as tears of fear and pain flowed from his eyes.

Michelangelo squeezed the handle of the knife with his left hand and kept his revolver pointed at Winston's forehead. "Now... *where is Caine Kingsley?*" Michelangelo interrogated in a low and gritty tone.

"*I don't know!* I don't know! No one knows!" Winston informed honestly.

"There's always someone who knows something," Michelangelo corrected as he twisted the knife.

The blade began to spread the flesh and bone in the center of Winston's hands, cracking and tearing as he let out a scream of agonizing pain. The men winced in fear, some dropping their aim slightly. Michelangelo's face hardened with an angry frown, his eyes furrowing into an enraged tilt.

"Tell me where he is, and this is all over!"

"I don't know! I don't know! I swear!"

Michelangelo let out a growl, then began to move the knife forward and back in his hand, slowly separating the skin. Winston screamed louder than before as blood covered the knife, his hands, and parts of the table. "*Icarus,*" he let out. "*Find Icarus!* He can tell you everything you want to know!" Michelangelo eased up a bit. "He's the only man who's been given a location," he continued, the other men re-aiming with sighs of disappointment. "He rides with three other men, the four horsemen!"

"Where?" Michelangelo questioned, Winston's tears and groans of agony replacing his response. "*Where!?*" Michelangelo repeated more viciously, twisting the knife further, snapping Winston's hand bones, and stretching his bleeding flesh more open.

"They just left a town called Guarida Del León!" He cried. "That's all I know! That's all I know! Please, stop! That's all I know," Winston revealed, sobbing. The porky man at the bar sighed. "Ya'll know we have to kill them both now," he reminded.

"It'll be the last thing you do," Michelangelo warned.

"Whoa, whoa, whoa, easy now, gentlemen," an unseen voice interrupted. He walked out onto the balcony with heavy footsteps, both black revolvers aimed at the men by the windows. "Let's just take a minute to breathe."

A few of the men at the far end of the bar, nearest to the windows, adjusted their aim to the black man in the black Ringo hat, puffy black winter coat, black gun belt, gloves, jeans, and boots.

"That's the Brother of Grim," one man said, dividing even more of the attention of the men below. "What's he doing here?" Another asked.

The attention was now evenly divided between the hunter, soldier, and weasel.

"All good questions that will all have answers in time, but before we get on to killin' one another, why don't we just take a minute to think this *through?*" He looked down at Michelangelo. "Now, my friend here has gotten himself into a tricky, albeit *stupid*, situation, but that does not mean we *all* should die over his outrageous actions!" He looked up at the men again. "I don't know about you, but I would much rather stay alive than get myself killed over a firefight that could be avoided! Now, whether you share this sentiment with me or not, one thing I know for sure is that nobody wants to be dead before the moment they expect themselves to die. That said, I would much rather *you all* be dead if it means my friend here gets to live. Therefore, as you can see, the deck is stacked. For those of you who don't know my reputation, one thing you should know is that if the Major General dies, you all die, and I will come out of this alive. That is a fact. Not a promise. Not a threat. Just a fact. So, I propose a way out of this where we all come out of this alive," he said, looking over to Michelangelo, continuing with, "And it begins with you putting the revolvers down and the Major General letting the little fella go."

Michelangelo noticed the Grim's arrival but didn't shift focus from Winston, who now had an inkling of hope within his eyes once again. The men in the saloon looked at each other briefly, then began lowering their weapons.

Michelangelo ignored the actions entirely.

"I thought you were retired, old man?" A man asked.

"Retire-*ing*. Still got some money to make on account of my last job going south," William humored with no smile.

"If we let the Major live, Icarus will kill us, or worse," a man by the window reminded.

"I'd rather take my chances with Icarus than the Grim," a man behind Winston determined.

The men lowered their revolvers entirely as the negotiations had come to a close.

"Now, Mike, this is the part where you let Mr. Riverbottom go," William reminded calmly.

Michelangelo heard no words, nor did he see any other man. Winston was Michelangelo's only focus. This was a shared sentiment on Winston's behalf, given that he had no choice but to stare at the soldier before him, hoping the pain and despair in his eyes would move him enough to let him go.

"What gives you the right to talk about him?" Michelangelo started. "What makes you *think* you have even the *slightest* weight of worth in this pitiful life you've lived, even to think of his name?"

"I'm sorry, Mike! Truly, I am! P-please just take the deal! I can make it right!"

Michelangelo let out a deep, angry, and breathy growl from his throat.

"Okay, okay, the deal then!" Winston reminded. "Remember the deal! Information for salvation, right?"

Winston's body shook with pain as Michelangelo stared blankly. The words Winston spoke came forth, but weren't enough to break through the sound of the rage-fueled fire in his mind. "You know what I hate about weasels, Winston?" He asked in a deep tone. "They prey on young, defenseless, tiny creatures. Whether sneaking into bird nests and killing the unborn to survive or thieving and scavenging what others have wrought, they will always be cheaters, liars, and pests."

"Mike," the Brother of Grim interrupted.

"They can't help it," Michelangelo ignored. "It's in their nature to be vile, to eat the weak. Anywhere and anytime, as long as it ensures they'll see tomorrow. But when a weasel meets a predator bigger than it, it runs and hides in the deepest hole it can find, waiting for its moment to come out again. But when the predator gets it in his mind that he's going to kill that weasel and end its life, it doesn't matter how long it waits; it will eventually get eaten."

"Mike, that's enough!" The Brother of Grim tried again, Winston's lips trembling with fear.

"So why don't I make good on our first deal, little weasel? Why don't I save us *both* the time and send you to the deepest hole I can find, somewhere where the holes burn hot, just behind the fiery gates of Hell, so that when my work on this earth is done, I will find you there again, even if only to feel the *satisfaction of killing you a second time!*"

"No!" Winston screamed.

"Ah, hell," The Brother of Grim readied.

Michelangelo pulled the trigger, blasting a round straight through Winston's forehead and out the back with a bloody stream. His head jolted backward, then forward as meaty chunks and blood splattered onto the men behind him. As Winston's body went limp, Michelangelo flipped the table he was on forward so it leaned on its side, letting Winston's body tumble to the ground while his hands remained stabbed into the wooden tabletop.

The Brother of Grim fired off two rounds from his weaponry, promptly zipping through the two men by the window. They stumbled a moment, then leaned backward as they reached for the holes in their chests, trying to hold in the blood that gushed forward, but were unable to. They fell forward onto the flooring behind them, thudding upon the wooden floor, dead. Gunshots rang out from every direction as the bartender dropped behind his counter, screaming in fear and sorrow as bullets riddled his building. Bullet holes popped into sight with explosions, filling in the riddling walls and furniture, especially the table that Michelangelo had put down and was currently hiding behind as cover.

He sank lower to the floor while bullets continued to splinter and explode the table's portion above his head, with only a few strays exploding into the wood beside him, the splinters and wooden pieces flying in every direction. He pulled out his left navy revolver and pointed both upward, clicking the hammers into a loaded position and waiting for his moment to return fire.

The Brother of Grim shot ten more rounds rapidly, with every bullet meeting its mark. The man beside Henry jerked backward as a bullet hit his chest, a spurt of blood shooting out until, eventually, another one came out of the back of his skull. Henry flinched as he watched the lifeless body fall backward onto the floor, as three more bullets blasted through the center of the fat man by the bar's chest. He clumsily toppled back into the bar counter behind him, sliding its front as a thick, bloody streak smeared behind him. The second man at the bar table took five bullets, shaking his body left to right as each one ripped through his torso. The last bullet shredded through the second man's lower stomach, forcing him to fall forward face-first, a pool of blood forming around him. William dove down to the balcony floor as bullets redirected towards him, each exploding the wooden floor around him and blasting holes through the ceiling above.

Henry grew furious and, appropriately directing his fury, charged toward where Michelangelo was taking cover. He stood, both revolvers aimed, but within seconds, his eyes widened in surprise. Henry grabbed Michelangelo with one hand, lifted him off the floor, and slammed him into it. He dropped his revolvers as he gripped Henry's massive arm, air shooting out of his body. Before the soldier could think, Henry lifted him off the ground again, grabbed his left leg, lifted him above his head, and launched him through the wooden wall. Michelangelo blasted through the wall and toppled through the snow, coating him in the freezing powder as he fought the painful daze. He reached his hand to his head to feel for injury, noticing his navy blue Hardee hat had gone missing. Henry effortlessly stepped through the opening in the wooden wall as Michelangelo wobbled to his feet before a large and thick pine tree, focusing on Henry as best he could. He looked behind Henry, noticing his revolvers were inside Alcy's Point, then quickly reached for his hunter's knife. As he felt the empty sheath, he remembered it was lodged firmly in Winston's hands. Henry's face contorted in anger as he picked up the speed.

"Great," Michelangelo complained, struggling to breathe.

Henry's right arm swung with a broad and loud birth, prompting Michelangelo to dodge underneath and hear the weighty meat stick whoosh by his head. Michelangelo used the force of his leg, upper body, and arm to smash his fist into Henry's ribs, then redirected that same punch to his right knee, dropping him to the ground and enabling Michelangelo to grab the back of Henry's head and smash it into the pine tree before him. The soldier tumbled backward, still trying to catch his breath, as Henry shook his head, stood, wobbled for a moment, then turned around, unfazed. He looked down at Michelangelo while he looked up in disbelief. "Seriously!?" He breathed.

Henry smiled.

Michelangelo charged the most powerful punch he could and struck it across Henry's face, which nudged slightly to the right, only making him angrier. Henry turned with a twisted face of rage as he walked forward, grabbed Michelangelo again, and launched him to the right into the saloon with a loud slam. The soldier dropped to a seat in the snow, barely able to see, then quickly tried to get up. Still, before he could fully rise, Henry marched over, grabbed him by his shirt and leg again, and lifted him above his head.

Michelangelo braced.

Henry launched Michelangelo through the saloon's exterior wall, exploding it and sending wooden and glass shards in every direction. The bartender curled into a ball on the floor, ducking underneath Michelangelo, who slammed into the backside of the wall underneath the bar's counter. The counter's lip hung over him, protecting that area from most of the falling glass. The smell of alcohol fumigated the room as the liquid from the broken bottles soaked into his clothes and the floor around him. He looked at his coat, torn and cut just a bit, then noticed the blood dripping down from his cheek, slit from a stray shard of glass. It was then that he felt the pain that coursed through his body, seemingly squeezing and pressurizing his muscles and bones as he twisted and turned in pain, doing his best to recover as quickly as possible. Amid the lack of focus, his right elbow bumped the bar counter, unhooking the double-barreled shotgun hidden underneath it, landing it firmly on his lap with a heavy plop. He held the gun weakly as he focused his vision, snapping the barrel open and noticing two slugs loaded within. He clicked the shotgun closed and looked through the hole he had just made, then to Henry, who was walking through the first one.

He reached down and grabbed Michelangelo's left ankle, yanking him out from under the bar counter and hitting his head on the counter's bottom in the process. Henry rosined his meaty fist behind him as Michelangelo flicked back the shotgun's hammers, aiming it at Henry's chest and giving Henry pause. The gun boomed as both barrels launched pellets through Henry's chest, spraying blood and launching him backward onto his back. Blood seeped through Henry's shirt while Michelangelo caught his breath.

In the time since Michelangelo had exited and re-entered the saloon, the Brother of Grim had reloaded his revolvers with the bullets attached to his blackened gun belt. He flicked the revolvers shut and, using the distraction of the shotgun sound, stood and aimed his right revolver at the last seven men. He aimed from the hip, pulled the trigger, and flicked his free hand against the hammer twice. They hit one of the men by the window, piercing his heart and painting the windows behind him red. He fell forward limply. The other man beside him took notice and then redirected his attention to Michelangelo, who was now limply standing on his feet. He aimed his revolver at the soldier, but not quicker than the Brother of Grim, who flicked his hand back against the hammer three more times, sending three heated bullets into his opponent's gut. Michelangelo noticed this man, who was now dropping his aim and teetering. He began to drop his aim as his facial expression turned blank. Taking advantage of the moment, Michelangelo pulled back his arm and launched the shotgun like a flipping sword, the barrel end smashing into his face. His head flicked backward as he tumbled into the window, busted open by the brutal impact of the flying metal, and succumbed to the bullets that filled his stomach.

Michelangelo hurdled over the bar counter and ran in the man's direction, his body starting to lean forward limply. Gunshots erupted behind the soldier as five men fired at his moving target, one of whom was primarily focused on the soldier, exploding the wooden wall just behind him. Michelangelo slid over the table, slammed into the man, and flipped around, using him as a meat shield for the oncoming bullets. They thumped and splatted into the body, making it flick and twitch as Michelangelo made himself as small as he could. As he did, the Brother of Grim aimed his right revolver forward and fired off his last two rounds. The first one hit the shotist's chest, stumbling him a bit, and then the other hit his head, jerking it to the left as he slowly slipped over to the floor.

Michelangelo looked down at the feet of his meat shield and noticed its standard revolver on the floor. He leaned down, picked it up, and as the meat shield's life had entirely faded, he carried its weight. The other four gunmen redirected to the Brother of Grim, which let Michelangelo drop the body and take off running sideways, shooting the three rounds that were loaded in the revolver by rapidly flicking the hammer with his left hand. Two bullets zipped through one shooter's heart, and the last found itself in another one's leg. That one flinched over in pain as Michelangelo dove behind his initial table, dropping the spare revolver and grabbing his two navy ones. Bullets flew by Michelangelo from the other two men, while William marched down the stairs and shot the right rib of the man who had been shot in the leg. The rib-shot man collapsed to the ground, allowing William to fire off two more suppressing rounds to get behind the left side of the fireplace.

The two men, untouched, turned to William in the center of the saloon, and in that instant, Michelangelo stood up and let off five booming rounds. The man closest to the table flicked to the right, then to the left, and the right again as the three searing pieces of metal made contact with his left shoulder, his right ribs, and his right upper chest. The last man took two bullets to the chest, forcing him to fall backward as his gun fell to the floor, hitting with a metallic thud as his hands reached up to hold the blood that came pouring from his chest cavity. The soldier hastily walked over and aimed his right revolver forward while his other revolver remained in his left hand. The last man fell to his knees as Michelangelo stood above him, the barrel of his gun pointed at his forehead. His eyes widened as blood oozed from his mouth, fear gripping his dying body. He looked at the soldier and tried to speak, yet the liquid forming in his throat would not let him. He slowly raised his bloodied hands to the side as the Brother of Grim turned around the corner of the fireplace to see what Michelangelo might do. The last man's hands shook in terror and pain as his lips quivered with blood dripping from his mouth. "Pl— please... I'm begging you—" he muttered.

Michelangelo pulled the trigger and blasted a hole clean through the last man's skull, his head flicking backward as his body fell to the floor. The thud led to an immediate and harrowing silence that the soldier and the hunter shared, both staring at the blood puddle behind the last man's head that began to form. The faint sound of fire crackling came back as the pitter-patter of blood did. Twelve bodies filled the saloon, and blood was speckled and splattered over the walls and floor as the winter's cold blew in. Snow lightly trickled through the bullet holes and gaping breaks in the walls, which landed gently on the floor inside. Michelangelo breathed heavily as blood dripped down his cheek, his busted lips resting and bleeding. The Brother of Grim was untouched and looked to Michelangelo with concern. Michelangelo, noticing this, turned and walked away from the body, holstering his revolvers without care and making way for Winston's corpse. The

Brother of Grim watched Michelangelo as he holstered his weapons; he did it slowly, with a sense of carefulness, so as not to alarm the soldier. The bartender slowly stood behind his counter, tears filling his eyes as he looked upon the mess in his saloon. "Why... why'd you have to kill 'em... why couldn't you just *walk away?*" He questioned.

Michelangelo paid no mind and instead knelt beside Winston's stabbed hands, attempting to pull his hunter's knife from the table that they were skewered to. William walked up behind the soldier slowly, keeping his distance while trying to close the gap.

"Not to fall in with The Bartender here, Mike, but... yeah. Why?" He asked. Michelangelo pressed his boots into the wooden flooring to improve his pulling position for his knife, firmly grasping its handle with both hands. "We had a deal," Michelangelo replied sarcastically, ripping the knife and Winston's hands from the table. He reached over and grabbed Winston's jacket, cleaned the blade with slow and steady wipes, and then looked up at William. "He broke it," he reminded.

William shook his head. "I suppose you're referring to the old deal, not the new one."

"What else?" Michelangelo responded, annoyed.

He looked to his left and noticed his navy Hardee hat beside him. He leaned over and grabbed it from the floor, quickly placing it atop his head. Wasting no time, he turned and made for the saloon's front doors.

"You ain't no saint! You're a vile man, just like the rest of 'em! Just as wicked and easily as unjust!" The bartender yelled at the soldier.

Michelangelo stopped and turned his head to the bartender, still in tears due to the state of his saloon. Giving what little empathy he could, he considered the bartender's grievances. "It took me years to save up to renovate this place," he continued. "What am I supposed to do now? How will my kids eat? Might I tell them it was the great 'protector of our nation?' Some soldier who brings as much shame to his uniform as he does to everything he's meant to stand for? *All for what?* For *vengeance!*" He sobbed. "You know what I hope for, Major? I hope someone puts a bullet in you just the same as the rest of them. All you vile and wicked men, involving the rest of us in the wars you wage! Why must we pay for what they've done; why must we pay for your injustice?"

The bartender broke down, crying on his bar table. Michelangelo pondered the question but figured it was pointless to share the truth of his motives, given the bartender's state of mind. He was not asking in hopes of getting answers but to express his disdain for the soldier. He had already decided that this mission Michelangelo was on was no more than a mission for revenge, which the soldier knew it was not.

"Tell me, bartender," he started. "You sleep guiltless knowing that you pay for your children's food with blood money? Or do you pretend you don't know where their money comes from?" The bartender looked up. "I reckon you consider this a blessing rather than a curse, considering it was only a matter of time before they took your blood, too. Your kids will be fine now. You will, too." He looked forward out the saloon doors. "Figure it out like the rest of us."

Michelangelo walked out of Alcy's Point. The Brother of Grim followed distantly behind. Before he left, he took pity on the bartender and walked over to his counter. The bartender looked at him, somewhat angry but seemingly disgusted. William took out twenty-five dollars from his pocket.

"This won't cover much, but it's the best I can do to try and make up for my friend's behavior." William compromised, placing the bills on the counter.

The bartender looked William up and down and then at the money on the counter. He took the money and turned around, placing it in his money box underneath what was once a wall of alcoholic beverages.

"Didn't know a black man could have such generosity," the bartender commented as he sniffled and composed himself.

The Brother of Grim forced a smile as he squinted his eyes, composing himself. "You treat all folks who offer you help like this?" he questioned. "No. Just some," the bartender clarified. "But I am grateful." William gritted his teeth as the bartender turned around, happy to take the Brother of Grim's money but unhappy to see him still standing there.

"You know," the Brother of Grim started again. "Sometimes I think about the past, about who I was before. I wonder if the man of violence is gone, and this new man of diplomacy has taken his place. On days like today, it's all I can think about. I think to myself, 'It's a shame that when I visit that old man, when I'm forced to relive my past, other people end up dying.' Then I wonder, 'What's one more? Who would know? Who would tell?" He gestured to Michelangelo outside by pointing his thumb backward. "Would he? Probably not! So then I think, 'Well, what would happen if the good ol' blood money bartender just so happened not to survive a shootout with villainous scum. Would anyone ever know?'"

The bartender gulped.

"What do you think, bartender?" Grim reminisced threateningly. "If you were in my shoes, what would you do?" The Bartender looked quietly at the men's bodies and then back at Grim, who was now resting his right hand on his revolver handle, waiting for the bartender's response.

"I think folks like myself are grateful for your generosity and hospitality," the bartender corrected in an intimidating tone.

The Grim forced a smile and rested his right hand. He stood tall and was content with the bartender's answer. "See. Was that so difficult for you?" Grim finished.

Grim turned and walked over the bodies as he went outside to the bitter cold of Northern Arizona, shaking him to his old brittle bones that wanted to rest. He closed his black bear fur jacket and tied it with the buttons. He was an old man who had survived sixty years of age, so the thickness of a coat like that, mixed with the black winter gloves he just put on, was an absolute necessity. The Grim had grown a full beard, which was bunched up two inches off his face. His hair had grown in a curly puff, sticking out significantly behind his ears. The grey in his hair peppered his beard and head hair, slightly showing underneath his black Ringo hat.

The Grim stepped off the steps of Alcy's Point and looked to Michelangelo, who was now finishing up releasing the horses that belonged to the twelve dead men inside the saloon. Once done, he swiped his gloves clean, walked over to Bleu, checked her straps, and ensured they were ready for departure. Grim noticed the haste and figured it was time to have a conversation. It appeared he didn't have much time. It was pitch black outside, and the winter's wind howled as snow fell through the air. Even the light that shone from Alcy's Point was overpowered by the endless wall of the forest's void, which left only a tiny bit of light to dance upon the snow that was swallowed into the white-laden ground below.

William sighed. "Given what I just witnessed, I think the best thing we can do right now is have a conversation."

"I have no interest in conversing with you, William," Michelangelo replied, still focusing on Bleu.

"So whose interest trumps whose? I'm heavily vested in the conversation."

Michelangelo turned quickly and powerfully, staring down the Brother of Grim, who to him was William, like an apex predator might for a challenger. William stood motionless as he analyzed the situation, wondering if he had misread Michelangelo.

"Why is it you're *really* here, William?"

"I'm here to help you, Mike," he backed up slightly and tried to ease Michelangelo's anger by motioning for him to relax with his hands. "I know I have done nothing that would lead you to trust me, but I am asking you to... just this once." Michelangelo gritted his teeth as he debated whether or not to believe him. "Not because it's best for *me*," he continued. "But because it's best for you." He shook his head. "I— I hope you take this in no offense, but... I mean... look at yourself, Michael. You're on a rampage, leaving a trail of bodies everywhere you go and nearly getting yourself killed each time you do it. More than that, I mean... I hate to ask the same question as poor, dead Winston, but I gotta know: why are you doing this? Killing all these men in this manner. What's it all for?"

"I don't have time for this and certainly don't have time for you," Michelangelo answered, ignoring him as he turned back to Bleu.

"You gotta give me something here, Mike. Anything," William followed. "Is it really that simple? Is it vengeance? Or some noble quest to right wrongs? Collecting debts? What?"

Michelangelo stopped once again and looked back at William with an annoyed straightening of his eyes. "It's more than just vengeance, Bill."

"Is it? Because from where I'm standing, those bodies in that saloon say otherwise. We could've spared them, Mike, but you chose to kill every single one of them, especially after Winston mentioned Thomas."

Michelangelo paused momentarily, letting out a deep sigh at the mere thought of Thomas's passing. A heavy pain draped over Michelangelo's heart as he reflected on the loss of his younger brother. It was relatively fresh, given that only a little over four months had gone by since he had died. He sighed.

"I won't lie to you and say that Thomas's death doesn't have a part in all this, but he is not the only reason I am out here. Winston was a dead man before I ever walked into that saloon."

"Because of what he did in 1887?"

"Because of what he did a few weeks ago."

William's head tilted in confusion. "Weeks?" Michelangelo shook his head. "In a way, I wish that he were doing what I found him doing in 1887... that would've been far less severe." He looked back up at William. "He and those other men there were following orders of 'the one they call Icarus.' Going around, town to town, and killing people."

William clenched his jaw. "For what?"

Michelangelo clenched his. "Their beliefs. Thomas's mess was nothing compared to what's happening right now. Innocent people are still dying by the hundreds, and no one's doing anything about it."

"And you think that's on you; you think you can end it?"

"No. There isn't any end to evil, Bill, but you can fight it."

"Fight it? It's not much of a fight if you're one man against an army."

"Tell that to the rest of them."

"Or we could tell the government about it and let them do this *legally*."

Michelangelo let out an annoyed laugh. "Seriously? This, coming from you?" He shook his head. "What's the government's work ever done for the people, especially the dead? How about the people Icarus and his men are heading up to right now? The government gonna help them? Did they help the folks of Saintsfire or Ciudad de Cristo, among dozens of others? It work out for them just like it worked out for Thomas?"

"*Thomas* was an outlaw, Michael. Whether you want to admit that or not, he was a wanted man who *killed* people, just the same as these men do. Now, he died a good man, and there's no denying that, but do you *really* think that if he had lived, he would've been thought of as 'The Saint of Salvation'? He hurt people, Mike. Innocent people. His death was his redeeming quality."

Michelangelo's body tensed as his fury furnace lit once more. "Why are you here, William?" William noticed this and slightly changed his tone. "Look," he sighed. "I'm just trying to help." The soldier scoffed. William continued, saying, "I am sorry about what happened. It could've played out so much differently, but it didn't. I won't deny that, but we can still make different decisions today to fix the damages of the past and mend the world of tomorrow."

Michelangelo let out a passive chuckle as he looked down and shook his head. "I can't tell whether you're a snake in the grass or a sheep-clothed wolf on the prowl," he looked up with rage. "But one thing I know for sure is that you *reek* of lies." He gritted.

"Mike—"

"Don't *Mike* me. Where do you get off talking like we're still family? You think you've earned that privilege again?"

"Whether you like it or not, we still are. That's how family *works*."

"Oh yeah? What about Thomas? You talk to him like he was family before you stabbed him in the back?"

"Stabbed him in the back!?"

"Don't play dumb with me, William."

"What are you implying?"

"I'm not *'implying'* anything!" He shook his head, looked away swiftly, and then looked back. "You know, I've been entertaining you like a man entertains a mosquito, meaning that eventually, with the right repellent or swatting, it goes away, but you, my friend, are like a fly—"

"Oh, brother."

"A pest that refuses to go away, yet here you are, somehow still sticking around."

"Because I've come to help you, Michael. Is that so hard to see?"

"*Yes! It is!* You helping me the same way you 'helped' Thomas?"

William sighed.

"Sigh all you want, but I believe the words coming out of your mouth just about as much as I believe your story about Mt. Restmoore."

"Oh, okay. Well, in that case, *please* elaborate on the fallacies of my story."

"You mean how you 'just so happened' to be at that same mountain at the same time that The Brothers of Boudiclare were? How you conveniently showed up after Thomas killed them and then proceeded to try and claim the bounty?"

"Which I was honest with you about."

"And if I had not shown up, would you have still been honest?"

William shook his head. "It's not like that, Michael."

"Right. It isn't like you set Thomas up because you didn't have the stones or wherewithal to kill Thomas yourself."

"I didn't kill Thomas!"

"Didn't you, though?" Michelangelo said, stepping toward William powerfully, the hunter slowly and carefully stepped back. "The kids told Peter everything, Bill. They told him how you dropped them off with Tommy, knowing good and well what was going on with all this believer-killing business. And unlike you, Tommy was no child killer, not even indirectly. You set him up, set them *all* up so you could cash out of the business." The soldier stopped inches from William's face. "At least that's how I figure it." He paused. "You're nothing but a coward in a suit of intellectual armor—a killer just the same as the rest!"

William looked down and noticed Michelangelo's hand gravitating toward his hunter's knife, unbeknownst to him. He looked up swiftly. "I never planned on them killing Thomas!" He lied.

This gave Michelangelo pause for a moment. "I find that hard to believe. How did you expect him to survive what you put him against?"

"Clearly, you didn't know the extent of your brother's abilities."

"And you have *forgotten* the extent of mine."

"The point is, Michael, that though I did not plan on his downfall, I didn't plan on his survival either."

"No, the point, Bill, is that you planned on a paycheck, and you put the lives of family, *our family,* and *children* on the line so that you could get it and run off to your little dream home in Florida. That still right?"

William was taken aback by Michelangelo's memory of the Florida home, given that it was something the hunter had mentioned decades ago. The soldier noticed this in William's micro-expressions. "I'll tell you like I told Winston," he continued. "I remember things. I figured you might remember things the same way, but apparently, you're happy to forget how things played out. More importantly, Thomas was family before he was ever a bounty."

William stepped back slightly, putting his arms out in a sacrificial declaration. "Michael, look at me! I'm here! I'm here now, trying to help you and make things right! How much more family could I be than I am right now?"

"And, what, you think that'll make things right?"

"No, that it'll at least be a start."

"Right, since you're here now, I'm supposed to forgive and accept you after everything you've done. 'Just bring you back into my life. That it?"

William huffily dropped his arms to his sides, slightly shaking his head but not looking away, waiting to see if Michelangelo would accept the offer. "I'm just trying to help you, Mike. Trying to make sure that your story has a different ending."

"So that's your means of business, then? That's why you haven't left, because you want to 'save my life?' "

"It's as I said. I just want to help."

"You want to talk me out of it."

"If that's what it takes, yes."

"Oh, it'll take a lot more than that." Michelangelo approached William again. "But since you want to talk, tell me the truth. Tell me this isn't some ruse to collect bounties?"

William looked between the soldier's eyes quietly as he placed his hands on his hips.

"Tell me it's not about the money." Michelangelo pried.

The hunter sighed. "I ain't gonna lie to you—"

"I knew it," the soldier confirmed as he turned his back on William and returned to Bleu.

"No, hold on, let me finish!" William pleaded as he walked after him.

"You're no different than four months ago," Michelangelo concluded angrily.

"You removed half the bounty, Mike! You paid me half for one of the most infamous gangs in the Arizona Territory and *robbed* me of my retirement! Disagree with my methods all you will, but that was wrong! Illegal!" Michelangelo rolled his eyes and shook his head, adjusting the bags on Bleu's rump. "What else would you like me to do?" William continued. "People are losing respect for me just as quickly as they're forgetting outlaws existed, and I know you can relate to this because you're just as much a phantom as the rest of us."

"Always running that mouth," the soldier said to himself.

"Can you at least understand that a man in my position needs to act now, or he will not have a tomorrow? And isn't that what it's all for, what it should be for, is a tomorrow?" At the sound of the curious comment, Michelangelo turned around haughtily. "All we've got is today, Bill. Except for those who are dead." They both looked at each other tensely in the snowy silence. "They don't have anything."

William nodded and looked down, sighing. He looked up again. "You're a hypocrite, you know that? What, so you can come out here for 'retribution' but acutely ignore or even manipulate yourself into believing that this has nothing to do with Thomas? Do you have no ulterior motive? Yet, when I do it, suddenly there's a problem."

Michelangelo sighed and looked off to the side. William proceeded.

"I'm here, Mike. Yes, for the money... but I'm here for you, too. I would say, primarily."

The soldier looked back. "You know you have a fascinating way of justifying your means with your ends."

"It's only human, Mike. It's what we do."

"It's what a dying breed does," he concluded, turning around and wiping the snow from his saddle.

"Exactly! A dying breed! Different times, Mike. What happened... it had widespread ramifications that I don't even think we can process—"

"That makes one of us."

"*But...* what we know is that I need money to survive, just the same as you need to bring death to wicked men. So... let's help one another as a family does, but rest assured knowing that I will try to stop you as best as I can."

Michelangelo said nothing, continuing to ignore William. "Look," the hunter finished. "I'm aware I made a mistake, that my selfishness resulted in where we are now, but I would not be here if I weren't trying to make things right. Let's be honest, at the rate you're going, I could follow behind you like I've been doing, let you do all the work, and collect the bounty... but I didn't do that. I'm here... for you."

Michelangelo looked down at the ground, planted his hands on his hips, and shook his head. He looked up and turned around to face the hunter, now sharing a compassionate look similar to the one he had given the soldier many decades ago.

"I know none of this will bring Thomas back," he continued. "But I'm not trying to. I'm just trying to make sure you don't join him."

"And I appreciate that, Bill, but you have to understand how much this situation stinks. Take a whiff from my nostrils for just a moment and see what you smell—"

"I know. I know. I've broken your trust beyond repair."

Michelangelo sighed.

"Let me make it right, nephew." William reminded.

Michelangelo sighed as he pinched the bridge of his nose, contemplating the idea of the Brother of Grim tagging along. Though he didn't want to admit it, he wanted, even needed, him to come along. Family was what he needed now, more than anything, but with a heart as equally broken as his trust, he didn't know if he could. That said, of all the people to join him on his quest, William was his best bet. Even broken, their bond was stronger than any other that could be formed in these lands.

"All right. You come along. Collect all the bounties, I don't care," he said, looking up. "But I need to know one thing, and I need you to look me in the eye when you tell me straight." He stepped closer to William. "Did you work with Kingsley?"

William squinted and tightened his jaw as he looked into Michelangelo's eyes, wondering whether the truth or a lie should come forward. What would come next if he told the truth? Given Michelangelo's current state, whose lives were at stake, and the outcome for all possible scenarios, William gave the best answer possible, though it was a lie: "No." Michelangelo darted between the hunter's eyes, skimming for deception in the old, wrinkly sockets.

He couldn't find one.

"And you don't know where he is or where I might find him?"

"No, I do not."

The soldier clenched his jaw and nodded. "Well, all right then," he finished.

He mounted Bleu, letting William turn and do the same, first letting out a high-pitched whistle to Betsy, his horse hidden behind Alcy's Point.

"I know I might sound like a broken record, but have you thought this through? Hunting down Caine? Killing as many men as you're killing? I mean, at this point, it doesn't even seem like you have an inkling of self-preservation in doing it... Especially after this little stunt in the saloon."

"Yes, I have a plan."

"I figured as much; I know you're smarter than this." William turned around. "But you're getting reckless, and that tells me either the frostbite froze your brain or you planned on dying here tonight."

Michelangelo looked up.

"Am I getting warmer?"

"I'm just getting tired," he said, looking down and adjusting Bleu's reins.

"*Or* you've realized that this fight is bigger than you can handle, and you may not be willing to fight it anymore."

"Maybe," he started, casually looking up with kinder, more welcoming eyes. "But now, I've got the Brother of Grim with me. I doubt death is something I need to worry about."

William nodded gently as Betsy rounded the corner, trotting towards him heavily, the ground thudding beneath her hooves. She was a large and loyal Clydesdale with hooves the size of heads and a body the size of a small wagon. She had once carried William's bounties in a stagecoach for multiple purposes. Still, with the shortening of business and a newly developed plan, William decided to abandon the stagecoach and adopt a single-rider approach. Betsy was black, coated in coal-like darkness. She had a large black saddle upon her back, with black saddlebags filled with ammunition on each side. A scoped rifle with a black shoulder strap on her right side was attached to the saddle. It had a blackened steel and wood frame, presenting an intimidating appearance that was enough to make any once-upon-an-outlaw think twice about breaking the law.

This was the reputation of the Brother of Grim, but to William, it seemed his reputation had lost its power. His rifle was just a rifle; black was just a color, and the Brother of Grim was now William Davidson. This lack of identity scared him, but it also opened up new opportunities and ideas.

It was Thomas's parting gift to him, and he wouldn't take it lightly.

As he thought about this, he stuck his left foot in Betsy's stirrup, pulled himself atop her, and adjusted himself in the saddle, stiffly and slowly. Michelangelo did the same with Bleu, only far more easily, turning her towards Guarida Del León. They both stared into the night.

"This path you're on only ends in darkness. There's no winning for you in this. No satisfaction, no joy. You may attain your retribution, but you will not win. You can't win. And I'd prefer it if you didn't die in the process." William tried.

"All paths end in darkness now, William. It's only a matter of which path you choose to take on it. But I figure... the more these monsters lie buried in the ground, the more others may be able to prosper," Michelangelo replied, looking at the hunter. "No one will have to feel what I felt, or more importantly, feel what these people are feeling. This mission... It's not just about me. It's about them. And if I am to die, I'd rather die fighting for something worth fighting for than whatever else I've been."

William looked at Michelangelo and nodded once. The hunter looked forward at the trail before them, ready for the coming journey. Michelangelo followed suit, but before he did, he looked down at a dark brown leather cowboy hat, rugged in its years, topped with a brown strap that held it in place around the base. The brown strap was tied together in a braid-like fashion just above the brim. It was Thomas's hat, carefully tied just below Bleu's reins upon her saddle. Michelangelo looked at his fallen brother's hat and placed his hand upon it as he had done many times before. He moved it slightly, making sure it was well attached. William noticed this and sighed only loud enough for him to hear, feeling more regret than grief.

As Michelangelo caressed the hat, he thought about the vengeance he had brought upon the Arizona North. He wondered if it was truly the punishment of wicked men or perhaps the punishment he gave to himself. Maybe the punishment was equally distributed and equally earned. Despite Michelangelo, the soldier, being sent to do retribution's bidding, he could not be sure of the truth. This was a common theme in his life recently, for even with William, he didn't know whether or not he was telling the truth, although he was inclined to believe him.

There were many inclinations that the soldier accepted through great inclination these days. Regardless, he knew he could not win this fight. He knew he was doomed the moment he started, but he could not let the hands of the law handle this injustice, this evil that had plagued the people of this free land with such horrifying atrocities. He felt fire and fury rush back into him as he remembered his mission, leading him to tap Bleu with his right heel and make way for Guarida Del León.

Unfortunately, one day ahead in travel, there was one who was already preparing for his arrival, who would challenge the very base of the believer's faith and the lion that rested amid his pride. He was as mortal as any man, yet seemed not to walk among them.

He was a man of infamous renown, known by the name Icarus.

CHAPTER 2

Thought to Bring Peace and Sow Only Good

eople talked about the town known as Little York. It was a town built on the cusp of a new age and had developed accordingly. The roads were paved with fine blackened stone that lay a path for horse-drawn carriages. The horses clopped up and down these brick-laden roads, and the city folk dressed in fine winter linens. The people walked up and down the sidewalks in front of the buildings, some made of wood and nails, and others, newer ones, made with red brick and dark-brown mortar. The town was so beautiful that even the sheriff's office was stunning in its presentation.

The General Store was a simple yet clean building, and of all the buildings in the town, it most closely resembled the Old West: it was a small, wooden store that had modernity being built around it, slowly but surely encroaching. It was a tiny shack that starkly contrasted with the times, hanging on by a whim and only moments away from being forgotten by time. The front of the store had two large windows that allowed for peering in, placed perfectly and evenly on each side and centered beside the dark wood door.

Although the store was a relic, it was not alone. Horses carried passengers with the same description, and the store owner was similarly frozen in time. The horses waited for their riders as they stood before the horse ties of the town: thin metal poles that stuck out of the sidewalks before every business. Each was masterfully topped with a golden-colored horse's head as a hitch, shining and seeming polished despite their constant use. Not a day went by that a horse wasn't attached. The hitches led into the sidewalks made of grey, hand-poured concrete, freshly paved in perfect squares, and designed for maximum visual appeal and walking convenience. The only wear the sidewalks had seen was that of the fancy shoes that clicked upon them, thereby maintaining their new and fresh feel.

The people notably walked on the sidewalks, and each man and woman took on particular characteristics that the town's culture had created. Men walked with a sort of elegance in a nonchalant strut and did not seem to mind the world or the people around them. Their clothes were expensive and delicate, consisting of dark top hats paired with long, black winter coats that reached just below their thighs. Most men wore a monocle just above their mustache that the bartenders and barbers had trimmed and shared. It was combed, thin, twisted in style, bent upward at the ends, and waxed to maintain its form. They favored classic white button-ups and black slacks, paired with shined black dress shoes to match. This was often what many would call 'Little York culture,' illustrating the substantial amount of money that passed through. The women were dressed in wide, vibrant dresses made of reds, blues, purples, and greens. Each wore a fur coat made of fox or mink, the skins of the creatures commonly looped around their necks. Both the women and the men walked about as though they owned the town, and, in all fairness, most of them did.

Clouds of grey and white filled the heavens above, and the town's rooftops were packed with clumps of snow, solidified by the freezing temperatures. The winter snow only added to the beauty of Little York, dropping delicate details of white upon the town to accent its darker, more earthy colors. The blizzard that came the night before had painted the town white, and though it had now calmed, it continued to work its artistry. The snow fell in a slow, quiet way that was peaceful and chilling. Icicles hung from every building's lip, and the ones from the theatre's sign were particularly massive. The Aland Theatre was a large, thirty-foot-tall building named after the acclaimed director who had impacted far more souls than any mortal could count through her inspirational plays, performances, and musicals. The theatre's sign was placed at the top, the letters slightly raised over the lip of the roof, making for a bright and clear signal that every member of the town, and even abroad, could see. This theatre was the tallest building in Little York and was made of excellent red brick, with two wondrously accenting windows; its borders were painted with delicate gold, on each side of the massive crimson doors that led directly into the lounge. The windows let in light from the outside world while also allowing the outside world to peer in, as the yellow and orange light electrically shone upon all those who would walk in front of it.

To the left side of the Aland Theatre was the barbershop, a small business that was a mere one story, topped with a flat roof. The shop was large enough to accommodate five men, who came in regularly for haircuts to maintain their dashing good looks. An Italian-made barber's pole proudly twirled its cylindrical red, white, and blue, just beside the painted red, white, and blue lettering in the window that read 'Obed's Barbershop.' The shop was painted a light, earthy green, and the window was rectangular, with crystal-clear glass, allowing everyone sitting comfortably inside to be seen. The front door was beside the glass on the furthest left side, and the barber's pole hung above the front door. The passersby would watch through the large window, seeing many men getting the hair of their heads trimmed while the thick part of their beards was styled.

Just beside Obed's Barbershop was the second-largest building in all of Little York: the Hotel Emilda. It was a grand and beautiful two-story building, made of red brick and darkened black mortar, handcrafted as though for the upper class but designed to appeal to travelers who wandered through, needing food and rest. The hotel's roof had a flat, square top, and just below it, on the front of the building, was her name painted in bright yellow with a maroon accent to complement the bold font. A dozen glass windows were evenly placed down the front, with red curtains hung inside.

At the base of the building was the most eye-catching section: a large, dark wood, double-door entrance with two large, golden doorknobs. Beside it, and on each side, were two massive windows stretching nearly to the end of the hotel's front. Like the barbershop, the windows provided a glimpse inside Hotel Emilda's interior, which featured beautiful, modernized decor. Fine leather chairs, enriched wooden flooring, walling, ceiling, and a chandelier above fancy wooden tables stationing dozens of men and women eating their gourmet meals. However, the most appealing aspect of Hotel Emilda was its view. If one were to go to the hotel's second floor, they would be treated to an incredible sight overlooking the land before them: the snow-covered peaks known as Mt. Sorrow.

The Mount Sorrow Mountain Range was as tall as it was wide and was primarily black. However, this season, one would notice the mountain's white snow inching closer and closer to the ground from the top.

To the right of the Hotel Emilda were the ides of nature's end, the wet, snowy mud flattened and plowed, the small patches of snow building where it could, just ten feet past. Nature fought against the inevitable expansion of Little York into the dark green beyond, where dense pine tree forests stretched high and far, obstructing most of the town's visual features, save for the Aland Theatre.

On the other side of the street, before the hotel, were massive piles of trimmed wood, tied together with old rope, stacked in empty, muddy, and snowy lots reserved for future real estate development. Not much construction had occurred since the snow began to fall, and given the sudden arrival of winter, the constructors were forced to store the materials in the best way they could, though most were now damaged or destroyed. The General Store was the only building that stood on the other side of the road for now, nearest to the surrounding snowy woodlands. Its backside led directly into nature's territory, and before it and to the right was a vast, circular, open street of black brick and mortar road, acting as a communal center, where individuals walked and gathered, the horse-drawn wagons passing by and avoiding the improperly placed pedestrians. Its intended use was to expand three more roads, similar to the one that had already been built. Evidence of more roads being built could be seen on the circle's borders, surrounded by snow and mud, save the Sheriff's Office, which bordered the outer edge of the circle.

The Sheriff's Office was a large, white, wood, marble-accented building with a prestigious design. Pillars stood in its four corners, while the top of the building took on a strong, square, and firm image. The windows on the front of the building were simple squares, complemented by two large, white, seven-foot-tall wooden doors. The Sheriff's Office was the fanciest building in Little York, and that was intentional. They wanted to ensure that any outlaw or civil disorder across these lands would understand that this town was not to be messed with.

Little York took after its older predecessor, which gave light and hope to the surrounding world. All sorts of folks would come and go, making a name for themselves in light of the changing world, embracing the new, and throwing out the old for the betterment of one and all. However, some individuals did not conform to this ideology; some stood out more than the rest, preaching on a soapbox just outside the Aland Theatre to those who would listen.

"Now, I know we've been here for a little over an hour, but I wanted to end the message with one more passage," Leonardo announced, clearing his throat. "O' Lord God, to whom vengeance belongeth; O God, to whom vengeance belongeth, shew thyself. Lift up thyself, thou judge of the earth: render a reward to the proud," Leonardo recited from memory. "Lord, how long shall the wicked, how long shall the wicked triumph? How long shall they utter and speak hard things? And all the workers of iniquity boast themselves. They break in pieces thy people, O' Lord, and afflict thine heritage. They slay the widow and the stranger and murder the fatherless. Yet they say, The Lord shall not see, neither shall the God of Jacob regard it. Understand, ye brutish among the people: and ye fools, when will ye be wise? He that planted the ear, shall he not hear? He that formed the eye, shall he not see? He that chastiseth the heathen, shall not he correct? He that teacheth man knowledge, shall not he know? The Lord knoweth the thoughts of man that they are vanity. Blessed is the man whom thou chastenest, O' Lord, and teachest him out of thy law; That thou mayest give him rest from the days of adversity until the pit be digged for the wicked. For the Lord will not cast off his people, neither will he forsake his inheritance. But judgment shall return unto righteousness: and all the upright in heart shall follow it. Who will rise up for me against the evildoers? Or who will stand up for me against the workers of iniquity? Unless the Lord had been my help, my soul had almost dwelt in silence. When I said, My foot slippeth; thy mercy, O' Lord, held me up. In the multitude of my thoughts within me, thy comforts delight my soul. Shall the throne of iniquity have fellowship with thee, which frameth mischief by a law? They gather themselves together against the soul of the righteous and condemn the innocent blood. But the Lord is my defense, and my God is the rock of my refuge. And he shall bring upon them their own iniquity, and shall cut them off in their own wickedness; yea, the Lord our God shall cut them off. Psalms 49."

Leonardo loved visiting Little York. He loved the lifestyle and feel of this new-age haven. He would often stare at the bright lights upon the buildings at night and dream of what it would be like to live among the lavish. This was because he was led to believe that he and his brothers were never meant to be men of earthly fortune, that it was a lifestyle not meant for them.

Leonardo had five brothers, known as the Brothers' Five, until he joined the band of brothers, making them the Brothers' Six. The people of Little York gave them this name, and it was by the locals alone that they were known. That said, Leonardo earned them their small portion of 'fame,' standing up on his soapbox and preaching to the people, usually leading with a recited scripture. He had been doing this for many years, with his brothers standing beside him, either deaconing, praying, singing, or guarding, all de-pendent on what Jordan had best judged. Leonardo was an eighteen-year-old man who had not yet seen the horrors of War. He was relatively sheltered and had only been ex-posed to the best sides of humanity. Even the rich, though snooty, appreciated, adored, and favored what Leonardo did, often perceiving him as a celebrity. More so, not only was Leonardo a celebrity in the eyes of these people, but he was slowly gaining a wider repu-tation throughout the Northern Arizona Territory. Some thought him a showman, while others considered him a conman. A majority saw him as a legitimate evangelist, while a few, though radical, saw him as a prophet.

It was a heavy load for a young man to bear, but it was one he did with pride.

He was five feet nine inches tall, and his hair was a black, wavy tuft. It was long with a short ponytail. He had a trim beard and mustache that barely extended off his face, with a bit of scruff starting to come in. His skin was tanned, a result of his Mexican descent, and he lacked physical strength. That said, he did have one benefit to his physical makeup: though smaller than most and malnourished, he was remarkably handsome, as evidenced by the waves of women who made up his audience.

He wore a light brown leather jacket that was torn and filled with holes. The jacket buttoned down the middle, its dark brown buttons lining the right side. Underneath the coat, he wore a white button-up shirt left unbuttoned two buttons from the top. It was tucked into his weathered black jeans, and at the bottom of those were a couple of leather, winterized ankle boots tied up to his ankles in all their handcrafted, brown leather glory. Leonardo's jeans lay on the outside of his shoes, making the ends of his jeans wet and frozen.

He looked over his brothers quickly before he continued his sermon, remember-ing that his brothers didn't share his blood. They were united by a bond made by their faith, not their genetic makeup.

Javier Salamanca was a short spitfire, ready to fight at a moment's notice. He wore clothing that rarely fit him, as he was too small to fit most of it. But a godly man's life is often poor, and these gentlemen fit that description perfectly. They didn't have the money to contradict such statements, and Javier's look matched this description. His old jacket was made of black cloth, patched together with different worn-out jackets that he had come across over time. Beneath his coat was a union suit, a faded and stained white color worn underneath his blue jeans. The pants had patches of all the same colors sewn in, and at the bottom, much like his younger brother, he had ankle-high, brown leather boots of the same making. They were the warmest items he had ever worn, which was not saying much. Javier was a Mexican man, and he was twenty-eight years old, having been with The Brothers' Six since they had been called The Brothers' Four.

Judah Warnsworth was a twenty-five-year-old intelligent man who often managed the brothers' funds. He primarily focused on the money they would need for their people back home, their trips to Little York, and, on infrequent occasions, to bordering towns. Judah was a man of analytics and wit, though, ironically, he was perceived as one of the simplest. He was five feet eleven inches tall and slim in weight, but broad in bone structure. He had brown hair combed upward in the front as best as possible, held in place by hair oil alone. He was a white man with a flat mustache that kept his lip in check, and for his clothing, he wore a long black tailcoat that had seen better days. The bottom of the tailcoat was torn beyond repair, and the tailcoat itself was tattered with numerous holes. The buttons on the front had fallen off, and the tailcoat was held closed by a makeshift belt of black leather that Judah tied around his waist when needed. He wore a white button-up shirt underneath his tailcoat, paired with black cotton suspenders that featured a white stripe down the middle, attaching firmly to his blue jeans, which were hand-me-downs from his neighbors in the village. His jeans were too big for him, so he wore suspenders to hold them in place. He wore the same brown leather boots as his brothers, which went up to his ankles, though he tucked his jeans inside his shoes, keeping his jeans dry and his pants somewhat presentable.

They were too long for him.

Lee Solomon was a large and burly twenty-six-year-old man who was perceived to be what many would call 'the muscle.' He was a whopping six feet and two inches tall and was broader than a barn. Lee didn't wear a jacket because he claimed he didn't need one. Instead, he wore a grey, white-striped button-up that somehow managed to fit around his chest despite its large size. He had blue cotton suspenders connected to a familiar pair of blue jeans, and the suspenders stretched dangerously tight as they covered his belly. Many did not let Lee's belly fool them, for underneath the plump of Lee's build was a man with two hundred pounds of pure muscle. His shoes were the same as his brothers', and his attitude was positive. He was an Asian man and a bald one, too, for the only form of hair that rested upon his face was his thin, black, full-faced beard and eyebrows of all the same color. Because of this, Lee's appearance was often misleading, hence the reason he got the job of a deacon, or 'bodyguard.' Though Lee was as big and burly as he was, his heart was far bigger, and he was as much a man of love as he was of muscle. He didn't have a violent bone in his body, and he was thankful for this because, despite his job of protecting the very important and highly sought-after Leonardo DelMuerto, his muscles had yet to be used for self-defense.

Luke Elderberry was a twenty-three-year-old Hispanic man who stood at five feet four inches. He was incredibly athletic, making him a thin yet toned man. He often ran from place to place before the brothers. He was the scout, and though he was short, he was quick. Luke had short, curly hair bunched tightly to his head and a thin mustache beneath his visually gifted eyes. His skin was caramel-colored brown, and his eyes were as brown as the winter mud, though they shone bright and handsomely in the light. He wore an all-too-large jacket made of furs and assorted hides, hemmed by the brothers' hometown damas. Luke wore a loose blue button-up shirt with specially tailored jeans that were snug against his body, requiring no suspenders and allowing him to move with maximum speed during his constant running. His brown leather boots matched his skill set. They had specially modified insoles, all done by the handiwork of El Damas del Cuero or, to the English-speaking ear, the Ladies of the Leather, a name the brothers had given to their hometown seamstresses.

The final item Luke always carried with him was his binoculars. When Luke ran, he wrapped the binoculars tightly around his right hand, and when he was perched upon his outlook of choice, he hung them around his neck. As good as his eyesight was, the binoculars enabled him to see clearer and further, faster as he nested upon the rooftops of any town the brothers were in. He was an observationalist and often helped strategize the safest approach for the Brothers' Six to preach.

The circumstances of the time had left no room for mistakes or arrogance, and though they trusted in the Lord, they did their best not to tempt Him. Jordan often took on this responsibility and was the one to start sending Luke to the towns ahead of them to ensure they were safe, given the rise in popularity of Leonardo's name, particularly among dangerous parties. He wanted to prevent wicked men from committing any evil act, especially considering those who had recently gained an infamous reputation.

Jordan didn't ignore the acts of Icarus, and though they were intimidating, if not terrifying, that didn't stop the progression of the Word that the Brothers' Six had been given to fulfill. Thus, they would do it regardless of what or who hunted them, but as a leader, it never left his mind and plagued him even into the late hours of the night.

Jordan Helmsman was a man of stoic stature and courage. He stood six feet tall and had a solid, athletic build. He wore a dark blue coat made of cotton cloth. Beneath this was a light blue button-up shirt, left unbuttoned with one button undone at the top. He wore black suspenders attached to his black jeans and brown leather shoes. Jordan was the leader of the Brothers' Six, though he preferred to see himself as more of a guide. He was a wise man, full of valor, looking out for his brothers far more than himself and always keeping one eye on Leonardo. Jordan ran what some might call a 'tight ship' and only traveled as he felt led to, spoke as he felt led to say, and led as he felt led to lead. Because of this, Jordan was often found praying for the proper guidance and leadership for his brothers. He was a Hispanic man, and his hair was wavy and black, with grey streaks already starting to show, even at the young age of thirty-three. He was clean-shaven and had light blue eyes, with his hair kept and combed to one side, as circumstances allowed.

These were the Brothers' Six, and before Leonardo, they had traveled to many places to preach to anyone who would listen, using scriptures from a war-torn bible. They were missionaries, taking the gospel to border towns miles away, sometimes leaving for months, as they had to walk to each destination. However, these shorter visits to Little York were beneficial practice for Leonardo, especially since he had now become the group's leading preacher. Though they all could preach, not many would line up to hear them, but because of Leonardo's eloquence and handsomeness, when he stood up to preach, a whole town would line up to listen to his voice.

"We are living in dangerous times," Leonardo started, looking around at the crowd gathering, his thick Hispanic accent coming through. He smiled. "But the times have always been dangerous. Whether you're a believer or not, we can all agree that danger *is* ever-present. I know you've heard the scriptures, but I want to focus on a specific passage today, particularly from my opening." He puffed up his shoulders with confidence. " 'O' Lord God, to whom vengeance belongeth, shew thyself.' " he paused momentarily. "We must face the adversary; we must *face* the coming storm, but that does not mean we are enactors of vengeance. No sir. No ma'am. We are *servants* of *Christ*." He stepped off his soapbox and slowly walked in before the crowd, making gentle eye contact with a few audience members. "Bad men exist as they always have, just as the Word of God has. The word of God has not changed from then, nor does it change now." He looked at a young, attractive woman and winked at her. "God is the same, yesterday, today, and forever, and on these words, we stand firm." He looked at a middle-aged man and comfortingly put his hand on the man's shoulder. "Though we hear of men enacting vengeful, violent acts, we are not of those men; though there are merciless killers, we are not of those kin." He removed his hand and continued working the crowd. "We are all children of God and should carry ourselves as such. Now you say, 'Well, Leonardo, they're killing us! Should we not defend ourselves? Remain defenseless?' That's not what I'm saying. What I'm saying is that you have no reason to fear. You are the sons and daughters of God; the enemy cannot touch you! You are impervious to the enemy's advances; best of all, to those who believe in God, you're saved!" He turned his back to the crowd as he made his way to his soapbox, then stood upon it, facing them again. "Those who seal their testimony with blood in the name of Jesus Christ shall receive their reward. They have earned salvation in the perishing of their persecution. For the rest of us, we could only be so lucky. So grateful! But until then, we should ensure that we are saved, that *you* are saved." He smiled widely and pointed to the crowd. "Believe in Christ, for he is the way, the truth, and the life."

The crowd clapped lightly and nodded agreeably. The younger women leaned over to one another, covering their mouths with their hands, only letting the tops of their flushed smiles peek over as they murmured with a flirtatious whisper. Leonardo noticed this and preached on.

"If you cannot believe in God... then believe in me! You are aware of the gifts and talents I possess. Trust in what I say, trust in what I do, and look to me as your example!" Some women in the crowd cheered. "I mean, come on, let's be honest: I'm the last remaining bible of Arizona, am I not? I am here to tell you the truth! So, come unto me, and I will share *all the things* that will give you strength!" He clenched his hand into a fist and leaned toward the audience. "I will teach you courage and bravery. To fight these battles and wars as God has commanded us to!" He leaned back casually, resting his arms. "And if evil wishes to come, I say let it. It cannot touch my soul, it cannot touch yours, and it is well within our power to send evil *right back* to where it came from!"

The audience cheered. "Not by seeking vengeance," Leonardo continued. "No. We must let vengeance be in the hands of the Lord!" The crowd let out a few hefty amens. "Those *minuscule men* out there, those killers of believers? They have declared war on the

Lord God, and He does not forget His enemies nor lose any war! So believe me when I tell you this: He will have His vengeance!"

Some of the crowd erupted into cheerful clapping, while others clapped cautiously, looking around as they nervously clenched their jaws. Leonardo accepted the praises, regardless of the anxieties, raising his arms upwards as the claps and shouts came forth. Jordan looked over to Leonardo, his jaw tensing as anger filled his squinting eyes. Leonardo smiled wider, letting out a confident laugh. Jordan looked over to Judah, standing beside him, prompting him to look back at Jordan. They both shared a familiar face of aggravation.

"We need to go," Jordan ordered.

"Agreed."

Jordan looked at Lee, who looked back at him. Jordan gave him a slow but powerful nod. Lee nodded back, then walked toward the crowd, raising his arms to the side and ushering them away with slow, waving motions.

"Oh, come on. We're just getting started!" Leonardo jokingly protested, working the crowd further as he laughed and gestured.

Jordan turned around and looked at Luke, perched atop the Aland Theatre. Luke raised his binoculars, looked around slowly and carefully, then looked down and gave Jordan a thumbs up. Jordan turned back to Leonardo, still soaking in the praise of the remaining audience. "God bless you all! I know it was a short sermon today, but let that not detract from its sweetness!" The crowd began to dissipate. "Believe me, I am as surprised as you are." Only three beautiful young women were left now. "Please come again," he said to the distant members. "We will return soon!"

The young women turned, seductively showing Leonardo their backside as they kept looking at him. "Bye, Leonardo," one said, the tip of her fingernail gently placed between her teeth, the rest giggling and smiling as they waved with their fingers.

"¡Adiós, hermanas! Until I see you again!" Leonardo replied with a teasing smile and a wink.

Jordan grabbed Leonardo by his right arm and yanked him off his soapbox.

"Ow! Hey, come on, Jordan!" Leonardo protested. "What's gotten into you?!" Jordan said no words as he continued to pull Leonardo toward the tall pine tree forest just beyond Little York's communal center. Leonardo continued to grunt and pull away, using his little strength to push Jordan's hands off his arm.

It was to no avail.

The brothers walked behind them, looking at the scene and then at each other, letting out slight but hidden smiles as they had done many times before. Luke ventured down the sides of the Aland Theatre, hopping from pipe to pipe and climbing between ledges or upon uneven brick until he hit the ground with a light and precise pounce to a roll. He stood, jogging after his brothers as they entered the forest, making their way to their home, Guarida Del León.

Jordan chunked Leonardo into the blindingly white forest, Leonardo stumbling through the uneven terrain. "A simple 'let's go' would have been nice," he bit. "Would you have listened?" Jordan questioned. Leonardo rolled his eyes and scoffed as he continued to walk forward, Jordan slowly making his way beside him.

The snow had covered the ground and the surrounding pines, turning their needles into frozen points. The wood was frozen solid and filled with patches of blown-in snow, and its branches held snow piles that occasionally fell when the weight became too great. Long and dark pine trees stretched to the sky, growing further apart and slightly thinner than others in the Arizona Territory due to the higher elevation. Little twigs stuck out from the frozen snow around, and the footsteps of the Brothers' Six crunched and creaked with every booted intrusion. Tiny snowflakes floated from the grey clouds above, unendingly in the bitter temperature. The air scraped frigidly against the brothers' faces, as the absence of sound created an empty, almost harrowing feeling, only broken up by the occasional sprint of a rabbit or deer escaping into the snowy woodlands.

The brothers walked around, Leonardo and Jordan quietly, like ghosts, not wanting to be seen. Instead, they ignored the ankle-high snow crunching and the freshly fallen snow fluffing up as their feet treaded through. Despite the insulation of their boots, their feet froze to the bone, motivating them to distract themselves with conversation as they distance themselves well away from the brothers behind them.

They walked in silence.

"You'd think winter would be over by now," Javier complained, shivering and rubbing his arms with his hands. "Sure, if it were a normal winter," Judah informed.

"You know what the problem is with you all? You need to put on more weight. You're all so... tiny." Lee joked. "How can we get more meat on our bones when you're eating it all?" Javier poked.

The group let out a cold laugh as their lungs chilled on a mid-winter's day.

"I wasn't joking... I'm asking seriously." Javier continued, confused.

"Just b-be glad you all ha-have meat in general," Luke replied, shivering.

"Well, look on the bright side, Luke. When we die from hyperthermia, the wolves will most likely eat you last," Judah joked.

"How is that a bright side?"

"Hey," Jordan butted in. "No one's getting eaten today. As long as we keep moving, we'll stay warm."

"I'm already cold," Javier rebutted.

"Then move faster."

Lee chuckled in his throat. "Yeah, like as much as you move your mouth."

"Not scientifically possible," Judah joked.

The group laughed warmly. Jordan was slightly grieved.

"Look, we need to focus more on saving souls rather than poking fun at each other," Jordan scolded.

The group's smiles faded slightly as they looked at each other, now more serious.

"Come on, Jordan," Luke defended. "They're jokes. We're just trying to lighten the load a little bit, that's all."

Jordan sighed. "I know. I know. I'm just saying that talking about the Lord comforts me. That's all." Judah turned around, looking at Jordan as he walked backward. "A time for laughs and a time for tears, huh?" Jordan looked up, reciprocating a slight, understanding smile that Judah now sprouted. "More like a time for peace and a time for war."

"I get it," said Judah, turning around. "Still, telling a joke sometimes. It would be good for you."

Jordan released a little air from his nostrils. "I'll keep that in mind."

Judah looked up and examined the land before his brothers. "Easy now, gentlemen. We're almost home. Just another two miles—"

"In freezing temperatures," Luke interrupted.

"In freezing temperatures," Judah agreed begrudgingly. "Before we get home."

"Well... look on the bright side, speaking in the words of a wise and humorless man: 'Walking through snow builds character.'" Lee poked, looking back at Jordan, who looked up at him and smiled, shaking his head.

"Oh, yeah. I can really feel the character being built," Luke breathed, shakily, and sarcastically agreed.

"But this rate, we'll have a character for days, so much so that it'll be packing onto us." Jordan punned.

The brothers slowly turned around as they continued to walk backward. "Did you just make a joke?" Javier questioned.

"Yes, yes. I know. It might as well rain," Jordan said, half-smiling. "Oh, God," Luke said, putting his hands together in a prayer-like formation as he looked at the sky. "Please, oh, please let it rain."

The group turned around. "Well," Judah started in. "I guess the frost hasn't bitten your brain after all."

Lee tilted his head back to Jordan. "Let me know when it does, and I'll give you a big hug."

"Thanks, big guy."

"Aw, aren't you both cute? You and your brotherly love," Javier jabbed, letting out a raspy and throaty laugh.

"Oh, you want brotherly love?" Lee asked. "I'll give you brother love."

He reached his arm over, grabbed Javier around the shoulders, pulled him in tightly with little effort, and lifted him off the ground like a grown man might lift a toddler.

"Hey! Hey! Put me down!" Javier demanded, flicking from side to side to no effect.

The brothers laughed as they looked at the two.

"Lee," Jordan intervened. "Put him down, please."

Lee did as he was told and placed Javier on the ground. Now, more riled up than ever, he marched ahead of the group.

"As simpatico as an elephant and a mouse," Judah commented.

"No! We are not 'sim-pah-tee-co,' as you call it," Javier rejected, making fun of Judah's American accent.

"Hey. Take it easy," Jordan corrected.

Javier rolled his eyes and slowed down, taking his spot beside Lee, who hugged him gently and genuinely. "Hey," Lee said, looking down at Javier. He looked up. "I'm sorry," Lee apologized. Javier let out a light smile and looked forward again. "Eh, it's fine. I know you're just messing around." Lee let go.

"I bet you're feeling warmer now, though, huh?" Lee asked.

Javier looked up, his eyebrows furrowed in a face of confusion. "You know what... yeah. I forgot about the cold entirely."

The group lightly laughed as they continued their march, but as they did, a cold breeze roared in the air. The trees swayed slightly as the snow on their limbs fell sporadically to the ground. The brothers pulled their jackets together and squeezed them as close as possible to their bodies, stopping in their tracks. It was so cold that the wind cut through their jackets like a knife, making them nearly useless. Judah turned to look at Jordan, who had taken notice of the falling snow, holding out his hand and catching a single snowflake.

The size had gotten bigger.

Jordan looked up at Judah as he looked around them, noticing that the flakes were now falling far heavier and quicker. Judah sighed, disheartened that, as far as this storm was concerned, the never-ending snow would not stop any time soon. The brothers looked around them, noting the snow that fell heavier and larger from the thicker and darker clouds. They looked to their shoulders, noting the small piles of snow that started to form on them. The following winter's microstorm had begun, and from the looks of it, it would be as unrelenting, deadly, and depressive as the previous ones. Each of the brothers noted their breathing as it grew heavier, each breath emerging in thick, white clouds.

Luke let out a sigh as his countenance slowly fell. "It never ends, does it?"

Judah looked over to Luke and put his right hand on Luke's right shoulder, smiling compassionately to encourage him. "Hey," he said. Luke slowly looked up. "Winters and summers, mountains and valleys, clouds and sunshine. All come and go in their due season." Judah recited.

Luke half-heartedly smiled. "As one ends, another begins."

"New beginnings bring new endings."

"The sun will shine upon us again," They both finished.

Judah embraced Luke, gently wriggling him side to side as the rest of the brothers pondered the poem. The clouds got darker.

"We need to keep moving," Javier firmly reminded.

"Agreed," Jordan added. "You all go on ahead. Leo and I will catch up with you in a minute," he ordered.

The brothers turned and looked back at Leonardo and Jordan, then at each other, their faces bearing a serious expression. Without a word, they waded through the trail within the pines that led them home. Leonardo looked off to the side, crossed his arms, and kept his eyebrows straight as Jordan turned his whole body to face him. Leonardo's mouth was tightly shut from his anger and annoyance.

"Leo," Jordan started with a soft but stern tone.

Leonardo didn't reply. Jordan sighed, then, fully stern, said, "Leonardo."

"What?" Leonardo responded quickly, keeping his body turned away from Jordan.

He dropped his hands to his side, his mouth opening slightly from the irritation, his eyes taking on a look of concern. Jordan analyzed Leonardo's body language and adjusted his tone again, making it softer and more approachable.

"I just want to talk," Jordan comforted.

"You always want to talk."

"Well, maybe if there wasn't something to always talk about, we wouldn't need to do so much of it."

"Or maybe if you focused on literally anyone else other than me, you would realize that there are others who could use your 'talks.' "

"I do talk to other people, Leo. I talk to the people in the village, in Little York, your brothers. You know that."

Leonardo scoffed and rolled his eyes. "You know what I meant."

"What? Do you feel like I single you out?"

Leonardo turned around. "Yes! You can't deny that it seems more often than not that you're having conversations with me!"

"And why do you think that is, Leo?"

Leonardo turned away again. "Because I 'keep making mistakes,' " he said, rolling his eyes and crossing his arms again.

"Look, you say it like it's not true or like you disagree, but deep down, I know you know I'm right. Not to mention the attitude."

"I just don't understand why *everything* is a mistake to you." He turned around, resting his arms. "And also, I wouldn't have to take an 'attitude' with you if you weren't constantly badgering me!"

"Badgering?"

"Yes, badgering."

"Okay, first of all, all I want to do is talk to you."

Leonardo started turning away slowly. "Sure."

Jordan grabbed his shoulder and gently turned him back. "Why is that such a crime to you?"

"Because, Jordan, we never 'have a conversation.' What do you want to talk about this time? My preaching or my appearance or something else I did wrong?"

"*Yes! I do!* Why would I not want to talk about that? Why would I not want to help you? Be the man I am supposed to be for you?"

Leonardo sighed and shook his head, looking away.

"Look, Leo, you have a *gift*. A magnificent one, and gifts are so much more than something you show off. They're like the unique swords God makes especially for us; we use His word, His whetstone, to sharpen them. Then, once they're ready, we learn how to properly and responsibly handle it unto mastery. We don't carelessly throw or tout it around and certainly don't use it out of pride and vanity." He released Leonardo and stepped back just a bit.' "Leonardo... these conversations are not for me to ridicule you or to take out my frustrations on you... They're to help you."

"The problem is, with you, it's the same thing repeatedly. You *refuse* to learn."

Leonardo looked up. "Well, maybe I just have a bad teacher."

Immediately, his heart was saddened when he realized that what he had said had hurt Jordan, who was now staring in silence as he looked between Leonardo's eyes. Jordan looked down, then away, and out into the distance of the pines. "I know you hate it when

I get on you for things." He paused, then looked back at Leonardo. "But Leo, it's my job to look out for you. It has been for years now. As much as you might hate me for it when you mess up, I have to correct you... Because I love you." He looked down, closing his eyes with an angry tightness. "And *still*, after all the lessons and mistakes, you *still* don't get it." He looked up. "What have I told you about how you preach? When you preach, you bring people to Christ. *Only* to Christ. Not to Leonardo DelMuerto or the gifts thereof, but to *Christ*."

Leonardo nodded his head slowly as he sighed and looked down.

"I don't hate you, Jordan."

He looked back up.

"Hm," Jordan said playfully. "Could've fooled me."

Leonardo let out a half-cheeked smile. "I just don't get how you don't see that I am bringing people to Christ. I mean... I have the entire Bible memorized in my head. All of it was photographically memorized scripture, verse by verse. For lack of a better word, I'm the last remaining bible of the West. Too many of these people, I am God to them."

Jordan sighed and shook his head as he kept eye contact with Leonardo.

"No, Leo, you're not. You're just a man, flesh and blood like the rest of us. You're not some great someone above all, and you're certainly no man to develop a God complex. You're a servant of the Lord. That's all. A mouthpiece who should be humbled even to be *thought of* in a time like this. A time of tribulation and persecution." He reached out and put his hand on Leonardo's shoulder. "God chose you to go out and bring the people to *Him*, not for you to stand on a soapbox and redirect the praise back to yourself." Leonardo shrugged off Jordan's hand. "Oh, come on, Jordan, that's ridiculous."

"Ridiculous? Are you serious? You were taking the praise today. 'Matter of fact, you take praise more than you give it and desire worship more than worshipping!"

"That's not true."

" '*Not true?*' Was I the only one by the soap box today, seeing you eyeball those women more than you're own woman?"

Leonardo forced out a nervous laugh.

"Uh-huh," Jordan continued. 'You think I didn't see that on the soap box? 'See you soon, sisters,' " he mimicked.

"Just, hang on a minute—"

"No, I will not 'hang on a minute.' Not only are you a son of God who stands before people as a representative of Him, but you are also an *engaged man* who will soon marry a wonderful young woman who loves you very much! Why don't you at least give her the respect *she* deserves if you aren't going to respect yourself?"

"Jordan—"

"Or at least leave her so you don't hurt her anymore."

"*Jordan! Okay!* I get it. I hear what you are saying."

They looked at each other in silence. Leonardo sighed, looking away, examining the snow that was rapidly falling. He looked back. "Can you at least admit that the people are encouraged?"

"*Encouraged?*"

"Yes!"

"Lord, have mercy," Jordan grieved, rubbing his face grievously with his hands as he sighed.

"They're emboldened, Jordan. Brave! They're ready to face the very real and very present and very *dangerous* adversary! Is that not what evangelism is for?"

Jordan stopped rubbing his eyes. "Evangelism is for the gospel, Leo. That Jesus Christ is alive. And yes, that should embolden people and make them brave, but not when it comes from a man who is *neither.*"

Leonardo was taken aback, silenced. Jordan shook his head. "You are prideful, arrogant, and self-righteous. The latter, most of all! You *tempt these men* like snakes in a pit, thinking that you're above them on some mighty ledge." Jordan stepped close to Leonardo, pointing his finger and pressing it into his chest. "But you are not Leo; *we* are not. We are *in* the pit, and the only reason the vipers have not bitten us is because of the *grace of God.*" He stepped away, calming himself. "No one can prepare for what's coming, the people especially, not when you put more emphasis on the business than the Father who sent you on it. What about the Word of the Lord in their *hearts,* Leo? The new birth. The important things! Do they have those? If they were to die today, where would they go?"

Leonardo watched silently, his heart pounding as Jordan shook his head and looked at the ground. "It is undeniable that you can preach a motivational sermon, Leo. I won't deny that." He looked up into Leonardo's eyes. "But what happens when the Devil walks up to their door? What happens when he asks them if they're willing to give their lives for the God they say they serve? Will they testify or reject something they have not even *begun* to know? Whose fault will that be?" Leonardo gulped. Jordan sighed. "As wonderful as your words are... they are death compared to God's."

Leonardo stayed looking silently, his breathing intensifying.

"I'm just trying to do my job, Jordan... just trying to help. Trying to help them understand the faith."

"And those are all amicable things... but the people don't need *religion,* Leonardo. They need God's doctrine. They need the Word, Jesus Christ. Not some watered-down evangelical *speech.* Not a show you put on for the praise and attention."

Leonardo clenched his jaw.

Jordan's eyes filled with sorrow. "The path you lead these people down is the path you will be responsible for. Ask yourself if you believe what you said today would save those people if the wicked men you taunted showed up tomorrow. Do you believe that it would save them? Do you believe it would say *you?*"

Leonardo's heartbeat pounded relentlessly in his chest. Jordan shook his head and looked down at the snow beneath him, his voice trembling and his heart beating the same. "You know nothing of these men, of what they can do. You haven't seen it... haven't heard it." He looked up. Leonardo slightly flinched backward as he saw the faint fear in Jordan's eyes. "The stories you hear are nothing compared to what's coming, and you tempt the Devil to lay claim upon this land? You tempt evil to come our way, the *people's* way?" He clenched his jaw. "I have seen what they're capable of. Believe me when I say you are *not* ready for them."

Leonardo thought about what Jordan said, wondering what he could have seen and heard. "I understand what you're saying, Jordan. All right?" He amended. "I'm doing my best, just as I know you are." He paused for a moment, thinking back. "I know you feel the need to be my parents... but I'm growing up now. I'm not the same four-year-old boy you found fourteen years ago; I'm starting to take care of myself. I know I'm not perfect, but I'm trying. I will try to be better, I promise you. It's hard when you bear the weight of this world on your shoulders," he reasoned.

Jordan sighed as he realized that some, but not all, of what he had said had reached Leonardo. Looking at him for a moment, he contemplated a change of strategy, taking a more compassionate approach.

"It's not your job to be perfect. It's not your job to bear the weight of the world on your shoulders," Jordan eased contemplatively. "But I understand what you mean, and I know you're doing your best. He looked over at the brothers, who were far away now, then looked back at Leonardo. "Come on. Let's catch up."

The two walked side by side as they made their way to their brothers, now thirty steps ahead of them. They conversed with one another, doing their best to ignore the discourse.

"What do you mean it's not our responsibility to bear the world's weight on our shoulders? To be perfect?" Leonardo asked Jordan, who smiled at the irony. "All that scripture in your head, and you still can't figure out the mystery of it?" He joked.

They trudged through the snow a few steps further. "We don't have to carry the weight of the world on our shoulders because the Lord carries it for us... only our ego and reliance on our mind make us believe *we* are the ones that do the saving, that are perfect."

Leonardo nodded a few times. "Okay, but we're made perfect by the Spirit."

"But imperfect in the flesh. You'll never change that."

Jordan looked over with a half smile. "That's the point of grace." He looked forward again. "When I was your age, I believed I could carry the world. I soon found out that it's not only impossible but also exhausting. Then, I grew a little older, met you, and thought I could carry your weight throughout this world my whole life, carry you on my shoulders as the Lord needed me to, and for a while, I could." He nudged Leonardo with his left elbow, looking over with a smile. "But I've come to find out that's pretty exhausting, too."

Leonardo let out a breathy laugh as he looked away from Jordan and then down to the snow with an embarrassed smile. Jordan looked forward again. "The point I'm trying to make is that the Lord is our strength. He's the perfect one. Not any of us." He looked over again. "As much as I might try, I will never be your perfect father. I'm beginning to accept that now." Leonardo looked up. Jordan smiled with pain in his eyes. "But I can try to be a great older brother."

Leonardo smiled back, his eyes sharing the same pain, and the two looked forward again. "I can see that my pride has grown in you, and I'm sorry. A part of me feels like I'm playing catch-up all these years later and that it might be too late to do so because, as you said, you're growing up. You're a young man, and it is time to make your own decisions." He sighed stressfully. "I guess the main point I'm trying to make is that the hard truth is that my brothers and I... we won't be here forever, Leo. Judah, Lee, Javier, Luke. None of us will last forever. There will come a time that arrives much sooner than you think." He looked at Leo as Leo looked back. "Forever isn't always, you know." They looked forward again. "When you stand alone to face a dangerous world, these moments that we share of correction and scolding might just save your life. I don't do this because I want to pick on you; I do it because I love you."

The two looked at each other, this time more accepting of the other. "Whether by faith or blood, I'll always be your older brother."

Leonardo nodded with a smile on his left cheek as Jordan raised his left arm, inviting Leonardo in for a hug. "Any day now," Jordan joked. Leonardo rolled his eyes and leaned in, hugging him embarrassedly as Jordan squeezed him hard, pulling him close to his heart. "Good. Now, you say, 'I love you, too, Jordan.'" Jordan poked. "I love you, too, Jordan." Leonardo reciprocated, fully smiling now. "There you go. I was beginning to think you weren't going to say it."

The two released as Leonardo thought about all that Jordan had sacrificed to care for him, how he had taken on the responsibility of caring for him when Leonardo was a child, or how he had loved and guided him through all manner of situations as he grew up. He thought about how well Jordan had done, in his mind, and how, though he was a great older brother, he was also a great father, despite his feelings to the contrary. Leonardo considered his love and was grieved, given that he hated how he had such trouble expressing it, or any of his emotions, for that matter. Still, he was thankful that Jordan knew this was the case and thus met him halfway, as he did just now, never asking for a great expression, but whatever he could convey.

"You'll be all right, Leo. Whether we're here or not, I'll still believe in you. I know you'll make the right choice in the end."

Leonardo looked up to Jordan as he considered this strange statement, the snow crunching and giving beneath them. "I'll do the best I can," he comforted. Jordan let out a few nods. "That's all we can do."

"'We are troubled on every side, yet not distressed; perplexed, but not in despair; persecuted, but not forsaken; cast down, but not destroyed; always bearing about the body the dying of the Lord Jesus Christ, that the life also of Jesus might be made manifest in our body.'"

"Which one is that one?"

"First Corinthians chapter four, verses eight through ten."

"Nice."

"Yeah. 'Makes a little more sense, now."

"Does it?"

"Oh, yeah. Some grumpy old man elaborated on it for me, and it all just clicked."

"Yeah, well, consider this a lesson in how old and grumpy men are usually right."

The two laughed as they made peace with each other, catching up with their brothers. They readied for their final hike through the hills that led to their village.

The Brothers' Six were at the latter end of a tiring mission, feeling the wear and tear on their bodies. However, for Jordan in particular, the wear and tear was deep, but more than anything, it was the excuse he would give when asked about his tired and weary face. Leonardo knew Jordan was dealing with something more, but couldn't place it. It had been evident for quite some time now, and though he had asked, Jordan always dodged the question. Leonardo thought about how he had heard Jordan in his unpleasant rest late at night, plagued by nightmares or sleeplessness. This had only increased for the past few weeks, going from every so often to nightly. Leonardo worried for his older brother, knowing he could do nothing to help him with these curses. He considered Paul's penning on infirmities, reproaches, necessities, persecutions, and distresses—that some people are burdened with different ailments so that the power of God may rest upon them. For some, this was depression; for others, it was a physical ailment, but for Jordan, it was anxiety, and if that was the case, then there was nothing to be done.

The Brothers had turned their attention to Jordan and Leonardo, for the two had walked close enough to make their presence known.

"So, how does your bottom feel after that spanking?" Judah asked humorously.

"Don't you have some math to do?" Leonardo responded, rolling his eyes.

"Déjame ver, una buena nalgada se mostrará a través de los pantalones!" Javier dicho'd, as he looked back at Leonardo's bottom.

"Translation?" Judah requested.

"It doesn't really," Leonardo replied.

"He basically said that a good spanking shows through the pants," Luke translated.

"... huh."

"Yeah. Either way, it's all right, kid. We've all received a spanking or two."

"More like two hundred," Javier butted in.

"*Regardless*," Luke cut off. "I think the point Javier is trying to make is that we all had a bit of a wild side growing up."

"Luke, what could you have possibly done that was wild?" Leonardo asked genuinely.

"Oh, I was a kleptomaniac."

"Was?" Jordan corrected.

Javier laughed. "I wasn't a maniac, but Luke is right: I had a wild side too, believe it or not."

"Oh, we believe it," Lee reassured.

"As do his past girlfriends," Judah remarked.

"Ha, ha, very funny. Hey, that reminds me: how's your mother doing?" Javier bit.

"Oh, great, now that the toddler-sized man isn't around to trip her up."

Javier forced a smile on his face. "You know, Judah, as good as having a big brain as your might be, there is one bad thing."

"Oh? And what's that?"

"The bigger the brain, the easier for me to *knock your head off!*" Javier screamed, jumping at his brother but being quickly apprehended by Lee, casually bear-hugging him with both arms and holding him off the ground as he unleashed flying fists.

"*Hey!* Easy." Jordan calmed. "Jordan, stop antagonizing Javier. Lee put him down... that's embarrassing."

"Especially after being called toddler-sized," Leonardo agreed.

Jordan shot him a look, then looked back at the brothers. "Okay, we have a bit of a trip, and clearly, we're all very agitated. Why don't we sing a song to calm ourselves down?"

"Which one did you have in mind?" Luke questioned.

The Brothers' Six had traveled many miles around, hearing many tunes from many worshippers. One of them was a good friend of Jordan's, a woman known as Bennie J. Wilson. Ms. Wilson was a marvelous lyricist who had been working on a hymn for quite some time, and upon hearing of such a hymn, the brothers immediately fell in love with it.

"Hold to God's unchanging hand," Jordan started.

"Hold to God's unchanging hand," Lee continued.

All of the brothers except for Leonardo joined in.

"Build your hope on things eternal," they sang.

"And just hold to God's unchanging hand."

Leonardo looked around at his brothers and smiled at the group. Although their singing was abysmal, the tune they played from the heart was beautiful.

"Trust in Him who will not leave you."

"Whatsoever years may bring."

"If by earthly friends forsaken."

"Still more closely to Him cling."

He thought about his brothers, these men who were the only family and friends he ever had. He thought about how he could win anything, take on anyone with them. Whether it be war or the devil himself, with his brothers, he was ready. *That's just the word*, he thought. *War.* He knew he had a spiritual one raging within him, but up until Jordan's recent comments about him not having them always, he had chosen to ignore it. He placed his self-advocacy, his responsibility for making the changes he needed, on them, believing that they would overcome his issues at his side. He misplaced his love for God with his love for them; strangely, their reciprocity of that love only enabled it. *Pros and cons*, I guess, he thought again.

He knew he needed to learn to separate his love for his brothers and, more problematically, himself from the love of God. Though their bond was forged in love and faith, they would all need something more for the moment they would leave each other's side, though if they had a choice, they would stick together until the end.

Nonetheless, Leonardo quietly joined his brothers in the chorus as they sang to Guarida Del León.

"Hold to God's unchanging hand."

"Hold to God's unchanging hand."

"Build your hope on things eternal."

"And just hold to God's unchanging hand."

In wonderful and lifted-spirit unison, they marched home, courage overtaking them. This was the courage Jordan knew they needed for the battle that was soon to come, having an evil most hellish carried out by wicked men of the same caliber, these inhuman members that could barely be classified as a part of humanity, being led by their chief of devils, the man known as Icarus.

That said, though he drew closer, enmity did the same. Icarus knew little about this opponent or how quickly he was approaching. He could not fathom how relentless he was, how deadly he had become, and how well within his grasp Icarus remained. No imagination could be tantamount to the rival that, to many, was seen as more revenant than mortal, that many knew as titles rather than his name, in life and before death.

To them, he was the soldier, the major general, and even the reaper, but above all, he was known as the Saint of Retribution.

CHAPTER 3

But Evil, Once Hidden, Came Traveling Thence

uarida Del León's sun had begun to set, and the snowfall
had thickened in size and quickened its fall as it coated
the land. The flakes fell quietly and consistently upon this
land of nowhere, the wind silent and the temperatures
dropping moment by moment. The people of the small village may have had reservations
about the temperature, but they were thankful for the lack of wind. In such a spot, even
a single gust of wind could mean a blizzard, which in turn meant a significant risk of
mortality for the elderly who lived there. The village was a thriving yet dying one, miles
away from any civilization, built upon the backs of the aforementioned elderly when they
were not so, but instead were strong, able, and young. They were diverse people from
many lands and walks of life. Some were white men and women from further north, while
others were Mexicans from the south, making the most popular population the Hispanics
for the three generations following.

The people of Guarida Del León came from lands as diverse as they were; yet, despite their differences, they all had something in common: each place they left, they fled, knowing that those they left behind did not want them. They were outcasts thrown to the wolves, sometimes literally, and gave meaning to the metaphor. Despite their rejection, they found sanctuary in Guarida Del León, for, despite the village's insignificance, it was alive and simple. The definition of humble beginnings with endings that were just the same, having found its cycle for nearly a century now.

The town's mystery lay in its vast inconsequentiality. It was unknown, though it had so much to offer. The people who found lodging there had done so by sheer accident or, in their words and belief, by the omniscient grace of God. All who found it were not only a few, but they also felt that its location was best kept as it was: a secret.

The cabins of Guarida Del León had a unique style; each one was comprised of the available materials provided by the surrounding nature and the culture and craftsmanship of the carpenters. Long logs from the surrounding pine trees were fastened with rope and ingenuity. The trees' tops and bottoms had been sawed off, leaving the bark intact, which built the cabins into a square-like design with a matching roof. Many animal hides covered the rooftop, where the space between the pines would not fully connect. The natural formation of the pines was rugged, uneven, and irregular. Though it prevented anyone who stayed inside from freezing, it didn't stop them from being cold, but at least kept the snow outside. The roofs were covered with clumps of snow, only solidifying and growing in height as the winter weather's relentless nature proceeded. Seven cabins around the village had all come together in a wide U formation that circled Guarida Del León's bonfire.

The cabins' doors were barely doors at all. They were made of large sticks, as big as a leg bone, and tied together with the same rope that held the building together. The rope was then used in the corners on the left side to tie it to the living space, creating a working hitch that ensured the doors stayed firm, withstanding the winds that beat against them.

On the sides of some cabins, some fences enclosed little gardens, and though they were used in the summertime, each one now was as dead as winter, for they were covered in thick, snowy white. For the cabins, there was no garden; clothing lines would connect from one stick to another, on the right side of the buildings, actively drying the clothing of the individuals who lived within them. Still, washing was hardly done at this point of the season, for the clothes would never dry in the winter's open air, and instead would freeze to an icy solid.

There were homes in Guarida Del León that were not made of wood, but instead of solidified clay, locally called adobe. The adobes were built by hand and made of the surrounding brown earth; thus, the adobes were a tannish brown color and took on the shape of domes. The interior grounds of these adobes were dug into the world, creating a living space that maintained a constant temperature, making them cooler in the summer and warmer in the winter, especially when compared to their neighboring cabins. In front of the adobes, there were stone tools to make bread and tortillas for the village. Many a molcajete sat inside the adobes, paired with many tejolotes. Thus, the most common source of food that the women would prepare was that of grains and corn gathered from their tended gardens.

The adobes were an art and a science, mastered by the Mexican people of Guarida Del León, and the entire village came to appreciate them for their wonder and beauty.

The women of Guarida Del León were gatherers, workers, and keepers, while the men were hunters. This created a specific dependence among villagers, and each one held up their end of the bargain to survive. They were more of a tribe than neighbors, for they were a family of individuals bound by familiarity and faith—rejects sent to live among others akin to them, and they loved each other for it. Leonardo found the faith that bound the villagers of Guarida Del León an odd thing to note, for it appeared that almost all who found their way to this unknown village just happened to believe or would eventually believe the very same as the inhabitants already within, which, though coincidental, seemed entirely implausible. Still, he chalked it up to the Brothers' Six great ways, worth words and good-hearted preaching. Most admired the charm of their preachings, where no church was laden, which were often spoken through tumultuous weather, and the opposite; evangelism around the bonfire, teaching upon a resting stump. The brothers preached messages of faith, hope, and salvation, and warmed both souls and bodies.

For the people of Guarida Del León, it was one of their few blessings, if not the only one, that they were able to eat good food and hear good sermons.

The bonfire built at the center of the village was a large and vibrant one that loved to dance. Rocks were laid around it in a wall-like formation, some stacked two feet high while others were only a rock's distance above the ground. The bonfire was constantly lit in the wintertime, providing warmth to the local inhabitants who were closely housed nearby. But on nights like this one, when the Brothers' Six were expected to arrive, the bonfire was especially lit to shine through the night. It was a beautiful sight to behold, for it was a sign, a light that read 'home' in the eyes of the troupe of missionaries, but meant a little bit more to Leonardo and took on a slightly different name, with a very different definition of home.

Leonardo walked over the hill to look at the village from a distance of thirty feet, gazing upon all the grace that this distant hill could offer. This overlook was lined with tall pine trees that reached to the grey and darkening sky, surrounding the entire front side of Guarida Del León and providing a visual shelter from almost everyone passing by. The Brothers joined Leonardo, slowly walking up behind him, gazing upon their home that warmed them in different ways. The afternoon sunlight had shone over the brim of Mt. Sorrow, stretching the sunset's brightly colored reds, purples, and yellows down below to the village. A bright, shining orange light blanketed it entirely and shone over the top of Mt. Sorrow. This light show was a rare occasion, given the constancy of the snowstorm, but alas, it was a gift for the sun to peek through the grey, clouded skies, though it continued to drop its heavy snow.

Jordan looked up and examined the mountain that he had grown to love. It was a vast mountain range that took up the entirety of the sky behind the village. It looked as though it were a painting, masterfully brushed upon the canvas of the heavens, far too vast and far too tall for any human mind to comprehend. Mt. Sorrow's peaks reached high into the grey and were constantly covered in the whitest of snow. Its base was a blackish grey that was only seen where rocks and trees had not grown, or the snow had not yet fallen. Below the mountain lay a vast, far-reaching valley, connecting seamlessly with Guarida Del León in an ocean of white. In this valley, snow was forebodingly overwhelming, with a bitter and blinding presence that extended for miles. The only sign of differentiation was the river that rested a hundred feet from the village. It was a small river that could nearly be called a stream, and now had a frozen, icy top that had formed over it. The villagers had smashed a large hole in the top of the bucket to catch fresh water and, when necessary, rainbow trout, supplying all the nutrients needed to survive, particularly for the elderly.

Jordan looked down at his people and smiled, appreciating his humble life that was as lost to time as it was to man. He loved it, though he knew the reservations that some who sought greater things might have.

Leonardo thought about a life greater than the one given to him as he looked down at Guarida Del León. Numerous thoughts of unfulfillment plagued his mind, as his disappointment continued to grow. He didn't know what he wanted entirely, but he knew he wanted more than *this*. He could do more than this; he had a gift that was greater than this, and often felt that this humble lifestyle was far beneath him. As he neared the point of his mood being ruined by his thoughts, he saw his definition of home come into view, making his thoughts disappear. This home was his treasure, which no amount of fame nor fortune could replace; a jewel that was as beautiful as she was heavenly, only accented by the afternoon's rays.

It was his soon-to-be wife, Sophia Rivera.

Sophia leaned against her cabin with her right shoulder. Her long, red skirt stretched just below her knees and waved in the afternoon winter breeze. Her arms were crossed, and snowflakes had begun to gather in her hair, as she stood there with a gentle smile, waiting for Leonardo. He smiled back as he took in her sweet as the springtime blossom beam, warm enough to heat the most frozen heart. Her hair was long, straight, black, beautiful, and soft as cotton. Sophia's skin was the color of a sweet caramel brown, and it glistened perfectly in the afternoon sun like glazed pottery. Her blouse was a puffy, white, long-sleeved one, filled with decorative red and blue designs sewn precisely upon the front of the blouse, twisting in numerous circular patterns. Beads hung from a patch upon her front, which was sewn into the blouse with red string.

Sophia softly swayed her hips, which in turn made the beads sway too; both movements worked to calm her anticipation as she waited for Leonardo. Her sleeves held tightly to her wrists, as the fluffs of the cuffs poofed out over her hands. Leonardo's heart began to pick up the pace, and as he noticed her hands, he remembered their soft and comforting feeling, one he often longed for. When she would hold Leonardo's hand, he felt like he was safe, like for a moment, nothing else in the world mattered. Leonardo's eyes slowly lifted from Sophia's hands to her chest and then to her eyes, doing his best to remember the beauty in their brownness. To him, they were as elegant as they were affectionate.

It was well known and even agreed upon that Sophia was the most beautiful woman in Guarida Del León. Although there were not many women in the village to compare her to, it was even further speculated that she was the most beautiful in the land. To Leonardo, who had indeed seen other beauties in the land, he didn't care. She was enough, and the enough was more than enough.

Sophia gently raised her hand beside her chest and gave Leonardo the signal to come closer with a gentle curling of her index finger. Leonardo donned a sincere and flirty smile. Sophia reciprocated and added a wink, biting down on her lower lip happily. Leonardo's heart raced as his left eyebrow raised mischievously. Sophia giggled and lifted herself from the lean of her cabin, only to walk around the corner and into her home. Leonardo stared on romantically. The rest of his brothers stared at him.

"Something you'd like to share with the class?" Judah laughed.

"Trust me, you don't want to know," Leonardo half-joked.

Jordan picked up a pinch of snow from Leonardo's shoulder and flicked it at his face. Leonardo flinched away, smiling. "Hey!" He exclaimed.

"A little bit of cold 'water' to keep your head on straight." Jordan joked, smirking and shaking his head. Leonardo made it down the hill. "Yeah, yeah. You all act like you were never about to get married before," Leonardo humored with a smile.

"I have never been about to be married before," Javier pitied.

"One day, big guy. One day," Lucas falsely sympathized, patting Javier's shoulder patronizingly.

The brothers chuckled as they began their walk down the hill to their respective wives, save Javier.

"Leo," Jordan began, "Make sure you're back to the cabin before nightfall."

"Relax, I know the rules," Leonardo responded with an attitude.

Jordan shook his head. "And yet," he said in a hushed tone, "he refuses to follow them."

"One often calls into question the arbitrariness of the rules, Jordan," Judah jumped in.

"Who's one?" He asked, looking knowingly at Judah. "You's one?"

"Yes, me's one. *Smart* ones."

"Mm," Jordan nodded, looking forward again. "Well, Leonardo is one who needs rules; otherwise, he'll get into all kinds of trouble."

"I don't think it's Leonardo you need to be worried about," Lee joked.

"Sophia is a good girl. She would never."

The brothers all stared at Jordan in silence, having just seen the same thing he and *especially* Leonardo did.

"Whatever! They're going to be married soon. It's fine," Jordan begrudgingly closed as he walked ahead, a worried cadence in his step.

The brothers quietly chuckled as they walked into the village behind him, going their separate ways in the town. The ground of Guarida Del León had become a reddish-brown mud that reflected the light from the bonfire in the gleam of the melted snow. Thus, the boots of every villager needed to stay mindful of where they tread, and more importantly, where they placed their shoes once they went into their homes. This was especially true for Leonardo, for Sophia had a particular dislike for dirty shoes in freshly cleaned cabins.

He walked up to Sophia's cabin, his shoes squishing through the muddied ground, as he ran his hand through his hair, frantically fluffing it. He raised both hands as he felt the snow in his follicles, quickly attempting to remove any buildup that had found itself frozen within his locks. Once he had done this, he brushed the snow off the shoulders of his leather jacket. Sophia's front door opened with a wild inward pull, surprising Leonardo and stopping him in his tracks. Sophia's silhouette flickered in front of the fireplace's dancing light, accenting a warm darkness upon the front of her face, leaving Leonardo speechless.

"Guapo?! Realmente eres tú?" Sophia flirted, pretending to be shocked as her hand daintily and sarcastically rested on her lips.

"Si mi amor, soy yo," Leonardo flirted back, rushing forward for a kiss.

"Sophia!" Jordan interrupted, "Como estas?" He continued with a light tone, approaching Leonardo from behind.

Sophia's eyes lit up as a smile graced her face. "Tio!" She exclaimed, pushing Leonardo aside with excitement, and leaped onto Jordan, hugging him tightly. Jordan smiled widely and hugged her back, then gently placed her back on the ground. She grabbed his face excitedly and looked over it to make sure he was alright. "Tuviste un viaje seguro?" She questioned sweetly.

"Si, sobrina, si." Jordan responded softly. "Mija. ¿Tu padre siempre construye muros tan delgados?" Jordan questioned.

Leonardo rolled his eyes and brought his right index finger and thumb to the bridge of his nose, looking down with a hard squint in his eyes. Sophia smiled as her mouth opened in shock. She smacked Jordan's shoulder lightly and slowly stepped back and toward Leonardo. "Don't worry, Jordan, we won't speak a word about you," Sophia redirected with a mischievous laugh.

"Uh-huh. Yeah. You know what I mean," he gestured to the walls of the cabin with his index finger. "Thin walls. Very thin."

"Don't worry, Jordan, this is no weather for anything but conversation." Sophia eased, looking flirtatiously at Leonardo as she gently caressed the snow off his shoulders.

"I agree. As a matter of fact, you two had better bundle all the way up. Put on as many clothes as possible. Vestido de pies a cabeza,"

"Yes, Uncle. Yes. Speaking of, don't you have a wife to be 'bundling up' right about now, or should we all continue to freeze outside?"

Jordan shook his head, trying to hide his smile and failing. Sophia did the same, pursing her lips together as hers came out on the sides. Leonardo lightly smiled as he looked between the two. He admired their relationship and wondered how Sophia did it. She was the only human being alive who could pacify such an uptight Jordan. Truthfully, it wasn't all that much of a mystery. Jordan loved her, and she loved him, and the bond they had built over time was enough. In a way, Leonardo was jealous of this bond they had, for it was one he had worked so hard to attain, though it was never granted.

"Clothes. On." Jordan finished, gesturing to both of them as he left, making his way to his cabin.

Leonardo shook his head as he slowly walked backward to make his way inside Sophia's cabin, turning to take it all in and see what she had done with the place since he had last been there.

Sophia's fireplace had a chimney made of rock and clay, standing firm in the middle of the wooden cabin and extending through the ceiling. This centered fireplace provided light to the central room, filling the cabin with a warm, dim, and orange glow. Inside the fire was a freshly placed kettle, filled with water. In front of the fireplace, to the left, lay a small cloth, ready for use in cleaning. Three feet in front of the fire, which crackled ablaze, was a small, round, grey-stained table, made of finely cut wood and supported by three legs. The legs came down from the table's center and sprouted outward in three directions to support all of its sides. Beside the table, there were two handcrafted chairs, placed on each side, with a color of grey stained wood, a round back support, and a simple flat seat, supported by four legs that held each corner. Upon the table was an old lantern with worn, silver metal, unlit, and lacking oil, its handle lying lightly on its side.

Leonardo looked at the rest of the cabin, examining the other rooms in total. Each room was built on either side of the fireplace, and each was complete with an old wooden bed and animal hides. The room on the left-hand side contained a small, single-sized bed, constructed of creaking wood and filled with a multitude of thin, dusty, and unmade bedding. The single bed contained a single pillow, flat and dirty, just as it was. Though, regardless of this bed's simplicity, it was kept and cleaned, to the best of Sophia's ability. To the right of the fireplace was a room with a queen-sized bed, presenting itself in the same manner as the room to the left. Despite this, there were a few differences in this room.

On the floor, ram and deer hides were laid to act as carpets, while simultaneously providing warmth for those who walked upon the freezing wood. There was a dresser next to the bed, containing Sophia's clothes, and upon this dresser was an old but cleaned mirror, large and oval in shape, balancing upon the wooden wall that gently supported it. Below the mirror was a brush that had been freshly used, grey in metal and filled with a thousand tiny tan bristles. The dresser was cleaned and well-dusted, just the same as her bedding and the rest of her home. It was a simple yet beautiful place, built by the hands of the carpenters who founded Guarida Del León, who were her parents.

Hector and Hermosa Rivera were both carpenters in their lifetime and had helped construct the rest of Guarida Del León similarly, hence their similarity in build. The two were held in high regard, and even still were, especially after their passing. It had been nearly two years to the day since Sophia's parents passed away. Sophia always found it fitting and sweet that they had passed together, despite the tuberculosis.

Leonardo calmly shut the door behind him. Jordan entered his cabin, keeping a close ear on the one next to him as the afternoon settled into the night. Sophia stood by the fireplace and placed another log on the fire. Leonardo stood just in front of the front door, staring at his beautiful fiancée. Leonardo rubbed his hands together, generating as much heat as he could, as Sophia slowly continued to build the warming fire. He walked toward her, already feeling the warmth soak through his flesh and into his bones, even if in the slightest. Sophia lifted her head as he got closer, sniffing loudly and playfully.

"Qué es ese olor?" She looked at Leonardo with a mischievous smile. "Eres tu?" She questioned, pointing her finger and lightly sticking out her right hip.

"Very funny," Leonardo replied with a half smile, rolling his eyes.

Sophia faced him fully as he continued to face her. He rubbed his shoulders as they locked eyes, his body beginning to warm more now. Sophia slowly raised her right hand to his face and felt his frozen skin with her palm. She glided her thumb across his cheek, staring into his eyes with a loving calm. His face was pale in complexion, frozen solid, and his lips were slightly purple.

"The winter is beating you," Sophia noted as she continued to caress Leonardo's cheek softly, her countenance slightly falling.

Leonardo could barely feel her hand through the numbness of his skin, but treasured her caresses all the same. He had often felt that though her fireplace burned warm, the smooth touches of her hand were far warmer. He closed his eyes softly as he embraced her hand, realizing that many heat sources could warm his frozen body, but there was only one that could warm his freezing heart.

"The winter isn't what's beating me," Leonardo remarked.

Sophia let out an airy laugh through her nose, smiled, and dropped her hand to his. "Who? Jordan?" She asked sarcastically. Leonardo's eyes slowly opened. He let out a smirk, then a sarcastic shrug, then clasped her hand with the tips of his fingers. "Who else?" He replied begrudgingly. Sophia lightly shook her head and smiled sweetly. "You know he loves you," she comforted. "Yeah... I know," he agreed with a sigh.

A romantic silence fell over the room as the two looked at each other lovingly. Sophia sprouted a cheek-to-cheek smile as she bit her lower lip and continued to sway. "Besides," she started again, lightly punching his left shoulder with her free hand. "Even if my uncle doesn't love you, I do, and that is all that matters." Leonardo laughed airily, releasing her hand and rubbing his shoulder, letting out a playful 'ow.'

"Good," he breathed. "Because I do, too."

"You do?"

"I do."

"Hm. I'll believe it when I hear those words on our wedding day."

Leonardo laughed as he usually did, taken in by her sense of humor. "Now sit down," she commanded. "Let me get you well again." He did as he was told, eyeing the chair he usually sat in. It was on the right side of the table and had been pulled out, leaving it for him to sit in. He grabbed the backrest of the chair and turned it even more outward to line it up with the front door. He turned and sat down in the chair, waiting for Sophia to come over. She had made her way to the fireplace and was examining the blackened kettle placed within the fire, now at a slight simmer. The water was warm to the touch, but not so much so that it would burn her fingers, or more importantly, Leonardo's face. She picked up the rag beside the fireplace and used it to grab the handle of the kettle. She pulled it out, walked back to Leonardo, and placed it on the table. She made her way around him and stood in front. She smiled lovingly, impassionately, and, as she had done dozens of times before, opened the kettle's lid and let out the steam, which was made even more evident by the coldness of the room.

"You better keep your boots off my table. The next man who violates that rule is going to feel my wrath," she warned.

"*Your* wrath?" Leonardo humored.

She rolled her eyes. "Or, at least the wrath of a thousand suns. Whichever is more potent."

Leonardo chuckled as the warmth of the cabin finally broke through to his bones, making his skin feel puffy, but more importantly, making him realize just how tired he was. He leaned his head back and relaxed.

"When did you become such a wrathful woman?" He asked with a smile.

"When certain *men* kept putting their boots on my table," she replied.

"Do you think you'll ever become forgiving?"

"If certain *men* stop making the same 'mistakes.' "

"I see there's a clear emphasis on men, here."

"One man in particular." She stopped wiping his face and looked at him sharply. His eyes fluttered open. "Mine," she clarified. He sighed, nodded agreeably, and closed his eyes again. "I know," he yielded. "I know. It's becoming a habit of mine."

"Becoming? No, it is a habit of yours." She wiped his face a little harder. "Forgiveness is for me, but it's in the going forth and sinning no more that the balance is weighed for *you,*" she continued less humorously.

"John eight eleven? Yeah, I know the words. I've been cursed to memorize the entire text."

"And yet," Sophia continued, raising her right eyebrow and placing her left hand on her hip, "with all those memorized, you still choose to ignore more than half of them." Leonardo sighed, putting his hands out to the side. "Like I said. It's a curse." Sophia shook her head, dipped her rag, and went back in for cleaning. "It's what you make it, my love. In the right hands—your hands, it could help a lot of people."

"Oh yeah?" He questioned. "How so?"

"Well, for example, let's say there was someone who wanted to hear John chapter eight right now. Then, you would be there to recite it perfectly to give words of life."

She looked at him and raised both eyebrows as a smile flowed across her face. He smiled back, sighed again, and with a slight roll of his eyes, closed them, and went to the scripture in his mind.

" 'Jesus went unto the mount of Olives," he started, "and early in the morning he came again into the temple, and all the people came unto him; and he sat down, and taught them. And the scribes and Pharisees brought unto him a woman taken in adultery; and when they had set her in the midst, they said unto him, Master, this woman was taken in adultery, in the very act. Now Moses in the law commanded us, that such should be stoned: but what sayest thou? This, they said, tempting him, that they might have to accuse him. But Jesus stooped down, and with his finger wrote on the ground, as though he heard them not. So when they continued asking him, he lifted up himself, and said unto them, He that is without sin among you, let him first cast a stone at her. And again he stooped down and wrote on the ground. And they who heard it, being convicted by their own conscience, went out one by one, beginning at the eldest, even unto the last: and Jesus was left alone, and the woman standing in the midst. When Jesus had lifted up himself, and saw none but the woman, he said unto her, Woman, where are those thine accusers? Hath no man condemned thee? She said, No man, Lord. And Jesus said unto her, neither do I condemn thee: go, and sin no more.' "

Leonardo noticed that a certain peace had fallen upon Sophia. He knew that, with him and the brothers gone, it had been a while since she had heard any words of life. He could tell that even that short passage had edified her enough to bring her to a certain calm. His gift had made way for that, and it was then he understood, if only a little more, the significance of it. She looked at him with a much calmer countenance. "Thank you," she said, leaning in and kissing him on the forehead. She dipped her cloth into the kettle once more, soaking it in warm water that dripped into the steaming liquid. She twisted out the water from the rag back into the kettle, the sound of water droplets dripping into the pot. She leaned over and cleaned the dirt and grime off his temple, nose, and eyes, now primarily focused on the outward uncleanness. His smile slowly faded as he looked at her eyes, though she did not look back. Reflecting on the importance of his gift, its misuse, and his conversation with Jordan, he felt a deep conviction. He gulped gently.

"I need to tell you something," he started anxiously.

"Oh?" Sophia replied.

"I, uhm. Look, I want to start by saying these are Jordan's conclusions, not mine, and I don't entirely think they're true, but since he brought it up—"

Sophia stopped cleaning him and looked down at his eyes, raising her left eyebrow and waiting for him to quit stumbling over his words, or even slightly own up to his mistakes.

"Or, maybe I'm confessing because I feel guilty because I *did* do it."

"And what 'it' is that?"

"I—" he gulped, "I flirted with some women while I was preaching."

Sophia slowly raised her eyebrows.

"In fairness," he continued, "they started it."

She tilted her head, her eyes fully wide.

"... but I am at fault because I did it back."

She shook her head and rested her facial expression as she did, letting out a slight smile. "That doesn't surprise me."

Leonardo was shocked at her response. "You're not mad?"

"Of course I'm mad, Leonardo, but I'm more disappointed. I also know that you're a flirt. It's in your nature. It's not a good nature, but it is in you."

"It is? I am?" He asked in disbelief. "How do you know?"

She put the warm rag on his left cheek and held his head in her hands as she gently looked into his eyes. "It's a tone—a slight thing; an inward thing. For example, a woman walks up to you and flirts with you. So, instead of turning away or expressing your disinterest, you respond just a bit nicer than a disinterested man would. You can't see it because you refuse to, because a part of you, a nature in you, likes it."

Leonardo said nothing as he realized his supposed flirting was indeed quite blatant. Sophia smiled painfully as she continued. "I've known that about you for a while... but, you're saving grace is that you've never followed up with any of them. You still don't, and instead, you chose to follow through with me. I call that love, even if it's stupid of me to do so. I believe that you're a good man; that unfaithfulness is not who you *really* are. You are a romantic, a man of love. Of passion and emotion. You are a rarity, and most importantly, you are mine. You are in love with me." She looked between both of his eyes. "Right?"

"Yes, I am very in love with you," he reassured hastily.

Sophia dipped her rag into the kettle again, ringing it out once more, then wiped his forehead. "I believe you. I believe *in* you, but I also believe you are a man at war with yourself, in one worse than any: you are in a war for your soul—diablos y ángeles tiran a tu alma. Te debates entre ser un hombre de fama y fortuna, o un hombre afortunado sin fama. You are torn between being a man of God who sends souls to Christ or a man of his own who sends men to the Devil." She dipped the rag again. "But in you, I see the potential for a righteous man. A man who, despite his backslidings, chooses to serve the Lord still. Besides your mistakes, you still get up and do your best for the people." She held his face with both of her hands. "I love that man. I want you to *be* that man, to *work* for that man, and it starts in the simple things." She caressed his right cheek. "If a man can learn to keep his boots off the table, then he can learn to bring food to it and many others."

Leonardo glanced between her pleading eyes and remembered why he cared for her so much more than all the women that could ever wander the earth. She knew who he was, or who he tried to be, and knew just how to speak to him to get him to see it. On the same token, he knew her in a way that no other would be able to. She knew what to say when he was feeling down, and he did the same. She could give mercy where mercy was needed and tough love where it was required. In his mind, he and Sophia were made for each other, written within the heavens like the stars that were placed before them. Their relationship was destiny, come Heaven or Hell.

"You know it was that wild streak in me that made your father not like me so much," Leonardo joked.

"That's only because you reminded him of him," she corrected, as she looked deeper into his eyes. "Do you really see that man in me?" he questioned. She thought for a moment, enjoying the silence and the subtle sincerity in the question. "What do you see in you?" She asked in reply. He sighed. "I don't know... I don't know," he answered honestly. Sophia smiled softly. "Then I guess we'll just have to wait and see," she breathed, a flirty sigh escaping her. "Either way, I think that whoever Mr. Leonardo DelMuerto is, he will be a great man who will affect many people."

"For better or worse?"

"That's what I'm going to sign up for."

Each was completely entranced with the other's gaze, Sophia hovering over him, bringing her lips closer to his.

Leonardo hesitated.

"And what if you're wrong?" He doubted.

She sighed, dropped her head, then slowly lifted it with a closed smile, slightly tilting her head to the right. "Then we will be wrong together." Leonardo smiled and sighed back, his worries only lessened somewhat. Finally, she leaned in slowly and kissed him gently, the fire crackling in the nighttime silence.

"Okay, time's up," Jordan interrupted, opening the door. Sophia quickly stepped away from Leonardo and stood stiffly beside him, wiping her lips as Leonardo pursed his. Jordan looked at the two. "Well, you two look perfectly innocent."

"I mean, I was going for a picture of purity, so if you bought it—"

"Yeah, I'm not buying anything." He pointed to Leonardo. "You. Up."

"All right, all right. Relax," Leonardo eased, collecting himself and standing calmly. "No fornication was had."

"Mhm," Jordan believed.

Leonardo touched Sophia's hand with his one more time. "Hasta la próxima, mi ancla," he farewelled. "Hasta la próxima," she responded with a soft smile.

Leonardo started making his way to Jordan, but was slightly put off when he noticed the somewhat more serious look on his face than usual. He gave a quick wave to Sophia and then quickly grabbed the door handle. "Goodnight, Sophia." He said. "Goodnight, Tio." She responded with a light, red-cheeked smile.

Leonardo walked past him and out the door. Jordan gently but quickly closed it behind him. " 'You ever heard of personal space?" Jordan antagonized, closing the door behind Leonardo as the brisk seven o'clock air cut through his skin once again, instantly undoing all the warmth that Sophia had just done. "I was just about to ask you the same thing," Leonardo tossed back.

Though this comment infuriated Jordan, there was no time for Jordan to deal with it now, for the two were needed at the bonfire. The fire's smoke reached high into the clouded and snow-filled night sky, melting any snow particles that might get caught up in the heated cloud, and the ones that didn't fell to the ground and made a thick, dark brown, mushy mud that often coated the villagers' boots. The brothers sat beside the bonfire on hefty, long, damp logs with mud mushed around the bases, resting and waiting for Jordan, Leonardo, and Javier to arrive. They gazed into the fire's bright, red, dancing flames, which warmed their frozen flesh as the pine wood within released a wonderful, smoky aroma. Leonardo and Jordan walked up, each of their steps making a squishy, wet splat, prompting the brothers to look from their enchantment and up at the latecomers, though remaining in their focused silence. The only noise that could be heard was the crackling of the bonfire, which filled the empty forest valley with light and life.

"Where's Javier?" Jordan asked, looking around hastily.

"He's a bit busy at the moment," Judah informed, gesturing with his head to the left in the direction of an adobe.

Jordan looked and saw Javier and a village woman, named Esmeralda, conversing privately. His eyebrows raised quickly, as did Leonardo's. "I was going to get him, but... it seemed a bit... wrong," Judah said.

"No, no. You made the right choice." Jordan looked back at Judah. "How long have they been talking?"

"Since we got back," Luke answered.

"Oh, they've been talking far longer than that," Lee commented.

"How do you know?" Jordan asked curiously.

"I mean... look at them," Lee added.

They all looked at the two, taking note of their flirtatious body language.

"Why didn't he tell us?" Jordan continued.

"Some people prefer privacy," Judah answered.

"Imagine the thought," Leonardo agreed, looking at Jordan. He rolled his eyes.

"Regardless," Jordan continued, "I'm happy for Javier. It's about time he found someone to make a home with."

"I agree," Lucas added. "She is a bit old for him, though."

"Only by ten years," Judah defended.

"Ten?!" Leonardo restated, shocked.

"Well, age is just a number, after all," Lee joked.

"In wine and cheese, maybe," Judah reminded.

"How old is she anyway?" Jordan asked.

"Forty-three," Lucas answered.

"*Forty-three?*" The brothers realized in unison.

Javier and Esmeralda turned at the commotion, the brothers awkwardly staring at the two in silence, Lucas letting out an uncomfortable wave. Esmeralda giggled as Javier rolled his eyes, only to look back at her and gently say goodbye. Javier walked over to the bonfire with a quick pitter-patter haste, the brothers waiting for him, smiling yet trying to act aloof.

"So... friend of yours?" Lee questioned as Javier arrived.

Javier rolled his eyes and chose silence.

"You know secrets don't make friends," Lucas piped up.

"No, but they sure do work great for making more than friends," Javier responded defensively.

The brothers cheered and razzed him, Lucas grabbing Javier's shoulders and shaking him violently as the other brothers smiled and clapped. Jordan smiled too, happy that Javier had finally taken some steps toward a more fulfilled life.

"All right, let's get started," Jordan said. "I don't want to be here all night. As a matter of fact, this will only take a minute." The brothers settled down and looked at Jordan, adjusting in their seats with a slight shiver. Leonardo sat beside him on the log opposite the brothers. "I know the nights only started, but I want to make sure we get plenty of shut-eye before the morning rolls around. That means we will all go home and get some rest after this. We're waking up bright and early tomorrow before the sun rises; that way, we can head up to Little York with plenty of light in the day."

The brothers murmured and looked at each other. Jordan noted their disapproval.

"Jordan, what? We *just* got back. We haven't even had a chance to rest, to even eat," Leonardo objected.

"I know, I know. I know. But, going off previous intelligence from what Judah has reported, the word from the world is those men haven't been anywhere near the towns we're going to in a good long while. This is the perfect time to head south."

"*What?!*" Leonardo objected. The rest of the brothers' murmuring worsened.

"I'm just offended that you sent Judah on an information run and not me," Lucas butted in, attempting to release some tension.

"Look, we had our reasons," Jordan deflected. The brothers calmed and listened more intently. "Look, you guys know just as much as I that we've been planning this trip for a long while. *This is the time.* Those people need Christ more than ever, particularly more than the rest. We have the money, we have the experience. We're ready." The brothers nodded and mumbled agreeably. "Look, I know I'm asking a lot, and I know it's sudden, but you've seen what's gone on down there. You've read the papers. Their churches and their Bibles have been burned to the ground, some of them with believers in them. It's a war zone that has left a wake of destruction, but it is those places that we need the most. That is our mission. Christ first, everyone else second. Those people need an opportunity to be saved much more than the people here at Little York. Our job is to preach the best way we know how, and I need every single one of you to do it. I need you to be prayed up, packed up, and ready for a fight come tomorrow morning... if you'll join me." The brothers looked around in silence, their expressions agreeable. Though they had the illusion of a choice, they knew deep down they could not live with themselves if they hadn't gone. "These people have been through hell," Jordan continued, "but by the time we're done, they'll know that there's still a God that loves them, despite all this mess."

The brothers, save Leonardo, all nodded in silent unison. They then redirected their states into the depths of the fire. Jordan noted this discouragement and silently gulped, his jaw clenched. "This is going to be a long trip," he went on, "I suggest that tonight, you make your peace with the ones you love. We won't be seeing them for a while, so let's make sure they know we love them."

The brothers, except for Judah, who continued to gaze into the fire, slowly looked back up at Jordan, curious and contemplating the peculiarity of the statement. Jordan had never spoken in such final tones, and in noticing this, they also saw the lack of a smile on Jordan's face. This was a strange occurrence, not only because the brothers themselves were in high spirits, as they usually were, but also because the bonfire meetings were intended to be encouraging and positive in nature. Jordan would often smile and beam with optimism, making them ready for the coming crusade of spreading the gospel. But on this night, he was deathly serious and had left no room for the likes of jokes and tomfoolery.

Jordan noticed his brothers' change in spirits, as they began to look to him and grow empathetically discouraged. Thus, Jordan felt it fair that he express some of his thinking, within reason, and did so with a calming tone.

"Gentlemen... I have walked this trail with you many times. I've been blessed to have each and every one of you walk it with me. I have seen you all grow into fine young men, men who I am proud to call my family. Men of great faith; men who are good and faithful servants, who unwaveringly stand, not only by my side, but more importantly by the side of the Lord. I know I may have been harder on some of you than others," he looked at Leonardo, "but it's because I love you, and I only want what's best for you." He looked back up at the rest of them. "You and the beautiful families you will have one day," Jordan said, subtly gulping down tears. "We may not be brothers by blood," he proceeded, "but we are brothers by faith. I would give my life for *any of you* if the situation called for it. Regardless of what happens, come hell or high water, I want you to remember that. I am not *the* Helmsman; I'm just playing my part on this ship that our Lord faithfully directs. He is our anchor, captain, and all." He cleared his throat. "You are all everything I could've asked for in this life. I am honored to have led you into battle."

The Brothers looked to one another, then back to Jordan, each trying to interpret the inherent darkness in Jordan's speech, though it remained mysterious. Nevertheless, the Brothers' Six were touched by the uncharacteristically kind expression of feelings Jordan had let out, filled with knowledge only Jordan knew, which made the ominousness ever starker. Lee walked around his brothers and over to Jordan's side, wrapping his meaty right arm around both of Jordan's shoulders, giving him the biggest side hug he could, pulling him directly into Lee's ribs under his armpit.

"It'll be alright, Jordan. We've got your back just as much as you have ours. Whatever it is, whatever the mission, we'll do it just as we've done the others: together," Lee encouraged.

Jordan looked up at Lee and smiled. "Together," he agreed.

The brothers stood up and made their way to Jordan, following in Lee's suit. "Why don't we say a prayer?" Judah advised. "That's a great idea," Jordan furthered. As the brothers drew closer, Jordan looked at Leonardo as he slowly approached, his eyes fixed on his brothers. Leonardo actively avoided eye contact with Jordan to save himself from a punishing or disappointed glare, which was often the only gaze shared with him by his hardened older brother. Jordan knew this, but didn't want that to be the case this time. He slowly reached out and gently grabbed Leonardo's left shoulder. Leonardo looked up at Jordan, stunned, and locked eyes with him. He noticed the slight smile on his face, preceded by a nod of approval, as Jordan's eyes filled with comfort and sorrow. Leonardo examined every one of Jordan's micro-expressions, his attention fully gripped, having never seen this look on him before. Leonardo peered deeply into Jordan's eyes and saw the nightmarish torment plaguing his mind. He saw the stress that formed in Jordan's eyes. He wondered if he was somehow responsible for it, or if there was something else he didn't know that was causing such grief. His heart ached at the thought of the pressure his eldest brother was feeling, wondering if there was anything he could do to alleviate it. Without knowing what was plaguing Jordan, he determined that doing better was the best he could do, even though he had been trying that all of his life. *Maybe more will lighten his load*, he thought, wanting to do good while not understanding the evil present.

Leonardo looked around at his brothers, who stood about him, grateful for this brotherly bond that he had attained; this family that he could call his own, and from this point forth, finally would. He started to grasp the concept, to some extent, and understood what they did—the purpose behind it all. He smiled a closed-mouth smile and reached his left arm around Jordan's shoulders as well. Leonardo rested his left arm upon Lee's, for Lee took up most of Jordan's back, then raised his right arm towards Judah, who walked over to embrace the forming unity. Judah then raised his right arm and welcomed

Javier, leading Javier to walk over and hug Judah, which was quickly followed by Lucas, who locked shoulders with Javier. The Brothers' Six were now united in a line of connection, in place, ready for the event that would soon come to pass.

And so, given the understanding of what was to come, Jordan began to pray.

"Lord, heavenly father of the highest. You are the Great Decision Maker. We believe that it is you who guides us with your mighty hand, who leads us to those who are a part of your kingdom. Lord, we have walked miles on end, and we will walk many miles more, even if only to get that one soul. We are calling upon your mercy in this moment of great trial, as the adversary comes in like a roaring lion. We have done as you have instructed, and have sailed this ship into many calm waters. But now, Lord, we pray, as we are to enter into this thrashing ocean, that you would strengthen our hull so that our souls may not perish. Lord, strengthen our faith so that we may not leave your side. Give us love, so that we may not choose hate; remove the sounding songs of retributive sirens, so that we may have a sound mind; restore unto us the joy of our salvation, so that we may be free and live eternally, for though death may be the end in this world, it is only the beginning in yours. May you warm our bodies as we march through the storm, and heighten our spirits as we embrace the unknown. We are trusting in you now, Lord Jesus. In your name, we pray. Amen."

The brothers went to their respective wives and did as Jordan told them. Leonardo, on the other hand, went to his wife-to-be, said goodnight, and retired to Jordan's cabin, to the same bed that he had been sleeping on for fourteen long years. He had bunked in a separate room, there beside Jordan's, and often stared into the cabin's ceiling for many hours of the night, dreaming about a future shaped to his liking. That night, though, as he lay down on his bed, slowly drifting off to sleep, he thought about Jordan and the ominousness of his speech. He had sometimes heard Jordan wake suddenly in the night from what appeared to be nightmares. He wondered if that was the origin of his anxiety or if there was something else entirely, something strange he was not sharing. Just beside him, staring into the same cabin ceiling and refusing to drift to sleep, Jordan lay awake as well. He refused to sleep in fear that he would have more hellish and horrid nightmares. It was only then that he began to realize that, even awake, the nightmares persisted. Jordan recalled the stories that the paper had been sharing, and though he liked a good story, he couldn't bear the idea of the one they were telling - one of darkness told far beyond the graves of those within it. *The only saving grace,* he thought, *is that the darkness holds as great a message as the light that far outshines it.* It was then that he realized the stories were no longer fiction, but fact; that the nightmares had become a reality. The immaterial did not only lurk within the night, nor the pages of the paper, but now lurked within the day in the very forests they once called safe.

The Brothers' Six had made ready for their journey, but they had not made ready for what was to come. Jordan could not possibly have prepared for the evil that dawned, the one that survivors called Icarus—an evil creature that no average man wished to encounter.

CHAPTER 4

Planting a Seed and Reaping It Hence

he Brothers had left upon the early morning's rise, for the sun had not yet shone upon the day, nor overtaken the latter night. They had left in the same manner as they had for many years prior, and thus, it was believed that the status quo remained intact. Nothing was out of the ordinary.

It was with the rising of the morning sun that the day took on a different feel, and the fiddler of the hour began to play a different tune, one that many believed to be an eerie introduction to its threatening harbinger.

The brothers had been gone for five hours now, and Guarida Del León was left unprotected. The silence that came with the fog drifting into the valley seemed not only to mute all nature but also to wash out the sun itself, letting barely any light shine through. Not much could be seen through it, and for he who dared walk into it, there was only a short distance in front to be seen, with only the silhouettes and shadows of the familiar made out. It was almost as dark as the blindness that came with the darkest night, only aided by the dead bonfire that had fallen to a smoky smolder. The light of the sun, though shining through the winter's sky, was consumed by the colors of dark and faded specters. The grey of the clouds engulfed the heavens and darkened the morning's haunt, as snow fell with slow and silent caution, joining with its silent spectators that coated the ground.

Alas, this was the reason for the Firestoker, an older man with a thin grey mustache and a face full of wrinkles from his many years of service. He exited his humble adobe, built just beside the bonfire's pit. He looked up at the silent sky, letting the flakes grace his face and help to wake him up. The little white light that shone through revealed his old and torn, grey fedora, with a white feather sticking out from the side of the dark grey band that wrapped around the base of the headwear. He grabbed one end of his grey scarf made of scratchy wool and wrapped it around his neck, just over his large grey jacket of the same uncomfortable material. The Firestoker wore buckskin chaps over his black jeans and dark brown leather boots, handcrafted by Las Damas del Cuero. The Firestoker was the shortest man of the Guarida Del León, standing at a delicate five feet and four inches. Still, despite his age and size, he was the strongest of the men who lived in the village, at least in heart, and was kept limber by his constant working of the bonfire. He was a Mexican man—a man of his people, and he did his job out of his love for them.

The Firestoker looked around and noted the shortsightedness that came with the morning's presence, and though he could not see far beyond Guarida Del León's houses, he still admired the beauty. He waddled over to the side of his adobe as he let out a quiet prayer thanking the Lord for another day of life, finishing just before making it to his shed, where the bonfire wood was found. It was made of untrimmed pine timber, small in size but numerous in structure, held together by leather wrappings firmly tying the roofing and the supporting legs together. It had no walls, yet, despite this, the snow did not enter too far in from the sides, and the dried wood was stacked tightly and neatly underneath.

As snow continually built upon the roof, the villagers alongside the Firestoker constantly stacked wood under the shed. It was of the essence given the winter's unending and unyielding lordship. If one were to fail in this job at such a pivotal time as this, then the people of Guarida Del León would have no warmth, no means to cook, and thus, no life. This was believed even before considering the vast population of the elderly, who comprised most of the village. The Firestoker pondered these thoughts with great concern as he grabbed two logs from within the shed, holding one in each hand as he turned and made his way to the bonfire. He gripped them as best he could with his old and shaky hands, and with all his effort, he waddled with a stiff haste to his smoldering responsibility, tossing the two logs into the ash-filled pit, leading the ash to burst and poof in the pit. He wiped his hands together and took a minute to breathe, noticing that this time it was a little bit harder, given the logs were a little bit heavier—the only discernible difference between this trip and the previous ones taken over the dozens of years prior. He let out a half-cheeked smile, chuckled, and slowly took a knee. He leaned over and blew into the bonfire's pit, igniting the embers to a bright orange shine that slowly faded back to their darkened dim. Over and over, he blew, and over and over, the embers lit and dimmed, until finally, he sprinkled on some pine kindling. Then, a tiny flame grew. Quickly, he grabbed his tiny log filled with pine kindling, tilted the kindling into the flame, and let that catch fire with just enough time for him to place it into the pinewood pile. The smell of pinewood smoke filled the air as the flames crept underneath the barken flesh. The Firestoker smiled, then put his hand on his knee and slowly rose to a stand. He rubbed his freezing hands together, removing the dirt and mud that had gotten onto them. He looked over his bonfire side to side, ensuring it was fully set.

He gave a pause.

A look of consternation overtook his face as he examined the log on the back end of the bonfire that faced toward the open and foggy emptiness. He tilted his head and slowly limped around, making his way to one log that was not only out of the bonfire but had barely been touched by the fire. He stopped in front of it, his back facing toward the emptiness, his brain rationalizing what could have caused this massive log to stumble.

He took his boot to the log and tilted it slightly, examining the unburnt sides. *Must have happened early last night,* he thought. Even still, what he couldn't make sense of was what could have knocked over the log. Then it occurred to him: what if it was not a what, but a who? The Firestoker felt the hairs on the back of his neck begin to straighten, and a chill, unrelated to the winter's freeze, ran up his spine. He looked before him and looked over the village as best as he could; the fog blinded his every glance and engulfed every abode. He looked to the pines and saw nothing; calmly but swiftly, he diverted his attention to Mt. Sorrow and noted its absence. His heartbeat increased as he let out a controlled gulp. Despite knowing he was the only soul awake at such an hour, he could not shake the idea that he was not alone, that there was a presence there with him, watching, waiting in the unknown. Even then, it felt like more than this, like not just one, but many sets of eyes peering down on him, living but not. The Firestoker clenched his jaw as the unfamiliar feeling crept closer. He felt like a deer when a pack of wolves closes in on its prey, and as he slowly reached his right hand up to his rapidly beating heart, he located the center of the feeling. He slowly turned around to the wall of fog behind him, seeing nothing in the flesh but something else in the spirit. He squinted his eyes at the landcloud as images in the mist began to take form. First, it was nothing more than a black smudge; then, it appeared to be four abnormally tall men; finally, it became clear that there were four figures on horseback, standing and watching within the veil of the fog.

"Fantasma," the Firestoker whispered under his breath as he stared at the motionless figures, their horses whipping their tails occasionally. He angled his head side to side as he tried to get a read on the spirits, realizing that each one's head stared forward, looking down on him alone. He noted their cowboy hats and puffy, long-worn coats that floated down to their sides. He continued to study the figures as they studied him back. The Firestoker remembered how his mother had told him to deal with specters, and thus, he stepped forward in a kind yet cautious manner. "Puedo ayudarlos hermanos?" He asked kindly, his voice firm yet welcoming.

They gave no reply.

He adjusted uncomfortably as he repositioned himself in front of his bonfire, facing down the riders in a more defensive stance, as he attempted to try again. "¿Qué los trae por aquí?" There was motionless silence from the figures once more, until after a nearly five-second pause, the figure to the left gently turned his head to the right and looked out at the valley behind the housing, then calmly back at the Firestoker. "En inglés, hermano. Para mis hombres," he ordered, revealing a Cajun accent. The Firestoker's eyebrows curled in a concerned curvature, for it was now abundantly clear that these were no ghosts, but men. He wondered if they had come seeking refuge, but even then, if that were the case, why were they hiding? His heart began to race heavily, and he took on a slightly more angry tone, readying to speak the best English he could.

"Why you walk here?" he asked loudly.

The figure sat motionless again, then, without breaking eye contact, lifted his right leg off his horse and splatted down into the wet snow beneath him. He stared for a moment, gazing at the old man and scrutinizing every detail of his person with intense focus. He started walking towards the Firestoker, slowly and steadily squishing and sloshing through the snow as his spurs clicked with every step. The Firestoker's heart beat quickly, as the uncertainty of this stranger began to grow all the more threatening. The Firestoker's eyes slowly began to rise as the figure walked closer, growing taller with every forward step, and broader in all the same manner. His black cotton jacket came into view, the left side unbuttoned, swaying side to side with every one of his calculated steps. The Firestoker took one step back as the figure approached; the sun's clouded shine made him clear as day, flesh and blood, regardless of his darkness being better suited to the night.

"I walk where it is I must, firestoker," the figure answered. The Firestoker gulped, cowering back slightly, as he started looking over every detail of the man.

He had worn a simple set of attire, nothing stunning or eye-catching, so as not to draw attention to himself. Regardless, a considerable amount of time had passed since this man had begun his reign. Thus, stories had spread far and wide, attaching a legend to everything he wore, making it his unmistakable identity. Upon his head, he wore a blackened stampede hat with a bullet hole perfectly shot through the right side brim. Upon the base of this hat was a red leather string that looped around in a braid, decorating the base in a faded red. From what many could tell and what little pillow-talk had gathered, he was thirty-three years old and had begun to show wrinkles around his squinting eyes. His eyes were a light brown color that took on a near-orange and yellow hue in the center, especially when met with the sun's shining, the very few times he walked in it, rather than in darkness. His skin was a lighter tan, and he was a Cajun man. His face was clean-shaven, with a single scar just above his right eyebrow and running down his face through his upper lip. His lips were slender, and his face was lean, though he was not in any capacity scrawny. He was a toned man, packed with muscle, standing at five feet and nine inches. His body was dense, and his mind was sharp and sly.

Around his neck was a red necktie, tied with a knot in the front and looping around the back. Below the necktie was an old white union suit, faded with time and destringing around the collar. The union suit's buttons were unbuttoned two from the top, showing his firm chest beneath it. Over his union suit was a brown sheepskin leather vest, winterized and sewn by a set of hands that no one else had known. The pants he wore were black, faded over time, making them more grey than black in certain spots. His jeans had begun to fray around his left knee, and the shin and ankle sections showed no improvement. Icarus' boots were light brown in color and were scraped, battered, and dirtied all over. They were coated in the mud and blood of the many miles and men he had met. His pants bloused loosely over his boots, and on the back of his pants were small inlets cut into the lower leg of the jeans, allowing his spurs to poke through. His spurs were black steel spurs in the shape of a sun, and they were patterned with slight traces of his horse's dried blood. His gun belt was made of brown leather and was faded just the same as the rest of his clothing, which had been weathered by nature and, more than anything, time.

The Firestoker examined the fading brown-leather gun belt, which had no bullets, and found it odd. The man had a silver revolver with a brown handle holstered at his right side, with the material of both equally faded. Scrapes and scratches coated the metal, and grime, composed of dirt, smoke, and blood, replaced the fading paint. It appeared that the figure had a certain indifference when handling his revolver, and as the stories went, that checked out: he did not rely on weaponry, but used it as needed. It was well known that he preferred alternative methods of handling. The Firestoker looked behind the revolver and saw a large Bowie knife, made of blackened steel and mahogany wood, that was perfectly placed together, fading all the same. He noticed that though he knife's handle was worn, the blade was kept at a slicingly accurate sharpness. His eyes glanced over to the figure's left hip, noting a special leather loop attached to the gun belt, holding a branding iron that hung down to just below his left knee, dangling from his gun belt where there was usually a revolver. The loop had a metal button sewn into the leather and was thick enough to hold the weighty iron, despite being a clip that he would squeeze together to secure the two leather flaps.

It was when the Firestoker saw the face of the iron that his anxieties reached their peak, and his worries came to a climax, clearly being made visible in his expressions and body language, for the iron's face was a cross, half an inch thick and blackened from previous use. The Firestoker looked to the iron and began to breathe heavily, now stepping back closer to the bonfire, while the figure let out a knowing smile. The man stepped forward, startling the Firestoker, who tripped backward as he fell toward the growing flames that had now gone ablaze. The figure reached out his long and firm arm, grabbing the older man by the collar and holding him steadily just above the heated bonfire that inched closer to the Firestoker. The man stepped closer to The Firestoker, collar in hand, as the Firestoker's eyes darted between the branding iron and the figure's eyes, now only a few inches away from his, looking down on him mercilessly.

"You know who I am, don't you?" He questioned knowingly.

The Firestoker's heart beat relentlessly as he solidified who it was he was speaking to, for the look of this man was the same as the stories the Brothers' Six had told him. "Icarus," the old man let out shakily. "That's right," he replied. "Ain't no ghosts here, partner. Just me." He stepped backward just one step, pulling the Firestoker away from the flame and releasing him, allowing him to regain his footing. The other horseman hadn't budged since Icarus had begun walking, yet the Firestoker darted his vision between the horseman and him. It was then that another emotion had entered his heart of horror, for though fear grew to its peak, so did his anger. He knew what was more than likely to happen next, and in light of this, also knew that this was his home, and the people within it were his family. More so, at this moment, the Firestoker had remembered one of Leonardo's sermons and had found a new boldness because of it.

He remembered that they should not fear these men and their presence, for all is in the hands of the Lord.

The Firestoker looked up into Icarus's eyes, and with an angry and confident gaze, he made ready for the events that were set in motion. "You do not belong here," he let out in an angry, poorly pronounced tone. A smile formed on Icarus's face. He found the Firestoker's misapplied confidence humorous. "You smile like a hungry dog! Waiting to be fed a bone!" the Firestoker continued. "What?" Icarus let out with a chuckle.

"You walk in here like this is your home! It is our home! God gave this to us! Do you know who it is we are?!"

"Do I know who you are?" Icarus questioned, his smile fading. His mouth changed to a closed, straight expression, as his eyelids squinted angrily. He leaned in. "Why is it you think I'm here, firestoker?" The Firestoker realized that this point was not only a good one, but mortifying. "This was no accident," Icarus solidified.

The Firestoker let out a shaky breath. "God will not allow you to take this place. He will not allow you to hurt his people!"

Icarus's smile snaked into his cheeks once again. "Hermano, He already has."

The doors from the wooden cabins flew open as large and vicious men pulled and tossed the villagers outside their homes. Some were still in their sleeping ware, others were clothed in sheets, all were letting out screams of terror. The men were thrust or punched from their homes and launched to the wet, muddy ground with fury, rendering most nearly unconscious, enabling the captors to grab them by their hair and hold them up. The women suffered the same treatment, only they were ripped from their homes as they clawed desperately at their captors.

It was to no avail.

They were launched into the freezing, wet mud as well. The Firestoker looked around at the sudden commotion. In a panic, he looked to his own home. The doors flung open, only to see his old and fragile wife tossed in the same manner and with the same violence. After all the women were on their knees, the captors then synchronously pulled them by their hair, holding them in such a way that they barely touched the ground on their knees, forcing out a multitude of painful screams from the women and men, who were grabbing at their hair.

"Stop this! Stop!" The Firestoker commanded, looking at the people, who were now coated from head to toe in the wintry mud, the snow continuing to fall upon this once-hidden land. Suddenly, a ferocious and fearless yelling could be heard from the houses behind the bonfire, gaining the Firestoker's and Icarus's attention. It was Sophia and Reyna, Jordan's wife, fighting the men who had intruded into their homes.

The doors burst open from each of their homes, and Sophia and Reyna came out flailing. Sophia scratched and clawed at the man who had lifted her from her waist, and faced her forward towards the village, carrying her like one might take a large dog. Reyna, on the other hand, came out armed and of her own accord, holding a log in her hands with her back facing Guarida Del León. The man in front of her laughed as he teasingly jumped towards her, toying with Reyna as she swung the log towards him. The man in front of Reyna was a large and towering one, whose shoulders and head barely fit through their front door. Yet, undeterred by his size, she fought on, knowing her life depended on it. All the men who had now infiltrated the village began to chuckle to themselves as they held their prey, looking on at the commotion and enjoying the show as the individuals in their grips sat crying in pain. The villagers shifted on their knees, attempting to gain any form of balance as the muddied snow stung their skin. Their hands held their hair as the men kept it pulled tight.

Two older women came forth from the adobes, too old to be hard on yet young enough to take orders. These women were known as Las Damas del Cuero, and they were the village's eldest members. Rather than being pushed and shoved, the damas were herded and guided by the animalistic men behind them. They were instructed to walk as quickly as possible to the circle of villagers gathered around the bonfire. As this happened, Icarus watched Sophia and Reyna fight on, for the will of the women entertained him. "And who might this be?" He called out to his men, corralling Sophia and Reyna. Sophia growled and twisted back and forth wildly in the air.

"Don't you say a word to these dogs, Sophia!" Reyna ordered.

Icarus rolled his eyes. "Harley, would you be so kind as to quit your playin' and teach this woman some respect?" Icarus ordered.

"Sure thing, boss," Harley understood.

Reyna swung her wooden log at his head in hopes that this time it would land a fatal blow. The log swung through the air. Harley grabbed it with one hand, stopping it full force, leading Reyna's eyes to widen. He pulled the log away, but she held on, squeezing the log with both hands, sending her forward just before he pulled it from her. Harley quickly countered, grabbing the back of Reyna's head and using her momentum to launch her face-first into the front of her cabin. It smashed with a meaty crunch, only for her to immediately fall backward, motionless and bleeding. Sophia looked at Reyna's motionless body as her face swelled and poured forth blood from a large gash in her forehead.

"Reyna!" Sophia let out in terror.

The villagers screamed as they looked at Reyna's body. "Good lord, Harley... she alive?" Icarus asked mockingly. Harley leaned down and checked Reyna's pulse, and noticed it was beating quickly. "Plenty. Just a little flustered is all," he joked. "Good. In that case, bring her over here with the rest." The men chuckled once more to themselves as Harley picked up the unconscious Reyna, plopping her body over his shoulders. Icarus looked at Sophia. "Her, too. Quit playin' and let's get this over with." The other man threw Sophia to the ground, and as she stood to sprint, his meaty arm wrapped around her throat, stopping her in her tracks. She started clawing and scratching again as her vision darkened in a circular pattern. Icarus looked back at Reyna, eager to make a point.

"Reyna Helmsman, I presume. Wife of Jordan Helmsman, who is, from what I understand, the leader of the Brothers' Six," Icarus clarified, looking back to Sophia. "Correct?" Sophia's eyebrows curled as her mouth gritted, nudging her shoulders forcefully into her captor's chest as she weakened. Icarus took note of this. "From what I understand, this is the same man who is closest to the one who goes by the name of Leonardo DelMuerto. That right?" Sophia stopped fighting for just a moment, let out a quick look of concern, then quickly continued to fight, keeping up appearances as best as possible. Icarus smirked. "I suppose it is."

The three other horseman hopped off their horses and began walking toward Icarus. "Good ol' Leonardo," he started again, looking off to the side, then abruptly back to Sophia. "I've been trying to figure out if he's supposed to be your husband or if he's just some boy in need of a mama, and you just so happened to fit that bill."

The other men and the three other horsemen that were now behind him all let out a condescending laugh.

"Eres la mitad del hombre que tu padre era, perro bastardo!" Sophia shot back.

Icarus laughed and clapped his hands together once, looking around at his men as they chuckled and joined him in the fun. "Well, looks like I struck a nerve!" Icarus mocked. He looked back at Sophia, who was still fighting with all she had, staring down Icarus like an angered lioness, her nose scrunched and her body ready to pounce. "You know what? I have a better idea for what we can do with you, Ms. Rivera. We gon' put you in a timeout. How's that sound? Yeah, we're gonna put you in a chair, tie you down, and make sure you don't get out. How's that sound?"

"Hijo de p—" Sophia began, but was shortly cut off by her captor's hand covering her mouth.

Icarus laughed. "Nice catch, Reg. While you're at it, why don't you give Ms. Rivera a rest? Lord knows she's gonna need it."

Sophia's captor smiled back at Icarus as his eyes took on a mischievous glow, as Sophia's widened in a panic. Reginald instantly tightened his forearm and bicep muscles, blocking the oxygen flow to her brain. Within seconds, her vision went completely black as her arms and legs went limp. Sophia's captor lifted her over his shoulders and turned around to enter her home, closing the door behind him, leaving the two in darkness.

Harley walked over to the rest of the village and dropped Reyna face-first into the mud, awakening her from her unconscious state. Freezing mud filled her gash, jolting her up as she gasped for air in shock. Harley wasted no time and grabbed her by the hair and pulled her upward, the same as the rest. The three horsemen now stood beside Icarus. He leaned over to the one at his right and proceeded to deliver instructions privately into his ear. "I'd like you to go into Ms. Rivera's home. Make sure Reg does exactly as I've said and nothin' further." The horseman nodded once and proceeded to walk towards Sophia's cabin, as all the individuals around watched in worry.

Icarus turned his attention to the gathered crowd and made ready to establish the ground rules of their situation. The villagers' eyes opened wide in horror as they gazed upon him, each one sharing a wild and terrified gaze, as he looked upon each. Icarus, having his fill of examining the villagers, looked back at the Firestoker in front of him, who had not moved as he was frozen in fear. Las Damas del Cuero had their heads bowed in prayer. The younger and middle-aged women were still crying quietly, as the pain from the pulled hair had subsided slightly. The few village men who remained looked at Icarus with terrible anger, their fists clenched as their hands held tightly to the captor's arms.

"Now," Icarus began again. "What was that you said about God's land and His people?"

The Firestoker didn't say a word.

"You know, under normal circumstances, I might've killed you already, but given the interruption, I'd say you've earned yourself a few more minutes of life. Now, luckily for you, firestarter, in those few minutes, I have found myself in a particular manner of thinkin'," Icarus emphasized, inching closer to the Firestoker's face. "Despite your name-callin' and God toutin', I'll offer you a deal. A real simple one, so even a foolish man like you can understand." He sneered. "Denounce your God in front of all your people, and I'll let you live. You don't? You die."

The Firestoker had expected this deal, for it matched the stories told of Icarus. Despite what he may have wanted, the Firestoker would not denounce his beliefs in this moment, even if it meant costing him his life. He angrily frowned and looked into Icarus' eyes with fear, noticing the sick fulfillment in his.

"I would rather face judgment here than be found guilty before the judgment of God," the Firestoker proclaimed.

Icarus leaned back and put his hands on his hips, raising his eyebrows while letting out an impressed frown. He looked to the villagers to share how sarcastically impressed he was, as they gave him their undivided attention. "Now, *that*," he started, pointing viciously, "That is a man of faith. A man of valor!" Icarus complimented as he slowly looked back at The Firestoker, clapping. "Bravo. Brava!" His clapping slowly ceased. "Elders. My." He looked back at his fellow horsemen. "They sure do make a great example, don't they?"

Icarus pulled his revolver with a quick flick of his right wrist and fired off a round straight through the Firestoker's left side of his neck. The villagers screamed in an echo of blood-curdling horror as the Firestoker's wife wretchedly wailed. Icarus looked back to see how accurate his shot was, witnessing the Firestoker reach for his neck to stop the blood from coming forward. "Oh, no, you don't," Icarus mercilessly commented as he grabbed the old man's collar and threw him to the right, sending the Firestoker over in a violent wobble, in front of the villagers so they all might see. Blood pumped through the Firestoker's fingers and slipped down under and over his hand. He gurgled as he attempted to walk forward, his eyes staring up at the heavens, darting in different directions in a hefty panic, unable to focus on any particular location. He fell to his knees and tried to keep moving, clawing at the ground before him while blood seeped forth from his mouth.

"Whew! Look at him go! My, that boy can fight now, can't he!" Icarus hollered humorously.

The rest of the men cheered and laughed at the entertainment while the Firestoker continued to crawl and bleed, doing his best to go towards his wife. Mud and freshly melted snow coated the front of his body as his wife screamed tears of agony, her right hand reaching out towards her husband. She clamored for his hands as the captor behind her held her hair tightly.

"*Roberto! Roberto! Mi Roberto!*" She screamed and sobbed.

"Come on, Robert! Go get her! Go get your woman!" Icarus mocked, speaking to the Firestoker like one speaks to a dog, his hands on his knees as he leaned toward the dying man.

The Firestoker, mustering all the strength he could, saw his wife and looked at her in her eyes, crawling a few feet closer to her, only to slowly bow his head and come to a stop. His face dropped down sideways in the mud, lifeless and oozing a puddle of blood from his neck and mouth. His wife cried as she looked upon her fallen husband; tears poured forth from her eyes, and mucus fell from her nostrils. Icarus holstered his revolver and directed his attention to her, ready to continue his act. "So, what do you say, widow?" She looked up at him fearfully and shakily. "You believe that hill was worth dyin' on?"

Icarus asked. She was frozen in fearful silence. He looked up at the man holding her and flicked his head. The man nodded, reached his hand down to the widow's mouth, and pressed against it with his meaty left hand, muffling her crying as tears streamed down his fingers. She grabbed wildly at the large hand upon her mouth, as the villagers watched in shock, unable to fully process what was happening. Las Damas del Cuero continued to pray, though now their arms shook violently with fear. Every man and woman who lay on their knees was crying and wholly consumed by terror.

"Roger, Blanco," Icarus started again. "Please grab some of the firewood that the firestoker so generously donated. I want a nice big fire for these folks to see. Remember to focus on the heat."

Roger and Blanco walked over to the woodshed and did precisely as Icarus commanded. They were two of the three riders who rode with Icarus in his travels and were the generals of his army. As Roger and Blanco walked over to collect the wood, Icarus now turned his attention to the villagers, making sure the stipulations of his contract were now undoubtedly clear.

"I want it to be known that *this* is what you are offered: Many of you may know me by story; many of you may know me by name, but now you will know me by experience, and nothing other. I am the one they call Icarus, and I am here to do your Lord's biddin'. Notice the wording on that, for it is very clearly and concisely said. My wording is placed as such so that every one of you understands exactly what is going on. Now, despite your village being quite a tricky place to find, it has been found nonetheless. That is because you cannot stop what is destined; you cannot stop God's plan. Remember that, as what is about to happen to you happens, remember that your *God* allowed it. Whether it be the harder or the easier, your destiny has come to pass," he placed.

Roger and Blanco walked to the bonfire with dried wood in hand, throwing four logs onto the flame, then turned back to Icarus. "Iron sharpeneth iron," he recited, "So a man sharpeneth the countenance of his friend." The two horsemen removed their branding irons from their hips and placed them into the fire. Icarus smiled, then turned and walked closer to his mortified hostages. "Now, as you can see, these here are brandin' irons. Got a cross on the bottom that'll soon be nice and hot, ready to be used to ensure we leave a reminder to all, particularly yourselves, as to what will happen here today. You all, by now, I'm sure, know the rules, but in the event you do not, I would like to make them clear." Icarus walked over to the branding irons in the bonfire and picked up Roger's, now heated to a dull red, making the heated metal smoke as he lifted the cross into the freezing air. "You denounce your faith, your God, before the firmament of heaven, and you will live. If you do not, then you will die." He dropped the iron casually and looked at the believers with a casual grin. "Either way... You will be branded with the choices you make today, regardless of what it is." He began to slowly pace toward the fire methodically, holding the iron behind his back with both hands, letting the trail of heat rise from just above the ground. "You will bear the permanent mark to all as to what the believer is rewarded with in their belief." He stopped before the bonfire and placed the branding iron back into the center of the flame. "Whether that be in God or not."

He turned back to Blanco and Roger with a swift ease. "Gentleman. Get to work." Icarus ordered as he made his way to Sophia's cabin. The villagers shifted and shuffled painfully as their horrified screams intensified, some more uncontrolled than others, while a few quietly begged. Icarus splatted through the mud and snow as urgency overtook him, remembering that Sophia was alone with some of his not-so-finest. With a quick flash, Icarus pushed open her front door and looked for anything that had been done in the home. To his ease, it was clean, without a single piece of furniture out of place. The fireplace was hot, freshly started, with Boaz, who was the third horse rider, casually leaning against the chimney, quietly watching over Sophia. Icarus looked over to her and saw that she was gagged and tied to her chair by the table, squarely in front of her fireplace, to ensure she stayed warm. On the other side of her table sat her large captor, who had carried her in and was now whittling some wood with his large, sharp knife, while Boaz entertained himself by gently rotating his iron. Icarus rotated his shoulders and stepped forward, closing the door behind him. The mud under his boots stuck to the wooden floor, and the snow that had fallen on his shoulders started to melt. Boaz looked up at Icarus with only his eyes, peering at him just under the brim of his black gunfighter's hat. Sophia sat motionless, staring at the ground below her, awake yet unmoving. The lasso rope was tied firmly to her agape mouth and lower chest, wrapping around her and the back of her chair, just enough to cause great pain and discomfort, with even the slightest of movements. The rope was prickly and solidly woven together, intended for use on cattle, but was also occasionally used on humans. It was thick, like a wire, and would bend the same, poking into flesh that found itself without a thick leather glove to hold it. Under no circumstances would anyone want to be bound by such uncomfortable material.

"Bo, Harley," Icarus started, "why don't the two of you be on your way? Go help out the boys outside. I can take it from here."

Boaz leaned forward off the fireplace as Harley stood to his feet, the two matching their pace in a slow and quiet step as they left the household, shutting the door behind them. Icarus looked to Sophia; she refused to look up at him, leading him to look closer at the lasso that had rubbed the sides of Sophia's mouth bloody. The blood from her scratches had stained the lasso's rope, while bruises and scrapes lined her arms and face. Icarus now looked past her injuries and instead looked to her spirit, noticing that her will was caving, but still present. She was tiring physically and spiritually, but her will still shone through. Icarus knew she wouldn't beg as easily as the others, and thus, it was her tenacity that he would need to target first.

He took off his hat and placed it on her table, then fluffed his short hair. It had been cut to a clean shortness on the sides, yet left longer on the top of his head. His hair was light brown and had a natural spikiness at the front, which was accentuated by him running his fingers through the front of his hair and fluffing it upward. He then casually walked over to the fireplace behind Sophia and detached his branding iron from its loop, placing the tip into the fireplace. As Sophia sat firm as a brick, looking at his hat with only her eyes, he did so. Icarus stood up straight, warmed himself by the fire for a moment as he let out a quick stretch, then made his way to the other side of the table, grabbing the chair that Harley was sitting in. Sophia darted her eyes down, remaining in stoic silence. He dragged the chair around the front of the table, the legs scratching against the hardwood floor in a loud and uncomfortable squeal. He placed it directly in front of her and sat upon it, facing her. He looked at Sophia's eyes, though Sophia continued to gaze down, angrily breathing through her nose. He casually looked at the frazzling of her, how some of it stuck up while small bits stuck to her forehead by the sweat, the same sweat that had dampened her clothes just as much as her head.

"You put up quite the fight, didn't you?" He asked.

She gave no reply.

Icarus raised an eyebrow with a curious gaze, his jaw shifting out a bit to the left side. Icarus was impressed with the young woman's determination. He sat quietly and listened to the fire that crackled within the cabin, looking around and familiarizing himself with the home. "Love what you've done with the place," he started. "Feels like a real home." He let out a forced smile as the sounds of screams rang from the village. A revolver shot rang out. Sophia flinched as the screaming and wailing intensified, the sounds of indiscernible threats being let out, with only the hateful tone being clearly understood. The sounds echoed through the valley, even to Mt. Sorrow, it seemed. Icarus sat back in his chair calmly, clasping his hands before him on his lap as Sophia sat quietly, shaking only in the slightest. Sophia's teeth bit down on the rope that gagged her; she breathed heavily and took on the vicious face of a fighter. Icarus leaned his head forward a hair as he studied her further.

"I've heard it said that it's the screams of a burnin' man you never get used to." He shrugged. "I think it's more the smell. That burnin' and blisterin' smell. It's unnatural, to say the least. Almost like God Himself wanted to make it clear doin' such a thing ain't natural."

He leaned forward, putting his elbows on his knees, his hands still clasped. "But the screams? I got used to those." He listened for a moment. "You used to 'em, Sophia? You gotten used to hearin' your people scream? Cry? Get put down like dogs?"

Another gunshot rang out. This time, Sophia didn't flinch, but her expression did harden with fury. Icarus noted this and waited for her to raise her eyes to meet his, but to his surprise, she did not, once again. He straightened his face and his sitting position.

"In fairness, Ms. Rivera, it is a rhetorical question, so there really is no need for you to answer. Not that you could, given the rope in your mouth." He chuckled to himself a bit, proud of his joke, then sighed and shook his head lightly. "Has it occurred to you that you are not outside like the rest of your supposed family?" Sophia's breathing skipped for a beat as the thought hit her. Icarus noticed and smiled. "Instead," he continued, "you are in here, beside a fire, talking to me. Yes, you are strapped and gagged with the most uncomfortable of ropes, bleeding and bruised... but you are here talking to me." Sophia slowly raised her eyes to meet Icarus', twisting her eyebrows in an inward turn and displaying a visual of angry confusion. "There she is!" Icarus let out with a smile. "Now you're probably wonderin' 'why me? Why does he need me? What could this crazy man with an army of foot soldiers want with an insignificant woman like me?" Sophia tilted her head slightly. "If you're not," he continued, "That is the question you should be askin'. Many might argue it's the only question you should be askin'." Icarus's eyes took on a darker and more sinister hue as his head slowly dipped forward, and he leaned closer to Sophia, invading her personal space and intimidating her slightly. Still, she didn't budge and instead continued to look into his eyes, waiting for the opportunity to strike. The firelight danced on the left side of his face, revealing the massive scar that connected with his hairline.

The other side of his face was darkened by the shadow that was cast from Sophia's head. "Truth is, Ms. Rivera, I don't need you. It's your fiancé I'm after," Icarus revealed, leaning back a bit in his chair. "Leonardo Del Muerto. Gifted young fellow. Not only that, but he's starting to become a bit of a celebrity around here, from what I've heard. So much so, he almost puts me to shame." He leaned in a bit. "See, the truth is, I think you and I both know that if Leonardo and I were left to our own devices, we'd be nationwide phenomena well before the month let out, given the way things are goin'. All this revival nonsense seems to be peering its ugly face again." Icarus chuckled. Sophia gave no reply, though her eyes had begun to tell of her curiosity. Regardless of this, her anger was over-whelmingly present, just barely disguising her confusion that was slipping through the cracks. Icarus shook his head as he smiled. "The world's different now, Ms. Rivera. The times aren't as simple or shallow as stealin' valuables or doin' train robberies. The pursuit of self-made freedom does not drive us. That's old age warfare that the world does not care about, and I couldn't care less, all the same. That is why I am after Mr. Muerto."

Icarus adjusted himself and sat straight up in his seat, looking over Sophia's face as her eyes followed him up. "The age of the outlaw is dead. If you look upon me and see only that, then you are poorly mistaken. I am not a freedom fighter waging war against my masters... I am waging war against the hypocrite who hides himself in his religion." He smiled eerily; Sophia's heart rate increased. "Nevertheless," he brushed off, resting his face, "this is indeed a war that you have found yourself in, only it is invisible to the naked eye and evident to the psychological one."

Sophia began to sit up slowly as the phrasing of Icarus' terminology discomforted her. "Seems you're ready to speak now," Icarus deduced. "If that is the case, then, in kind, I will remove the rope with the *intention* that you will speak reasonably and communica-tively." Icarus stood to his feet. "But first," he started, walking behind her and over to the fire. He stared at the iron, stuck deep within the flame, the cross turning a bright, shining yellowish red. He took in a heavy breath, letting out the air through his nostrils in a mo-ment of slight release. Sophia looked to the side, her eyes scanning the area, trying to see what Icarus was doing, slightly afraid yet fully engaged. "I want to restate that I am after your fiancé, Ms. Rivera, yet to attain him, I am going to need you to do something for me."

He pulled his iron from the fire. He walked slowly in front of Sophia, stood before her with a menacing downward gaze, then gently lifted his iron to her face, now only a mere twelve inches from her cheek, shining a searing light upon her skin. Her eyes widened as her heart pounded, the iron's heat reaching through the air, making its blistering presence felt despite the distance.

Icarus leaned down and in, putting his left hand on Sophia's left shoulder, and looked into her eyes with a hollow gaze, inching the cross closer to her face as his mouth turned to an angry frown. "You have two choices," he growled. "You denounce your faith, reject your God, and prove that you are nothin' more than a liar and a fraud, all the same as the God you say you serve, and I will let you live. But if you do not, I will brand you like the property you are, and kill you slower than *any* of your friends out there!"

Icarus squeezed Sophia's left shoulder with his left hand, the cross's heat intensifying as it got closer to her face. Sophia's eyes widened as her breathing increased, watching the upright cross approach slowly. "You think this burn is gonna be bad? You just *wait* until I'm through with you. I will bleed you *slow* and leave your corpse here to *rot* and *wait* for its lover, only for him to see what the woman he once loved has become: this bloated and broken and *fleshy mess*. And best of all? It will break him—his faith, he claims to have, his love that he holds to so dear? Even his very will to live! *All of it!*"

Sophia let out muffled yells as the iron cross burned into the lasso rope. Icarus continued to push the cross closer, and Sophia's left cheek started to blister quietly.

"You know it's true," he continued, "so what's it goin' to be, Ms. Rivera? Huh? *You tell me!"* The lasso rope around Sophia's face burned apart, snapping and releasing her from her gag.

"Wait! Please, wait!" Sophia pleaded, the cross mere millimeters from her cheek.

"Wrong answer," he rejected, grabbing the rope around Sophia's chest with his left arm, lifting her forward, then off the ground and slamming her backwards onto the ground in her chair. The firewood popped and shifted from the force of the slam as air shot out forcefully from Sophia's lungs. Icarus pressed his left knee into her right ribs, his right boot slamming beside her head. He held the rope firm as he readjusted the iron and placed it just above her skin once more, inches away from her face, her skin slowly blistering from the immense heat.

"You want to try again?" He asked.

"Okay, I'll do it!" Sophia yelled with tears forming in her eyes.

"*Do what?*"

"I'll denounce my faith!" She sobbed.

"Then *denounce it!*"

"I denounce my faith!"

"Not just your faith; *who do you denounce?*"

"God!"

He slammed her down again. "Say his damn name!"

"I denounce Jesus Christ!"

"Say you reject him!"

"I reject him!"

He got in her face. "Now say you're a liar and a fraud just like he is."

"I am a liar and a fraud just like he is!" She sobbed.

Icarus paused for a moment and, with a ferocious grit of his teeth, flipped the iron cross upside down, continuing to hover it just above Sophia's face.

"All you believers are the same: a bunch of hypocrites lookin' for the next best option to fulfill your own selfish needs, your *wants*, every one of your God damned desires. Ya'll love to do it in the dark, but now you'll be revealed for what you *truly* are, and you will bear your cross as you should have long ago!" Icarus gripped Sophia's forehead with a forceful grab of his left hand, holding her head as steady as he could with an intense and focused fury. "Bear your cross as I have borne mine, you make-believin' hypocrite." He pressed the upside-down cross into Sophia's left cheek, forcing a painful and blistering scream to come forth from her lungs. Her skin sizzled and singed underneath the iron, its cross pressing firmly against her. Sophia's tears fell upon the iron and turned into a sizzling mist, as Icarus clenched his teeth together with a wild and wide-eyed expression. Icarus lifted the iron and slowly lifted her to a proper sitting position without a struggle. He holstered his iron within the leather strap attached to his gun belt and clipped the strap firmly around the iron's handle. Sophia sat sobbing in terrible pain, her burn blistering and puffing in a bright pinkish-red hue. He unsheathed his Bowie knife and pointed it at Sophia. "But whosoever shall deny me before men, him will I also *deny* before my father which is in heaven," he quoted.

With a flash, he cut the lasso rope and freed her. She fell to the floor in a weakened and destroyed state. She crumbled and crumpled into a ball as she reached her hands to her face, covering the upside-down cross but doing her best not to touch the skin. Icarus stood above her, now holstering his Bowie knife, and finished the next part of his plan. Sophia wept as Icarus grabbed his hat from her table, placing it atop his head and adjusting it as he looked down on her. "It'll not be a wonder to me how you believers can spend your whole lives sayin' you believe the word of God, yet the moment that one of you gets pressed to the ion, suddenly every bit of the good Lord is worth denouncin'." He shook his head. "Was it worth it? Is spendin' the remainder of your life in misery only to go to hell worth it? Was Leonardo worth it?" He chuckled. "My goodness, I nearly forgot about the poor boy. I wonder what he'll think of all this. What might he say?"

Icarus turned around and made for the front door, opened it, and paused a moment as the brisk winter's air flicked his skin. He turned his head slightly back to Sophia. "Don't leave. It'll only make things worse." Sophia looked up at him as tears poured down her face. He looked back and down at her, letting out a cold and twisted smile. "Be seein' you real soon, sister."

He slammed the front door behind him, immediately making way to help finish off the remaining believers in the village. Sophia dropped her head to the floor, covered her face entirely, and sobbed. The tears stung her freshly scorched flesh that now and for-ever would show an upside-down cross. She lay there for many hours, thinking about what she had done, the decision she had made, and the ramifications that it brought. She wondered what might have been the better decision, why, at that moment, she had chosen Leonardo over the Lord. She asked for forgiveness, though she felt she didn't deserve it, knowing that it didn't matter anyhow. From the little scripture she knew and the scripture Icarus had recited, she figured she was as good as condemned because of her choice. She wondered if she could have made the other decision anyhow, for she could not bear the thought of leaving Leonardo alone, especially with such a sight as her mutilated corpse. She knew what he was like and what it would do to him, and knew that with how drasti-cally their lives were going to change, he would need her now more than ever. The war that was coming was not a forgiving one. In the end, there were no sides that won, no man to walk away the victor, for the blood that was shed upon the homeland and abroad required an ever-increasing price to be paid, a price that many soldiers have faced the front lines of war, being killed and forgotten.

Regardless of whether a soldier is a friend or foe, their lives are taken so that others may retain their freedom, and in this case, though it was as spiritual as it was physical, the same applied.

Sophia understood this, just as she understood that people are ever so keen on forgetting the past; thus, it is hard for those in the present to fight for the future. Nonethe-less, soldiers are born and bred for such occasions, and they are willing to fight the greatest wars, and thus, are destined for the battlefield. They are men and women made to fight an overbearing evil that is hellbent on waging war against the children of their nation, some-times taking on the form of men like Icarus, who had created hallowed ground in Guarida Del León. Still, by the laws of warfare, this ground would not be the last one hallowed, for one cannot wage war without the assurance of an adversary, and Sophia rested on this.

Without her knowledge, an adversary had most certainly arisen.

At first, some thought that an appropriate adversary would have been an opposing army, ready to march on and fight the hundreds that opposed the people. However, in time, people would come to understand that, on rare occasions, there may only need to be one man. One who is willing to stand against a tyrant for the greater good of those he tramples over. One man, one soldier who is willing to face the forces of evil upon the very battlegrounds he has chosen, dressed for the occasion and ready for the fight.

This man, this soldier, was Michelangelo St. Hart.

CHAPTER 5

A Preacher by Day, A Soldier by Night

and clouds lifted from that dark day of the north as the snow fell in its uttermost silence. Icarus and his men had left long ago, within the hour of the morning's first rise. Those who remained in Guarida Del León wept profusely, and the bonfire had burned down to a smoky, ashy smolder. A constant stream of smoke rose from the wasted wood, and the bodies of the villagers were left out in the frozen, muddy open. Those who were killed lay in the same place they'd been kneeling, and the survivors cradled and cried over their bodies. The pale faces of the dead faced up to the clouded sky, the mark of an upright cross branded into their cheeks, and a bloody bullet hole bursting outward from their foreheads.

Among the dead were many old and grey who suffered long before their passing.

Those who lived bore an upside-down cross, proclaiming their sins before all of Man and heaven. The dead of this day were marked and remembered by the names they would be buried under in the valley behind Guarida Del León, left to be forgotten, with their last image being a dale of tombstones: Victoria Salamanca, Iglesia Barajas, Bonnie Montecarlo, and Reyna Helmsman. These women were Las Damas del Cuero and were the eldest villagers, except for Reyna. As for the men, their tombstones would read: Roberto Barajas and Raul Cruz, the latter being the Firestoker whose wife survived. There were once twenty-three villagers within the village of Guarida Del León, but after their encounter with Icarus, only seventeen remained and gravely mourned. Despite Icarus and his men being long gone, Sophia had not left her home. The only sound that came from it was her breathy crying, which was not at all unique to her on this grey and snowy morning.

As the people wept, two figures approached from a distance, now riding where Icarus and his men had once ridden in. The silhouettes took on the shapes of a soldier and a hunter, both looking upon the destroyed village, but the soldier was unfazed by either the brands upon the people or the dead bodies. His horse wasn't bothered by the imagery either, casually splotching through the snow and mud as her rider led her to. The hunter's horse shared a similar sentiment, walking just as calmly as her rider rode attentively, more concerned with the soldier rather than the battlefield before him. He looked at the soldier's stern face, watching as he analyzed the scene, looking for a threat. The hunter was grieved to see the face that had overtaken the soldier, for it was a face he had worn all too often and had significantly grown familiar with.

It was the face of a man who had seen far too much war.

Some of the villagers had looked up, noticing the two approaching. They began to stumble away fearfully, worried that more persecution was imminent. Others were still mourning the loss of their loved ones and remained huddled over the stiffening bodies.

"I take it you've seen this before?" William asked, concerned.

"Somewhat. In all honesty, these people got lucky. Usually, what remains is far harder on the eyes." Michelangelo answered.

William looked at the desolation as he and Michelangelo entered the village,

William going around the right side of the bonfire, Michelangelo around the left. Seeing Michelangelo's uniform, the villagers who were cowering away eased, and the remainder who had not noticed them looked up at the passing men. Quickly, they rose to their feet and shambled over to them, begging for help. "Ayúdanos! Ayúdanos, por favor!" One middle-aged woman cried as she raised her hands towards William, gently gripping his leg as he continued to ride through. Bleu and Betsy slowly stepped toward the center of the village, occasionally looking down at the frozen dead and the clamoring alive that were below.

"Mi amor, quédate conmigo," the Firestoker's wife cried, holding her husband's bloody head in her arms. Michelangelo looked at her, then the blood that coated the Firestoker's neck, and the bullet wound that caused it. He then looked at the cross branded into his face, noted its upright position, and then looked at the rest of the people as he moved forward. There were many more screams of agony heard from nearly every member of the village, save a few men who had walked over to the Firestoker's woodpile and were collecting wood to reignite the bonfire. Michelangelo stopped a few feet in front of Sophia's house and turned Bleu around to face the bonfiremen. William joined him just beside and leaned forward to rest upon the saddle's stirrup. The men turned around and looked at the soldier, who in turn looked at their faces and noted the upside-down crosses branded into them. Michelangelo sighed, knowing what the symbol meant, though at this point it barely bothered him, having seen the same symbol on a multitude of faces dozens of times before.

"Gentlemen," he started. The two looked him up and down, taking note of his uniform and status. "Major," one replied.

"You got names?"

"'Course we do. My name's Jameson. This is Jack."

"Howdy, Jack."

"Howdy."

The bonfiremen looked at each other slowly, then back at the soldier.

"'Can't say we ain't thankful for you being here, but I gotta say, major, it does seem odd, you being here like this," Jameson investigated.

Michelangelo nodded his head casually. "Yeah. I hear you."

"The U.S sending in soldiers to help?" Jack questioned.

"Not exactly. But I am a soldier nonetheless."

The two men nodded their heads lightly. "So, how can we help you, Major?" Jameson asked.

Michelangelo paused for a moment. "I need information. I'm looking for a man who goes by the name of Icarus. Last I was told, he was headed this direction... by the looks of things. It appears I was told right."

"Told right, sure. Told on time? I'm not sure about that. You missed him by nothing more than a mile; he left not but four hours ago. He and a small army of men."

"Which direction?"

"Just on up the hill there," Jack replied, "following the trail to Little York. About an eight-hour trip if you go on foot."

"They on foot?"

"Most of them, but... not all of them," Jameson responded. "A few dozen men were walking, maybe, but not the four horsemen."

"These horsemen: describe them to me. What did they look like?"

"Well, I mean, the men were nothing notable of any sort, but the horses... they were something strange."

"Yeah," Jack interjected, "One was a white Arabian, the other was a black colored steed... dark as the night."

"One was a cherry red," Jameson added, "and that Icarus fellow, his was nearly the color of fog itself. Like a pale color... having albino eyes."

"Almost sounds made up."

"I agree, Major... I agree. But I assure you he's as real as the devil himself."

"Which is also a point to be debated."

Michelangelo sighed and looked over the camp. "And Icarus, what does he look like?"

The two men briefly looked at each other, shrugged, and then went back to Michelangelo. "Middle-aged man, maybe. Clean-shaven and with short hair, wearing clothes that just about anyone would wear." Jack answered.

"Except the sheep skin vest," Jameson clarified. "That's a handcrafted piece... haven't seen anything like it."

Michelangelo looked back as he honed in on the unique detail. "Any other pieces of clothing that stuck out to you?"

Jameson gestured to his face quickly and shamefully. "Branding irons."

"Like what's used for cattle," Jack said.

"The iron is molded into the shape of a cross. Every one of the horsemen had one."

"None of the others?"

"Not that I could tell."

Michelangelo nodded lightly. He stared at their brandings for a moment, prompting both men to look away in shame. The corners of their mouths curved down in a saddened gloom, as their eyes shared a hollow darkness. The fresh horror the men had experienced had been burned into their minds and faces, taking on a pink and red, fleshy hue that bubbled into the shape of an upside-down cross.

"I've heard the stories," Michelangelo started. "Seen this happen in more places than just yours." He stopped looking at the markings and looked at them. "It's a terrible thing. Dozens of men would've done what you did. It's important you know that."

They smiled and sighed, finally able to make eye contact with Michelangelo.

"Pardon me," William joined, "but did you say twenty-four men in that army?"

Jameson and Jack directed their attention to him.

"Give or take a few," Jack confirmed.

William looked at Michelangelo. "Sounds like quite a lot of men for an army of two."

Michelangelo rolled his eyes and looked at William.

"You are free to leave at any time."

"Oh, I can leave, but I wouldn't say I'm free."

"And you remain bound by your convictions, not mine."

"Somewhat."

"Besides, it won't just be 'an army of two.' We'll have a cavalry."

William curiously scrunched his eyebrows and straightened his face. Michelangelo redirected his attention to the men who had already turned their attention to him.

"You all have weapons?" He started.

"Mike," William protested.

"Let the men talk, Bill." Michelangelo stopped, shooting him a threatening look in his eye, then turning back to the men. A moment of uncomfortable silence passed as he looked back at the two men. "Whenever you're ready."

Jack and Jameson looked at one another, then back at Michelangelo. "Well, sure. Everyone here came armed. Most of us had to, " Jack informed.

"Why's that?"

"Most of us traveled some rough road to get here," Jameson filled in.

"Mhm."

"You think your people know how to shoot?"

"I know for certain a handful do, including myself."

"Mike, you can't be serious," William attempted to stop.

Michelangelo looked over, more threatening now. "Very serious, Bill. Very serious." He looked back.

"The union isn't coming for you boys. 'Far as we know, my nagging bounty hunter and I are the best chance you got, and even then, it more than likely isn't enough."

"I see what you mean," Jameson caught.

"Rest assured in knowing that I do have a mission, and I will do whatever it takes to complete it... Right now, that's starting to look a lot like you all helping me in the fight."

The men nodded their heads. William shook his head, looking away.

"You all fighters?" Michelangelo asked.

"Not by experience or by nature," Jack replied.

"Are you willing to be?"

The men looked at one another, then back at Michelangelo.

"Sure. I'd say so." Jameson answered.

Michelangelo nodded his head, then turned and made way for Bleu. He adjusted himself in her saddle and turned her toward the village before him, looking at the rest of the villagers who had slowed their cries and instead began to look more at Michelangelo. William looked over to him as well, sharing an expression of disdain as he waited for him to reveal his plan. Michelangelo grabbed Bleu's reins and sat confidently.

"People of Guarida del León: My name is Major General St. Hart. I am a Union soldier. I have just had the privilege of speaking to these men here about your previous encounter with the man they call Icarus. First and foremost, I would like to extend my deepest condolences to you. I am no religious man, so I can't say I understand the gravity of such a matter... but I know any amount of degradation done, big or small, is a degradation too many. Being forced to bear a mark that is as painful as it is humiliating is an injustice not only to you, the people, but to us—this country, and the very principles it was founded upon." He paused for a beat, ensuring everyone was listening. "I am no saint, though my name may suggest otherwise. I am no keeper of the law, and I am certainly no savior. I am a soldier; one who has found himself amid your war, pain, and tragedy, particularly today. This event is one of dozens that I have wandered upon. To me, this is no different than the town I found last week, or the village I will find tomorrow, for there are wicked men all over the Arizona Territory, and they all follow this Icarus, and passionately do his bidding. There are far more found dead in this great land than the dead who lie here. In most cases, they were treated far more harshly than you, which is not to diminish your experience, but paint a picture. One that I hope will motivate you and help you understand my perspective and mission. Know that I am not here to tell you that this tragedy does not matter, but that this tragedy is of great importance. For this pain you feel, both the physical and emotional, has been felt by hundreds of others, and will be felt by hundreds more. Unless... it is stopped."

The villagers began walking toward Michelangelo. Their crying had stopped, and their expressions had started to shift, for they had gone from a morbid sorrow to an intrigued and angered countenance. Michelangelo saw the growing flame and continued to kindle it.

"I am aware of your faith. It is the very thing that has landed you in this position. We know very little about the motives of the man who has done this to you, but we do know this: you who remain... You have made your faithless decision; you who remain do not believe as much as you say you did." He shook his head and let out a slight smile. "God damn the man, but he does know how to get results. My point is, at least to me, it is clear that you value your flesh more than your faith. This is not meant to degrade you, but the truth. I do apologize for being frank, but as I understand it, your decisions today have tainted your reputation before God and the rest of those who did not denounce Him. This fact should anger you, and if it does not, I question whether you survived this deathly encounter." He clenched his jaw, looking between the eyes of all the villagers who watched him. "I am no theologian. I am no preacher. I am a soldier. I see the tactics of war, and I understand their outcomes. The outcome of what happened here today can only be a battle. If your reputation is stained, then what sense is there in trying to clean what cannot be cleansed? I know the act of killing is a sin, but I wonder if inaction is a greater one. Suppose you are truly lost, then fight not for yourselves, but for those who may face a similar fate. Isn't the law of a believer to fight evil? Is it not your responsibility to help save those who must be saved? If I were to align with any law, it would not be the laws of men, who would see wicked men kill thousands before hanging them till dead. Instead, I would align with the laws of God, who will take an eye for an eye and rain vengeance upon the wicked, from what I know." He nodded confidently. "I am no religious man. I am no preacher. I am a soldier, and when I look upon you who have been brutalized, broken, and murdered, I see the makings of me in you." He raised his fist. "Pick up your arms, and fight! Not for ourselves, but for those whom we've lost, and those who are found losing! Join me, and fight these monsters, and send them to their graves so that they may not make a hundred more!" He lowered his fist as the villagers began to speak to one another in an agreeable manner. "And for those of you who think yourselves no soldier, might I remind you that the soil on which you stand was won by the same hands that plowed it. Farmers, villagers, and simple men fought and died so that others might be free. If you, men and women, share with me this sympathy for justice, then I promise you, you will see valor in this act of war; you will see honor before the end!"

The villagers had taken on a vengeful gaze, the very same one Michelangelo had been wearing for many moons. This army of a few, which had previously been left as victims, was now instilled with newfound purpose. They had all been convinced that if they could not live as the believers they once were, then they would die as the soldiers they could be. Though they were all above the age of thirty, they still believed they had the fire to fight, and maybe even the manpower. The villagers consisted of eleven men and six women. Of the women, two were above the age of fifty, and four were between the ages of thirty and forty. Of the men, ten were in their forties, and the remainder ranged between their fifties and sixties, though some appeared to be in their seventies. This was all Michelangelo needed for his plan. It was more than enough for him to work with.

William had other thoughts on the matter.

"We fight for this," an older woman determined, "we fight for our people!"

Michelangelo forced a smile as he nodded his head once, looking upon the villagers who had aligned with his plan, and they nodded in agreement.

"Then, ready yourselves. Find your weapons and all the ammunition you can carry. Today we march for Little York... and tonight we fight the enemy," Michelangelo ordered.

The villagers disbanded as quickly as they could. William stared at Michelangelo, who looked over his small army of fodder, of villagers who had decided to fight a war that wasn't theirs to fight.

"You sure about what you're doing?" William asked.

Michelangelo turned to William, angered not so much by the question as by the very insinuation of William's findings.

"Bill, of everything I need right now, your judgment is not among them." Michelangelo ignored.

"Why? Because it makes you uncomfortable?"

"Because it comes from a hypocrite."

William huffed and shook his head. "I'm only concerned for you. That's all. You and these people. Them more than you."

Michelangelo looked at the people, noting the ill-equipped individuals he had recruited. "They want to fight, William." He coped. "I'm just assuring them along."

William gated up beside Michelangelo. "No, you want them to fight, Mike. I see what you're doing. That big ol' speech about fighting for others and fighting against evil. That isn't their fight, Mike. Hell, it's not even yours, yet you come out here trying to convince yourself as much as these people to bleed and die for it."

Michelangelo looked at William with a firm face of consternation. "It is my fight, Bill. It is. You know why." He looked forward. "I won't be having this conversation again."

"Yet you should. You want to get both of us killed, fine. I'll follow you to hell and back if it means I'm taking care of you, but innocent people?" William looked at the crowd of villagers. "These people are not soldiers, they are not fighters, they are *civilians!*

Simple folk, and in this case, nothing more than cannon fodder... and you know that." He looked back at Michelangelo, who did not turn, but looked down as he clenched his jaw. "You recruited these people just so they could be blown away... so that you and I might stand a fighting chance because you don't care about the war, you just want Icarus... and you and I both know why you want him. You're fighting wars of fabrication that are nothing more than a squabble among people we have no place among."

Michelangelo turned and faced William. "You know, I figured you, being in the war, would know better than anybody the importance of this one."

"I know the importance of law, Mike: law and *order*. Look, I will be the first person to tell you that our laws ain't perfect and that beyond a shadow of a doubt they need a hell of a lot more work, but they are the closest thing we have to society. They retain civility. It is all that separates the men from the monsters. Without them, you get anarchy."

"Anarchy?" Michelangelo looked forward. "You mean like this?"

William sighed, his shoulders stooping. Michelangelo looked back. "That's what your law allowed. Explain to me how your law is much better."

"You know what I mean, Mike."

"Yeah, I know what you mean, and I don't agree."

"But can you at least agree that your means and maybe even your motives are... misapplied?"

The two shared a short pause.

"It's not too late, Mike. We can still turn around, we can stop this... we can just go home."

Michelangelo turned to William with a sadness in his eyes and harshness in the corners of his mouth. "What home?"

William looked between Michelangelo's eyes, understanding the meaning. "War is my home," the soldier started again. "I feel *right* at home. I couldn't care less what you or anyone thinks of what I do. Uncle Sam? The news? Let 'em talk. Let them *bicker*. Let them disagree. That's what they're good at, anyway. That's their job, is it not? To say a whole hell of a lot and not do a damn thing? I mean—" Michelangelo let out an angry chuckle. "This is rich, isn't it? You, of all people, defending your 'people of the law' after how they treated you? How you're treated now that they no longer need you. You're just as much a pestilence and a grievance as the outlaws you once hunted, if not more, on account of your skin. Yet you align with them? What does 'the Grim' have to say about this? Or, why don't we take a moment to consider the black men and women who are still working like slaves up in the south because the law doesn't trickle down to those who think it doesn't apply to them, to people who are 'under the law' and found a way to enforce slavery by the penny on the pension? That's your law: an idea that is more lawful than meaningful to those it's meant to protect."

William nodded. "For now."

"For now?"

"Yes, for now. These things take time, Mike—"

"I can't believe I'm hearing this."

"—And when men like you do things like this, it takes longer!"

"When the bureaucrats take their time, innocent people die!"

"And more will in the long run if you keep on with this!"

"My keeping on works!"

"The law works!"

"For who, Bill!?"

"It works for me!"

The two men stopped as they realized they had raised their voices to a shout, and a handful of villagers had started to pay attention to them. They looked around, waited until the people returned to their business, and then looked at each other again.

"Just because it doesn't work for you, doesn't mean it won't work for everybody else," William finished.

"And that's exactly your problem, Bill. That's what your problem has always been. It's all about *you*. You don't care as long as you benefit, and as long as you're benefiting, you don't care if innocent people continue to die every day. That this continues to happen every day, and men like Icarus are allowed to continue without any accountability. You say it's all for the greater good of tomorrow, yet you neglect the evil of today. And you can live with that?"

William shook his head and sighed, looking down for a moment. He looked back up. "If that's what it takes." He looked around at the people. "Mike, I know it's bad. I'm not ignorant of that. I know that, maybe deep down, you do care about all this... that there's more to it than Thomas." He looked back at Michelangelo. "But take a word of wisdom from an old man: times are better now than they've ever been. They will get better. I've seen it. It's not always pretty. Most times, it requires the extermination of the old to make way for the new. The outlaws were an example of that. But take it from an old man, a black old man: things are better. They *will* get better."

Michelangelo nodded, sighed, and looked out over the village. "I know... I know."

They sat in silence for a moment, Michelangelo gazing out at the landscape with his eyes but drifting in his mind, William gazing at Michelangelo with a broken heart.

"I look around and all I see is death, Bill," the soldier started. "Injustice. Pain. All caused by the ignorance that comes with fabricated bliss. I fought and would've happily died for that bliss... but now? All I feel is cold. Numb. And I look at these people and all I see is the cold, and the numb, and the pain, and the death, and I can't help but wonder, 'Who's going to stand up for the people?'" He looked at William. "Who's going to stand up for the ones it doesn't work for? Who *makes it* work for them?" He looked back. "This? This isn't working. Not for me, not for them, and certainly not for long. The law... It's working against them, working against me. Everything in my being regrets what I did for it. The innocents I killed, the orders I followed, were lawful yet had no morality." He looked back at the hunter. "I killed people that we once classified as threats that today we'd call innocent, the same way I'm killing these men that are threats that are innocent until proven guilty."

William nodded. "I know, Mike. I know. Of anyone in this world that could ever understand, trust me, I do. I know it doesn't always make sense... that it's not always fair... but it's the best we've got." He looked forward. "I care about these people. I do. I'm not going to sit here and pretend that what's happening isn't horrible. I fought in the war for these people, for all people. Black men, white men, Mexican men, Indian men. All men. American men." He gestured forward. "This is what we got. It's what I got: a black man-made bounty hunter who achieves success by nothing short of a great deal of luck, skill, and opportunity... and this fresh Hell we've stumbled across."

Michelangelo nodded. "Perhaps, then, both are true."

"Both are true... but the trueness of them was found in the ability to choose that truth. These people? You can't tell me they 'made their own choice' when you come in here twisting their minds like that, making them feel like the only way they can redeem themselves is by pulling the trigger. That's not fair."

"They know what they're doing. They know the consequence."

William sighed. "Just because you're not the one putting the gun to their head doesn't mean you're not pulling the trigger.

Michelangelo looked back at William. "These are good people, Mike," he finished. "Flawed, but good. Don't do this to them."

William looked at the coldness that fell upon Michelangelo's face. He could tell he was in no place to be convinced. He knew he had already made up his mind. To William, Michelangelo seemed blinded by his undying thirst for blood, for the crimson payment he felt due, and he grew ever more worried for his vengeful nephew. William leaned back in his saddle as his eyebrows shifted into a worried frown. Michelangelo looked forward, leaning on the stirrup of Bleu's saddle.

"I've been where you are, you know," William started again, "Gone down this same road." He looked off into the distance. "Some wars, Mike... some just aren't worth fighting. Some require a price that outweighs the prize."

"Yeah, and you would know."

"I would. I won't deny that." William leaned back in his saddle and crossed his arms. "You know, that war, Michael... It's twisted me up inside ever since. Demoralized me so deeply that when I ponder taking a man's life, my ponderance is not whether or not I should do it, but how I might benefit from it. It has made me selfish and bitter, and cold as the falling snow, as you said." William hesitated. Michelangelo turned in the hesitance and the intrigue of the commentary. "So much so," the hunter continued, "that I was... willing to send Thomas through a Hell that would cost him his life for it, for my idea of justice." He stopped for a moment, his heartbeat increasing as he looked between Michelangelo's eyes. "This path... I know where it takes you. That's why I'm here. You and I... we are the same. I am your revenant from a future that you can still avoid if you listen. This war you're using to fuel your vengeance... it only ends one way. Mine was legal, and look what it did to me."

Michelangelo looked into William's eyes and noticed the years of pain and emptiness caked around each one. Still, he was not persuaded, and instead, had waxed more furious as he usually did when someone mentioned his brother.

"You know, I've been wondering that: how does a man like you 'end,' Bill? After doing all you've done. You say this is where the road leads, that this is where it ends, yet you're still living. So, where is that stopping point? When do you pay for what you've done?" Michelangelo questioned.

William stared quietly for a moment. "I suppose I'm paying for it now."

"Are you?"

William went silent again.

"Yeah. That's about what I figured." He paused. "You know, I think I know when a man like you, men like *us,* pay for what we've done—really 'end' as you call it. Or, at least how. Cold and alone, destined to greet the souls of all whom they killed, not because of the war but because of their selfish desires," Michelangelo foresaw. "What you don't seem to get is I know that, and I *accept* that, Bill. I know why I'm here. I've accepted the consequences of my actions. I've seen my future specter and embraced his eerie presence. The question I find myself asking is why you haven't done the same, why your convictions end with you living." He looked forward. "I'd imagine Icarus's convictions don't. Not with the way he's *clearly* committed himself to them." He shook his head. "Men like us have all killed the innocent, and we've all made mistakes; only some of us preach against the repayment of such sins and align with the current sinners in the name of 'peace,' though we all have the bill headed our way."

William's eyes straightened as he really listened to what Michelangelo was saying. "Mike, there are reasons to keep going, to start over. You don't have to punish yourself for what's happened, what you've done."

Michelangelo looked back. "Then who will? Who makes men like us pay? Men like Icarus?"

He looked back. William took a minute, his heart aching with pain. It was for this reason, this first assumptive reason, that William had come for Michelangelo. Honestly, deep down, he did want to help his nephew, knowing that if anyone understood what he was going through, it was him.

"Just don't be so blinded by your thirst for bloody justice that you cannot see whose it is you're spilling," he finished.

"Blood's already been spilled, Bill. Now it's only a matter of what it should be spilled for, and whether we let it go to waste," Michelangelo finished.

No matter how hard William tried to convince Michelangelo, his impasse was too harsh to overcome. William looked down at the ground below him and let out a slow and huffy sigh. He shook his head and thought about leaving his nephew's side. He wondered if, at this point, it was best to cut his losses and save his life. He thought about leaving behind the role he had chosen to play: the voice of reason, a conscience, if you will, that Michelangelo had gone deaf to. Knowing this, he knew that more than likely Michelangelo would not survive, and his last surviving family would die with him. That said, he wagered that it would keep innocent blood off his hands, a thought that grew more appealing to him with every second, but was quickly squashed by the overwhelming weight of guilt and regret that plagued his heart, painting the dark canvas of his soul with crimson complement.

He could not escape who he was, being the Brother of Grim, by any other means than redemption. Who could not ignore the fact that it was he who once sought vengeance upon all, taking on the form of monetary success and bloodshed, leading to the death of Thomas St. Hart.

Thus, though William did not want to fight in Michelangelo's war, he did want to fight in the battle *for* Michelangelo. William figured that if he could win the war for his heart, he would be truly victorious, even redeemed. William prayed he might win this one before another storm that would force William to cross his moral lines, one that he knew was coming, as it had come many times before. He committed to his restitution and let out a loud sigh, looking forward at the village the same way Michelangelo was.

"If you take this fight to Little York, the news'll be nationwide by the week's end. Then Roosevelt and all his Union will know exactly what you've done," William reminded.

"That's what I'm counting on," Michelangelo informed.

"Can I count on something from you, Major General?" Sophia spoke up.

William and Michelangelo turned abruptly to the quiet and attentive woman who was now standing in front of her cabin, her hands clasped together in front of her skirt, and her bare feet inching towards the two in the mud. William and Michelangelo looked upon Sophia's face, seeing the upside-down cross was singed into her. They looked at each other, then back to her, unsure what it was Sophia had heard, and even more so, what she wanted. Her eyes were puffy and red, her body bruised and scratched from a recent beating. Michelangelo was taken aback by her, almost amazed at her resilience and uniqueness, even in how she addressed him.

"I heard what you said," she started, "All of it. And to be honest, I don't know if you're a good man or a bad one because of it… But you're here. You're what we have, and I-I require your services."

Michelangelo said nothing; he only looked at Sophia in confusion.

"My fiancé is out there," she continued. "His name is Leonardo DelMuerto. Do you know him?"

"Yeah. I know him," Michelangelo responded softly.

She began to cry again, her lips tightening together, doing her best to choke down the tears that had started to come again. She sniffled, then breathed out through her mouth, controlling the waterworks.

"Help him. Save him, please. Bring him back to me. Icarus, he-he's going to kill him, or worse, I-I don't know. That's who he's after. That's what he said. He wants Leonardo." Michelangelo looked over the young woman and, for the first time, was at a loss for words. "Please," she went on, "if you can save him. He's all I have. I'm all he has. Maybe, if he lives, he can fix all of this. Fix us. Maybe everything will be okay," she pleaded, tears falling again.

For a reason not yet known to Michelangelo, the pitiful sight of Sophia had bothered him deeply, profoundly, so much so that his cold heart was able to feel some heat again. He thought about his newly acquired mission, one that added more to his motive for the war, not only with Icarus, but with himself. "I'll do the best I can," he comforted softly.

Sophia nodded her head and let out a slight smile, wiping her tears from her eyes and turning around, walking back inside her cabin. The soldier looked to her, and though he was still confused by the mission presented to him, he was open to its new, more inspiring feeling. William looked over at Michelangelo and noticed, for the first time in a while, that his heart had begun to beat, even if softly. The hunter let out a cornered, cheeky smile. "Michelangelo St. Hart," he commented humorously, "you might just have a soul in you yet."

Michelangelo turned to William with a somewhat amused expression, his left eyebrow lifting. "Don't get used to it."

"Oh, I won't. I won't."

Within the moment, the villagers came forth from their homes armed with their best weaponry and winter clothing, ready to make haste for Icarus and his men. The villagers were a small militia prepared for the challenge of war and had accepted its potential outcomes. The major general looked around and took note of them, all while giving a satisfied nod. William, however, looked over the villagers the same and saw nothing but the walking dead.

"Alright. We've got a lot of ground to cover and a short time to get there. Let's get going," the soldier ordered.

With this, the villagers who remained, save Sophia, had begun their march towards the town of Little York, led by the soldier and the hunter. This conflicted pair was aligned, despite their differing morals, as each worked for the greater good, regardless of the methods they used to achieve it.

Whether it was known to William or not, Michelangelo did think about what he said, though it rarely made any ground. Truth be known, there were many pieces at play in his motives for fighting in the holy war he found himself caught up in, but they all seemed to align with one outcome: killing Caine Kingsley. He was willing to do anything to ensure this happened, even if it meant fighting a war. Still, it was Kingsley who provided a means to Michelangelo's end and made sense of all the other complications that came with it, which the soldier struggled with inside.

Knowing that he was gaining on Icarus gave him hope that he was gaining on

Kingsley, and the quicker this war was over, the faster he could finish his primary mission. The plan was to subdue Icarus and attain Caine's location, the last bit of information he needed to complete his quest.

At least, that was the plan, but plans are much like trains in that they are a series of moving parts that continually run upon a track laid before them, and a train with many moving parts requires many unmoving hitches; hitches that can either keep the train together, or just as easily derail it. Hitches that have taken many forms, but here, took on the forms of four men that would soon be remembered as the soldier, the hunter, the bastard, and the preacher.

CHAPTER 6

Wars Often Fought Bring Blessings or Plight

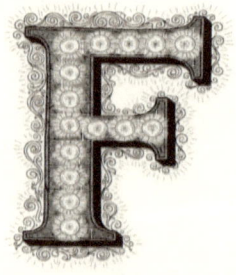 lakes fell upon the streets of Little York in a silent pat-
ter, coating the brick-laden streets in a river of white, the
blackened brick frozen over spontaneously with ice glistening on the street where snow had yet to accumulate.
White powder filled in between the cracks and solidified into piles atop the many buildings that lined the street. It was late in the afternoon, and the sun had begun to set upon
a day as cold as the souls who hid within it.

The Aland Theatre's sign shone brightly into the darkening day, lighting up the
sky in a beautiful yellow, with a hint of orange that complemented its glow. The street
lamps were lit up all along the street, and the buildings had now turned on their lamps
to light their insides. The street lamps sprouting from the ground shed their light on the
occasional horse-drawn carriage or wagon that clopped through. They also shone upon
the people of the late afternoon, who had gone out for their stroll. The General Store had
no lights to shine upon it; however, it did borrow light from the Aland Theatre directly

across, and had four lanterns that reached outward from it, placed in the corners inside. The interior of the Aland Theatre let light upon the streets as well, lighting the face of the General Store brightly via the theatre's front doors. Regardless of this, no one could quite see into the General Store, given that the afternoon light began to lessen and dim.

It wasn't nighttime exactly, but it was the just-before-night hour that had enough light to make everything visible, but merited turning the lanterns and night lights on nonetheless.

Little York was the same as it had been a few days ago, and had found itself as peaceful as it always was, particularly in the fading of the afternoon's light. The people of Little York were dressed in their finest winter best, as most of the town was, save a few. The local populace did not favor this particular bunch. They were seen as a stain better to be ignored than recognized, which wasn't hard, given they spent most of their time lurking in the shadows. Even the Brothers' Six tended to ignore them, not out of malice, but simply because these men, whoever they were, made it clear they didn't want to be seen, nor spoken to. That said, although the brothers didn't dress as nicely as the rest and looked more like the men who hid, the people of the city accepted and welcomed them, for they had grown fond of Leonardo's preaching.

Nearly eighteen hours had passed since the brothers had left Guarida Del León, and Jordan had determined that their temporary base would be the Aland Theatre. On the rooftop, Lucas roosted in his nest, watching over Little York and all that surrounded it, ensuring there were no unknowns entering. He would occasionally peer over the edge and look down through the lights of the Aland Theatre's sign to check on the individuals who walked the streets, just as Jordan was. He and the brothers were in the front lobby, for the time being, waiting for the right time to leave, which Jordan could not place, though he tried desperately. To compensate for this, he looked through the theatre's windows vigilantly, analyzing every person and checking to see if any were suspicious or threatening.

The theatre's lobby interior glowed a warm red, featuring a glistening red carpet and walls made of the same redwood. The ticket master waited within the glass casing behind the brothers, contrasting with its golden painted metal, also made of reddened oak.

The Brothers' Six waited, bored, most tracing over the red carpet and wooden walls time and time again, counting the frays in the fabric or the wooden pallets that made up each section, then, once done, counting and re-counting again. Lee leaned against the wall, and Javier sat in a chair, each twiddling their thumbs as they waited in the same position they had been for many hours now. Judah leaned beside the ticket master's booth, gently flipping through the pages of a book he was reading. It was titled "The Lions That Hunt, The Wolves That Follow," by George Oden. Meanwhile, Leonardo sat on the floor, leaning against the wooden wall, as he stared at the lights that made up the glass chandelier at the lobby's center. He shifted his gaze between that, his brothers, and then back again. He went from the chandelier to Jordan, whom he had looked at many times before, and was bothered by the strange behavior Jordan was exhibiting. He was more cautious than usual, and this bothered him. It was not normal behavior.

Judah had noticed the same thing, casually looking up from his book, then slowly to the clock that rested above the front door, revealing the late-night hour of eight fifty-three, then to Jordan. He let out a sigh, shut his book, letting out a dusty and hollow thud, and held it in his right hand. He then started walking towards him. Jordan gazed through the icy front window, quickly glancing at the different people, more shifty now, analyzing their features as though he were looking for a specific thing.

"Jordan," Judah interrupted.

Jordan didn't answer.

"Jordan," Judah interrupted again, more sternly.

Jordan turned with a quick and piercing look. "What?" He answered, agitatedly.

Jordan saw the sternness in Jordan's lips and the anxiety in his eyes that had manifested in the form of dark circles. It took him back, so much so that he had to take a moment to compose himself and gather his thoughts.

"I may not be as wise a man as I may seem," he started, "but I know that eight hours in a theatre is... peculiar when it comes to our ways of doing things."

The two shared an awkward silence. Jordan sighed and shook his head, looking back out the glass slowly. Knowing his brother, Judah decided to pry. "Jordan, if there's anything I need to know... anything I can do to help, you can talk to me."

Jordan looked down, shook his head lightly, then slowly turned to Judah again. The brothers had noticed the commotion. Each one didn't move a muscle or change their expression, instead pretending they weren't listening as they eavesdropped on the two. Truth be told, they were all worried about Jordan's behavior.

His eyes softened. "I don't know, Judah," he lied. "Something just doesn't feel right."

"Doesn't feel right, how?"

"I don't know," he lied again, hushing his tone. "I can't put my finger on it."

Judah looked between his brother's eyes. "Maybe the problem is that you're looking for something to put your finger on."

"No, no," he rejected sharply. "This is different."

"How is it different?"

Jordan looked out the window cautiously. "We don't belong here."

"Don't belong? What do you mean we don't belong?"

"It's hard to explain."

"Jordan, we have come here twice a month for years... the people know us, the guys are comfortable... you're the only one who seems to have a problem with the established norms."

Jordan whipped around quickly, trying not to draw any attention. *"This is not normal,"* He rejected sternly. He quickly looked around at the brothers who had all looked up, then promptly went back to 'ignoring' him. He looked back at Judah, hushing his tone again. "This is *not* normal. That's what I'm worried about."

"Worried? You've never worried before."

"Yeah. I know."

"You know that, but you don't know what's making you so paranoid?"

"Seems that way."

"You just can't place it, huh?"

"Yeah."

"Hm." Judah paused. "Maybe you could start by not lying."

Jordan sighed, his front slowly falling with his countenance as he realized his jig was up.

"You know," Judah started again, "I trust you with every fiber in my body. I have for a long time now. But Jordan, something is wrong. I have no idea where you plan on having us stay tonight, if you plan on having us stay at all. I don't know what's going on with you, and I'm the brains of the operation. One thing I do know is this: if we don't leave now, we won't be leaving at all, at least not tonight. You and I both know just as well as anyone that the cold freezes far quicker at night than in the day, and that's without constant snowfall. That begs the question, 'What is the plan?' Do we leave now, or are we sleeping outside on the sidewalk?"

"Mr. Salliere will allow us to stay here—"

"Mr. Salliere has been generous enough. You and I both know that, as nice as he is, we've stretched his kindness a bit too far by asking him if we can stay in his theatre entrance for the time we have. I *doubt* he'll extend that kindness to letting us sleep in his lobby, and even if he did, I wouldn't want him to. We are pushing his graciousness to its furthest extent, for reasons that none other than you appears to know, so either start telling me the truth or start making decisions."

Jordan looked back out the window and glided his gaze over the passersby. "I made a mistake, Judah," he said at a volume only Judah could hear. "For weeks I've been...

having this nightmare about us and the people. In it, I walk out of my home in Guarida, and I look over the town, and" he gulped. "I see the people... brutalized and horrifically killed with crosses burned into their cheeks. Those who were alive had one up-side-down, the dead ones had it right-side up." He looked at Judah with faint tears in his eyes. "But most horridly of all... I saw us, with bullets in our heads and upright crosses in our cheeks, lying there in the mud, and Leonardo was above us, held captive by these three men who were forcing him to watch." Great fear took over Jordan's face. "They had these branding irons, and they made him watch. And he cried... and they laughed." Judah's eyes widened as his mouth twisted in horror. "And then it went black. I don't know what happened next."

Judah gulped and shook his head, doing his best to remove the images from his mind. "Jordan," he cleared his throat, "you've been under tremendous stress. That's just your subconscious, you know? It's taking those stories we've been told and pushing them out, making sense of them."

"It wasn't my subconscious, Judah."

Judah paused, his face taking on a more stern look. "What are you saying?"

"I'm saying that it wasn't my subconscious. It was something more. Every time it was something more."

"Like what? Like a vision?"

Jordan looked up, ashamed yet honest. Judah's eyes widened as his breathing quickened. "Just to be clear," he said, gently raising his hand toward Judah, "you're saying you had a vision, multiple visions, from God, assumptively, showing that *this* was going to happen?"

Jordan nodded lightly. "Yes."

Judah looked around, panic overtaking him. "Jordan, what— what about the people?

What about our *wives*? We should *be there* for them. We need to be there *now!*"

Judah calmed his hysteria and did his best to control his breathing by taking deep, slow breaths, thinking about the people of Guarida Del León, and seeing the face of his wife. "Why?" he asked. "Why would you do this?"

"I know it was a mistake—"

"You're damn right it was a mistake."

"I wanted to keep Leo safe! You know how important he is."

"He's *not* more important than our people."

"He is what this country *needs*. You know that. As far as we know, he's all that it has left."

Judah shook his head, breathing angrily.

"Regardless," Jordan concluded, "What's done is done. Now all that matters is keeping Leo safe. Besides that, it is just a vision."

"Right, the *one gift* that you have other than leadership, and it's 'just a vision,'" Judah angrily chuckled.

Jordan bowed his head. "I know that we can't change what's coming... that we can't stop it. I just thought that there might be hope of keeping him safe if we changed what I had seen. That there would still be a chance... even if in the slightest."

"You didn't change fate! You worsened it!" Judah criticized quietly, his finger angrily pointing. Jordan nodded his head. "I know," he agreed.

Judah composed himself, then looked at Leo. "Still, I understand why you did it." He looked back. "I just wouldn't have done the same."

Jordan nodded. "I know." He looked up. "You asked, I answered. I owe you that much. "

"God knows I'm the only one you could tell," Judah affirmed sternly, shaking his head with an angry scowl. He looked at the brothers. "We need a plan. We have to keep moving." Jordan stepped away from the glass and began to think. To this point, he had not done so, for deep down he knew that whether it was by Jordan's hand or the hand of

God, one way or another, Icarus would find them soon enough. That said, with Judah's encouragement, he figured that maybe it was worth it to fight fate once more.

"Alright, Leo and I are going to walk across the street to the General Store. We'll get some supplies for the road. You keep an eye out, and when you see us exit the store, you and the boys come outside. From there, we'll hightail it as fast as we can to the next town over. No hesitations; no questions." Jordan looked at Judah. "That work?"

"Yes. That works," Judah agreed sternly.

Jordan nodded a few times, then walked past Judah as he took post by the front window. Judah couldn't help but feel betrayed, or at the very least that Jordan was a liar and a traitor. He understood his reasoning, but couldn't shake that he had still made the decision he did. He wondered if it was his shock that he was trying to navigate, rather than the situation itself, and he prayed that the visions Jordan had were nothing more than a figment of his imagination.

Jordan looked over at Leonardo. "Come on. We gotta go," he commanded.

Leonardo stood to his feet and joined Jordan at his side, and quickly the two walked to the theatre's front doors. Jordan thrust the double doors open, and the winter air scraped across their cheekbones as the two walked out onto the sidewalk, their boots sounding with an empty, hollow clop as their leather heels hit the blackened brick. Jordan looked to the left, then to the right, ensuring that no one suspicious was approaching. Leonardo did the same, only he was looking for horse-drawn carriages and the like, as he usually did; this time, however, he was a bit more focused on Jordan's behavior rather than the behavior of the individuals in the street. With quick haste, Jordan pulled Leonardo along with him as the two walked across, interworking their way between horses and carriages, while hastily walking into the general store. The bell above the door rang out with a light ding as the salesman behind the counter stood as firm as a plank, watching as Jordan and Leonardo slowly approached him. The general store's interior was filled with a wide variety of supplies, all of which were ready for purchase. The right side of the building had wooden shelving on the wall, each one filled with stacks of canned goods, consisting of fruits, vegetables, and various beans. Below the shelving, there were candies and alternative canned goods, each separated by moderately thick planks of wood, which acted as boxes built upon a long wooden platform, as large as a counter. The roof of the store was flat and square, made entirely of wood that had the same texture as the flooring that thudded beneath their footsteps. Each step Leonardo and Jordan took made itself known with a thick, hollow sound, which slightly echoed off the walls, for there was no other soul within. Leonardo and Jordan looked over the goods and proceeded to the left side of the store.

On the left side was a series of items for self-care and survival. In one wooden bin, built atop cabinets, was a series of shaving razors, each one made of shining silver and featuring a red and brown wooden handle. Within the bin beside these was bait to put on the end of one's fishing rod, in case one were ever in need of going fishing during a season such as this. In the third bin was a handful of pocket watches and pens, patterned and neatly placed for excellent presentation. Above them on the shelving units were different bottles of alcohol, all labeled with their respective titles, facing forward. Beside the shelving units, on the left and right sides of the building, there were two windows. Leonardo peered out of the one on the left, examining the space beside. He turned to the right window and noted the same emptiness. Jordan cautiously turned his head to the front windows that made up almost the entire front entrance's exterior, looking deep into Little York's street. The front windows were adorned with a marvelous printed title, featuring the words 'General Store' in red and yellow dead center.

He looked back at the goods and squinted slightly as the four lanterns that hung from the four corners of the building did their best to shed light despite the night's coming fall. The orange and dingy light shone through the store, while the electronic lights of The Aland Theatre reached through the front. The sun's fading light shone over the earth, giving the sky a menacing purple and dark blue hue. The store was kept and lit, yet even then, Leonardo could not help but smell the faint, musty odor of dust and old wood.

The salesman stood behind his counter at the back of the store, rising to his hips. On top of it was a cash register, which was black and full of metallic buttons, similar to those of a typewriter. The counter was positioned against the right wall, and the wall curved around the corner, extending directly behind the counter. The counter had enough room for the salesman to stand and plenty of lip for storage underneath. Leonardo looked at the salesman and smiled, waving kindly with a slight smile on his cheek as the salesman cautiously returned the wave. Leonardo turned his head in a bit of confusion at the reaction. Leonardo rubbed his shoulders for warmth as a draft came in, then quickly looked at the direction it was coming from: a hatch in the ceiling that required a ladder to get atop it. It was behind the counter, square, and just above where the Salesman stood, complete with a wooden trapdoor handle, presumptively, though Leonardo could not tell currently because the door was wide open. The ladder was coming down from it, just behind the salesman, popping out just beside where the counter ended, standing in front of the wooden back door that led to the outside world. This was unlike other general stores, though Leonardo figured this one had it because it was a moderately tall building in Little York, as were the rest. Jordan noticed that Leonardo was distracted and looked at the door too, feeling the winter's chill as well, and wondering at the sight similarly. He walked up beside him and stared at the ladder, then the hatch. "You've never seen that before?" He asked, looking at Leonardo. "I don't think I ever cared to notice," Leonardo replied honestly. Jordan nodded and shrugged his head, finding the commentary fair. "Honestly, I haven't noticed it much either. Usually, the hatch is closed with the ladder on the wall, but it appears our salesman here has decided to cool off a bit," he joked, smiling with a couple of light chuckles and making eye contact with the salesman. The salesman forced out some nervous laughs, causing Jordan's eyebrows to slightly furrow and his smile to fade slightly.

Snow fell through the trapdoor opening, sparkling in the lantern's light as it collected on the wooden steps of the ladder. The salesman stood tensely, the same lantern's light shining upon different angles of his face, and as Jordan continued to discern him, his suspicions heightened. The salesman was stiff as a board and shaking from the cold, or as Jordan had assumed, even something more. Leonardo walked over to the apples beside Jordan and admired their assorted, multicolored presentation. As he approached the salesman, he casually placed a couple of cans of fruits and vegetables on the counter. The salesman shakily reached for the register and began punching numbers into the machine, slowly but accurately. Jordan's eyes followed the movements, then slowly made their way back to the salesman's face. He placed his elbows on the counter, leaning in toward him. "Evening, Fitz," he greeted. "Evenin'," Fitz greeted back. Jordan waited for the usual greeting that the salesman had done hundreds of times before, yet it never came. He nodded as his heart began to beat slightly quicker. "Quite the night for a draft, don't you think?" He joked, gesturing to the open door with his head. Fitz let out a nervous laugh and a smile as beads of sweat slowly rolled down his head. "You feeling sick?" Jordan investigated. In a panicky fumble, Fitz pressed the wrong button on the register and let out a muffled curse. Jordan stood up straight again, concluding that something was very wrong. Fitz looked up at the ceiling for a flash, then back to Jordan, dipping his head and leaning in slightly. Jordan leaned in the same. "I ain't supposed to talk to you," Fitz whispered in a shaky and fearful tone.

Jordan's eyes widened as he leaned back, his heart racing as his breathing tightened. Leonardo picked up an apple and walked beside him. "We got enough money in the budget for one of these?" He asked, looking up and then to Fitz. He glanced between the two quickly, awkwardly reading the situation. He stopped on Jordan's face and was immediately troubled. It was as though he and Fitz were communicating in silence, with the only discernible word coming from Jordan being 'Why?' As though he heard, Fitz answered again, "I-I shouldn' even be lookin' at you, Mr. Helmsman, let alone tellin' you these things." Jordan placed his arm in front of Leonardo, then slowly and quietly began to step back. Fitz looked just behind the two, then his eyes widened as his breathing abruptly stopped; he then looked back. "It's the Devil, Mr. Helmsman. The Devil."

"Jordan Helmsman; Leonardo DelMuerto. Why don't the two of you come on out and join us for a little chat?" Icarus called out.

Jordan's heart sank as he turned rapidly to the front window, keeping Leonardo behind him as he looked at the very same devil Fitz had identified, standing in the middle of Little York's street, his hands placed proudly on his hips. Leonardo turned to see what Jordan saw, wondering who had called them out and if it was the same threat he had heard of many times before. *Surely not,* he thought, though Jordan thought otherwise, and as Leonardo caught his thought, he dropped his apple and slightly hid behind Jordan. They stood quiet and still, their breath slowly increasing with exasperated speed. Neither said a single word; instead, they thought only of what to do next.

Icarus waited for them to do as he planned, as his dozen armed men did the same, all around him, each holding a rifle and ammunition to spare. To Icarus's right, the three horsemen that followed him sat atop their destructive steeds, with Roger riding closest to him. His horse was the rich, cherry-red one, with its hooves, mane, tail, and nose all charcoal black. Next to Roger Wilcox was Blanco Salvador, and the horse he rode was a snow-white one that blended in nicely with the wintertime snow. The Arabian's hair was as white as the fur underneath it, and the saddle atop the beast was a black leather seat that was old and worn as the days were long and shallow. Beside him, Bo Liverpool on his charcoal-black steed. Being the last member in the lineup, his job was to hold Icarus's slightly yellowish and pale horse. It was an odd-looking creature, and its fur was not that of any colors upon a color wheel. Instead, it was as though it were an allusion to color, only to fade consistently. The hooves it walked upon were faded black, and its hair was the same pale yellow.

To Jordan, the most striking feature concerning these men and their beasts was not so much the men and the beasts themselves, nor the coloring of the creatures they rode upon, but how the men had dressed, for they looked no different than the average man. There was no fancy attire, no identifying marks, no clear indicator that these men were followers of Icarus, as gangs usually did. As far as Jordan was concerned, they were hardly dressed any differently than his brothers, for their clothing was old and worn, too, like any other nobody from nowhere. More horrifying than this, as Jordan looked closer at the faces of the men surrounding Icarus, he realized that he did recognize them, having seen them many times before at Leonardo's sermons, including the one he had preached the day before. These were the men who refused to speak to anyone, the ones hiding in the shadows, and now, far too late, it all made sense.

The Aland Theatre's doors burst open with a mighty and loud kick. Jordan's eyes shifted off the sixteen men before him to the commotion, as did the townspeople who watched, stepping back in a fearful jolt. Large, burly men came forward with four of the Brothers' Six in hand, each one being held with their arms behind their backs, being pushed forward by the pain in their shoulders. The brothers were furious and fought with all they could, especially Javier, who fought the most violently. Yet, regardless of their fighting, it was all to no avail, for the men holding them were far bigger and far more violent, and made up of meaty, massive muscle. Following behind this group of captors was another one of Icarus's henchmen, holding a gagged and wrist-bound Lucas. In the fading daylight, Jordan made out the blackened right eye on Lucas's face, seemingly done by a large and unseen fist. The men brought the brothers to the middle of the street right beside Icarus, lining them up next to one another and forcing them down to their knees harshly, the frozen brick smashing into their knees. Giant palms gripped their shoulders as Icarus examined them, slowly making his way over with methodical clomps, his spurs clicking threateningly across the bricks. He donned a smile as he looked over his victims, waiting for Jordan and Leonardo to show their faces.

"Surprised to see me? I know I would be if I was you: a couple of overconfident believers, such as yourselves. That don't surprise me, though I can see why you would be surprised." Icarus chuckled. "None of us expect the Devil to show when we talk about him. Hell, most of us don't even believe he's real until he shows his ugly face." He paused and smiled, facing the General Store. "Kinda funny, ain't it?" He continued to saunter toward the brothers. "Yes, we are all so keen to disbelieve in the Devil... until he is standin' right in front of us. Only then, in the sheer absurdity, does the Devil become believable." He looked up at the brothers. "And when the Devil becomes believable—" They looked up at him. "He becomes scary." He looked toward the General Store again. " 'Course, if you can see the Devil, that also means you can kill him, which raises the question: if you could *kill* the Devil, would you?" He smiled. "Would you stop, evil? I know I would. I guess that's why God only showed Himself once. I mean his *real* self. And what was the first thing humanity did when He did that? They killed Him. Imagine that... killing God; killing The Devil."

Icarus waited a moment for a response. He smirked and huffed in a bout of irritation, shaking his head and then looking back to the four brothers behind him. "Ya'll seein' where I'm goin' with this?" They scowled. He scoffed, then looked back at the store. "You know, conversations are only as entertainin' as those who engage in them. Why don't the two of you come on out of Mr. Maguire's store before you start boring me?"

Once again, there was no reply.

Icarus looked down and sighed, now irritated, flicking his right hand in the air to signal his men. Two men with rifles in one hand and reins in the other casually clopped two hunters' wagons over from the left side of Icarus, each one drawn by the backs of two massive black horses heavily clopping upon Little York's street. The wagons were made of blackened wood and lacked a top to cover them. The sides of the wagon were two-foot-tall rims, and below them were two large wagon wheels that bounced and thumped roughly against the blackened brick below. The horses pulled the wagon up behind the brothers, as Icarus looked over to them and made note of the arriving transportation. The men on the wagons wore a similar murderous look, their faces a mix of indignation and viciousness, ready to kill at Icarus's command. The two drivers jumped down from their respective wagons, holding their rifles in both hands as they walked over to join Icarus and the rest of his army. Icarus impatiently looked back at the General Store and noticed that the night's darkness had fully taken hold. The town of Little York was now only lit by its street lamps and The Aland Theatre's shining sign, mixed in with the faded light of the lanterns that hung inside each building. Snowflakes fell with an eerie stillness, gradually picking up speed. Icarus looked inside the store and used the lantern's light to see who was hiding within. He made out three silhouettes, though he was unable to interpret which one belonged to Leonardo. Nevertheless, he had now confirmed they were there, and this further tested his patience. He rolled his eyes and walked over to Lucas, pulling out his revolver from his holster.

"Listen, I normally don't ask twice, much less three times," he said, hovering over Lucas. "So I'm goin' to make this real simple for you." He pointed and pressed his freezing revolver into Lucas's left temple, moving his head slightly to the right. Lucas let out a muffled groan as he bit down on the rag that gagged him, closing his eyes and preparing for death. Leonardo's eyes widened. "Lucas! No!" Leonardo lunged forward past Jordan as his instincts took him over, but with little to no effort, Jordan gripped the back of Leonardo's jacket, pulling him backward as he turned, placing both hands on Leonardo's shoulders.

"Jordan, what are you doing?! *We have to go out there!*" Leonardo struggled as Jordan's hand pressed against him. He said nothing, and this, combined with Jordan's uncharacteristically physical approach to detaining him, caused him to stop and look Jordan in the eyes. Jordan raised his right finger to his lips, hushing him, as they listened.

"I want you to know, Leonardo, that I'm addressin' you," Icarus started again. "So, I'm makin' this very simple for you: come on out here, show your face, and I'll make sure these brothers of yours keep their brains inside their heads. Or... you can wait inside and I'll show you just how artistically inclined I am by paintin' the streets with your brothers' blood. It's your choice, Leo, but the clocks tickin'."

Leonardo lunged forward again, but Jordan's hand pushed him back even harder. Leonardo's face twisted angrily as Jordan held him down. *"He is going to kill Lucas!"* Leonardo forced. "He is going to kill *you!*" Jordan corrected, gripping Leonardo harder.

"We can't just sit here, we have to do something!"

"*You* will do nothing!"

Leonardo stopped moving as he took a moment to look at Jordan, noticing the pain and sorrow in his gaze. His eyes frowned with the cheeks on his face, while the grip on Leonardo's shoulders eased, and the two looked at one another. Both breathed heavily as they matched each other's gaze, Leonardo slowly piecing together what was said, as Jordan pieced together what to say.

"You cannot go to that man," Jordan started. "What he wants from you, what he's after... You cannot give it to him. He *will* kill you." He sighed. "*This* isn't your fight. Your fight is with principalities, not with men. You take what we've taught you, what the Lord has taught you, and you do everything you can with that. That has always been the point of all of this. It's you, Leo. You're all these people have left." Leonardo looked between Jordan's eyes as he did his best to bear the weight of the words he said. "That's what I need you to do, Leo. No matter what happens."

Leonardo shook his head. "No, no! We can fix this, we can— we can get out! God will—"

"*No*, Leo. God won't. *This* is God's will. It always has been. Your problem was you were never willing to accept it; you always wanted to control it."

It was true; Leonardo was not willing to accept the will that Jordan alluded to, and when he thought about it, he considered the idea that Jordan was right about this being a previous issue as well. He looked to the army outside, which had grown in number. He wondered if there was anything he could do; if there was anything that could stop this unfortunate fate from unfolding. But alas, Leonardo relented, for he began to face reality—the reality that there was truly no escape. Leonardo looked back at Jordan only to realize that Jordan had not stopped looking at him, for Jordan wanted to cherish this moment with his youngest brother, if it were the last.

"I can't," Leonardo admitted.

"Yes, you can," Jordan encouraged.

"No, no, *I can't.*"

"Yes, you can!" Jordan grabbed his shoulders and squeezed. "You have to!"

Leonardo froze.

"Please..." Jordan pleaded. "I've done everything I can for you... Now it's time for you to return the favor to the people. Believers, non-believers, friends, family. You're all they have left."

"But I'm scared, Jordan... I'm scared."

"I know." He eased his squeeze. "I know it's scary, believe me, and in all honesty, it doesn't get any easier to handle, but the good news is that the gift you have is from God, and it's from God to the people. You need to be alive to give that to them. Without you, without the gift... the faith will be lost. That's why, if you trust Him, God will protect you. He'll protect the gift as long as He needs to. But if that man gets his hands on you, he'll destroy everything we've been working towards; everything the Lord has been working towards... it'll all be over."

"You can't do this—"

"I *can* do this! More importantly, I will." He breathed. "Just know that no matter what, I've always loved you. I tried to do right by you the best I could. I want you to remember that, and promise me you'll return the favor."

Leonardo hesitated.

"Promise me," Jordan reiterated sternly.

"I promise," Leonardo said, unassuredly.

Icarus rolled his eyes. "Couple of amateurs, every single one." He pulled back the freezing metal hammer on his revolver, loading a bullet into the barrel.

"Okay." Jordan looked back at the front door, then to Leonardo once more. "Go behind the counter and don't move. You leave when I give the signal," Jordan instructed."

"What signal?" Leonardo questioned.

"You'll know it when you see it." He looked out the front window. "Don't move, don't even breathe, if you can. Then, when the time comes, you run and don't look back. Let the Lord guide you." He looked back at Fitz. "You defend this boy with your life," he ordered. Fitz nodded, a nervous wreck.

"Jordan," Leonardo interrupted. Jordan looked down and began pushing Leonardo back toward the counter. "I understand what you're saying, I even agree... but I'm not just gonna sit here and let all of you die."

Jordan placed his right hand on Leonardo's left shoulder. "It's not up for discussion," he finished, using his left hand to pick Leonardo up from his legs and toss him over the counter backwards. Leonardo attempted to regain his bearings as he adjusted himself behind the wall, curling out from his awkward position, and finding himself just under the lip of the counter. Jordan marched to the front door of the General Store in a huffy and tall stature, as Icarus watched, waiting for the two remaining members to walk forward. He stopped in front of the door and put his forehead against it, breathing slowly and closing his eyes as he let the chill of the windows numb his forehead, praying a quick prayer.

Jordan threw open the door, walking out to face the army of men before him with the audience of townsfolk watching in the background. Icarus dropped the aim of his revolver and slowly released the hammer, holstering the weapon and analyzing Jordan. "Finally," he mocked, tilting his head at a slight angle to the right and squinting his eyes, a half smile forming on his face. "You know, you don't really strike me as a Leonardo. I'd say you look more like a Jordan."

Jordan stopped as Icarus approached, walking directly in front of him and prompting him to look down. Both stared each other in the eye.

"I'm all you're going to get," Jordan said.

Icarus let out a light scoff as he smiled fully. "Well, color my intelligence insulted, Mr. Helmsman! Either you think I'm dumb, or you are as dumb as they say you are!"

The army around Icarus laughed, Jordan doing his best not to let Icarus's jab emotionally take him. "Maybe I should ask the brains of the operation," Icarus continued, turning around. "What's his name?" He asked Roger.

"Which one?" Roger answered.

"The walking library."

"Oh! Judah."

"Judah!" Icarus said, turning around with a menacing smile.

"You sure do like to hear yourself talk, don't you?" Jordan criticized.

"Yeah, well, it's moments like these where I get to have the most fun," Icarus paused. "But you're right, Mr. Helmsman. Why waste time?" He rested his hand on his revolver handle. "Let's be clear: your boy ain't goin' nowhere. If you think he is, you are *horribly* mistaken." He gestured with his head behind the General Store. "I'm guessin' you saw the back door in the store leadin' out towards the backwoods? Yeah. I got men, about twenty feet off the trail, there waitin' for Leonardo to make his great escape. And, given my men saw both of you walk into that store, and I confirmed that myself, I doubt that he stands a fightin' chance, unless, of course, my men up and vanished out of thin air." He laughed, his army of men joining him. "So... either he's still in *there*, or he'll be out *here* in just a moment. How quickly and violently that happens is up to you."

Jordan clenched his teeth, his cheek muscles flexing on both sides. "You can have the biggest army in the world, but it won't save you from God's wrath," he prophesied.

Icarus stopped for a moment, tilting his head. "The wrath of God?" He questioned. "What do you think I am, Mr. Helmsman?" He began to pace around Jordan. "You and your people's empty threats of 'God's wrath,' prophesied to me many times, and yet, it is He who has allowed me to do this to all of you." He stopped in front of Jordan. "He will allow me to do what I am going to do to you. That's God's wrath, Mr. Helmsman." He clicked his tongue. "You wanna know what's a *real* threat? You want to know the real 'wrath of God'? Death. Death is a promise, one we are all given the day we enter the earth, and it is that very *promise* we cannot avoid. So, in my perception, though this supposed wrath of God you claim prophetic authority over may come for me, however it may be interpreted in its subjectivity, you can be certain that it's coming for you *first*. It'll come for all of your kind well before me, for it is I who will be making sure of it."

Jordan was taken aback.

"On that, we agree," he concluded. "But, no matter what you do, no matter how hard you try... you'll lose. You can kill all of us, but you can't kill God."

Icarus smiled tensely, squinting his eyes and squeezing his hands subtly. "That's where you're wrong, parson."

He launched a powerful punch into Jordan's stomach, toppling him over to his knees, the air leaving his lungs, leaving him gasping for air. The brothers watched helplessly, trying to stand and wriggling in the hands of their captors, but to no avail. Leonardo watched from behind the General Store counter, frozen in fear as Icarus pulled out his revolver again, aiming it at the back of Jordan's head. He pulled back the hammer with a loud click, then looked to the store one final time. "Last chance, Leo!" He called out. "There's no way out of this. Not for you, your brothers. *No one!* Now, I'm willin' to let your brothers go on account of you comin' out, but if you *don't* get out here in the next thirty seconds, I will blow a hole so big in your brother's head a man a mile away would be able to discern his final thoughts!"

"He's lying, Leo! Don't listen to him!" Jordan yelled. "To live is Christ and to die is gain—"

Icarus cracked the revolver across Jordan's face, dropping him to the ground. Leonardo flinched as Icarus leaned down, picked up Jordan by his hair, and held him up again, now pointing the revolver at the back of his skull. "You wanna keep testin' my pa-tience?! Fine, go ahead! *See what happens!* I'm givin' you the front row view!" He roared. "Five seconds on the clock! *Five, four—*"

"*Three!*" Michelangelo yelled out, rising over the lip of the General Store's roof, aiming his Flintchester repeater down at Icarus' chest, along with William and the sev-enteen other men and women of Guarida Del León. Michelangelo was armed with the Brother of Grim's repeater. It was black and had a black leather shoulder strap. It had a scope on the top that was the same color, allowing for much farther shooting. He also had a double-barrel shotgun loaded and holstered sideways by its shoulder strap, from his left shoulder down to his right hip, and carried it on his back. William held his two revolvers in his hands, while the townsfolk had their rifles and repeaters aimed at a dif-ferent man below. William had his sights on two of the horsemen. Icarus's army raised their rifles in a quick surprise, the horsemen drawing their revolvers and aiming back at Michelangelo and William. Icarus looked up from Jordan and slowly dropped the aim of his revolver, holstering it.

This intrigued him.

Icarus did not expect these fighters, the hunter, the soldier, and the men and women he had just finished branding. He looked upon them in wonder as his eyes float-ed across the roof. The light from the Aland Theatre lit up their faces as the snow fell gently all around. "Now this is a surprise," he taunted the eleven men and six women aimed over the rim of the General Store roof, primed and ready for post-branding ven-geance. "Still, I must admit: ya'll clean up nice," he joked. He looked at William, curious as to who he was, then looked over to the one he had heard of before. "Evenin', Major," he greeted, motioning with his right hand for one of his men to come get Jordan. A man of Icarus' army walked over and grabbed him by the shoulders, dragging him next to his brothers and waiting for Icarus's following command. Michelangelo flicked the loader of the repeater, sounding off a threatening warning to Icarus below.

"Let the men go," Michelangelo ordered.

Icarus nodded slowly as he puckered his bottom lip and placed his hands on his hips. He pondered the command, turning and looking at the five brothers, then back up at Michelangelo. "You're early. I will admit that this is far more unexpected than... whatever this is. Don't get me wrong, I was expecting you to arrive eventually, but this... well. Here you are!" He subtly and quietly gulped.

"You expect to get a hole in your chest, or was that also not a part of the plan?" Michelangelo rebutted.

Icarus chuckled. "That's the Saint Hart wit I keep hearin' about."

"What else you hear?"

"That you're real mad! And I don't blame you." Icarus eased the tension in his shoulders. "Look, Major General St. Hart—soldier of soldiers, as I've been told: listen. I understand why you are a vengeful man. Believe me, in those regards, you and I are not so different. But this... business you've involved yourself in, this holy war." He put his arms out to the side. "You don't need to be!" He dropped his arms. "Yeah, I've heard the stories, and trust me, I've had my share of anger toward you because of them. It's hard not to when the stories are about your men. These horrifying, violent, and bloody stories... the stuff of nightmares that even a man as wicked as I would not do. It's impressive, honestly. Good to see our tax dollars are goin' toward whatever the hell it is they taught you." He smirked. "Even I find myself lyin' awake at night thinkin' about the blue boogyman, the vengeful Major General St. Hart. But this... this is real. Here you are! In the flesh! The Devil himself." He flicked his head up toward Michelangelo. "The stories true?"

"You're getting real close to finding out," Michelangelo threatened.

Icarus stopped for a moment and reconsidered his taunts.

"Listen, Major, I'm drivin' at a point: I may not look it or leave evidence to think it, but I am a man of reason... If you give me a minute, I might just be able to prove it to you." Michelangelo said nothing. Icarus continued. "Based on what I've heard, this war you've decided to fight, I mean, truly, it only concerns you in the context of Caine Kingsley. Does it not? You've been jabbing knives into kneecaps and splitting bellies like butter for just that, as it's been told me. Therefore, it behooves me to inform you that you findin' Caine Kingsley, in context to me, is mutually beneficial! Here's the problem, and it truly is a simple one: you have come at a *very* inopportune time. A bit early, as I said. Now, look, I am willin' to look past that and give you the information you need, but it is only I who can provide it to you. None of these other fellas has it. So, here's my offer: take you and your uhm... 'army', back to Guarida Del León. Once I'm done here, I'll meet you there and provide you with all the necessary information. Whether or not you want to kill me after attaining that information, well, that is your prerogative, but... I assure you. If you just *let me finish this*, I will give you the location of Caine Kingsley. You have my word."

Michelangelo took a moment to ponder the thought in silence. "How good is that?"

Icarus pointed back to his army with his thumb. "Ask them."

Michelangelo continued to think.

"Besides, even if I'm lyin', I have no doubt you'd be able to find me again."

He weighed the appeal of the absolution in exchange for the lives of the Brothers' Six and all that had come before them. He debated the exchange of information for Icarus's potential liberation, weighing all the horrible things Icarus had done to the one who started it all. Though it made sense in Michelangelo's head to get Caine's, he knew that if he did, he would be proving William right: that this war was never about justice, but revenge. Deep down, he knew that it was about more than that—it was about both.

It was about retribution.

"I only have one mission, Major," Icarus hurried along. "This is it."

Michelangelo nodded. "I think I'll have it my way. That's worked so far. So, why don't we go back before the bullshit, and this time you sincerely *hear* my offer: let the brothers go, and come with me, before you and the rest of your men die."

Icarus's shoulders dropped as he let out an annoyed sigh, looking down and shaking his head. He looked up again. "Unbelievable," he said to himself. He didn't want to kill Michelangelo—by all means, he respected him, but he also could not compromise his mission. He looked to the Brothers' Six, then back up to Michelangelo, letting out two sharp whistles from his lips. The Aland Theatre's rooftop moved with life, revealing eight more men armed with rifles, all primed and aimed at Michelangelo and the villagers. The theatre was higher than the roof of the General Store, giving them a deadly advantage. William aimed his revolvers at the horsemen and shifted them over to the rooftop men, as the village folk looked between the men in the street and the men on the roof, realizing their odds of survival had drastically shifted against them. "Mike..." he warned. "I see them," Michelangelo batted off. Fear overtook the villagers as Michelangelo remained unmoved. It was at this point that Icarus had thirty-four men, ready to kill the soldier's small militia.

The Aland Theatre's bulbs lit up the underside of the rooftop, men's faces, as the night fully darkened the scene. It was much harder to see each one now, which did work to Michelangelo's advantage. Regardless, it was clear to everyone involved that Icarus had the upper hand, and as the snow softly fell upon villager and warrior alike, Icarus smiled.

"I'm tryin' to be reasonable here, Major General," he tried again. "It truly does not work to my advantage for you to be dead. However... if you *insist* on dyin', right here, right now, I will oblige. I'll complete my mission, just as I am sure you'll complete yours. Please reconsider. While you do, I am going to talk with my trusted advisors and allow you the opportunity to do the same, to consider your options."

Icarus turned to his horseman and chatted quietly as William leaned over and did the same to Michelangelo in a stern whisper.

"Mike, you need to consider what it is you're being offered here. The situation changed. We are outnumbered, outgunned, and are in *way* over our heads, much more than we were before! We knew there would be men... but this is a damn fortress! The psycho says it's in his best interest that you stay alive, so let's take the gamble, cut our losses, and wait it out. Worst case scenario is we go back to the village and come up with a different plan!"

"You actually believe that slime ball?"

"I didn't say that; all I said was we should reconsider."

"Ah, yes, let's consider the maniac, William."

"If it means changing course from this suicide mission, by all means!"

"He can't be reasoned with. As far as we know, if we leave him now, we may never find him again. I'm not about to let that happen."

"But if we don't take that chance, it is a *fact* that every single one of these people will die!"

Michelangelo looked at Bill coldly. "Have you forgotten why they're here?"

Some villagers, besides Michelangelo, shot him a side eye of concern, then refocused on the men before them. "Besides," he continued, "Let's not pretend it's the people's lives you're worried about."

"Well, heaven forbid that a man have life preservation."

"I'm not asking you to stay, Bill. I never did. You want to leave? Then leave, but I'm not leaving without the kid."

"The kid?" William thought for a moment as Michelangelo looked over, letting just a bit of light peak out from behind his cold, dead eyes. He looked back down his sights. "The kid and the information. We leave now, we might lose both."

"And this is... you being honest? Not just another excuse to justify your means?"

"If we leave the kid, God only knows what unspeakable things this man will do to him. On that standard, I'm sure you can agree that the actions of staying are justified. Besides that, all these fools are in one place, right here, right now. We can end this today."

"So the missions changed? This isn't all about Caine?"

"It's evolved."

William weighed the thought of this new side to Michelangelo, which he had thought had been dormant for a long time. He wondered if perhaps this thought to save Leonardo came from a place of redemption—a place that, of all the men William had ever known, he had only seen in Michelangelo's younger brother. Perhaps the evolution of the mission was something more deeply rooted in his soul. William looked down the sights of his revolvers once more, the villagers breathing heavily as their heart rate accelerated, the presence of death breathing a cold breath down their necks that was far colder than the air around them.

Icarus turned back Michelangelo after finalizing a new, soldier-inclusive plan with his men. He placed his hands on his hips and stood confidently, waiting to hear the soldier's decision. "So," he beckoned, "What are we doin', Major?"

"Not a damn thing different," Michelangelo decided.

Icarus blew an angry burst of air through his nose as fire shot through his body, similarly to how a dragon might have done the same. A begrudged smile overtook his face as he shook his head annoyedly. William clenched his teeth; Icarus did the same. Michelangelo remained calm amid the tension, as focused as he had ever been. Icarus slowly nodded while looking at the ground.

"You know," he started, looking up, "a few months back, I had read in the paper that these two kids had made it out of Arizona." Michelangelo tensed. "Supposedly," Icarus continued, "they had the last remainin' bible in the United States. It was a grand story, an American legend, some called it. I believe it even made national news." He began to saunter to the left. "Because of that story, that Bible, this country has seen an awakening of spirituality that will more than likely change its entire structure going forward. It was a small fire... but it has now grown into an unstoppable force." He stopped and smiled. "For better or for worse." He sauntered back to the right. "However... there was one thing I couldn't understand at first: I thought to myself, 'how does an outlaw turn against his family, to save a couple of insignificant believers?'"

Michelangelo tightened the grip on the repeater, his finger slowly tightening on the trigger. William did the same. Icarus noted the slight tension in Michelangelo's shoulders and continued. He began to believe that his plan just might work.

"I thought that maybe it was just sheer, stupid bravery or that internal need to feel better about all the bad things you ever did—for 'salvation.' The spiritual pardon that saves us from our accountability. Or... perhaps it was a higher calling. Maybe, in summation, you could call it a bleeding Hart, punctured by the charity case of a couple of kids." He stopped in front of Michelangelo. "Or maybe he just didn't have the stones to put 'em down himself. Lost the nerve." Michelangelo's breathing intensified. "Now, in my opinion," Icarus continued, "After meetin' just one of the two Saint Hart brothers, I think I know exactly what it was that happened. The way I see it, you and your little brother got somethin' in common. Somethin' that the *press* left out." A snide grin slithered across Icarus's face. "In my opinion, you're both just a couple of fools runnin' a fool's errand, pickin' pointless fights upon burnin' hills that you've deemed worthy of dying on. The story of the Saint Hart brothers is not one of inspiration; it is a story of the foolish, dyin' the same way they lived: as *merciless fiends*, harbingers of death that have reached their will's end, sent to bring death to all unfortunate enough to find themselves in their path!"

"Oh, God..." William prayed.

"Show me what you've got, soldier," Icarus said to himself.

Michelangelo let out a loud and bellowing yell as he pulled the repeater's trigger, firing a bullet straight into Icarus's center chest. The shot connected with a twang and flew off into the woof of the General Store in front of him. Icarus launched backward to the ground as Michelangelo raised his head from his aim, looking down at Icarus, confused, as Icarus did his best to escape and regain the air in his lungs. Rifles and revolvers blasted from every direction as every standing street soldier sent heated metal through the sky at the opposing members. Michelangelo watched Icarus in a state of great dumb-foundedness. He had not shed any blood, and instead, though in pain, got to his knees. A bullet whizzed by Michelangelo's head, as another zipped through the lip of the General Store's rooftop, flying through one of the village men's heads, jerking his head backward as blood and brain shot out the back in an outward splooge and spray. He slowly top-pled backward to the roof, thudding against it as a crimson puddle formed behind his open skull. The village women on the roof shot at the men atop the Aland Theatre, each hitting their targets in succession. A bullet soared through a man's heart on the rooftop with a jerk of his upper left chest, sending him backward and instantly rendering his body limp as he fell to the ground. Another man, upon the Aland Theatre rooftop, jerked to his right as a bullet exploded within his right shoulder, throwing him back and onto the roof as a bloody puddle formed behind him.

Icarus' men in the street shuffled across it, gathering William's attention and shifting his focus from the roof to the street, firing his revolvers in an alternating fashion, and each round hitting its intended target. One of his bullets sliced through a street man's lower stomach, while another obliterated another one's skull beside him. The meat of his forehead sprouted outward as blood shot forth, dropping him to the ground in a quick and lifeless thud. William followed up his next shot with a shot to the other man's belly once again, staggering him backwards and forcing his body to its knees, leaving him to paw at his bullet-ridden stomach as it poured forth blood from the holes, then made its way out of his mouth. Michelangelo noted one of Icarus' men trying to lift Icarus from the ground, as Icarus struggled to get up. He cracked the repeater's loader and blasted a round straight through the side of Icarus' helper's head. The helper's head bobbed side to side as his body fell onto Icarus, meaty chunks spraying onto the black-bricked street be-side him. Michelangelo loaded another round in and aimed it down at Icarus once more. However, he was interrupted by William, who tackled Michelangelo to the rooftop.

Bullets blasted through the wood and air where Michelangelo was standing, launching pieces of obliterated bark above them. Little wooden flakes shot everywhere in front of Michelangelo's face as he looked up at the village woman who was shooting next to him. Multiple shots riddled her body and jerked her to the left and right as rifle rounds meatily ripped through her body. She slouched forward, her rifle falling from her hands, as a final bullet whizzed through her forehead and thrust her backward onto the rooftop. William looked behind him and saw another village woman's head flick violently to the left, a bullet shooting down through her right cheek and bloodily splattered out the other side. Her arms went limp, her body toppling over to the side, the village men yelling and firing their rifles as quickly as they could for suppressive fire. William quickly stood beside them and aimed his revolvers forward, shooting the men on the Aland Theatre's roof. Other villagers shot at Icarus's men in the street, nearly ripping the men to pieces. One man's leg popped open as the bullet ripped through with a shredding red spurt, and as he fell to the ground screaming, another bullet immediately ripped through his mouth and blasted out the back of his lower head, killing him as he let out a bloody and limp gurgle. As that man fell lifelessly, another was shot through the back of his left chest, throwing him forward with a rapid jitter, as the bullet ripped and rattled in his rib cage in a merciless ricochet, similar to the man beside him who had a bullet fly through the right side of his head, blowing open the side and bouncing around inside, mincing his brain. The bleeding bullet hole oozed blood as he toppled forward, smacking into the street, dead.

William quickly disposed of the men on the Aland Theatre's rooftop with the seven remaining bullets he had loaded in, each one making their mark, spurting blood over the theatre's lights, painting the light that covered the town with a sickening red hue. Blood dripped down the lights as the bodies toppled forward, backward, two toppling over the theatre roof's lip and crunching into the ground. The last man atop the Aland Theatre somehow managed to retain his life, despite being shot in the center of his chest. Blood seeped from his gritted teeth. William noticed he was still alive, looked down at his feet, and saw the village woman's rifle. He picked it up, flicked the loader, and blasted a round through the rooftop man's chest once more, wobbling him in place as his neck and spine tried to stay up, only for him to fall forward off the Aland Theatre's roof as well, hitting the brick street below with a splat.

Gunfire blasted all around William, a bullet catching his hat and launching it off his head. The hat flipped through the air and landed roughly on the General Store's roof. William dove to the ground; Michelangelo launched up, shooting at the men who had shot at William, providing cover. The villagers rose with Michelangelo upon the rooftop and fired as many bullets as their rifles had remaining to suppress Icarus' men below and potentially focus on the Brothers' Six.

The men holding the Brothers' Six had launched on top of the seemingly pro-tecting them, only now they ripped them off the floor, and began forcing them into the hunter's wagons. The horses reared as Jordan, Lucas, Javier, and Judah tried to fight their captors, who punched, kicked, and launched them. The horses neighed as Lee was tossed in the other hunter's wagon by himself. One of the villagers noticed this and aimed his rifle at the men loading Lee from the back. With a white flash, he shot and hit this man in the back of his leg, dropping him to his knees. Lee saw this, kicked that man in the face, and began tussling with the other captor.

Jordan looked at the General Store. *"Leo! Run!"* he let out before the butt of a rifle cracked him in the back of the head, knocking him out cold.

The other brothers saw this and quickly made for the man who had done this, but were met with the same violent treatment. Lee saw this, and in the moment he was distracted, he was also hit with the back of a rifle and rendered unconscious. The villager aimed again but was immediately met with a round to the chest, stumbling him back-wards. He looked down, blankly pawing at the wound as it began to fill his shirt with blood. He fell backward off the side of the General Store roof, only to smash headfirst into the ground below him.

"Get them the hell out of here!" Icarus yelled at the wagon drivers and loaders as they finished loading the brothers' unconscious bodies. He slammed through the General Store's front doors, still trying to breathe.

Michelangelo looked to where the villager had fallen, looked at the man holding Lee's leg, and fired a round through the back side of his head. The man's head jolted forward and forced him to fall forward to the ground below him. He then redirected his attention to Icarus as Icarus painfully stumbled toward the General Store entrance, grabbing at his chest as the men who were helping him up released him and armed themselves. Michelangelo cracked the repeater and aimed it at Icarus's shoulder. Wood exploded in front of him as another round zipped by his left ear, both being fired by the men previously helping Icarus. He flinched and dove backwards as the incoming fire rained around him. *"Bill!"* He yelled. William looked over. Michelangelo slid the rifle across the rooftop to him. The remaining villagers applied suppressive fire.

"I'll cover you; you cover me!" Michelangelo suggested.

William grabbed his repeating rifle, pulled twelve repeater rounds from his pocket, and loaded them into the weapon one by one, flicking them in with a forceful ease. Michelangelo grabbed the rifle of a fallen villager and stood, shooting more rounds in the direction of Icarus's men on the ground. One of the villager women twisted to the right as a bullet severed her right neck, then another punctured her right lung, sending her tumbling forward. The village woman next to her turned quickly. *"Sar—"* she started, as a bullet launched through the back of her head and out of her left eye, cutting her off. She fell forward just like her friend before her, right next to her, though she was still alive and choking on her blood. Blood filled her lungs, and the hand that was holding her neck, as Michelangelo shot three of Icarus's men with three consecutive shots, each bullet landing accurately in each man's chest. The three toppled backwards towards the street, as blood shot out of their backs, spraying the streets in blood, giving he black brick a glisten of crimson as the bullets ripped through.

"Hya!" A wagon driver commanded.

The riders whipped their horses into a trot, which led the hunters' wagon containing the Brothers' six to leave rapidly. William rose from behind the cover of the General Store's roof lip and loaded his repeater, Michelangelo diving next to him.

"The horsemen are leaving with the brothers!" Michelangelo yelled.

"What do you want to do?" William questioned, yelling back.

"Make the damn shot!"

The villagers rushed forward, firing suppressive fire as Michelangelo and William rose above the lip of the General Store's roof, aimed their weapons, and quickly fired rounds at the hunters' wagons, which bounced violently upon the uneven brick. They were at the edge of the street, where the street gave way to a forest. Both the hunter and the soldier stared at the two in their sights, quickly losing sight of them in the dark, but as they honed in, to their surprise, a man on the hunting wagon was shot in the shoulder by its driver and was sent plummeting to the ground, left unconscious. William and Michelangelo dropped their aim, raised an eyebrow, and looked to one another.

It was odd, to say the least.

A bullet whizzed by William's ear, slicing through a male villager's lower chest, crippling him forward as his hands reached the wound. They both ducked under the lip of the roof as his weak body plopped onto the General Store's roof, leaving him to bleed out and squirm, slowly, unto death. This was no different than the woman who was shot in the neck and the lung, who now stared blankly, blood oozing from her mouth and coating her neck, as her bloody arm went limp and plopped to the side, no longer trying to stop the bleeding from her neck.

Icarus stood from his lean upon the produce shelves and pulled his revolver from his holster. He lifted it with his right hand, his free one holding his chest as he painfully wheezed, fighting for each breath. Fitz raised his hands toward Icarus. "Please, please don't! I told you everything! I have the boy; he's here, he's—" Fitz begged.

"Oh, shut the hell up," Icarus said, silencing, pointing his revolver, and shooting through Fitz's forehead. His head jerked backwards with a flick, blood spraying onto the wood behind him, his body stumbling backward into the wall, then slowly sliding sideways to the ground, his mouth and eyes agape. His body thudded directly beside Leonardo, his lifeless eyes looking into his, prompting him to cover his mouth with his hands, doing his best to conceal himself. He continued to look into Fitz's lifeless eyes, frozen in fear, as the bullet hole in his head let out a droplet of blood, now streaming down toward the ground.

Icarus unbuttoned his sheepskin vest, revealing that beneath it was a leather chest piece, square in shape with rounded corners, and featuring leather straps that tied tightly around the edges. The armor covered the most vital organs in Icarus' chest, for within the leather there was a thick piece of metal, three layers deep and weighing a hefty fifty pounds. This armor didn't stop all bullets at all angles, but it would help protect him against the few rounds that hit him in the most critical areas. The metal was held within a leather swaddling, and it was connected to leather straps designed to maintain the armor in place. Two leather straps went over his shoulders, and additional leather straps around the waist attached to the bottom of the piece. The straps had met in an X-like shape on his back, providing a tight fit to keep the armor firm, while the front of the armor offered a heavy protective weight. Icarus had once seen a man use this idea to avoid being shot in a duel against five others, and recognized the potential for further development if it were refined.

This man, Icarus, had never been given a name; thus, Icarus would never give the man credit, but he would nonetheless develop the idea and have one crafted that was better, more mobile, cleaner, and more comfortable. He removed the straps as he took the leather-covered metal off his body, pulling the leather shoulder straps over his head and throwing the metallic piece to the side on the ground with a thud. He breathed heavily, listening to the gunshots that rang out. He looked to the bullet hole in the leather armor, for a ripped leather opening had been made where Michelangelo shot him. He flicked open his revolver barrel, unloaded the recently used bullet, then reached into his pocket, pulled out bullets, and loaded one single bullet into his revolver at a time, slowly.

Fitz's eyes began to unfocus as more blood dripped to the floor, now puddling and inching toward Leonardo. He gagged and shuffled away from Fitz's corpse, getting closer to the counter's wooden wall as quietly as he could. In his horror, Leonardo's caution slightly left him, letting his left boot smack against the frame of the counter, letting out a loud thud, clearly heard. Icarus's eyes darted in Leonardo's direction.

A wicked smile graced Icarus's face.

He started walking toward the counter, flicking the loaded revolver closed, but keeping the gun aimed at the ground. "Upon his rock, he proudly stood," he recited, "Thought to bring peace and sow only good. But evil once hidden came traveling thence, planting a seed and reaping it hence." His boots creaked on the wood as he walked to where Leonardo was, Leonardo doing his best to keep quiet, covering his mouth with both hands as Icarus drew closer. "A preacher by day, a soldier by night; wars often fought bring blessings or plight. Though taken heed bring calm to thine sway, death follow quickly to the prayee and prey." He was now at the corner of the counter, and methodically curled his fingers over the counter's back lip, gripping it firmly as Leonardo watched helplessly. "For whether thine heart be of lamb or of lion, the unworthy shall fall at the foot of Orion. Taketh wide birth of he burned by the son, or findeth thy soul be quickly undone." He slowly, methodically began to look over. "Tales, like this, told must end in much sorrow; take heed of the lesson, ye world of tomorrow." He began to look toward Leonardo, his face as dark as midnight's black. "For though resting bones make quick solution, mind the price paid for your retribution."

Michelangelo dropped through the trapdoor of the General Store's roof and slammed down in front of Icarus with a slight bend in his knees, inches in front of him. Icarus slowly looked up at Michelangelo's darkened face as he slowly began to rise above

Icarus. The wood beneath Michelangelo let out a loud, squeaking creak while Michelangelo stood powerfully upright; the shadow on his face, under the brim of his hat, slowly slipped away. Icarus's eyes widened as he looked into Michelangelo's eyes that glared down at him, almost inhuman. It turned out the rumors were true, and he was as tall as he was wide, even more than Icarus. He was four inches taller and four inches wider—a wall of muscle.

It was then that Icarus understood why the men who survived him feared him so, why the stories struck fear in the same way, for then, Icarus also learned the meaning of fear, and for the first time in a while, felt a familiar terror.

Michelangelo's mouth curved downward in a rage-filled twist, drastic enough to be seen through his beard, for his hair curved down the same.

"Do what you're gonna do, soldier," Icarus welcomed, gripping his revolver.

Michelangelo, obliged.

He let out a grizzly yell as Icarus aimed his revolver forward to fire. He smacked the revolver out of Icarus's hand, launching it to the wooden floor. He grabbed Icarus's aiming hand and slammed it on the counter, then quickly grabbed Icarus by the throat and pushed him backwards. Icarus struggled to retain his footing, stumbling as Michelangelo powered him as he wanted, maintaining complete control of Icarus. He slammed Icarus's back into the General Store's front wall beside the window, rattling the entirety of the store. Icarus held on to Michelangelo's wrists with both of his hands, in an attempt to hold himself steady as oxygen ceased to make its way into his lungs. He gritted his teeth, trying to think of a way out as Michelangelo pulled Icarus forward and violently slammed his head into the wall, then proceeded to hit his ribcage, his face, then his ribcage again. Icarus, now dazed, took his hands and balled them together, bringing them down in a weighty smash upon Michelangelo's forearms.

It didn't work.

He tried again and again, repeatedly slamming his fists down as Michelangelo hit him over and over, until finally, with one final smash, Michelangelo released, and Icarus launched his right fist into Michelangelo's right cheek. He stutter-stepped backwards as Icarus proceeded forward, viciously grabbing Michelangelo's jacket and reeling his fist back, only to pound Michelangelo's face with his fist, rapidly and repeatedly. Each hit connected with a meaty, painful, and busting blow, forcing Michelangelo's head to jerk backwards with every punch. Yet as Michelangelo regained his balance beneath him, he reached up and caught the next punch coming from Icarus firmly in the palm of his hand, looking at Icarus angrily in the eyes as his widened with surprise. Michelangelo slammed his forehead into Icarus's forehead and upper nose, letting out a moderate crunch and sending him backwards into the food section with a stumble. Michelangelo raised his fists to his chest as his head regained focus. Icarus did the same, tripping side to side on the food cabinet, feeling the dizziness Michelangelo was experiencing as blood oozed from his nostrils.

Michelangelo walked forward heavily, his breathing turning into growling as Icarus breathed fearfully. The soldier swung at Icarus's face, allowing Icarus to duck under and land three powerful punches into Michelangelo's ribs. He tumbled forward and into the wooden fruit shelves, forcing him to drop his fists and catch himself on the shelving unit. Icarus twisted around and grabbed the back of Michelangelo's head, only to slam the bridge of his nose down into the wooden cabinet with vicious momentum. Michelangelo's nose split with a spurt of blood on impact, shooting blood out from the injury that instantly bled. The cabinet's bottom shelving had cracked off, sending fruit forward to the ground as Michelangelo dipped to his knees, disoriented, his hat flying off his head and onto the floor. Icarus wrapped his right arm around Michelangelo's throat and held as firmly as he could, squeezing with both of his arms. Michelangelo gripped Icarus's arms as he began to choke the air out of him, the soldier's vision slowly beginning to darken. Icarus gritted his teeth in a fanged expression.

"All you had to do was walk away!" Icarus reminded.

Michelangelo roared and launched to his feet, ramming the top of his head into Icarus's chin with all the force of his legs. Icarus stumbled backward slightly and loosened his grip just enough for the soldier to grab his arms and jump up and backwards, slamming the two to the floor with an impact so powerful it toppled the alcohol bottles on the shelves to the ground. They fell and smashed around Michelangelo and Icarus, a few rolling beside them. Michelangelo turned around and knelt over Icarus, gripping his left shoulder and pulling back his right fist. Michelangelo shot his right fist into Icarus's face three times, busting Icarus's lip, shooting blood forth from it. His nose bled more, and his eyes began to blacken along with his cheekbones and chin. Michelangelo continued to ruthlessly beat Icarus, the alcohol from broken bottles seeping into the wood and their clothes.

Michelangelo stopped punching, looked over to a broken bottle top, quickly reached for it, and slammed the sharpened glass toward Icarus's right shoulder. He grabbed Michelangelo's forearm with both of his hands, holding it shakily as the bottle's sedated end inched closer to Icarus' right shoulder. *"Where's Caine Kingsley!"* He roared through his blood-soaked teeth. Icarus looked over to a small shard of glass at his right side, then back to Michelangelo. He clenched his teeth and prepared himself for pain as he accepted what needed to be done. He removed his right hand from Michelangelo's pressing arm, letting the broken glass of the bottle stab into his shoulder, forcing out a loud and painful scream. Quickly, he gripped the glass shard beside him and thrust the short and sharpened edge into Michelangelo's left ribcage. Michelangelo reeled back as he let out a yell of pain. He pulled the bottle top from Icarus' shoulder and stumbled to his feet; Icarus stumbled to his feet quickly, grabbing an unbroken bottle of Gin from the floor on his way up. Michelangelo stumbled a bit, holding the small shard of glass in his hand. He squeezed it, yet before he could pull, Icarus smashed the gin bottle across his face, pouring stinging alcohol over his cut nose and eyes. A shard of the glass had broken off and slashed a gash into Michelangelo's right eyebrow, which was instantly filled with alcohol and blood.

Michelangelo stumbled back and to the side once again, now grabbing his face as Icarus wobbled to and out the back door, slipping into the walls and barely able to hold himself up. He whistled for his horse as he trudged through the snow, and in the next moment, his pale steed swooped in, picking him up and enabling him to retreat.

For the first time in a long time, Icarus was afraid, and though he had not been killed, he nearly was, having been beaten within an inch of his life, knowing that, if Michelangelo had the chance, he would have finished the job. This alone was enough to put the fear of God into Icarus, and this bothered him deeply.

Michelangelo grunted angrily in pain. He wiped the alcohol from his eyes and looked at the motion at the door: four of Icarus's men entering. He looked at them and sized them up, noting that one of the men had already sustained a severe injury in his left shoulder—a gunshot wound given at close range.

The soldier breathed heavily as blood and beverage coated his face, nearly blinding him amidst all the liquid. He looked down at the wooden flooring, the liquid dripping and dropping off and into the puddle of alcohol that surrounded him. A broad, bated, and angry frown spread across his face, his left hand coming up to wipe the alcohol and blood once more, which was quickly flicked from his glove onto the ground. He reached down to his ribs and clenched the shard of glass, then yanked it out with a quick pull, shooting pain up the tenderness of his side. The glass shard dripped with his blood as he reached down with his right hand and unsheathed his hunter's knife. He angled both pieces towards the men in front of him, leading the metal of the blade to glint in the lantern light. The men glanced at one another with a fearful haste, then back to Michelangelo, as they fidgeted in place and readied for the fight. Michelangelo stood starkly, holding both weapons at the ready, while his injuries dripped crimson flowlines from his nose and eyebrow. His breathing intensified as he worked himself into a huffy rage. The men's hearts pounded.

Michelangelo looked up, yelled, and lunged forward, plunging the shard of glass into one of the men's eyes, sending the other men back to their bottoms in horror.

On top of the General Store, William was shooting his repeater blindly into the darkness, for the only things that could be seen were those who were lit by Little York's lights. Flashes of gunfire sparked in the darkness as each army fired blindly into the night. Still, the war outside was almost won, for very few soldiers remained to fight it. William and the remaining villagers had gunned down four more men, dramatically swaying the tides, in a way that none believed was possible. Still, William knew the battle was not yet won, and there was still a little more left. One of Icarus's men rushed across the street, clearly in William's sight. He shot the running man through the side of his left ribcage with a quick and controlled squeeze, the running man reaching for his gunshot wound in a painful grimace, only to immediately fall to the ground dead. William looked up from his scope and quickly scanned his surroundings, searching for the next target or potential location where one might be. There was no gunfire, nor even a sound, only a strange and unnerving silence that had fallen upon the town. The remaining villagers on the General Store roof began to stand, as each one looked around in confused victory.

"Is it over?" A village woman asked.

"No! Get down!" William yelled as a bullet whizzed through the air and ripped into the woman's left leg, bursting her femoral artery.

She screamed as her friend fired rounds back at the flash from the darkness. The rest of the rooftop warriors ducked as William noted where the shot had come from, peering through a bullet hole fired in the General Store's lip, attempting to ready his next shot. William smashed the lip's bullet wound open with the stock of his repeater and rested his repeater barrel in the rugged wooden opening. He lay on his stomach and used the freshly made hole as a support for his aim, hiding behind the lip of the roof for cover. Another gunshot blasted from the darkness, from the exact location as the last, clearly outlining the man in the flash, as his bullet sliced through another village woman's neck, the wound shooting forward blood in thick, quick spurts. She grabbed her throat and aimlessly waddled to the side, sitting down hard and leaning against the wooden rooftop lip, her head immediately slouched forward. The village woman bleeding from her femoral artery was now holding her wound as tightly as she could, though this did not stop the extensive bleeding.

William had his shot and, based on the flash, took it. His repeater let out a flash and a bang. The hidden sharpshooter's body flopped forward into the street light as William gripped his repeater and rolled over to the right. A bullet immediately exploded through the lip where William was and ricocheted off a gun on the rooftop. The round twanged against the gun's metal and flew through the side of the arterially bleeding woman's head, flicking her head to the right and dropping her body sideways, lifelessly. The village man beside William took a shot and clipped the shooter, who killed the last remaining woman. Though the shot was good and undoubtedly accurate, this village man was immediately met with a bullet to his collarbone that sent him to his knees. He yelled in pain as the other eight village men took fire at where the bullet had come from. William noticed the shot's location as well and shot another one of Icarus's men dead center, while the village men who were shooting took all the fire. Only two of Icarus's men remained, and between the two, they had shot and killed four of the villagers who stood their ground. William looked at their bodies as they began to crumble on the roof, some dying far slower than the others, while others toppled over instantly, lifeless. William's breathing intensified as he looked at all the blood. He gripped his heart that pounded a million miles an hour, then refocused, shakily reaching into his pocket and reloading his repeating rifle again.

Michelangelo ducked under a coming blow from a fighting man by the back door, as the man with a glass shard in his eye squirmed on the floor, squealing, reaching for his bleeding eyeball as blood coated his shaking hands. Michelangelo plunged his knife into the fighting man's stomach and ripped the blade sideways, gutting him as he stood. He removed the knife and twirled underneath the gutted man's arm and stood behind him as the man took both hands to his belly, feeling strange bumps inside his shirt that were not there before. Michelangelo booted the gutted man in the center of his back, sending him forward into the other two men by the front door. The two men by the door stared in horror, shaking and terrified by the brutal nature of the soldier. They threw the gutted man onto the floor; blood spilled from his belly and began to puddle beneath him as he twitched. Michelangelo flicked the knife into the air, caught the blade with his index finger and thumb, and threw it into the right man's chest cavity, leaving only a small portion of the handle sticking out. He wobbled backwards, his eyes widening, staring at the blade as the man beside him flinched back, stumbling to the ground again. Blood formed in the back of his throat, his hands slowly pawing at the blade, grabbing the blackened wood handle. Michelangelo shifted his focus to the man who stumbled; he saw this, fearfully rose to his feet, and picked up a large vodka bottle on his way up. Michelangelo stomped forward with a hefty and murderous haste. He screamed and raised his bottle weapon high; Michelangelo grabbed his wrist and pushed him back toward the window. Just before reaching it, he punched the man's nose, jerking his head back with a rigid flick, forcing him to hang on to any form of consciousness. Michelangelo looked to his right and noticed the other fighter had ripped the blade from his chest, blood oozing from his mouth and chest. He started to walk toward Michelangelo with murderous yet misguided intent. *"No, no! Stop!"* The man in Michelangelo's grip screamed, reaching his hand forward. Michelangelo turned back to his captive and grabbed the alcohol bottle he held, smashed it on the wooden shelves beside him, and turned to the other, barreling toward him clumsily.

Back on the General Store roof, William cracked the repeater and loaded in a round as he looked to the village man who lay beside him, and noted the injury the one had sustained. The crimson liquid flowed from his collarbone. The village man had crawled to lie beside William and was resting his head behind the lip of the roof. He looked at William and clenched his teeth in pain, as William looked back.

"I count two rifles. Can you still fight?" William asked.

"Yeah... yeah, I think s—" the village man began as a bullet blasted through the lip of the roof and shot out through the village man's right eye.

The villager went limp; William flinched back, wiping the blood that had spurted from the man onto his face. He stared at the villager's face that now had a gaping, dripping hole. He refocused, looked at the two remaining village men beside him, noticing that they had stopped shooting.

Their preservation of life was now far greater than their will to win.

Their faces and clothes were coated in the blood of their friends and loved ones. Their eyes were wide, staring into oblivion, and their mouths were frowning with a terrible fear. William breathed, his exhaustion and panic doing their best to take hold of him, as he formed a plan. William knew that these last men would no longer be able to fight, for their minds had been broken to the point that they could not function usefully on the battlefield. He determined he would do what was best for them.

"*You two:* I'll lay down some cover fire. You get the hell out of here and find yourself some place to hold up! Not back where you lived, and certainly not here... but go somewhere. Got it?" William ordered.

The two men, the ones Michelangelo had first spoken to when he arrived at Guarida Del León, looked at William and, in unison, silently agreed, nodding to William as he nodded back to them, gripping his repeater and readying himself for the final shots. "Go!" he barked, whipping around and standing to his feet, firing repeater rounds in the directions he assumed the enemy would be. The two village men stood and bolted for the roof's end, running for their lives. A shot from Icarus's men sparked in the darkness as the bullet slammed through one of the village men's lower backs. He tumbled forward painfully, flipping forward over the roof's edge to the ground below, slamming into the snow on his back. The other man jumped off the roof and landed in the uneven snow, cracking his left ankle and rolling into the white powder. William noticed its direction and redirected his aim, firing a round through the second-to-last man standing for Icarus. A gunshot boomed from the left, leading pain to surge through William's left side. The bullet had grazed his left ribs, causing him to wince and recoil in pain, stumbling a bit, then firing back at the location the shot came from, just beside the store. William grunted in agony, falling sideways onto the roof as he placed his hand on his ribcage, feeling the faint drip of blood. He guided his middle and index fingers across and let out a painful sigh of relief as he realized there was no wound. Icarus's final man now redirected his attention to the surviving villagers and began marching after them as they attempted to make their escape.

The village man who had hurt his ankle was pulling his shot friend backwards through the snow, limping and fighting against the freezing white powder that coated them both. The shot villager grunted and attempted to hold up his head, as his damaged body started to succumb to its injuries. The last man of Icarus rounded the back corner of the General Store and made for them with a relentless quickness. Jack looked up as Jameson continued to drag him, seeing him bolt his rifle with a fluid click.

"Jameson, run!" Jack yelled.

Jameson stopped. He looked up, his eyes widening as Icarus's last man aimed his rifle and fired a round, booming through the center of his head. Jameson's head flicked back, toppling his body backward into the thick fluff of the snow, spraying the white of the ground with droplets of red. Icarus's last man loaded another round with no hesitation as Jack gritted his teeth, pulling himself up to his elbows, and watching as he waited for his death. Icarus's last man aimed at Jack's face, and with no hesitation, a revolver round exploded through the front of Icarus's last man's skull. Jack flinched and backed away as a bloody mist coated his face. Icarus's last man dropped the aim of his rifle and looked down at the ground beneath him. He dropped to his knees and then fell face-first into the snow, enclosing his body within it.

William leaned against the back corner of the General Store, his right hand holding his side and his revolver in the other. He started limping over to Jack. "Can you walk?" He called out. "Y-yes," Jack answered. "Okay. Get to it," William ordered, reaching down and pulling him over his good shoulder, allowing the two to walk to the center of Little York.

"I want to go home," Jack said, "Jameson and I need to go home."

"We're gonna get you home," William comforted. "We'll get you both home."

Inside the store, Michelangelo ducked under the incoming flying blade with ease, releasing his grip on the man he had and dodging the one charging him, sending him toppling forward, and plunging the blade into his fellow man. The man screamed as Michelangelo noted the clumsy man's exposed throat, immediately zipping his broken glass bottle across it. Liquid red sprayed over Michelangelo's face and the face of the last remaining enemy inside, the soldier standing straight up and immediately wiping the spray from his eyes. The slit-throat man toppled forward into the candy shelving and slammed chest-first into the wooden frame, then slowly slid down it as dead as the rest. He looked up and noticed the man by the window, who was clutching the blade in his left lower stomach in pain. He saw that the soldier had put his attention on him and clumsily went for his revolver, fumbling at the handle. Michelangelo slowly pulled his shotgun from his back and clicked the hammer. The man saw, raised his fumbling hand forward, and let out, "No!" before Michelangelo fired a single shell through his chest, bursting it open and launching him through the window, the glass crashing onto the street along with him. He slammed backwards onto the brick street and toppled, then stopped sideways with a sudden halt. The soldier looked down at the man as he breathed heavily, staring at his corpse in the street, waiting for any other movements. Once none came, he turned around and looked at the last man—the one who had a shard of glass in his eye, still writhing in pain. Michelangelo slowly walked over to him, his shotgun held in both hands, and his right thumb flicking the other hammer to a loaded position. The glass-eyed man raised his left hand as blood dripped down his face like paint, oozing over his mouth down to his neck. Michelangelo raised his shotgun towards the man's face, aiming down the sights.

"I have information!" The man pleaded.

Michelangelo spoke no words and looked up from the iron sights, realizing that this was the man who had been shot off the wagon earlier.

He listened.

"Icarus," the one-eyed man started, "he went to the Hillberry Settlement. It's an old, tall building, thought to be rundown and abandoned. If you go there, you'll find him and the brothers."

Michelangelo nodded his head, leaning back and resting his shoulders as he dropped the shotgun down to his hip, retaining his aim. "Thank you."

The one-eyed man's only eye widened. "Wait, wait, *no!*"

Michelangelo pulled the trigger and boomed the shotgun's slug forward into the man's head, exploding it into meaty bits. Chunks and droplets of maroon matter and meat launched in every direction, particularly onto the wall behind what was now a bloody stump. His hand dropped limply, his fingers twitching, as his head now leaked a fountain of red blood that Michelangelo stared at remorselessly, suppressing the thoughts that came with what he had done. He stepped forward and made for the back door, only to stop just before exiting, right before the light lantern cascaded around him, creating a dark silhouette for the one left to see: Leonardo.

The soldier was covered in blood and meat from his hat to his boots, his clothing stained red from the victims that all dripped the same color. His shotgun had tiny droplets upon the black metal, and his face was painted crimson, with barely any olive shining through under the swipe of smeared blood around his eyes. His beard and hair were riddled with wetness, and the tiniest bits of bloody flesh had found their way into it. He lowered the aim of his shotgun with his left hand and held it by its base with his right.

Leonardo had covered his head with both of his arms, tense and in the dark under the counter. His breathing was heavy and fearful, loud enough for Michelangelo to hear. The silence of Little York helped in this matter, for after the battle, there was not a sound. The soldier was used to the familiar sound of hallowed ground, for his life was filled with it and the death it required; strangely, it was one of the only moments he found peace from the relentless burdens that preceded such a silence.

Michelangelo looked over and under the counter, seeing Leonardo quivering, Fitz's blood soaking into the right side of his clothes. Leonardo stared at the soldier in horror, thinking that this was his final moment, for before Leonardo was the outline of a bloody and horrific creature. Leonardo's eyes frantically glanced over the soldier, his breathing so heavy that his shoulders rose and fell with every breath, like a grizzly bear after hunting its meal. Michelangelo didn't realize he was striking fear into Leonardo's heart, and once he noticed that he was the cause of Leonardo's reaction, he humanized.

"Easy, kid. I'm here to help," he calmed, holstering his shotgun over his shoulder, taking off the glove on his right hand, and reaching it forward to Leonardo. As he did this, Leonardo's breathing slowed; he saw the blues of his soldier's garb, now seen in the lantern light, as well as the blood that covered a majority of it. Despite this understanding of a protector rather than a destroyer, Leonardo was still traumatized. "You can come out now. It's alright," Michelangelo comforted. Leonardo didn't budge. Michelangelo sighed, dropping his outstretched hand, then looked at Fitz's body. He moved the ladder out of the way and stepped behind the counter, gripping the corpse around the waist and shoving the body over. Leonardo looked away as Michelangelo then grabbed the torso and did the same, pushing it into the back corner of the counter. Michelangelo bent his knees and rested as he balanced on his toes, squatting next to Leonardo. He looked at him and let out a bit of air through his nose.

"Are you Leonardo?" Michelangelo asked calmly.

Leonardo hesitated. "Yes."

Michelangelo nodded, looked down at the floor, then off to the side, in a slight, playful manner. "I hear you're kind of famous." Michelangelo looked back through the side of his eye.

Leonardo let out a slight smile from the corner of his mouth and looked to the side. "Seems that way."

He looked back. Michelangelo reached out his unbloodied hand once again. "I'm Michelangelo St. Hart. You can call me Michael or Mike. Most people do."

Leonardo marveled at the name, for it was similar to his, and this comforted him. More than this, he had heard about the story of the Saint, the outlaw who went by the same name. He reached out and grabbed Michelangelo's hand, shifting out from under the counter, only to be helped into a standing position. He looked at the soldier again, now able to put the disturbing sight before him more at ease as he started to gain his bearings.

"Do me a favor and look at me," Michelangelo instructed. Instantly, Leonardo's head started to drift to his left, to the store that was filled with blood and bodies. Michelangelo shielded his eyes with his hand. "Nope. Nope," he corrected, "Right here." He guided Leonardo's head back. "There you go. Right at me."

Leonardo breathed and calmed himself as he looked at Michelangelo. "So you're a St. Hart brother?"

"Sure."

"Like Thomas St. Hart?"

Michelangelo's heart saddened as he nodded. "Yup."

"In all my days... I never imagined! It is an honor to meet you."

Michelangelo nodded, confused. "Well... all right then," he accepted. "Listen to me. I need you to prepare yourself. All right? You're about to see a lot of dead men, brutally dead men. It's going to be rough, but you need to get through it. We need to get you out of here and keep moving." Leonardo nodded as he fought his eyes that were trying to peer to his left. "All right," Michelangelo finished.

The soldier turned and walked out the back door. Leonardo followed after him, though he immediately looked to his left, looking at the General Store that was filled with blood, alcohol, food, and bodies, the liquid being over the wooden floor and walls. The front, left window was busted open, and the bodies of four men lay brutally massacred. Leonardo took in the horrifying imagery, unlike anything he had ever seen before, searing itself into his mind forever. He tripped over a boot beneath him, and as he looked down at it, his eyes trailed up the body until his eyes looked upon its headless topper, the most scarring image of all. He gagged, failing to comprehend what he saw and rushing out the open back door of the store and past Michelangelo. He vomited onto the snow-covered ground. The soldier looked, paused, and watched. "Sorry you have to see all this," he apologized. Leonardo stopped vomiting for a moment, breathing heavily as he stared into the multicolored snow beneath him. The vomit steamed in the cold as he refocused his thoughts.

"Sorry, I just, uh... never read about that," Leonardo informed.

Michelangelo nodded. "Reality is often not as glamorous as the stories make it out to be."

Leonardo slowly stood upright, wiping chunks of vomit from his mouth, as he faced the soldier. "Not very saintly of you," he joked. Michelangelo let out a slight smile and a puff of air from his nose. "Whoever said I was?" He joked back.

"Well, your name, for starters."

Michelangelo's eyebrows bent in confusion. "My name? Well, I hate to break it to you, kid, but I'm more a soldier than I am a saint. To me, that's just a name."

"Yeah. I can see that. You're... a lot more violent than I imagined."

"Than you imagined? How long have you been reading about me?"

"Well, not you, but your brother. Still, the name is unmistakable. It's unique, you know? Either way, your brother is a legend, especially to people like me, and you, being a

St. Hart, or at the very least bearing the name, now have a reputation to uphold. You have the, uh, potential to inspire people by that alone. People like me and others. When we see you, we see your brother and your brother's a hero, so, as reason would serve, would you be." He looked back at the body inside the General Store. "At least that's the idea."

Michelangelo nodded as Leonardo looked back at him. "We may be brothers, but... I'm afraid we're far from similar. Other than the fact we're both killers."

"Well, that's certainly one way to look at it."

Michelangelo looked off into the darkness. "Listen... there was a young woman back at your village. She's alive," he said, chasing the conversation. "More importantly, she's looking for you. Sent me here to try and bring you back."

"Sophia? *She's alive?!*" Leonardo exclaimed.

"Yes, she is."

Leonardo smiled and breathed out a breath of relief, placing his hands to his head and turning to the open nature behind him. He turned back. "And what about the people?!" Michelangelo looked at Leonardo and straightened his eyes in a hardened expression. "No. I'm afraid not." Leonardo's joy quickly faded as he looked at the soldier, for the blunt truthfulness of the statement took him aback. "He killed them? Icarus, I mean," Leonardo asked. "Some of them," Michelangelo replied. "I rode through your village over eight hours ago, but by the time I got there, the Devil and his men had gotten there first. Those who stayed alive picked up arms and followed me here to fight... I doubt many of them are alive anymore."

"What do you mean by 'took up arms?'"

"They came here to fight, of their own accord. To fight for you and your brothers. They fought hard... from what I saw."

"No... no, no, no, no, they *wouldn't do that*, they, they can't do that, I—"

"Leonardo, if it's any consolation, those who lived denounced their faith and denied your Lord just the same as the rest. They came here to fight as a means to right their wrongs. They felt that it was the only option left.

Leonardo turned around and stared off into the distant, woodland snowland, for he was unable to comprehend how his people would do such a thing as this. "I know it's tough to hear," Michelangelo continued, "but it's the truth," he lied. Leonardo turned back around in a fit of fear, realizing what the soldier was saying.

"Sophia stayed?"

"Yes, she stayed."

"And she's at home."

"Correct."

"Then that means..."

Michelangelo stared knowingly at Leonardo, who stared back, confirming what he already knew. Leonardo marched past the soldier, not wanting to hear anything else he had to say. "Where are you going?" he asked.

"I want to see the roof," he replied, turning back. "If what you say is true, then they must have been those who were shooting up there with you, yes?"

"Yes, but you're not going to like what you see. What's done is done... it may be best not to make yourself familiar with it."

"I don't care. I want to see them with my own eyes."

Michelangelo sighed. "Believe me, kid... You don't."

"It's my decision!" Leonardo ignored, turning and making for the ladder.

"That it is," Michelangelo agreed to himself, reaching into his pocket and pulling out a package of cigarettes, letting one rest in his lips, lighting it with a matchstick. "But the you who made that decision won't come back," he finished, breathing in the smoke.

The preacher firmly placed the ladder back in position, leading to the ceiling hatch, and climbed it. He needed to prove to himself that what the soldier said was true; he valued that more than preserving his innocence, and he would do so at any cost. Thus, he stepped onto the roof and went peculiarly silent.

Michelangelo looked back at the General Store and gazed at a particular whiskey bottle next to the boot of the headless man, unopened and slightly cracked. He made his way in, picked up the bottle, and pinched the cork, popping it off with a light pull, allowing the fumes to seep into his nostrils and burn into his lungs.

Leonardo let out a painful cry that echoed through all of Little York. His knees thudded on the ceiling beneath him, and tears quickly followed. Michelangelo listened through the thin wooden ceiling and clenched his jaw as he empathized with his pain. He looked down and noticed his navy man's hat that had fallen from atop his head. Then walked over, picked it up, and wiped the blood and alcohol on it. It smeared across the hat, with only the heavy droplets flicking to the floor. Next to the droplets, however, was a strange piece of material he had never seen before. He placed his hat on his head and knelt, looking at the odd leather armor. He picked it up and was surprised by the weight. Thus, he held it with both hands as he examined it: the thickness of the metal plating, the ripped bullet hole in the leather that revealed it. "So that's how the bastard dodged me," he spoke to himself, looking over the straps and noticing they were made of the same dark brown leather. He examined the shape of the metal inside and saw that, although it was square, the edges had smoothed down to a soft, rounded corner, which ensured that the piece fit comfortably and safely. Michelangelo held it up to his chest and compared the size of the armor to his own to determine if it was an item he could potentially wear.

The armor was a perfect fit.

Michelangelo tossed it over his left shoulder, opposite his shotgun. He started to think of what else Icarus might have lost, and that was when he remembered the revolver that he had disarmed. The revolver sat on the wooden floor, its old and uncared-for disfigurement hidden amidst the multitude of liquid and debris. Michelangelo walked over and picked it up, looked it over, and shoved it into the back waistline of his pants. He figured he could learn something about Icarus, if anything, in the tiny details.

Michelangelo lightly pushed the front door open and walked onto the brick-laden street, as the brisk of the late-night snow fell upon him. Flakes fell and melted on his clothing, while his gloveless hand lifted his newly acquired whisky to his lips, his index and middle finger plucking the cigarette out just before the burning liquid coated his throat. The substance traveled down into his gullet, filling him with a calming and warming sensation. He lowered the bottle after an unhealthy swig and exposed his teeth in a grimace as he gulped down the fiery beverage. He placed the cigarette back in his mouth and looked at the battlefield he had fought in, noting the bodies that had riddled Little York. Twenty bodies coated Little York's street, and twenty-nine lay on the roof of the General Store and the Aland Theatre. The streetlights shone upon the scene, their glow reflected within the rivers of red. Bodies with bullet holes decorated the town, and blood filled the black lines between the bricks. What was once a symbol of a bright and hopeful tomorrow was now an example of a dark future come to pass.

History would not remember Little York as the beacon of a better world, but instead as a reminder of its brutality and bloodshed.

The town was empty, lifeless, and the only sign of life within it came from the bordering buildings, particularly Hotel Emilda, where it appeared that a majority of the people had taken refuge and were looking out the window. Michelangelo plucked out the cigarette again and took another long drink, then looked at the sky as he closed his eyes.

"Glad to see you made it", William greeted weakly.

Michelangelo looked at him and was pleased to see that he had survived. He was surprised at the relief he felt from knowing his uncle was still with him, but didn't dwell on the thought for long. He looked at Jack, whom William had on his shoulder. "Where are you taking him?" Michelangelo asked, taking another swig. "We're headed to the hotel. You?" Michelangelo looked at the blood coming from William. "I'll join you in a minute. I'm waiting on the kid."

"He's alive?"

"He's alive."

"Well, I'll be damned."

Michelangelo chuckled. "Maybe not just yet." He looked at William's injury again. "You okay?"

"Yeah. Just a graze."

Michelangelo looked over William's head, the tight, curly, balding, and salt-and-pepper color that trailed from his top to his beard. "A graze can be a lot for an old man." William smiled, legitimately touched that his nephew seemed to care again, even if in the slightest. "Well, I appreciate the concern, but it's not."

Michelangelo nodded and took another drink. William watched as his nephew then looked forward and stared at the battlefield emptily, his consciousness lost in the thoughts of a soldier's mind, ones that slowly distanced him from reality. William looked at the bottle and noticed that half of it was already gone, then looked at Michelangelo's face and sighed in his soul. He readjusted Jack on his shoulder. "See you in a minute?"

"Yeah," Michelangelo replied, his eyes still fixated on the emptiness before him.

William nodded and turned, limping toward Hotel Emilda and leaving Michelangelo in the eye of his storm.

Leonardo continued to cry on top of the General Store's roof, looking down at his pale people, those he never imagined would do this. They lay dead in their puddles of blood, upside-down crosses burned into their faces, staring lifelessly. Bullet holes riddled their bodies and heads, some too damaged to recognize, and all seeping crimson from their wounds.

Many thoughts raced through Leonardo's mind, but Leonardo only found himself focusing on one: *Why*. He sobbed, wondering how he had failed his people, how this tragedy had ever been made possible. He pondered this thought painfully and could not find a single answer. Thus, Leonardo finally sought someone he had not seen in a very long time, if at all: he sought the Lord. "Why are you doing this?" He prayed. "These people believed in you; they-they *worshipped* you. I preached to them, I encouraged them, and still... You killed them." He sobbed.

"I don't understand. I-I need to understand. I *need* to know that this is all supposed to be worth something, that this is supposed to prove something, that-that there is a reason that I am still here and they are not." Tears poured from his eyes. *"Why didn't you take me? If this is my fault, if I'm supposed to be punished for my insolence, then why didn't you punish me? Not my brothers... not the people! Nor your people! Me!"* He breathed through his tears. "I told them you'd protect them... that evil would not fall upon them, and it did! It fell gravely," he said, touching a corpse's hand.

He waited for an answer, a sovereign reply. There was none, only the sound of falling snow. "Their souls are lost, and you say nothing? What does this prove? What's the point? Is this my fault?" Leonardo choked.

He waited again, but still, *nothing.*

"Answer me!" He screamed, demanding from the heavens. Silence took over again.

Michelangelo heard the pleas and drank again, continuing to look at the clouds that covered the stars, letting the snowflakes melt on his face. Leonardo looked down at the General Store roof as his shoulders slouched in defeat, his eyes clenched, his mouth a tight line, and warm tears trickling down his cheek, chilling in the winter's cold. "Alright... fine," Leonardo conceded.

Michelangelo turned at the sound of boots with spurs clicking toward him, and to his surprise, he saw the sheriff of Little York, who had come out of hiding. The Sheriff was a much older man with a large grey mustache that was finely combed out to a pointed end. He wore a black helmet made of shiny metal, which was clean and well-maintained. He had a sheriff's badge symbol on his helmet, directly above a leather, black strap that held it in place tightly. The symbol was made of a golden, yellow metal, and the buttons upon his jacket were golden yellow, the same, running down the center of his chest in a double-breasted pairing. His coat was blue, with black cuffs that connected to fancy white gloves that were hardly soiled. Next to his chest buttons, a modernized badge made of golden metal was worn, taking on the shape of a shield with a sash etched across it. Beneath his buttons, a brown gun belt hung at his waist, with a golden buckle of the exact nature. On his left hip, there was a revolver that hung in its holster, and on the right, a black baton hung neatly down his side. His jacket stretched down to his knees and had a slit next to the buttons that ran down the side. The slacks he had on complemented his blue, for they were an intense black. They were well-pressed, and they complemented his dress shoes, which were shined and kept in neat condition. The sheriff was a pristine lawman in a pristine town and had walked upon the peaceful bricks of Little York many times before. But now, Little York was filled with disarray and destruction, and Michelangelo was the apparent, sole survivor.

The sheriff looked Michelangelo over and noticed he was coated in blood and flesh while standing amongst their bodies. He knew who Michelangelo was and wondered how he might best handle the situation.

"Sheriff," Michelangelo greeted.

"Major General," the sheriff greeted back. He walked in front of the soldier and looked at the surrounding bodies, then back at Michelangelo. "So... you're the rogue soldier I've heard about."

"Apparently."

The Sheriff slightly chuckled in his throat as he continued to look around. "You kill all these boys?"

"You asking me to admit to a crime?"

"Just asking in general."

Michelangelo looked around. "All of them? No. Most? Sure."

The Sheriff nodded and looked down at the ground, then up to Michelangelo with shame in his eyes, grateful more than lawful. "Listen, uhm. Look, I don't have any other way of putting this, so I'll just say it plainly: You saved this place. It may not seem like it to others, or to the bureaucrats who don't care, but it was only a matter of time before these men showed up. They were comin'. I-I know they were comin'. They've been here before. I just— I never thought it would end up going quite like this." He shook his head. "They would've killed the brothers and God only knows who else. Despite what the papers will say, or the law might think... today you did more than I ever could. And I am thankful for that."

Michelangelo took another sip of his drink and looked forward at the dead men before him. "Don't thank me for this." He shook his head. "Whether it be the blood of the innocent or the blood of the wicked, blood has been spilled here all the same. Bodies rot in your streets, and the history made here today will haunt this town forever. People won't forget. The nation won't understand. Today, to you, I might be a hero, but tomorrow or the day after that, I'll be a villain depending on the time, place, and those who remain." He looked at the sheriff. "Today you'll thank me, but tomorrow you'll damn me. Today you'll remember, but tomorrow you'll forget, and the reason why is that today I am the only man left standing, but tomorrow more will stand in my place—more who are more righteous, more worthy, more profitable, and once they come you will start to see the truth of this horrific matter; the *truth* that I am no better than the very men who lye dead in your streets." Michelangelo huffed in and blew out smoke from his lips. "Yes, sheriff, I am the rogue soldier who some believe has been sent here to kill the killers, but as the dawn breaks its seal upon the looking eye, all will see what is truly to be seen. It's the night that hides the demons that wait to be revealed." He took a drink. "One day soon, you'll wish you could forget me. You'll want to, and then I'll be the one that's forgotten." He breathed in one long breath. "Don't thank me for this. Don't thank anyone for any of it."

The sheriff listened to Michelangelo's words and looked at him in his moment of confession. He pondered over the mind of a man such as this, and how it had found itself in such a place of morbid reality; a place that held a truth that was only known to men such as him.

"Well," the sheriff started, "Good man or bad, one thing that we can agree on is that you are the one sent, and innocent people were saved. If anything, I am thankful for them."

Michelangelo looked over to the sheriff in a curious expression, noting that, for the first time in his life, someone had heard his truth and still accepted him. The sheriff respected Michelangelo more after hearing it. He let out a half smile and gave a quick nod as a slight sorrow in the deep pits of his eyes managed to come through. The sheriff noticed this and nodded back with a similar smile. "Listen, as far as I'm concerned, you were never here. I wager that by morning you'll be gone, so I won't worry too much about what the morning's light will bring."

"Thank you, sheriff." Michelangelo appreciated.

The sheriff looked behind the soldier and noticed an approaching Leonardo, who immediately. Michelangelo turned and saw him as well, particularly in the defeat of his shoulders that slouched toward the ground as he continued to walk forward.

"He alright?" The sheriff asked.

"I don't know," Michelangelo replied.

"If I were in his shoes, I wouldn't be."

The Sheriff turned to walk back to his building as Leonardo approached Michelangelo. "You both take care now," the Sheriff finished.

Michelangelo looked at The Hotel Emilda as William and Jack entered. Leonardo looked over to the hotel as well, following Michelangelo's lead. "I don't know about you, but a nice warm bath sounds good right about now," Michelangelo offered.

"I do not know if anything sounds good right now," Leonardo denied.

"We'll see if you sing that same tune once we get you one."

Leonardo looked at Michelangelo and smiled; with that, the soldier and the preacher began walking toward the Hotel Emilda. The snow continued to fall as the bodies in the streets froze, with no one in Little York daring to go outside, and most deciding they would not walk these streets again. Sadly, from this point on, the beautiful town of Little York would be populated by far more ghosts than people.

Not much more can be said about the town of Little York, for it is remembered for its massacre that occurred on this day, one so vicious and bloody that many would never forget it. Death was seared into the minds of those who witnessed the battle, and for those who hadn't but had heard, shared the same searing. Government authorities rallied their troops, as the names Icarus, Michelangelo, and Leonardo would soon spread across the nation. Their names would tell a story on the front-page printing that was grandiose, gruesome, and mortifying. The titles would differ depending on the paper's perspective, with some reading "Michael The Murderer" and others "The Saint of Little York." Some even read "The Saint Returns!" Amid the chaos, there was one title in particular that was printed intentionally by the *New York Paper,* one that caught the attention of two individuals who would take a specific interest in this bloodthirsty soldier. The title read "Saint Hart lives!" with a gripping subtitle that said "Major General Michelangelo St. Hart, Fights Holy War for Hunted Believers!"

Most, however, read "The Little York Massacre," which tended to be the consensus.

Some called Michelangelo a saint, while others called him a soldier or a madman, and each made valid points in support of their respective perspectives. Regardless of what the papers would print, neither the soldier, the preacher, the bastard, nor the hunter would pay any mind to it, for their battle together had just begun, and only one would remain, the victor.

CHAPTER 7

Though Taken Heed Bring Calm to Thine Sway

teaming water lifted from the tub that thawed Michel-
angelo's frozen bones. The dirt and grime upon his body
washed into the water as the blood of both his own and
others drained into the liquid. Michelangelo's nose, eye-
brow, and ribcage all dripped fresh blood, plopping into the water and dissipating almost
immediately. His flesh puffed in the warmth of the water, as the cold was replaced with
heat. The bath water was a creamy, white color, just tainted by the soldier's filth. The water
washed away the muck that had built upon him and cleansed the many months of bloodshed and mud that had caked onto him from his many months of war and travel.

The tub was made of the finest stainless steel, its innermost area shining with a
bright gleam in the dimly lit washroom. The tub was slender and had just enough room
to fit Michelangelo. His body was fully submerged, except for his arms, which rested on
the rims. The rest of his body warmed in the steaming liquid as the hills of cream colored
bubbles floated over the surface, filling the tub and piling up to the center of his hairy

chest. Steam filled the room and warmed his face, making the tub's room heated and hazy.

The outside of the tub was wrapped in a tight wooden frame, holding it together in a fitted design that complemented the fancy aesthetic of Hotel Emilda's washroom. It was a dimly lit wooden room, illuminated by only one lantern that hung in the center of the ceiling. Its small, flickering flame danced within the glass casing, casting the room's shadows and giving it a distinct softness. The lantern's light filled the room with a fading red and yellow, though it was dim, and it was only able to reach the bottom of the tub. The corners of the room were shrouded in shadow, whereas the ceiling was bathed in light reflected from the glass. There were no windows; instead, there were wooden walls, polished to a gleam and tightly fitted together, ranging in color from a darker brown to a maroon red.

To Michelangelo's right stood a stool made of masterfully crafted timber. Behind him, towards the back corner of the room, was a changing station of tightly sewn, tan cloth, set between metal. Upon the changing station's cloth were intricate, brown, and square designs, with triangles sewn into the center. The changing station was small in comparison to the washroom, but it was intentionally designed this way so that it could be left in the left corner. To his left, a short wooden table rested, lined up perfectly with his left arm on the tub. Upon the table were some metal scissors, a shaving razor, shaving cream, and a soft, white cloth, next to a small, cracked glass bottle of whisky.

The soldier lay his head back upon the brim of the tub, closed his eyes, and began to drift off to sleep in the room's silence. His muscles relaxed, and his mind was intoxicatedly close behind. Suddenly, there was a soft knock on the washroom door. The gold and engraved knob gently turned to the right, opening the wooden door slowly. "Come in," Michelangelo said sarcastically. A bathing lady had entered, peaking her head in the doorway.

"I'm sorry, sir, I don't mean to disturb, but I'm of the mind you may enjoy the disturbance," she informed.

Michelangelo looked up and saw the bathing lady and her beautiful smile, slowly fading the longer she looked at his blood-soaked face, the flakes solidifying, and the tiny bits of men's flesh trapped in his beard and hair. Michelangelo examined her attire as she stepped further into the room, this custom-tailored eye catcher of an outfit. The top was a corset that pushed up her breasts firmly, paired with a white, fluffy button-up, with a collar that flared around her collarbone and chest. Her skirt was made of fine red and black cotton, and the boots she wore were black, tied up to her ankles. She was a white woman, and her face and body were wonderfully eye-catching, accentuated by the bright reds, pinks, and whites she had painted on her face.

In the time Michelangelo had taken to examine her, she did the same to him, noticing his bruises that had formed around his nose and eye, and the cuts upon his nose and eyebrow looked horrifically large, made even more visually mortifying by the blood that flowed. She gulped. "Sir, do you care for a premium bath?" Michelangelo leaned his head back and closed his eyes again, nestling his fingers over the edges of the tub and sliding his body down deeper. "No. Thank you, miss. I can wash myself just fine," he dismissed. She nodded quickly, relieved as she began to close the door. "However," he started again, "I'd appreciate it if you got my clothes down to someone who can clean them. The leavings tend to stain."

She looked around the washroom with a confused and curious expression, then saw his clothes crumpled on the floor beside the door. The pile of clothes consisted of a navy man's jacket, hat, black gloves, black riding boots, and a navy man's pants. Each piece of attire had smears and sprays of blood on it, to the point that it had pooled around them. At the top of the pile was a white union suit containing only slight traces of blood that were all the more visible due to their whiteness. The poor woman gagged, quickly holding her hand to her mouth, and hurriedly picking up the damp clothes, walking out the door, and shutting it behind her.

Michelangelo smiled and breathed a long breath out of his nose as he committed himself to rest. This was a rare moment of tranquility for him, one he had not had in months. As his flesh had tenderized, the pain that came with his wounds worsened. He began to reach his left hand around, feeling the bruises and cuts that coated his body. He rubbed his shoulders, browned and blackened from the hits he had taken—his back and chest, the same black and blue. Then, he gently reached down to the gash in his rib, placing two fingers to feel the sedated flesh and the blood that seeped from it. He winced, thankful that he was not bleeding too heavily and that it appeared only an inch of the shard had made it in. He lifted his arm once again and looked at it, noticing the large scar that stretched over his left bicep. He started to think about the many times he had been cut and stabbed, then looked down at his chest to see the tinier scars there. He lifted his left leg, saw the wounds on his thigh, then rested everything and bent his left arm, stretching the soreness of the muscle that came with the healed injury. It was then he noticed the soreness in the rest of his muscles, his tired and beaten body that had spent months fighting recently, and years fighting historically. Still, in this water, in this moment, he rested, dropping his arm once more and letting his mind drift away in the water.

"Major General?" A soft woman's voice spoke through the door.

Michelangelo rolled his eyes with an airy push of breath through his nose, his patience reaching its end. "I already told you I'm not interested in your services."

"Fairly said, but I'm not here to offer you our premium services. I'm here to offer some conversation."

"What kind of conversation?"

"A meaningful one paired with a bath and no funny business."

Michelangelo pondered the offer. It was a strange one, and he hadn't had a meaningful conversation in a while. He wondered if this was possible for a bathing lady, and was so intrigued by the idea that he began to warm up to it. *After all,* he thought, *she is a stranger. If everything goes wrong, I doubt I'll see her again.* More than this, he knew the thoughts that plagued, cursed, and ate at him would come whether she was there or not.

He wondered if having someone else with him would make them easier to manage. He even considered—had hope in the idea that this conversation would make him feel better, or at least prolong his perdition.

He opened his eyes, lifted his head once again, and looked at the door. "All right, fine. Come on in."

With a quick entrance, a different woman entered the room, wearing the same uniform as the other bathing ladies who worked with her. He looked upon her and found that though she wore the same attire as the rest, there was something slightly different about her, almost troubling. This woman was not a worker like the rest, for she did not carry an enticing persuasion, but instead, a soft and gentle spirit, welcoming and kind. She softly closed the door behind her and looked at Michelangelo, examining the rugged soldier as he did the same to her. *What interest might someone like her have in a man like me?* He thought. It was then he realized something even more interesting: this woman was not phased by the busted and bleeding soldier before her, but instead, had a calm and happy expression, as though she was almost comforted by the gross familiarity. As she looked back at him, she noticed the soldier's intrigue, slightly cleared her throat, and controlled her heart.

"You do that makeup yourself?" She joked.

"Makeup?" Michelangelo asked, looking down, then at his bloodied face in his reflection. He smiled and let out a single chuckle, then looked back up. "Oh. I see."

The woman smiled, and his eyes softened. As she looked into his eyes, she found herself, once again, experiencing a familiar feeling. Michelangelo's eyebrows slowly drew closer as he felt it too, as she made her way over to the left side of the tub, collecting the wooden stool and carefully placing herself behind the soldier. He continued to look forward as he pondered the woman's familiarity, while she slowly and steadily prepared herself, her hands gently reaching over to grab the cloth that lay on the table to their right. Michelangelo's mind raced to find a connection as she continued about her business, for somewhere, in a dark corner of his mind, he knew he recognized this person. She stood at five feet six inches and seemed to be a strong, lean woman. She was Colombian, and her hair was as black as the night sky, and as wavy as the winter's breeze. Her skin was a rich, olive color, and her face was as beautiful as the night was long.

"Major General Saint Hart," she started. "You mind if I ask how a Major General finds himself all on his own?" She leaned forward and dipped the cloth in the water in front of Michelangelo, soaking it thoroughly, then lifted it, the soapy water flowing in a steady stream of steaming liquid that dripped back into the bath. She lifted the cloth above Michelangelo's head and gently wrung out the water, letting it wash through his hair. Blood and flesh trickled down the sides and rinsed onto his chest. She rinsed and repeated, and as Michelangelo relaxed, he changed focus from her familiarity to her question.

"I suppose the average 'major general' finds his way out here much like anyone else would," he generalized.

"And are you 'the average major general?' "

He smiled. "I suppose not.

She smiled as she dipped her rag once again and lifted it from the water. She reached down, softly held his left cheek, and began wiping away the chunks from his face. His heart slightly raced.

"I gotta say, miss, you're lack of blood issue is mighty unique. Maybe even a better conversation," he investigated.

"Oh, it's nothing all that interesting. I've just seen a lot of blood in my life, is all."

"Where does a lady like you get into the business of blood?"

"Anywhere she finds herself in the company of men like you."

He smiled. "That right?"

"It most certainly is," she smiled back.

Michelangelo paused for a moment, his smile fading. "West, by chance?"

She paused momentarily as she caught the peculiarity of the statement, for it was strangely specific, and worse, accurate. She continued cleaning him immediately, though he noticed the pause. "Most of us come from the West, you know."

"True, but there's a far smaller demographic that comes out of it familiar with blood."

She tensed slightly. "And who might they be?" She asked, continuing to wash his hair, the water beneath the bubbles looking more and more like red wine; his skin finally showed its olive color after not having done so for many hours.

"Well, doctors, rarely. Sheriffs, even more so. But in my experience, the most common are outlaws.

She nodded, and her heart began to race. "I used to patch up a man not too different from you. He would come in looking like this after some of his battles." She wiped his face gently. "To me, you're just another busted face."

Michelangelo nodded. "Was he a soldier?"

"Of sorts."

"Good sorts or bad sorts?"

"It depended on the day."

"I see. So you were a nurse?"

"Not exactly."

Michelangelo tensed slightly as he put the pieces together, then sighed gently through his nose. "This soldier of sorts: would you say he was a righteous man or a wicked one?"

She stopped and thought. "He was a righteous man among wicked ones. In the end, he stood beside the righteous—the most Holy, if you will." She sighed. "But none of that matters now. Both he and they have been dead a long time now." Michelangelo gently nodded. "I'm sorry to hear that. Dark days take the place of the fallen righteous man."

"So we have seen," she agreed. "And what are you? A relief to the dark days or one who extends them?"

"It doesn't really matter what I say I am; what matters is what you perceive."

The woman placed the blood-soaked cloth to the side, then reached over and picked up the small scissors on the stool, and finally looked back at Michelangelo, sizing up his ragged and long hair. After finding the place she first wanted to cut, she pinched a small patch that dripped down to the middle of his neck, and began her delicate trimming.

"I think you're a righteous man trapped inside a wicked one; a doer of evil possessing the body of a good man," she spoke honestly.

Michelangelo chuckled lightly. "You certainly don't mince words."

"I never have and I never will."

He nodded.

"Don't move!" She commanded. "I might trim you wrong!"

"Oh, sorry," Michelangelo apologized with a slight smile. Though he didn't know, she, too, was smiling. He pondered her statement as the sound of snipping hair continued in the silence. "Maybe you're right," he slightly agreed. "Though I wonder, who's the greater fool: the soldier fighting a holy war or the painted lady cutting his hair in Little York."

She stopped trimming his hair, put one hand on her hip, and pointed the scissors in his direction. "First of all, I'm not a painted lady... though I do dress like one as part of company policy." She started clipping his hair again. "My doors are not open for business, and my values remain uncompromised. Second of all, those are some mighty bold words for a naked man. You may want to mind your manners if you don't want more than your hair getting snipped."

Michelangelo chuckled. "Ah, those scissors are the least of my worries."

"Take your gamble, soldier. We'll see if you feel the same here in a few minutes."

A slight hint of sadness and guilt fell upon the woman as she jousted with Michelangelo. It wasn't so much the words or even the banter itself as the way he had done so with her, and she went back to him. She looked at his scars and bruises that covered his body, clumps of his freshly trimmed hair plopping into the water. "So. You any good at this soldiering stuff?" Michelangelo let out a little air from his nose. "How do you mean?"

"I mean," she said, sitting back. "Have you seen yourself lately?"

Michelangelo nodded. "Considering the many times it could've gone far worse, I would say, yes, I am pretty good at what I do."

She smiled and leaned forward, continuing the cutting. "How's that working out for you?"

"There are fewer bad guys in the world. That makes it work for me."

"What about everyone else?"

"Remains to be seen."

They both stopped and thought in the silence for a moment.

"So what *do* you do?" Michelangelo asked.

"I serve beverages at the bar downstairs," she answered.

"Oh. I must've walked right by you."

"You did. That's how I saw you."

"And that's what led you up here?"

"Something like that."

"So you know who I am?"

"Not other than the immediate news that's been getting shared around the bar." She clipped in silence. "No, it was more than I recognized you. Your face."

Michelangelo nodded, understanding what she meant. "You ever seen me before?"

"No. Not exactly."

Michelangelo's heart hurt, which was a strange thing for him to feel. This hurt bothered him, for he had not felt empathy in a while, and he wondered what was happening to him that caused it to resurface. "So," he redirected. "Why Little York?"

"Well, I won't lie, it wasn't my first thought. It was New York that I wanted to go to, but things didn't turn out the way I expected them to. About four months ago, I was pregnant, near a train station, but unable to reach it. I had just enough money to buy a train ticket and get out of here when—" she trailed off.

"When what?"

The woman stopped breathing for a moment, wondering if she wanted to share her revealing truth, not knowing that the soldier had already figured out who she was. She breathed again. "Then the law found me and chased me down. They ran me down for miles and miles, and the more that I tried to get around them, the more the bounty hunters, sheriffs, and deputies kept appearing, until finally I was able to hide here. The bartender downstairs—he's the manager—he gave me a place to stay, a job. He even hid me and kept quiet when the law and the hunters came looking for me. He understood my past and threw it aside, anyway. He did the right thing, all things considered. Thus, the plan I had, well. You know how they go. They don't always work out the way you want them to."

"No, they do not," Michelangelo agreed, having all his suspicions confirmed. "You must've done quite the heinous thing to have a state-wide manhunt set for you, to the extent they would chase you up north."

Her heart raced as she continued to cut his hair. "You could very easily say that, and then some."

Michelangelo nodded. "You mentioned you were pregnant." He paused a moment. "Did the baby make it?" He asked worriedly.

"He did. He's as well as the day he was born." She smiled. "I had him here, actually. In the hotel."

Michelangelo smiled out of the corner of his mouth. "What's his name?"

She smiled, a heavy sorrow in her heart. "Tomás. Thomas, in English. Tomás Santa Felina is his full name." She moved to the top of Michelangelo's head and continued cutting. "He's named after his daddy." Michelangelo's smile faded as his heart sank heavily.

"Thomas is a fine name. A good name. English or Spanish spoken."

"I agree."

Michelangelo thought about the moment he had found himself in. It was almost impossible for him to believe, and a part of him felt as though he'd rather not, but it was the truth, and all he could do now was navigate it. "And what might his mother's name be?" he asked, almost rhetorically. She adjusted herself and began cutting the front of Michelangelo's hair now, matching it up with the rest of his freshly trimmed do. "Rosa. Rosa Santa Felina."

Michelangelo smiled slightly as he heard the name, humored by the simplicity of the changed name. "Never heard of a Saint Felina. She must be new," he teased.

"Freshly made up, I'm afraid," she teased back.

He smiled, chuckling just a bit more. "If it's any consolation, the name doesn't go over any easier with a Hart behind it. People still find it odd."

"Oh, I've noticed. I kind of like that about it, in any case. The uniqueness of it to the point it bothers people."

"Sure, but it's not very good for blending in."

She laughed. "No, I suppose not."

He laughed with her. "Well, either way, there are worse things to be known as than a saint."

"I suppose... though I'm not sure the price of sainthood is worth the privilege of bearing its mark."

Rosa picked up the cloth once more and dipped it into the steaming water, only to twist it over Michelangelo's shoulders, washing the flakes of his hair from his skin. They slowly flowed down into the streams of red and white water, disappearing into the fading bubbles that surrounded him. His hair was now fully trimmed, with the front kept short to his head, leaving only an inch of length in the front. His sides were clean and flat, like a brand-new soldier who had just enlisted. All that remained was his massive beard, having grown for over four months now, filled with an assortment of debris. Rosa picked up her stool and walked over to his left side, now able to look into his hazel eyes, leaving him unable to hide any feeling he might have about her or their situation. She looked between them once again as he looked into hers, the two of them analyzing the actual person behind the mask, determining who they might be while being drawn to what they had in common.

"Those eyes," she sighed, looking away and dipping her cloth into the tub once more, then looking back up and wiping his face. Michelangelo looked at her in her eyes, now, as she focused on cleaning the mud, blood, and alcohol from his beard. She motioned for him to close his eyes, and he did, leading her to carefully wipe his eyelids clean, working gently around the gash in his eyebrow and the bridge of his nose.

"You know, the familiarity you look for, I cannot offer. My eyes may only be a solidarity for the ones you're longing to see... but they are not the same, only similar," he reminded, sorrowfully.

"I know... but still. There's something comfortable in the familiarity." She wrung out the cloth. "Regardless of whose eyes they are, I know them: they're good. They're kind, despite the rough exterior. They reveal the essence of their bearer. You both had that in common, among other things."

"Quite the dissonant statement to be made for a woman wiping the blood of dozens from a 'good man's' face."

"All the mud and blood in the world cannot hide the true nature of one's soul, just as strangers are not always as strange as they might seem, at first."

"So we're no longer strangers?"

"I'd say so. I'd argue we never were. We have a commonality."

"Had, Ms. Felina. Had."

Rosa nicked the cut on his nose, her lack of focus taking over. "Ow," Michelangelo let out, almost humorously. In truth, the pain was felt, but not too severe. She pulled back her rag quickly as she looked into Michelangelo's eyes, bearing her teeth in a worried state. Michelangelo gently opened his eyes and let out a smile to let her know it was okay. She breathed, smiled back, and continued with her cleaning.

"I'm glad to see that, despite how heartless you pretend to be, you are still just pretending. I know this might sound strange, but it's almost comforting to see a Saint Hart mourn. Makes me remember there are still people who feel in the world, though you have questionable means of doing so."

"You mean all the killing?"

"Yes, the killing. Hundreds have had their blood shed for the sake of you finding familiarity in the estranged that have been made by persecution. That's your grief, I wager." She wrung the rag, dipped it, then wiped again. "It's in grief that we discover a multitude of things about ourselves. Sometimes, if we're lucky enough, we even find a connection."

"So it appears."

Michelangelo closed his eyes and rested again. Rosa dipped her cloth into the water gently, then hung the fabric over Michelangelo's face, twisting and squeezing as she let the water flush over his face, rinsing the remaining traces of blood into the tub. She then took the dampened cloth and wiped away the remaining small, meaty chunks and blood from his beard.

"You'll have to excuse the insistence, Major General. Truth be told, you're the only other human being in our small part of the world that I've been able to find solace in." Rosa continued.

"So it's mourning you want?"

"Yes. If you'll let me."

Michelangelo opened his eyes to look at Rosa. She noticed, forced out a smile, and then stopped wiping his beard as tears began to well up in her eyes. She looked down at the wooden floor and clenched the bloodied cloth in her hand, letting it rest on the rim of the tub as she squeezed her eyes and her mouth, doing her best to hide her crying.

Michelangelo slowly reached over and clasped her hand on the rim of the tub, the tips of his fingers just barely dipping into her palm. She looked up at her hand, then over to him, letting out a saddened smile as a tear fell from her eye. He understood her grief. Truth be known, he was the only one alive who could have ever empathized with what she was going through. She gently squeezed his fingertips, then shook her head as the tears quietly flowed.

"I'm sorry," she apologized. "I'm sorry." She lifted her hand and placed the cloth on the table to her right, then wiped the tears from her eyes with the back of her hand. "I know this isn't what I promised you." She let out an awkward laugh. "I'm supposed to be conversing and cleaning, and I am currently crying." She reached over and grabbed the scissors again, then leaned over with both hands and started cutting chunks of Michelangelo's beard. He thought about how Rosa was feeling, how she was finally able to mourn. He wondered if he had done the same, at least to the degree that he began to process his thoughts and feelings. He tensed as he realized he hadn't, having no one for four months actually to do it with. It was then that he realized it was time to talk about his younger brother and the grief that came with him. Michelangelo knew this was the only kindness he could offer Rosa, and in reality, was the only kindness he could offer himself, the only kindness he felt he deserved.

"You know, Thomas always had good in him. As long as I can remember, he has always seen the best in people. He didn't care too much what any of us thought about it, either." He smiled, letting out a light breath from his nose. "We used to live with our mom and dad on a little homestead, if you could call it that. It was on the outskirts of the New Mexico Territory. We were farmers of sorts, but only of what we could manage to grow in our little garden. It was a dusty hell hole, our section, as most of that territory is, so our garden was never overtly bountiful." He smiled. "Tommy was always in that thing, though. Playing with the vegetables or just watching the grass grow. I believe he was nine years old at the time... just a young kid. I remember one day he was out in the garden playing with a carrot, holding it by its base with both hands and slashing it around like a sword while he made little swoosh sounds with his mouth. I'll never forget the imagination he had." His smile began to fade. "Unfortunately, the reason I remember that day so distinctly wasn't just because of that. It was because of the visitor who decided to come our way. He was a man who rode up on a large steed. Any other human being looking at him would quickly understand who he was and what he was after, but not Tommy. No, Tommy walked right up to him and began talking with him. 'How was your day?' He asked. 'What are you doing out here in the middle of nowhere?' But my Mama, Daddy, and I... we knew what he was about. When we heard Thomas talking outside, we didn't bat an eye much because it wasn't anything inherently unusual. Tommy was always talking to himself. It was when a voice responded that we realized something was wrong. My Daddy grabbed the shotgun on the wall, and my mother and I walked outside, staring down this man who was as rugged as the sands beneath him. He was a scum, that guy—a villainous bastard child of the West. You know the type. Those outlaws with their way of dressing and that arrogant aboutness that they had with them." Michelangelo sighed, clenching his jaw. "I ran over and grabbed Tommy while my dad aimed the shotgun at the outlaw's chest. They had a brief conversation that consisted of nothing more than questions designed to gather information." His muscles tensed. "I'll never forget the smile that man had as he left, trotting over the desert hillside. We didn't know exactly what he wanted. We didn't even know what he was doing; we only knew that we were alone, and much like any other wolf, he was going back for the pack to come pick off the sheep left alone."

Michelangelo shook his head and looked down into the bathwater. Rosa stopped cutting for a moment and listened. "My dad told me to take the horse to town and get the sheriff. He told me to go alone since I'd be able to ride faster without having to watch Tommy. I didn't think much of it, considering he was staying behind to protect the family and pack up whatever they could before they left. So, I listened. I ran outside and made my way to the family horse." He looked up and stared forward blankly. "I'll never forget the last words Tommy ever said to me. He was hiding underneath the porch with his knees tucked to his chest, cradling them while he stared at the ground. For the first time, I had seen Thomas afraid, and to me, that was far more frightening than anything. When even Tommy knew that the man was bad, that something terrible was coming, that was a reason to be afraid. 'Mikey,' he said, looking up at me. 'Are you gonna hurt those men?' I didn't know what to say. I just looked at him, baffled by the question. I couldn't make heads or tails of it... after all that he had seen; all that he had heard; all that he knew was coming, he was more worried about an outlaw than himself. He was worried someone was going to die, and that scared him. It didn't matter who it was. 'As long as I'm standing, I won't let anything happen to you,' I said. 'You have nothing to worry about. It's all going to be okay.' " Michelangelo looked at Rosa. "What a heap of lies that was." He looked away and at the corner of the room. "I've always found it appalling that we can lie to the ones we love, even if only to make them feel better for a moment, thinking it'll help, somehow. Sometimes, I wonder if we don't just lie for our sakes, because telling the truth is far harder than lying about what really might happen. I've thought about that a lot recently. I think about that day a lot, because, regardless of what I said, how hard I rode, and how quickly the sheriff and his five deputies returned with me, we were still too late. I came home to ten bodies, two of which were my mother and father, and the rest of which were those men. They had come back sooner than any of us could have expected, like they had been planning it for a while. My father stood his ground, but that wasn't enough." Michelangelo went quiet for a moment, slightly bringing his eyelids together. "The strange part was Tommy's disappearance. I for sure thought he was dead, but to my surprise, he was not. He was just gone. I thought the worst at first: that he had been taken by one of the outlaws or got hurt and run off somewhere. But as the sheriffs investigated, they saw that most of the outlaws had been killed by pistol rounds, not shotgun shells." He laughed, shaking his head. "Never in a million years would I have thought that another group of outlaws came in and saved him. Never in two million years would I have thought they would take him under their wing." He sighed. "What a horrible thing for a kid to witness... I doubt he remembered any of it, that his brain would allow him to." He went silent. "Sometimes, I wish my brain did the same, but it has not given me the same mercy. I remember everything. Every word, every work, every *worm*. There's not one day nor moment that I don't think about those men who killed my family; there's not one day that I don't think about the ones who had their hand in Thomas' death. Those Brothers of Boudiclare, as they were. But even then, the worst of it is, I don't blame them entirely. For the most part, I blame myself." He clenched his jaw. "Before I ever knew about the Boudiclares, I told myself that I'd never stop looking for Thomas. Never stop searching for him as long as I live, because though the odds seemed slim, and fate seemed sealed... I couldn't believe he was gone. It was as if I could feel him every day, so I did the only sensible thing I thought I could do to find him: I joined The Union. I joined in hopes of traveling the nation in search of him, finding any clues and hints as to his whereabouts, while simultaneously making something of my life for my country. I figured, 'Who better to join than the United States, the upholders of justice and keepers of the peace; these defenders of freedom and fighters of the law?' " He chuckled. "Doing things for your country tends to change the views you might have of it. Still, I figured while I was doing that, I could continue my search for Thomas. It was the perfect job for an eighteen-year-old orphaned boy, until I realized what it was going to cost me, and by then, it was too late. The things I would see along the way, the actions I would take, not because I wanted to but because I *had* to. It was all far more than I bargained for; it's all more than I can forget. Some things are so vile that your mind won't allow you to. They're so brutal that you can only hope your mind will grant you mercy when you wake up, especially if you managed to sleep through the night without having a nightmare. But that morning never came... and the nightmares never stopped. The nightmares about the land acquisition, about removing the natives, killing those who retaliated, and brutalizing the ones that survived. The unsatisfied men have their way with the women, and the violent ones have their way with all. Oftentimes... by the time they were done, there were no people left to send to the reservations. I didn't partake in any of those atrocities, but I didn't stop them, either. Therefore, though I may not have their sins on my soul, I was among them and shared in it nonetheless." He paused for a moment. "I did kill their warriors, though. I was just a soldier, then. I thought I was following the law, the justice system. I trusted that the government knew what they were doing was for the greater good. What I didn't know is that they couldn't care less who lived and who died. I think they preferred that the people didn't. To them, the natives' deaths were just one less variable in the equation that they didn't have to solve peacefully. Not that they were ever going to, anyway." He stopped again. "I have concluded that I am as much a killer now as I was then, only then I couldn't make sense of it. I couldn't quite figure out how we could kill the innocent and not be called killers. How could we lawfully kill those who did nothing to us, only to better ourselves and grow our way of life? How are we any different than the common outlaw? Why are we 'justified' in all of our actions if said actions are done in the name of manifest destiny? More than all this, how could I, still seeing this and believing differently, change anything? It was only when Uncle Sam decided that the time of the outlaw was no more that we finally got involved and restored law and order to those who had it coming. But even then, it was only because it was high time we collected on those territories we paid for. The U.S began building forts all over the country, which were meant to pose a threat to any who dared defy it. They were a message to those in their old ways: the old age is dying, and they would soon die along with it. We hunted hundreds of outlaws for months. We tracked every outlaw from Florida to California, with the instruction to keep them alive so they could be properly tried and prosecuted. However, once we came across most of the men and saw what they had done, there was no mercy left for them. Only frontier justice, which the government didn't seem to mind." He clicked his tongue. "We did save a few of the younger ones. I couldn't seem to quite blame them for what they'd done. They didn't know any better, and in understanding this, I had grown a soft spot for them. Because of this, the people had started calling me 'Michael the Merciful,' though I must admit that there was rarely any mercy. I suppose in a world where there is no mercy, any form of it is seen as a grand gesture." He thought about it for a second. "I think the people called me that because it made them feel more at peace with what was going on. When they saw me, they saw potential for mercy, despite my having actively chosen cruelty, and even in that, they were able to make peace with what would happen, because the men were wicked. The cognitive dissonance was alarming, and for me, it was even more so." His face hardened as his eyes got cold. "I had never felt more at peace than when I was killing those monsters; I was never more content with what I was doing than when I put the barrel of my revolver to their head and pulled the trigger. Every time I did, I felt as though another weight of the world had been lifted off my shoulders. Every skull I blew open was one less one an innocent person had. Every bone I broke only mended that which was broken in someone else, and in turn, doing these things had mended me... in some ways. These men who had lost their humanity had done things that I had not thought humanly possible. They deserved everything they had coming to them, and I was happy to oblige. But sadly... all the killing came to an end as quickly as it began. Despite our best efforts, the new world was starting to look an awful lot like the old one, because when all civilians saw was men killing men, women killing women, men killing women. In contrast, women killed men; this seemed no different than the days when they were trying to abolish slavery. So, we were instructed not to intervene until the outlaws could be properly apprehended; apprehended to be tried before the court of law, whether it be in the frontier or the city. We needed examples to be set before the nation and the people that we were civilized, and by God, the government was going to have it. No more blood in the streets; no more justice on the frontier. All that remained was the good, great law, which naturally came with a double-edged sword. This is the same law that I quickly found out allowed for monsters to massacre, especially if they had the money to do it." Rosa leaned in and began cutting his beard again as he sighed. "That didn't sit right with me then, and it certainly doesn't sit right with me now. I had pondered the concepts of what the law had allowed for, and found that we could slaughter every individual that stood in the way of manifest destiny, but could not harm the American people who did it for far less. No, they got a 'proper trial'. To that, I found myself asking, 'Are we not all Americans, the natives and the tyrants alike?' These tyrants that I've seen behead the defenseless and mutilate the weak." He stared forward, blankly. "These revelations are enough to kill a man. When you fight for something you no longer believe in, it destroys you. So, I gave up. Figured there was no more fight in me, especially for a coming era that seemed to distance itself from men like me. But just as I began to let go of my care for the world, as fate would have it, I ran into the Brothers of Boudiclare. I felt like my life had finally come full circle, and it was then that I realized I had forgotten my great commission in the first place. It was then I wondered what good any of it did? What was it all for? Didn't I do all this to find Thomas, or my purpose, or something in between? In the end, all I found was his corpse. In the end, I was the last one standing for reasons I still can't explain. Why was I left standing? Why am I the one who's left alive?" His eyes saddened as they drifted down to the water. "As I looked at him, it all hit me: that this law, this way of doing things, doesn't work for men like Thomas's killers; like the ones that follow Icarus. You throw the book at them, and they'll just burn it. You tie the noose around their neck, and the spirit escapes it." His face hardened with anger. "I am the only thing they respond to, and it is because what I do is *permanent*. When they meet me, there is no trial. There is no tomorrow. There is only the great beyond, where God may judge you. That approach works; it yields results. Everyone knows it, I know it, you know it. The government most certainly knows it, and the best part is, they'll let me do it. They'll let me do what I need to do because it gets the dirty work they can't do, done, and once they're done with me, they'll throw me to the wolves just the same as all the rest. They'll hang me just the same as the rest of the scum of this earth, so that I might swing in their stead, so as not to let 'democracy' die. And to be honest... I'm okay with that. As long as every single one of these wicked men is ten feet underground, I'll happily swing among them. It would be a sweet release from the hell I live in every day, because every day, all I see is Tommy. Every day, I remember that I'm still standing, and he's not, because I *failed* him, and there's nothing I can do to change that.

All I can do is make things right. It may not be what Tommy might've done or what he would've wanted, but it's the only way I know how. 'Those who are undeserving shall be departed. ' But Tommy? He didn't deserve this... I did. Tommy was the best of both of us. I should be where he is; I want to be where he is."

Rosa gently put down the scissors after listening to Michelangelo's monologue of thoughts. She looked at him worriedly as he looked at her, then sighed. She picked up the shaving cream and a badger brush, fluffed the tips, and whipped it around into the creamy shaving substance, carefully holding it to the wooden round handle. She gently brushed Michelangelo's jaw, coating his lips, chin, cheeks, and upper neck in shaving cream. She placed the badger brush back in its container, then gently grabbed the straight razor from the table. Calmly, she opened the blade and held its blackened wooden handle firm as she leaned forward and focused, her face only a few inches from Michelangelo's. She gently glided the sharpened blade down, letting out the faint scratchy sounds of hair coming off his left cheek.

"I know it's not much consolation," Rosa started, "but I am sorry for all that's happened to you, that life has mistreated you. I may not have seen all that you have, but I sympathize with life's cruelty. With the loss. I've lost nearly the same." She wiped the razor's cream and hair off on the rag. "I lost my family, my friends. My freedom, even. I know my variations of those things weren't much of any of it, but it was what I had... and it was good while it lasted." She readjusted the blade on Michelangelo's face, then shaved down. "Tommy was a good man. If you could've met him one more time, I think you'd be surprised at how alike the two of you are: two men afflicted by their past yet certain of their future. Only, in my humble opinion, I think the only thing certain about a Saint Hart brother is their uncertainty. It's in your supposed absolution that the essence of your uncertainty is made clear." She cleaned the blade again. "You two are men who, though you portray yourselves as thick-headed simpletons, are far from such a description. You both try to boil yourselves down to a couple of killers, but deep down, you know that you are far more than that." She slid light, gentle strokes above Michelangelo's upper lip. "Thomas was proof of that."

"I suppose he was," Michelangelo agreed.

"I keep hearing that word 'was.'" She sighed and wiped the blade clean. "I know it's the truth. It doesn't get easier despite having heard it dozens of times." She started shaving the other side of his face. "That said, I can personally testify that he was a good man. That's how he'll be remembered despite all he did before. He did what he did for something, and that's what I hold onto. That's my hope, I guess. That all this must be worth something. It has to be." She stopped shaving for a moment and softly looked Michelangelo in the eye. He looked back. "You say everything you did didn't matter, that it all wasn't worth it. That, since you're the last man standing, all of what's happened has been a waste, but what if you're just missing the bigger picture? The broader point?"

"Which is?"

"That there has to be something to what we do. Tommy believed that. He believed in those kids, so much so that he chose them over all of us... including me. At first, I hated them for it. It took me a while to reconcile that, but I did when I got to thinking that those kids were just as innocent as mine. Then, when I started looking outside myself, I realized that it mattered. Lucius failed. Caine failed. They were safe in New York, and what Tommy did mattered, certainly to them. Then, shortly thereafter, the United States regained its Bible and is now on the verge of a religious revival. Think of all those innocents who were being robbed: now they have something. I survived, my boy survived... that's something. I'm not sure we would have that if he hadn't done what he did." She cleaned the blade and leaned in, resuming her shaving. "The point is that it matters, and why we survive matters, and you may not agree as to whether or not you should have, but maybe that's not for you to agree upon, but for us to see and have hope in. I know I didn't, for a while. But eventually I realized that this life that I have... that's the something I got to have because of what Thomas did."

Michelangelo visualized what Rosa was saying and the broader, more spiritual or philosophical strokes she was painting. "With all due respect, Ms. Felina, in my view of things, that is just hope for the lost who are left over."

Rosa smiled, slightly laughing through her nose. "Well, you can believe that if you want to, but I refuse it. Honestly, I refuse to believe you believe that. After all Thomas went through, all he sacrificed, you think it was all for nothing?" She leaned back, looking at him again. "What about you? You think what you're doing now is all for nothing?"

"Thomas had a basic, if not flawed, layer of human empathy for a couple of kids that needed help. Nothing more. Anything more than that would be foolish to believe—"

"Oh, foolish? So does that make you a fool?"

"I was getting to that, but yes."

"So you legitimately believe that all—" she gestured down to the red-watered tub. "Of this is just meaningless? Just a fool being a fool? That it won't help in some way."

"I can't fully explain my psychology to you. It's not so easy to deduce."

"It is quite easy, Major General, it is the thick heads of men that make it hard." She leaned in, placing her elbow on her knee and pointing the straight razor at Michelangelo's face. He looked at it, then at her. "See, I believe that good men do great things for greater reasons—ones bigger than themselves. Reasons that allow others to live on and be made great by the power they serve. I believe deep down, you know that, and though you want to pretend you're just a cold-hearted man out for retribution, *I know* you know there's something deeper."

"Well, of course I do."

"Then explain it!"

"I know that what I'll do matters! I know it'll matter to the people who are being persecuted, for those who are suffering the oppression, but it won't matter to me because

I don't want to *survive* it!"

Rosa looked between his eyes in the silence, searching for a lie but finding only morbid truth.

"I'm hoping I don't," he finished.

Rosa nodded softly. "I didn't want to either for a long time. But then I saw the opportunity in my son. I saw what we could become if we took a chance on the life Thomas gave us." She smiled sadly. "I felt we owed it to him." Michelangelo looked between her eyes in silence. "Maybe," she continued, "you owe that to yourself, too."

Michelangelo sighed. "Is that what changed you?"

"Is what what changed me?"

"Thomas's death. Did it change you?"

She cleaned the straight razor. "It wasn't so much his death but what he did for, what he fought for. *Who* he fought for." She leaned in and started to shave the final bits of Michelangelo's face. "It was for the greater good, sure. The principle of the thing... but in a much more direct sense, it was for all of us. For you. He didn't give his life for nothing, as you might see it, or make a foolish decision under a fool's pretense. Tommy was no simpleton. No, he gave his life so that you and I could find what he found: true freedom. That choice cost him everything."

Michelangelo thought about what Rosa was saying and considered the subtext. "Do you think what I'm doing is wrong?"

Rosa stopped shaving him and looked down into his eyes just above his face. The vulnerability shocked her. She could tell this was something he didn't do often, and didn't want to mess it up. "I don't believe that's for me to decide... but what I can say is that it's entirely dependent on what it is you're fighting for. Don't get me wrong, what you're doing is horrifying and it will traumatize many people... but maybe that's what it takes. How else does God rectify an evil that has gone so far into darkness without sending someone far scarier than them?"

Michelangelo nodded. "I'm fighting for all of it—vengeance, the persecuted, for what's right, for myself, making sense of all this."

"Yeah, I gathered that. There's a reason for what you're doing. My only caution would be in remembering one thing."

"And what's that?"

"Vengeance is in the hands of the Lord."

Michelangelo smiled. "Who is it you think sent me?" He joked.

Rosa smiled a little as she shook her head, rolling her eyes and going back to shaving. "Well, then, whatever His will may be, let it be."

Michelangelo continued to look at her. "You really believe in all that? After everything you've done?"

"Why? You judging me?"

"No, no. I'm only curious."

"Hm. Well, frankly, after everything I've seen and the varying truths I've been convinced of in life, this is the one that makes the most sense for a person such as myself, which I guess makes sense. It made sense to Tommy, and so it makes sense to me."

"So you believe it because he did?"

"No, I believe it because he helped me understand the redemption that came with the belief."

"Hm." Michelangelo pondered. "I've never been able to believe in it, honestly, after everything I've seen. It's hard to do that when you've stared into the face of evil and seen it flourish, especially now. I don't understand how God could let all this happen."

"That's understandable. I'll be honest with you, neither do I, entirely. I'm not sure most people do, on account of the scarcity of Bibles these days. Who knows: maybe with them becoming more accessible, we can all start to make sense of it."

"Yeah. Maybe." He thought some more. "Either way, I do not believe that my soul is to be saved, though I know you may have done your best."

Rosa smiled, focused on the bottom parts of his neck.

"My soul is about as wicked as the ones I'm coming for," he continued.

Rosa looked at him with a sweet smile. "So was mine."

She cleaned her blade, now finished with her shaving. Michelangelo nodded and let out a thought-provoking smile. "Either way," he began again, "I will concede to the notion that I am exactly where I need to be. I am the one sent to destroy every one of those murderous maggots and leave their corpses as food for their friends. That's what I believe, anyway, and I will sleep far more peacefully tonight knowing that there are two dozen authoritarians and autocrats lying dead outside my window than I ever would knowing that I stood by and did nothing. I'm not bothered by the presence of death or by being a harbinger of it. I'm bothered by standing by and doing nothing, just as I have done too many times before. I am tormented by the knowledge that if I don't do something, no one will. The idea of failure mortifies me—failing them, just as I failed Tommy. I know none of this will bring him or the people back, but it will certainly make things even. It'll prevent others from suffering the same fate, and that's worth it to me. That's what I'm willing to commit my life to, or at least what's left of it. That's what I'm willing to fight for. I know it's not pretty; it certainly isn't glamorous, but when is justice really? When has it ever been?"

Rosa looked at Michelangelo with sadness in her eyes, her lips pressing together gently as she closed the straight razor and grabbed the rag. "A soldier's creed, if I ever heard one," she concluded, letting out a soft smile. Michelangelo smiled as she leaned forward, wiping his face clean of the extra shaving cream.

"Whatever you decide to do, Michael, I want you to know that what happened to Thomas was not your fault. You need to accept that. Thomas made his own choices just the same as you've made yours."

"Yeah... I suppose you're right."

"My, maybe there's hope for you yet, Saint Hart," she teased.

Michelangelo smiled. "Feels miles away, I'm afraid."

Rosa leaned back and took a moment to examine the new man Michelangelo's fresh shave had made him out to be. His chin was chiseled and strong, his lips moderately thin. She looked at the gash in his nose, then at the cut on his eyebrow. She placed her cloth down and began digging in her dress pocket, then pulled out a thin needle attached to an even thinner string. "Healing often is," she replied, raising the thread and needle. "Last bit to patch you up."

"That thing been sterilized?" Michelangelo asked worriedly.

"Really? *You,* of all people, are worried about whether or not I sterilized a needle?"

"It's not even the proper kind of needle and string."

"It works just the same."

"I'm pretty sure it doesn't."

"Oh, hush up."

Rosa leaned in and began stitching the agape bridge of Michelangelo's nose, sliding the needle into the thin parts of his flesh and slowly pulling the string through. Michelangelo grunted slightly as he gritted his teeth, doing his best not to focus on the pain of the stitching.

"You're afraid of needles, ain't you?" Rosa asked, smiling.

"I didn't say that," Michelangelo responded, smiling back.

"You didn't have to."

He thought for a moment. "Can I confess something to you?"

"Of course."

"I am afraid of needles."

"*What!? No,*" Rosa remarked sarcastically.

"Needles and swords, if you can believe it. Something about how long they are. It freaks me out."

"Well, we all have our fears, sometimes even unexplainable."

"Oh, yeah?"

"Yeah. I'm afraid of cows."

"Cows?"

"Yes! They're creepy! I hate their beady little eyes and the way they stare at you. You know they'll trample you if you let 'em."

"So I've heard."

The two laughed together, Michelangelo grunting a little as Rosa continued to tend to his wounds.

"You know, Tommy was always conflicted," she started. "He always felt lost and out of place. But the last time I saw him... he was at peace. He was home. Despite his gunshot wounds or his knowing his time was up, he looked at me, and I *knew* that he was going to be okay, that he had made it. I know he wanted the same for me. One murderous outlaw looked to another, and we had hope. And if there's hope for Tommy, then there's hope for me; if there's hope for me, then there's hope for you too. For all of us... It just takes a bit of faith to believe in something greater than ourselves, whether that be God or the principles we hold ourselves to."

Michelangelo considered what Rosa said. He wondered what it was that he might consider home, and where he might find it. He had spent years without one, so it seemed like more of a fantasy than reality, at least for a man like him.

"You make your home where you make your peace. That's the concept?" He asked.

"Ideally."

"I don't know if I can be at peace while men like Icarus walk this earth."

Rosa finished stitching Michelangelo and locked her eyes with his. "I know," she said with a smile.

She cupped his cheek with her hand, rubbed it gently, then stood, making her way to the door. Michelangelo sat in the lukewarm, crimson water and looked after her. New bruises had appeared on his chin, painting his jaw in black and blue. His right eye was black as well, but now it had red stitches sewn into his eyebrow and the bridge of his nose. Michelangelo adjusted his back, wiggling up in the tub as both his palms gripped the brim.

Rosa stopped before the door, gripping the doorknob. "I know Tommy's gone," she began again. "And you may not be the cleanest… but I'm glad that there's still a Saint among us. I sleep better knowing that." Michelangelo looked at Rosa as she turned to face him. "Lots of beauty can come from the saints. Their stories bring hope to us believers, so that we may have something to hold on to. When God is silent, which He often is, we can only hear Him through the stories that they tell —the testimonies they bear. That is what makes the Lord real, sometimes. We look to the Saint of Salvation and we're inspired—a story as beautiful as his reaps the very same love it sows." She paused. "But I wonder… what kind of saint will you be? What might the Saint of Retribution inspire? What'll it reap? Who will we look toward then?"

Michelangelo nodded, knowingly. Rosa opened the door, turned to leave, then paused and turned back again. "Look, I know you're a busy man and all with all this blood lust and vengeance business, but if you can, you should consider staying with us for a while. My son and I, I mean. We'd both appreciate your company."

Michelangelo smiled nervously. "Stay here? With you?"

"Well, the two of us. As an uncle, of course. Thomas could use *an uncle.*"

"Oh, Thomas could?"

"Yes, Thomas."

The two laughed again, Michelangelo doing his best to hide the fact that the idea tempted him, while Rosa did the same. They continued to look at each other, smiling in the silence, sharing that moment of bliss.

"I'll think about it," Michelangelo replied honestly, lifting himself from the tub.

Rosa looked away from him, covering her eyes, as he walked over to the changing station behind him. Water dripped in great puddles from his body as he thudded across the wooden floor, the weight of his muscles causing the wood to bend beneath him. She looked up and over her hands slightly, seeing only a little as she fought the urge to see it all.

In truth, both knew that Michelangelo wouldn't take the deal. The soldier had come too far to settle now, and Rosa, having met a Saint Hart before, knew that there was no chaining their minds once they had determined it was made up for justice. Still, she figured she'd try. To her, it was worth at least trying.

"Thank you for listening, Michael. I appreciate it. Truly," Rosa thanked.

Michelangelo walked behind the changing station and wrapped the white towel around him, looking thoughtfully at the dampened wood floor beneath him. He thought about who should be thanking whom, for Rosa had also made Michelangelo feel better and greatly enticed him with her offer of starting a family. However, he knew men in his position were rarely given such a privilege.

"Any time," he assured, walking around to see her again. "And thank you. Sincerely."

She smiled and closed the door calmly.

Michelangelo stared at the closed door as he thought about what Rosa had said: the concept of something greater, and where it was that his heart appeared to be, within this war. He knew he was at war with himself, the world, and injustice, but wondered which was the most important. Which was 'something greater.' Regardless, it had manifested in a violent and self-destructive summation, and would more than likely end in all the same manner if he did not change course. Still, he couldn't. His bloodlust was too great, and despite all that he had spilt, he was still thirsty. He looked down at the wooden floor and sighed, then made his way to his room, readying himself for a rest he had not had in a good long while. As he walked into his room, he dried his entire body, then lay in his bed, resting his head on the soft, silky pillow. He pulled up the covers and sheets of the same material and closed his eyes, letting the material carry his thoughts away. He wondered who he was meant to be, how his story would resonate with the millions who would hear it, and what his legend would become. He asked if he cared about how it affected those who believed and those who didn't, or how they might interpret his actions and determine if they were inspiring or diminishing. He wondered if the people would see him as just or unjust. Regardless of what conclusions he came to, deep down, he knew how his story would end: in death. As he lay there, thinking about the possibilities of the coming outcomes, he thought once more about a new piece to the puzzle: a young boy who had joined this venture and had true potential to be something greater, who could fight the good fight Rosa wished for Michelangelo. He wondered if this was what had intrigued him so much about Sophia, if this was why his mission evolved. He figured that if he were to fight wicked men, then the preacher could fight the wickedness that possessed them; if he could protect Leonardo DelMuerto so that he might fight this fight, then maybe Michelangelo would succeed in fighting for something greater. If the preacher could live through this story, perhaps not all of the testimony would be lost, for he could go forth and tell the story that Michelangelo knew he never could.

And he slept.

CHAPTER 8

Death Follows Quickly to the Prayee and Prey

ichelangelo walked down the spacious wooden stairs into the lower area of Hotel Emilda. The morning's sun had begun to shine over Little York, projecting a light blue hue over the mountainside that shone through the hotel's barroom windows. The windows were tall, wide, and rectangular, with a crosshair design through the center. The walls that held them in place were made of fine mahogany wood, the same material used for the floor. An assortment of animal skins covered the flooring, all placed in a particular location based on the size or extravagance of the creatures' tufts.

In the center of the bar parlour, there was a mountain lion skin, spread wide to show all its light brown fur that had been perfectly stitched together. Beside the mountain lion's skin, all around the solid wood floor, there were patches of boar's skin, blackened and round, and made only more prominent in their decorative style by the fireplace that shone its orange light upon them. The fireplace was a large and warm centerpiece, built into the left side of the building, between two windows that showed the barbershop. The chimney was made of rocks that were rounded and smoothed by the hands of builders and time alike, held together by mortar that was tan in color but firm in its solidification. The opening of the fireplace was shaped like an upside-down U, and it connected to a cemented opening at the bottom. The wood inside cracked and popped, giving off the scent of rich pine that filled the bar parlour with a warm, smoky aroma. On the opposite side of the room, aligned perfectly with the fireplace just beside the stairs, was a bar with an assortment of fancy drinks and meals. The bar counter was a wide, ten-foot slab of wood that took up the majority of the right side of the bar parlour. The wood of the counter was smoothed down and coated with a soft glaze, finished with a rich, cherry red that glistened in the reflection of the firelight.

The lip of the bar counter was smoothed and rounded, protruding ever so slightly over the edges to showcase its laced, wooden carvings that spiraled around the rim. The bar was supported by a mahogany wooden wall that stretched from the ground to the counter, covering its entire length. Behind it, an assortment of premium alcohols was displayed in beautifully crafted glass bottles. Each bottle was crafted by the finest glassblowers in all of Northern Arizona, containing various forms of brown liquid. From fine brandy to Romanian rum, each one glistened in the morning's light.

Michelangelo took note of the different beverages and tried to ignore their call to his thirst, something new that had developed in him recently. He shook his head slightly and ignored the spirits as he walked to the bar counter, grabbing one of the eight cherry red stools that were placed in front of the bar. He sat himself down, leaned forward against the counter, and rested both of his elbows on it. He held his freshly cleaned navy man's jacket in his inner elbow, which, now, only had splotches of light, dark-brown stains too soaked into the clothing to get out. His pants were clean as well, and they too had faint stains on them. The pants' legs were tucked into his black riding boots, now washed and shined to reveal the many scratches and dents they had. His jacket was unbuttoned, showing the light brown fuzz that made up the inlay, which covered his relatively unstained navy man's button-up shirt, tucked into the tops of his pants. The buttons of his shirt were a golden yellow and had swirly insignias on each. He took off his navy man's hat and noted the faint bloodstains upon the brim, base, and even the fine yellow string that complemented the attire. He remembered a time before, when this yellow string was bright and shining, tightly strung together and leading to a tidy end that elegantly hung on the front of his hat. But now, as he looked upon his headpiece, he saw that the time of cleanliness was gone, and the string was frayed and discolored. His clothes were also discolored; the navy blues had become a faded navy. His clothing was torn and weathered, with many stabs and rips within its cotton. He sighed as he pondered over the journey he had undergone so far, and how it was far from over.

Rosa walked over to Michelangelo. She was wearing the same clothing she had on the night before. Her night shift at the bar was barely coming to an end. To the right of her stood a bartender, cleaning his dishes by slowly rubbing his rag around the rim of the glasses, bringing them back to their once-perfect and premium shine.

"What'll it be, soldier?" She joked.

Michelangelo chuckled. "I'm not drinking."

"Not alone?" She cutely held up an unopened bottle of whisky, a slight flirtatious glimmer in her eye.

Michelangelo shook his head as a smile grew on his face. "No, Rosa, I'm just here to pass the time."

She shrugged and put the whisky away. "I suppose it's for the best." She looked back at him. "You don't strike me as a man who does that often."

"You'd be struck right." He looked around. "I'm waiting on someone. Two some-ones, actually."

"Oh, I see. And who is it you might be waiting for?"

"William Davidson," William interrupted.

Rosa froze; her body tensed with a quick squeeze, her head whipping quickly to the bounty hunter who approached her. Her eyes fixated on him while her mind raced to her resting child just beneath the counter. Tomás was hidden under the bar counter, swaddled in a makeshift crib made from a wooden box and cloth.

"Yeah. He's one of them," Michelangelo confirmed.

William stomped down the stairs heavily, making his way to Rosa's recognizable boots. William's boots thudded and spurred heavily as he made his way to the bar counter. The steps he took reverberated through the emptiness of the room, bouncing off its wide walls and high ceiling, only to be obstructed by a dozen mahogany tables. Michelangelo noted Rosa's tension and realized the cause was coming from William. He looked at William, who was now freshly cleaned, and wondered what it was William had done to Rosa.

William wore the same clothing as before, only his hat was now missing from the top of his head. His jacket, boots, and jeans were cleaned to a shiny black, though they were also lightly stained with blood. Michelangelo examined William's balding and grey hair and saw how the illusion of the Brother of Grim seemed to fade along with his hairline. He had never seen William as the character so many had perceived him as, as so many had feared him to be. To the soldier, William Davidson was only his uncle, far before anything else. Regardless, Michelangelo saw that William's presence struck fear into Rosa, and did his best to get to the bottom of the issue, given their obvious history. He adjusted his posture and turned his upper body toward the Brother of Grim as he stopped at the bar counter beside him. He placed his right hand on his right hip, just above the grip of his navy man's revolver, his left arm lying flat upon the countertop. Rosa remained frozen in fear.

"Morning, Bill," Michelangelo greeted.

"Good morning, Mike," he replied almost sarcastically.

Michelangelo nodded. "How do you like your coffee?"

"Black."

"Of course."

William looked from Michelangelo to Rosa, who was analyzing his every feature. William thought about the last time he had seen Rosa and the circumstances that had been presented during that moment. He thought back to a time far before this one, and how different things were. Michelangelo faced Rosa again, casually looking between the two and analyzing the tension that was present.

"Rosa, two black coffees, please," Michelangelo requested.

Rosa did not reply.

"Rosa. Hello?"

She shook her head. "Sorry, what?"

"Two black coffees?"

She went over to the coffee heater on the stove behind the counter and filled two cups. Michelangelo kept looking at her but spoke to William. "I take it you two know each other?"

"Yes, we do," William replied.

"You're not planning on taking her in, are you?"

"Not at the moment."

"She came back with the two coffee cups in hand.

"Thank you," Michelangelo said.

"Yeah, of course," Rosa replied.

"And a thank you from me as well, miss...." William opened.

"Santa Felina," she answered, looking over to William with less fear and more fire now.

William raised his eyebrows and tilted his head to the side as his bottom lip pouted out as he thought about her name. Michelangelo sipped his coffee, darting his eyes between the two over the rim of his cup.

"Santa Felina. Well, that's unique," William teased.

"It's the best I could do on account of you got my husband killed."

Michelangelo slightly choked on his drink, burning his lips in the process. "Ah. Dammit," he said, wiping his lips and shaking his fingers. William and Rosa looked at him as he looked up between the two. "Sorry, I just did not expect you to say that." They all stood in silence for an awkward moment. "You got any cinnamon?" Michelangelo asked. Rosa leaned under the counter, took out some powdered cinnamon in a small glass jar, and handed it to Michelangelo. He grabbed it, cleared his throat, and gently flicked some into his coffee.

William looked at Rosa again. She looked back at him, her traumatic response losing its effect. She quickly realized she wasn't in any real immediate danger, given that he was with Michelangelo, and more than this, her illusion of the big and scary Brother of Grim had been broken. Now, he was just a balding old man tagging along with a blood-thirsty soldier for reasons she could not figure out. "So, this is what's become of the big, bad Brother of Grim?" She antagonized. William was angry at first, but couldn't bear to keep it up—the performative act he had mastered in his many years of bounty hunting. When he looked in her eyes and saw the pain that rested in their sockets, his guilt overcame him, and he knew that, as much as it might irk him, she was right for feeling the way she did.

William sighed. "Listen, Rosal— Rosa," he corrected, "I know it won't amount to much right now, and maybe you won't even believe it considering the man you came to know me as, but I am sorry for what happened."

Rosa listened.

"I thought I was just doing my job," William continued, "but I wasn't. It was more than that, deeper than that, and I recognize that. I was blinded by greed and vengeance, the former more than the latter, and I used Thomas as bait to ."

Rosa thought in silence for a moment. She looked down at her son. "You saved mine and my sons' lives. I know that much. I'm thankful for that much, even owe it to you." She looked back up at him. "So, I believe you, mostly."

William nodded slightly, relieved. Rosa looked up at him with an angrier expression. "But... that doesn't change the fact that if I weren't with child, you would've killed me too. It doesn't change the fact that, despite you not pulling the trigger, it was you who got Thomas killed." She put her hand on the counter and leaned in close to the hunter. "And it sure *as Hell* doesn't explain the fact that it was *you* who was waiting for us with Caine Kingsley."

Michelangelo tensed, dropping his coffee with his casual attitude and looking toward William, his anger growing. "What was that?" He asked. "Oh," Rosa replied. "He didn't tell you? When my gang and I went back to tell Caine that we were done, the Brother of Grim was waiting there. Right there with him." She smiled wickedly. "It was almost as though the two were working together."

Michelangelo's heart pounded with anger. "You want to explain yourself, Bill?" He asked, interlocking his fingers tightly.

William laughed nervously, then quickly composed himself, conjuring up a lie. A part of him was thankful that Rosa did not reveal the whole truth, but the other part of him was afraid as to why. He couldn't quite place why she would reveal a half-truth, especially one as dangerous as this. "Rosa," William started explaining. "I am a hunter. I hunt. I had a hunch you and your boys were working with Caine, which Thomas only confirmed, so I followed it to its natural conclusion that just so *happened* to be accurate."

Rosa smiled angrily as she shook her head, looking down and then back up to him. "So that's the 'truth' then? You're just one hell of a tracker?"

"It ain't my fault that you and your boys were about as easy to track as a bleeding rhinoceros. The trail you all left traced right back to Kingsley. Easy as that."

Rosa sighed furiously. "You haven't changed a bit. You're the same greedy man that you were months ago, the only difference being now you're ten times weaker in body and spirit."

"Hey, Bill," Michelangelo interrupted. William looked over to him as his heartbeat picked up the pace. "You don't know where Caine is, right?"

William clenched his jaw as he looked into his nephew's eyes. "No. I don't."

Michelangelo breathed heavily through his nose as he began to piece the final pieces of his uncle's puzzle together. The two stared at each other in silence as she waited for William to get what he deserved. Truthfully, despite it all, she only wanted him to be honest. She wanted to know if he was as changed as he claimed to be or if he was still willing to lie for his benefit. With what she had seen, she determined that he was, and that his apology was empty.

"Michael," William started again, "even if I did know, you don't think he would've moved by now? He may not be on a wanted poster, but he is a wanted man. More people than just you want him dead. He wouldn't stay in one place; you and I both know he wouldn't."

Michelangelo nodded lightly. "Why didn't you kill him?"

"What? Are you *really* going to ask me that?"

"Clearly, you knew what he was doing. You tracked him down and deduced as much, so why didn't you kill him?"

"Well, this may be hard for you to understand, Michael, but some of us only kill within the confines of the *law.* "

"Was he not breaking it?"

"Not legally, no!"

"Oh, not legally?"

"Yes, Mike. Not all of us kill because it's the 'just' thing to do. Regardless of what he was doing, no law enforcement agency was aware of it. You can't kill a man without a contract for his head. Now you know that if there had been a contract for him, despite our previous connections, I would've handled him just the same as the Brothers of Boudiclare. You know that!"

"And you didn't think maybe reporting him would've been the right thing to do, so you could 'obey the law?' "

"With all the money and power he has, you think it would've mattered?"

"And you wonder why I'm doing what I'm doing."

"As someone who cares for the family you're doing it for, yes!"

"Oh, you want to talk about family? You, the guy who betrayed his 'family' for monetary gain?"

"How long are you going to lord that over me?"

Rosa huffed an angry laugh. "As long as it takes for you to admit you're a no-good lying killer," she interjected.

"Oh, that's high talk for someone with a reputation such as yours, Miss *Felina*. Might I remind you that the price on your head is higher than it was when I saved your life?"

"All right, enough," Michelangelo said, rubbing his eyebrows with his thumbs in frustration.

Rosa's anger boiled through her blood as Tomás began crying underneath the counter. The bartender noticed the interaction and glanced over slightly, then returned to cleaning his dishes. Michelangelo thought about what he heard and the information that had just been revealed to him. He thought about the potential new truth and what it could mean for the road ahead. He dropped his hand to the counter and leaned on it.

"Listen, we can all accuse one another until we're blue in the face, but it won't get us anywhere worthwhile," Michelangelo lied.

Rosa knelt and lifted Tomás from his tiny wooden crib, filled with a flutter of blankets that wrapped around his body. She swaddled him in a red blanket that protected him from the deadly winter's cold. Rosa looked at Tomás, bouncing and cradling him as Michelangelo looked at William. "Whether we like it or not," Michelangelo continued, "we don't have evidence to support any truth either way, or at least I don't. I don't know how it all played out, or what exactly you were doing during that time, and honestly, at this point,

I don't believe it matters. What does matter is that I am hunting *Caine*, and since you have stuck with me thus far and count on doing so, I will grant you that. We are working together, and it would benefit us to *keep* working together. Despite all there is to be said, and how much of the truth there is to be found, I will hear nothing further." He stood up from his stool and stepped closer to William. "But I will say this: if I find out all that Rosa said is true—that you were working with Caine and *knew* about Tommy's involvement with him— " he got in William's face, the hunter looking up as the soldier towered over him. "I'll bury you just the same as I bury Caine, in a hole so deep your legacy will be reduced to worm food." William looked between Michelangelo's eyes, unsure of whether or not he believed this threat. Regardless, this was the first time that he had threatened William's life, and he did not tend to take these types of threats lightly. If this was a legitimate one, as he perceived it was, then his odds had just shifted unfavorably. These were odds William did not agree to. Rosa looked up and saw William's smile slightly grace his face. It was one she had seen a few times before, a dangerously familiar one that, though similar, lacked its original threatening power. Though his smile was masterful, when she looked in his eyes, all she saw was sorrow, denial, and bitterness weighing them down. Gone were his fiery and vengeful daggers, seemingly replaced by dull and non-threatening weights. "Sure, Mike," William agreed. "Whatever you say."

Michelangelo clenched his jaw as the front doors opened, revealing a young, skinny, and poorly dressed boy, coated in snow from the recent snowfall, as he walked through. He looked around for a moment, saw William, then began walking toward him. Michelangelo, William, and Rosa all looked as the young man approached. "Your bounty wagon is here, Mr. Davidson," he informed. Michelangelo and Rosa slowly turned back to look at him. "I believe that's my cue," William said, smiling and walking past Michelangelo. "I'll be outside sorting out the bodies, determining if they're worth a dime." He turned around, walking backwards. "Who knows! Maybe we got lucky and killed one that matters." He turned around again and exited the door, the young man following.

Michelangelo shook his head as he looked after his uncle, still debating as to what he would do, having figured out the truth from what pieces he could put together, as footsteps creaked down the steps of the hotel. He turned around and looked at them, only to see Leonardo walking down, rubbing his eyes and adjusting his jacket with a yawn. "How'd you sleep, kid?" He asked. "Uh, good. Thanks," Leonardo replied.

Rosa looked at Leonardo, then back at Michelangelo. A slight smile formed in the corner of her mouth as she squinted at the soldier. Tomás was quiet now; she adjusted him to her right shoulder and patted him softly with her left arm. "So," she started, "How do you know Mr. DelMuerto?"

Michelangelo looked at her, noticed her smile, then let out a half-cheeked smile. "Circumstance, mostly. Fate, if you want to get spiritual."

"Oh, I see. 'Fate.' 'Circumstance.' " She chuckled. "How arbitrary."

He shook his head. "Okay, how do you know him?"

"He preaches here often. I listen to his sermons as often as I can."

Michelangelo nodded as Leonardo walked up to the bar counter. "Looks like you got yourself a fan, kid," the soldier joked. Leonardo looked at Rosa, who looked sweetly at him.

"I only mentioned I listened to your sermons. He's being exaggerative," she corrected.

Leonardo nodded, letting out a feigned smile as he leaned against the counter in silence. He couldn't get his mind off his brothers and was worrying about them relentlessly. As far as he knew, they were nowhere to be found, in a land unknown, seemingly lost in the winter's storm. Michelangelo noted this along with the dark circles under his eyes.

"I have some good news," Michelangelo said. Leonardo looked up and over quickly. "I can't be sure, but I think I know where your brothers are."

"Really?!" Leonardo replied excitedly, nearly jumping out of his jacket and looking up with desperation and hope in his eyes, hanging on every word of Michelangelo's.

"Where!?"

"Easy, evangelismo," Michelangelo said, reaching over and taking his final sip of coffee. "Last night, I interrogated a man who told me about a place called the Hillberry Settlement. It's about a day's ride from here. I figure that since it's in the direction that the horsemen left in last night with your brothers, that's probably where they'll be. More than likely, it's where Icarus will be, too. So, that's where I'm headed."

"Well, then, why are we here!? We need to go!"

"We?"

"Yes, we!" Leonardo stated as he began walking past Michelangelo.

"Slow down, partner." Michelangelo stopped, reaching out his arm gently to stop Leonardo. "You do realize you are the one man that Icarus wants? You need to stay here where it's *safe*."

"Look, you can either let me come with you and we can go together, or you can 'keep me here' and I'll eventually go alone, but you are not keeping me from my brothers."

Michelangelo looked into Leonardo's eyes and saw the truth in them. "Yeah, I'd probably do the same." He sighed, dropping his arm and shaking his head. "Can you ride?"

"Like a horse?"

"Or a tree; whichever you're more familiar with."

Leonardo smiled and rolled his eyes. "Yes, I can ride a horse."

"Good, because you certainly can't walk there." He looked out at the white-covered grounds outside the Hotel Emilda. "There are about two dozen dead men outside who are more than willing to donate you one. Find yourself a horse, then come and find me. I'll meet you in the street by the old man dressed in black."

Leonardo smiled. "Thank you!" He gave a quick nod and jogged for the front door, then rushed outside. He was unfazed by the winter morning chill or the snow that fell in large flakes. Despite the temperature dropping and the snow increasing, he was more concerned with saving his brothers' lives. He took off, jogging out of Michelangelo's sight as the soldier shook his head and turned back to a giddy Rosa.

"What?" He questioned defensively.

"Nothing, nothing. It's just sweet, is all," she replied.

"Sweet? What's sweet? I'm not doing anything sweet."

"Right. You're just helping the Brothers' Six because they're central to the whole murder-vengeance thing."

Michelangelo rolled his eyes and smiled. "It's Leo. I'm helping him, if you want to call it that." He looked at his empty coffee cup. "His fiancée came out of her home in a pitiful state, back at their village. I couldn't help but feel for her. I'm not sure why. Her face was... branded. Her eyes ran red from the tears." Rosa listened sorrowfully. "She asked me to bring Leo back." He looked up at Rosa. "I figured, why the hell not? 'Can't hurt to fit one good deed in amongst a hundred bad ones, can it?"

Rosa nodded slowly, then looked down at a sleeping Tomás. She let out an airy laugh as she smiled widely. Michelangelo took notice. "What?" He asked, smiling.

"I just find it interesting that a man who claims to be so cold finds himself being warm," she replied.

"Even the smallest of fires burns in the wildest of flurries. I suppose none of us is ever as cold as we claim to be."

Rosa looked at Michelangelo, hopeful of the warmth that seemed to grow within him. Then, a serious expression took over her face. "So... you think you can save the Brothers' Six?"

The soldier sighed. "I don't know. Even if they were there, or even alive, I don't know how I'd do it. Still, I wasn't tasked to save them; I was tasked with saving Leonardo. He is the only one I need to get home."

Rosa nodded her head slowly as she thought about Michelangelo's words and wondered if this was his honest confession or a refusal to accept a greater challenge.

"You know, I once heard a man tell me that home is where you make your peace;

home is where the ones you love welcome you and remind you of the reason you return. I used to have that, despite its brokenness and the wickedness that surrounded it. Despite all the evil that attached itself to us, we were still a family. Having love is one thing, but home... home is with your family." She looked down at her baby. "I was lucky enough to have the love of my life be my family as well. I had it all." Michelangelo looked into Rosa's eyes as she looked up at his. "I had that taken from me, ripped from me in minutes... now what remains is me and my son. Regardless of how horrid they were, they were still mine. Imagine the effect that would have on someone whose family isn't so horrid? A family who never deserved what they were getting, or ever expected to be treated as such." She paused a moment. "You may get Leonardo home... but without his brothers, he won't return. Not the same, at least. He'll come back to a shell of what his home once was... and that? That's not peace. That's a war that never ends. Believe that."

Michelangelo considered saving the Six Brothers; he pondered the impossibility of such a feat, weighed against the overwhelming responsibility of bringing the preacher home. He had not pondered thoughts like these in a long time, but he pondered them now as they grew more enticing. "You make a good point, Ms. Felina," he conceded. "I'll give you that. Look, Icarus and his men: they're smart, cunning. As far as I know, the brothers are already dead. I can't fix that, much less stop it from happening."

"And if they're alive?"

"If they're alive... then there's a chance."

"For the oh-so-smart great major military general?"

"Yes, for him," he smiled.

She smiled back. "I hear what you're saying. Maybe they're alive, maybe not. But if they are, maybe the impossibility of the task is worth the risk." She paused for a beat. "It's men like you that make the impossible possible. That's the Saint Hart legend." She looked at her baby. "The way I see it, you are Leonardo DelMuerto's only hope. You may be all he has left."

Michelangelo let out a slow and frustrated shot of air through his nose as he looked off to the side. "Yeah. I know." His mind wrestled with thoughts of selfishness versus selflessness, with the question of prioritizing the mission or the morality behind it. He wondered what was more selfish, anyhow, to prioritize one soul over the others or a few souls over the majority. *Maybe,* he thought, *it's possible to do both. Be selfish. Be selfless.* He turned back and grabbed his navy man's hat off the top of the bar counter and slid it onto his head carefully, ensuring he did not bump his freshly stitched wounds. "As much as I'd love to stay and chat, Ms. Felina, I have a job I must tend to."

She smiled, adjusting Tomás, and revealed his face. Michelangelo's eyes widened as he looked at the baby boy. He looked over the familiar features of his younger brother that had been passed down to his son. Tomás had a chiseled nose and hazel eyes that perfectly complemented his wavy hair. His skin was more of a darker shade, much like his mother's, and his cheeks were filled with a pleasant warmth and peace. Michelangelo looked at Tomás, and for the first time in many moons, felt a sincere feeling of joy. He noted the preciousness of the child and was glad that of all the deaths he had survived. As the soldier looked upon Tomás, Rosa looked at Michelangelo. She examined his tall and muscular features, the bruised and stitched face that was once hidden underneath his beard. She studied his chiseled chin and his morning stubble until, finally, looking into his eyes, she saw that comforting familiarity. She was torn by this strange affection, this feeling of guilt and of peace, one that, though bizarre, she liked, even if for the momentary peace it offered her. She determined that, if he would let her, she would care for him, even to hold onto some resemblance of the good from before. Still, she knew he wouldn't let her, that he had already made up his mind. Thus, she cared for him the only way she knew she could, at least for now: with a warning.

"Watch out for Grim, Michael," she started. "I know you don't have much reason to trust me, but I am *begging* you to listen to me when I say that the man who rides with you is on no one's side but his own."

Michelangelo nodded calmly. "I know. As much as it pains me to have him along, I'd be a fool not to admit that I can't do this on my own. I need at least one other man like myself to kill the remainder of these men, or at least the horsemen, and that would be Bill."

She sighed. "I understand."

He looked over to her comfortingly. "... Don't worry. It'll be alright."

She smiled appreciatively, though she wholeheartedly disagreed. "I just don't understand how you can walk beside that man after all he's done. All this mess we're in... It's because of him... Tommy's dead because of him."

He looked away from her, staring off into the distance. "I haven't made much sense of it either. Sometimes I feel like it's that part of me that wants Bill to be good, to be how I remember him. At other times, I wonder if it is truly just a violation of my principles for my benefit. Either way, one thing I will say is that this whole mess isn't *entirely* his fault. Sure, he's involved, far more than he's letting on, but at the end of the day, it all comes down to Caine Kingsley. If I don't get to him, this is all for nothing. Thus, Bill is a necessary evil tolerated to fight a greater one than he." He looked back at her. "But rest assured, Rosa, once this is all said and done, I will get him to confess the truth, and when he does, there will be justice. For me, you, Tommy, Tomas. Everyone who's suffered because of this."

Rosa nodded as her worried eyes looked to Michelangelo, for she feared for Michelangelo's life in light of this alignment with the Brother of Grim. "Just make sure you come back," she pleaded.

He looked between her eyes. "I will."

As he looked into her eyes, he wondered if coming back to Rosa was an option for him. She was pretty, and raising Thomas's son was something he would be more than happy to commit himself to. More than anything, he would take care of her, ensure that she was all right after everything she had been through. He would be happy to do it, or at least a part of him would. She smiled and gave him a final nod as he shook himself away from his thoughts, shelving them for now and making his way to the door. As he did, he looked to his right and saw the bartender at the opposite end of the counter. Suddenly, a temporary solution, or even an alternative idea, popped into his head, and thus, as an act of care for her, he made his way to him. The bartender looked up at the soldier as he approached, taking slow, powerful steps. He reached into his jacket pocket and pulled out three of his dollar coins, stopping in front of the bartender and laying the coins flat on the counter. He leaned into the bartender, who in turn leaned toward him.

"You run this place?" He asked.

"Yes. I am the manager," the bartender replied.

"Yeah? What's your name?"

"Mr. Landon."

"Full name."

"... Bozco Landon."

"Bozco?"

"Yes, Bozco."

Michelangelo smirked. "That's what they name fellas like you where you come from?"

Bozco stared, unamused. "Indeed," he replied, annoyed.

Bozco was a British man of great prestige and posture. His mustache was thin and well-kept, and it did not spread further than the reach of his mouth. He had a face that was lean and bony, the same as the rest of his finely dressed body. He wore a shiny black vest over an ironed white button-up, paired with black slacks and shoes that shone just as brightly. His hair was combed and parted down the middle, and it glistened with a shine made only by hair pomade.

"Listen, Bozco, I need you to do me a favor, and I want to stress that by favor I mean that I expect what I'm about to tell you to happen." He pointed to Rosa. "I need you to take care of Ms. Felina and her boy." He looked back, dropping his point. "If anything happens to them, I will place the blame solely on your head. Whatever happens to them, I will make sure it happens to you." He smiled. "We clear?"

Bozco leaned back with an appalled yet receptive expression, slowly shifting his gaze between Rosa and Michelangelo. He remained unbothered, yet cautious. "Why me, sir?"

"Because I know you gave her a job despite her background and the reward on her head. I know you lied about her not being here when the law came, and you have fully accepted her, warts and all." He nodded, respecting Bozco. "That tells me you're kind. That tells me you care. I'd wager you probably like her."

Bozco gulped. Michelangelo smiled. "No, it's okay. That's good. You're kind. You're here. Therefore, their lives are in your hands. Take it seriously. Take responsibility." He looked over at her and Tomás. "You may be all they have left after all is said and done."

Bozco's tensions calmed. "Thank you, sir." Michelangelo looked back. "No. Thank you." He looked behind Bozco. "You selling that bottle of brandy?" Bozco turned around, reached for the bottle, and then placed it on the counter in front of the soldier.

"Three dollars," Bozco said. Michelangelo lifted his hand and gave Bozco the dollar coins. As the bartender took them, Michelangelo looked up behind him and noticed the massive painting, one he had not seen before.

The painting was brushed in what appeared to be the finest oils. At the center stood a grizzly bear, its body covered in a mixture of light and dark brown fur. The grizzly lay lifeless on a large boulder, beautifully captured in its natural state, having a mixture of tonal blacks, greys, and whites that mixed perfectly. Beside the bear was a peninsula, giving sight to an ocean that spread far and vast as though it would never end, holding the sun that began to rise from its waters. The sea was hundreds of feet below the creature, which appeared to have been gazing out over this vast body of water. The sky above him consisted of beautiful and bright yellows, pinks, light blues, and reds. However, what intrigued Michelangelo most was the protrusion that sank deep into the right side of the bear's back; emerging from its back was a magnificent and sparkling sword that appeared to come from a time long ago. The sword had a golden hilt, the blade made of pure diamond, and a cross-guard that stuck out from the bear's flesh. The cross-guard took on the shape of what looked like bear claws, hooking outward like one might see on a knight's sword.

The soldier stared at the painting in awe, the art overtaking his focus. Bozco turned and looked at the painting, then back at the soldier, and then at the painting again. "It's called *Bearenstein's Legend.*" He said. "Wonderful piece, really, painted in fine oil from the Elizabethan era." Michelangelo turned to Bozco, curious. "Elizabethan?" He asked, uneducated.

"As in from the time of Queen Elizabeth."

"Oh," Michelangelo learned, looking back at the painting. "Pretty name."

"The artist's name is Dakota Rain," he said, looking back over to Michelangelo. "She was known for her medieval stylization in the arts."

Michelangelo nodded, saying nothing, gliding his eyes across the piece. Bozco glanced confusedly between the painting and the soldier. "Would you care to know its meaning, sir?" he asked.

Michelangelo looked to Bozco as he came to, then quickly glanced back at the piece, for though he was back in reality, he was still mesmerized by the handiwork and the strange connection he had to it. "Yeah. Sure. What's it about?"

"It is said that the painting is inspired by the story of the knight known as Stockton Bearenstein. Now, as I'm sure you're aware, most knights find themselves to be valorous. Brave. Sacrificial faceless men that are seen more as entities than they are as humans. But Stockton... he was a vicious man. Many saw him as brutal and violent. So much so that the term 'deadly' did not accurately describe him. He was... something far more. One day, he found himself on yet another rampage of justice when he killed a man who was greatly loved. This man died like the rest, but those who survived him were different, dangerous. His mother, known by the name the Witch of Locke, loved her son dearly, and when she discovered he had been slaughtered in battle, she figured his killer needed to be seen as the creature he was rather than the flesh he walked in. Thus, the witch cursed Stockton and turned him into a bear, condemning him to a life of animalistic existence. However, the witch was not entirely unfair, for she had left him one single hint as to how he might break the curse: 'Act as more man than monster when you are more monster than man, and the man will be seen more than the monster he is.' From then on, Stockton prowled the borders of the kingdom as the monster many had perceived him to be, still protecting those inside but never again as the man he once was."

Michelangelo nodded, his jaw half agape. "Huh," he huffed. "You got all that from a painting?"

Bozco laughed. "No, sir, from reading. The painting itself is simply the expression of the story."

"Ah, well, I suppose I appreciate the painting more than the fairytale," he said, looking back at it.

Bozco examined Michelangelo, then nodded silently. "Your name is Saint Hart, is it not?"

Michelangelo turned, intrigued. "It is," he replied.

Bozco nodded, looking at the painting. "Interesting."

The soldier huffed. "Why is that interesting?"

"Well, for a man so disinterested in fantasy, you have certainly taken a liking to its elements."

"Ah, it's just a nice painting, is all."

"I was not referring to the piece, Mr. Hart." He looked back at the soldier. "Art is never about 'the piece.' It is a connection on a level that only the appreciator may understand, exemplified before us by an individual we may never know. Fantasy or not, one might argue that the connection we feel is very real. Very prominent. Enough to entrap even the most bloodily lustful."

"Art imitates reality."

"Precisely. Though, in your case, good soldier, I would not only consider this piece an imitation, but a reflection. You are somewhat of a walking fantasy, Mr. Hart. A legend, if you will."

"Ah, to hell with the legend. I'm just a man doing what he feels is right."

"As most legends do."

Michelangelo smiled and shook his head. "All right then, Mr. Landon, you've piqued my interest: How does Stockton's story end? Clearly, something went horribly wrong."

Bozco looked at the painting again. "In some interpretations. In my view, I would say something went horribly right. You see, an army had risen against the king's kingdom and threatened all who had lived within. With Stockton gone, there was no terror to keep the terrible away, for without a man of war who raged upon wicked men, wicked men raged upon the innocent with war. Many had not heard of this monster known as the Bearenstein, but the Bearenstein had heard of them. His time in the wilderness had changed him, and his fight, though present, was no longer a fight for blood or justice, but was a fight for the people as a protector. Something deeper called to the Bearenstein, something some of us might call humanity. Somehow, this humanity remained, and the Bearenstein charged into battle, fighting valiantly amongst the horde, vicious in control. He took on the army of the enemy among his fellow knights. At first, they feared him, as any seeing a monstrous bear would, but when they saw the beast was on their side, they too fought valiantly. However, among the army of the enemy, the Witch of Locke was at the center. They all fought ferociously, the witch losing her hold on the kingdom. Eventually, it came down to her and the monster, fighting on the peninsula to the death. It was there that both killed each other, the Bearenstein sacrificing himself to the witch's hand to do what must be done, only this time, with righteousness. He mauled her as she stabbed him in the back with his sword, a trophy she had taken from the once-violent knight. It was the king's sword that the king had given him as a reward for the many fights he had won before. In her last moments, the malevolent witch realized that she was wrong about him, about the beast of a man that was now a man forever a beast, dying in this cursed form for the sake of the greater good. To her, this was a greater deed than living as a man again. In the end, she died unchanged in heart but changed in mind, and the Bearenstein saved the kingdom, crawling over to the overlook where we see her gazing upon the ocean, now more of a man than a monster, though many would not see it that way. That is, of course, the image displayed here: the *Legend of Bearenstein*."

Michelangelo nodded. "A bit dramatic, don't you think?"

"Maybe, though, the most important morals are. That's what makes them ring loud and true."

"And what's the moral of this one?"

"Even the most beastly men can have hearts of gold. However, I feel that it raises a far more important question: are we monsters with the hearts of men, or are we men with the hearts of monsters?"

Michelangelo pondered the thought as he looked at the piece. The question Bozco raised was interesting to him, though he felt it was phrased unfairly. One-sided, even.

"That sounds like a trick question to me, Mr. Landon."

"How so?"

"Because there's no answer to it. Not for something as complex as this. I think you're dead wrong. To me, this is a story of redemption—that no man is beyond saving, especially the ones willing to fight for what's right." He looked at Bozco. "That's knighthood, is it not? Isn't that what the king wants?"

Bozco smiled. "Precisely, Mr. Hart."

Michelangelo smiled, realizing he had been slightly tricked. "Ah, you're quite the clever man, Mr. Landon. Got me thinking."

"That is one of the many perks of this medium. It is, at the least, a vessel of thought."

Michelangelo looked back at the painting. "There is much truth to this, you know. This victory the Bearenstein attained. There isn't much victory on the battlefield without loss."

"As it goes, soldier. As it goes." He looked at the painting too. "Sometimes, you gain more in loss than you do in victory."

"Yeah. Most times, it isn't even about living: It's the sacrifice so others can fight on after us."

"And is that what you aim to do, major general? Sacrifice yourself in all of this so others can fight on after you?"

They looked at each other. "If that's what it takes," Michelangelo replied.

Bozco nodded, a slight frown forming. "I fear it will always take this for a man in your position. Nonetheless, I hope you get them all, Mr. Hart. You may not be a perfect man, but you are their perfect monster."

Michelangelo nodded once. He appreciated Bozco's understanding of his situation and his stance on the matter. This didn't make him feel better about what he had to do, but he heard more than anything. Bozco picked up his rag and continued to clean the drinking glass gently. Michelangelo looked down and noticed the bottle of brandy that was placed before him. He picked up the bottle in a slow manner, causing the liquid to slosh and slide around inside the glass. "Thank you for the conversation, and brandy, Mr. Landon. Apologies for my initial threatening manner. I'm not yet trained in any other way."

"I understand your reasoning and sympathize, Mr. Hart. No need to explain."

Michelangelo nodded, raised the bottle, and tipped it toward him, then turned around. "Be seeing you, Bozco," he said. "Likewise," Bozco replied.

Michelangelo exited the Hotel Emilda. The outside air was frigid, and the snow fell heavily. His body tensed from the instant bitter chill. He popped off the cork of the brandy, raised it to his lips, and took a warming swig of the beverage, attempting to numb himself from the inside out. The alcohol burned down his throat, though slightly less this time compared to the previous drinks. The liquid slid down into his stomach and slowly began to dull his senses. He dropped the bottle and looked around at the small town, searching for William and Leonardo. It was then that he saw the hunter walking among the bodies and examining each with the young man he had seemed to hire before joining Michelangelo on this feat. The soldier sighed, shook his head, then pocketed the bottle in his upper coat pocket as he made for him. He walked into the center of the now snow-covered street. It appeared that overnight, the snow had hastened into a constant, thicker fall, the densest of all the snow previously. The soldier looked past the buildings of Little York and into the distant horizon, noticing the wall of white that encased the town, consuming the forest that surrounded it, and mentally prepared himself for the coming chill.

He let out a sharp and quick whistle into the air, looking to his left. Bleu clopped toward him, her hooves flicking up the snow on the street as her legs powerfully trotted toward him. He turned to her as she clopped beside him, chuffing and blowing air through her nose excitedly. "I see you found somewhere to stay," he comforted. She usually did, although this time it appeared that she had been exploring a bit, as Michelangelo saw the light spots of snow. He put on his black gloves, then reached up to her and began wiping the powdered snow from her back, throwing clumps of the frost onto the street, where they plopped gently into the surrounding white.

She let out an annoyed, yet assuring burst of air through her nose, as white clouds shot from her nostrils. Michelangelo smiled as he looked over the young mare and thought of the many miles they had traveled together. She was a strong, loyal, and smart horse. Michelangelo was thankful for that, grateful that of all the horses to be given on this journey, he was given her: a force most formidable and unwavering.

As Michelangelo continued to wipe snow off her, his hand smacked against an unfamiliar new addition to her saddle: armor that he had recently acquired and placed upon her the night before. He lifted the plated leather off her and examined its square and rounded corners. He wiped the snow from its top and turned it around, studying it in all its wet state. He was discerning how a person his size could wear such a piece, or how anyone wore it at all.

The front of the armor was a metal plate covered in light brown leather, while the back was composed of many sewn-together leather pieces that interlocked closely, much like the strings within a shirt. Michelangelo examined the shoulder straps of the armor, which were connected to the thick leather and attached just above the leather-bound breastplate. He noticed that each strap was unbuckled at the ends, and also noticed that at the bottom of the armor, there were belts that buckled just below one's ribs, which made for a strange strapping maneuver. Michelangelo removed his jacket, one arm at a time, switching the hold of the armor between his right hand and the left, until he eventually tossed his coat over Bleu's saddle in an uncaring manner. He slid his head between the straps at the top, then rested the armor heavily on his shoulders. He shook and adjusted the piece to cover his upper chest over his button-up. He looked to his right side and grabbed the leather strap with a buckle just below his ribs, pulling it towards the leather back armor that held tightly to his back.

The leather had straps on the bottom, which he grabbed and slid through the buckle to secure them in place and hold the armor tightly against him. It fit comfortably, though it was heavy. It was an armor that the soldier found to his liking, and as he looked at the chest plate and noticed the bullet hole in the leather, he poked it with his index finger. It was right where his right lung was. He smirked as he admired the accuracy of the shot, then dropped his smile as he remembered that it unfortunately did not make its target. He determined that after he obtained the necessary information, he would not make the same mistake again.

He shook his upper body as he adjusted the leather straps that were tightly wound behind his spine. Though the tiny pieces of leather were bound together in small strips, their intertwining was not exactly the most comfortable feeling. The leather back functioned as a support for the heavy leather armor on the front, counteracting the weight and making for agile and dynamic movement.

"Could use a back slab of metal to counteract the weight further," Michelangelo critiqued as he looked at Bleu. "What do you think?"

He put his arms out to the side as Bleu stared for a moment, then shook her head as she blew air out of her lips. He dropped his arms, disappointedly. "Ah, what do you know?"

He leaned over and grabbed his coat, then pulled his arms through each sleeve. He buttoned the buttons over his armor, shielding himself from the cold while also ensuring no one knew of his new plating. He climbed atop Bleu and sat firmly in the center of her back. He grabbed the reins as he looked toward William, who now had summoned Betsy while he stood alongside his large bounty hunter's wagon that was parked out front of Aland's Theatre.

William's wagon was a large, black, and metallic pull, tall enough to stack four bodies high and wide enough to fit five. The wagon could fit twenty bodies on a good day, if one were ever so inclined to do so. Though under normal circumstances, this amount of storage would not be necessary. The wheels of the wagon were large, black, and made of a blackened wood that was worn by the miles of travel they had seen. The back doors were large metal doors that swung out towards the opener, allowing for one to be tossed into and moved from place to place with relative ease. The entire back of the wagon was made of the same metallic material and consisted of only walls with no windows to peer out and see.

Michelangelo clicked his tongue, guiding Bleu toward William, as the hunter stood beside Betsy with his hands placed annoyedly on his hips. Michelangelo noticed that William's hat was once again upon his head, keeping that character—the Brother of Grim—present and illusory. He looked over the dead bodies, frustrated.

"Any winners?" Michelangelo asked condescendingly.

"Not a one. 'Course, I wouldn't know for sure given you blew one's head clean off his body." William complained.

"Oh, you don't need to worry about him. He wasn't worth a dime. You can trust that."

"Yeah... none of these boys are, if I'm honest. They're all nobodies. Random freaks primed for the fight."

"Makes you wonder where they keep coming from."

William shook his head, sighed, then looked up at Betsy and climbed atop her with a grunt and a shaky pull. "A many a fool a cultist is," he concluded. He looked at Michelangelo. "So. What's the plan, soldier? I assume you have one."

"More like a location. 'You ever hear of the Hillberry Settlement?"

"Yeah. It's about a day's ride out of town. 'Matter of fact, it's a day's ride to and from there from any of the nearest civilizations."

"And your point is?"

"My *point* is that it would be unwise to travel to such a distant place with the weather as troubling as it is." He looked around. "White, cold, and near impossible to see much further than thirty feet." He looked back at Michelangelo. "Do you know what that means?"

"Yes, I know what it means."

"So then you know we need to stay until it passes."

"What, you afraid of a little ol' blizzard, Bill?" Michelangelo patronized.

"At my age, yes. Hardly any a-creature can survive a storm like that."

"Which means that Icarus and his men won't be doing much surviving or moving either, hence the reason we need to move now."

"And get killed."

"That's more of a personal issue for you, my friend. Leo and I will be fine."

William's blood boiled a bit as his breathing intensified. "You know, your blatant disregard for human life is somewhat irking to me."

Michelangelo rolled his eyes. "Oh, give me a break."

"No, no, I'm not talking about these men out here. I'm talking about the ones up there." He pointed to the rooftop of the General Store. Michelangelo looked over, his eyes widening, shocked by William's abrasiveness. "Uh-huh," William continued. "Were there deaths a personal issue for them, too? Do you think Leo would agree that their decisions were *personal?*"

Leonardo clopped up behind Michelangelo, noting the two men staring each other down in a tense, frozen silence. William looked over to Leonardo, then slowly dropped his finger, pointing. The preacher pulled his horse to a halt about five feet away from the two, looking between them a few times, waiting for one to speak. Michelangelo noted Leonardo's presence and proceeded to choose his following words very carefully, hoping that William would decide to do the same.

"We all got free will, Bill. You *chose* to be here. If you don't like it, you're free to leave. No one's stopping you. I don't know why we need to keep having this conversation," Michelangelo stated in a grittily angry tone.

"We will keep having this conversation until you hear what I'm saying: I am worried about you, Mike, about *me*. This ain't about the dead, it's about why they have died and why you are destined to do the same," William rebutted.

"Yeah? What else is new?"

"See! You don't listen! It's like talking to a wall. Your selfishness and desire for retribution put those around you in danger. Me, you, Leo. Think about it!"

Michelangelo laughed angrily. "You are such a damn coward."

"A coward? Really?"

"Yes! Don't try to make this about the kid, or you, for that matter. You think I give a rat's about *you*? After the blatant lies and constant manipulation?"

William smiled angrily. "Oh, okay. I see. So that's how it's gonna be, huh? After all this? You have one conversation with the common hotel whore, and suddenly all that we've been through means nothing?"

"That 'common hotel whore' has been more honest with me than you."

"How do you know?"

Michelangelo smiled, baffled. "How long are you going to keep this up?"

"As long as I have to save your life and maybe even mine! I mean, come on, think of the hypocrisy!"

"Hypocrisy?"

"Yes!"

"Really?"

"Mike, in case you forgot, she's an outlaw, hardly any different than the ones you've been killing."

"That's a bit of a straw man, don't you think?"

"For heaven's sake, son, do you know who she is?"

"Rosaline Dan Fillio: last remaining survivor of the Brothers of Boudiclare, and currently most hunted of all remaining outlaws in the Arizona Territory. Yes, I'm well aware of who she is."

"Then *why* are you listening to a lying, stealing, murdering, backstabbing individual that would do *anything* to preserve the life of her and her son?"

"Because I've seen the same kindness in her that Thomas has. Believe me, for a moment I considered it, but that kind of kindness can't be faked, and I know you saw it too because you let her live."

"I didn't let her live because she was 'kind,' Michael. I did it because she was with child. I may be a killer, but I will not kill a mother and her unborn, or any mother with a child, for that matter."

"But you'll happily kill your nephew and two kids as long as it pays well."

"I made a mistake! I'm here to fix it, or at least try! I've followed you through the

coldest of hells and the bloodiest of baths just to *ensure* that you don't end up as one of the many casualties this war has attained! I've been shot, nearly killed, and yet, here I remain: standing right beside you! Is that not enough to prove to you that I am here to *help?* Is that not enough to earn me, even the slightest inkling of mercy?"

"Not when I don't know if every other word out of your two-sided mouth is a lie. I don't know if you're here to help me or not because I can't trust you. I don't know if I'm riding beside 'good ol' Uncle Bill,' or the Brother of Grim that took his place. The same man who rides beside me and says he's here to help me is the very same man who has a wagon for corpses following him around, like some vulture following a dead man, waiting to pick his bones clean! How am I supposed to know that once the bounty is placed on my head, *you won't be there to collect it yourself?*" The soldier stopped, breathing heavily. "I will not grant mercy to someone I cannot trust. I can't afford it."

William took a minute, weighing honesty and deception. "You're my nephew, Mike. Isn't that enough? I mean, you've given far more to far less, all for the sake of kindness. What do I have to do to receive the same treatment that Rosa received, other than be kind? I feel as though I've *been* kind, yet you believe it's deceptive, so what do I have to do to convince you that I can change?" He stopped for a moment. "I know that's what it was. The reason you spared Rosa, I mean. Yes, she was kind, but it was the fact that her reputation, being who she was, could change. Could be a mother. See, now, you believe that people can change—you've seen it, and that goes against everything that you currently believe in. That's why she's alive. You believe there's good in even the most wicked of people, because you see the good that Thomas saw, the good that *Thomas* became. I know that doesn't apply to everyone, especially some of these men dead out here, but it is possible... and you know that. You saw it in Rosa, yet you can't reconcile it."

Michelangelo was silent. Whether he wanted to admit it or not, he knew William was right. William sighed.

"Why can't I be one of those few, Mike?"

Michelangelo blew a sad breath through his nose. "I shouldn't have to give that mercy to you, Bill. I shouldn't be here, having to hope that Miss Dan Fillio is the one telling lies because I can't make sense of anything else. I should know, beyond a shadow of a doubt, that it's *you* telling the truth. I should be able to trust you with every fiber of my being, but how can I? After everything I've seen, that I've heard, from you and others... how can I?" He shook his head lightly. "If I find out that what has been said is true, that my uncle is one of the most wicked men that I have ever known, that he had far more than a bounty hunter's hand in the murder of his nephew, there will be no mercy."

They stared at each other in silence for a moment.

"I don't want to believe that, Bill, but something inside me already does. I've only refused to believe Rosa because I want to believe you, but how can I when deep down I already know the truth?"

William thought for a moment as the two had once again come to an impasse. In truth, Michelangelo was willing to spare William's life if he would come clean. He almost found the idea of being alone far worse a punishment than living with this truth about his uncle. William, on the other hand, was led to believe he didn't have a choice. Either he could come clean and die, or stay quiet and do the same. Or, there was the option to leave. To abandon Michael and not look back. That said, this was not an option for the hunter for more reasons than one, the primary one being that he could not live with the guilt of his other nephew dying because of his decisions.

William did not give the confession that Michelangelo was baiting him into. He hoped, even planned, never to have to. Maybe, if he could succeed in taking down Caine Kingsley, he and his nephew could have an uneasy trust with one another once the dust settled. As for Michelangelo, he had his rock-solid assumptions, but needed undeniable evidence to take action against William or perhaps spare him.

William shook his head and sighed. "Look, Mike... you can believe me or you can not. I can't make up your mind for you. But regardless, I will stay right here beside you to ensure I have at least one nephew left after all this. I am only suggesting, as your uncle, that you stay indoors during this storm. Pitching you up against a whole army of men, that's one thing I do not doubt you can handle, but pitching you up against a blizzard? I can't be sure."

"My mind's made up, Bill," Michelangelo answered, disappointed.

William nodded gently. "Okay," he agreed.

Leonardo awkwardly looked between the soldier and the hunter as quietly as a mouse, trying to figure out what to say at a time like this. "So," he started, "you guys know where we're going?"

"Forward," Michelangelo replied, still looking at William.

He lightly heeled Bleu to the side, then forward with two clicks from his mouth. She went forward with a slow and steady gait, the vast tree line of pines beginning to spread widely before them, sprawling on for miles in every direction, with only one trail that led in and out. The trail was covered in snow, just like the pines and their forest, making the path nearly non-existent. William heeled Betsy forward as well to match Michelangelo's speed. Leonardo followed behind.

"So, are we alright?" William asked. "You tell me," Michelangelo replied. William stopped for a moment. "You say you'll kill me if you find out that Caine and I were working together. I get that. So, I'm only going to remind you of this once: there are many mistakes a man can make in this life. Don't make threatening me one of them."

Michelangelo smiled slightly out of the corner of his mouth as he squinted his eyes, like a rifleman might when focusing the scope of his rifle. "Looks like we have ourselves an understanding." He leaned his head back to Leonardo's direction. "You keeping up, kid?" Leonardo sped his horse up with a couple of quick kicks, enabling him to ride up beside the soldier and the hunter, matching their strut as they entered the woods.

"Yes. Doing fine, all things considered." He chuckled. "You know, this is going to sound ridiculous, but of all the people I could be going forward with, I did not expect it to be you, Major General St. Hart." He looked over to William. "And The Brother of Grim." He looked at Michelangelo again. "But I'm glad it's you. There are no two better legends equipped to handle this situation."

William's ears perked up as he had heard a name that he had not been called in a long while. "Legends, huh?" He asked.

"Oh, yeah. I've heard dozens of stories about the two of you. People talk, you know, especially in the town. Again, I thought it was just a legend but... here you are, in the flesh."

"The flesh indeed," William agreed. "So, what stories have they been telling?" Michelangelo rolled his eyes.

"Well," Leonardo continued, "as far as most people around here are concerned, you are the greatest bounty hunter of the West. From what I hear, you have single-handedly taken down some of the most feared and revered gangs that have walked the Arizona Territory."

"I wager history will tell it differently, but I'm glad at least one person will know the truth." He turned his head slightly to the side, amused. "I gotta say, it's a bit odd seeing such enthusiasm for a man of my profession from a believing boy such as yourself."

"Well, just because I do not condone the killing doesn't mean the stories are any less legendary."

Michelangelo looked over to Leonardo. "Careful of the legends you believe in, kid." He looked up at William. "Not all of them are worth believing in." He looked forward again, then opened his now far colder brandy, lifting the bottle to his lips, tilting his head back, and enjoying the substance as he closed his eyes. Leonardo turned and looked at William, who was looking worriedly at the soldier. As Michelangelo stopped his drinking, William looked down at Leo. "Look, we've got a long ride. Why don't I tell you the story of how I got my name?"

"The Brother of Grim!?" Leonardo asked excitedly.

"The very same."

Snowflakes fell quickly as the winter's blizzard continued to set, while the snow-covered pines consumed the three that made their way into the woods. Michelangelo dreaded having to go forward with the hunter who rode beside him. He wondered what his mission had become and what the state of his ultimate objective would be when all was said and done. Leonardo was certainly not a part of his original plan, and in all honesty, neither was William. Now, he had a job of babysitting and watching his back, potentially having to do what he did not know he could. On top of all of this, he now carried on the responsibility of saving the Brothers' Six, if there were any to be saved, all while attempting to capture Icarus so he could put an end to the sick oppression that plagued this state.

He looked up at the haze of white that circled them, only gaining more thickness as the coming blizzard settled in. He knew that if they did not hurry, it was possible that the blizzard could kill them, ripping the very flesh from their bones if they got caught within.

The stage was set, and the soldier, the hunter, the preacher, and the bastard were all readying for the coming confrontation, which would be known as "The Hellfire at Hillberry," the battle that turned men into monsters and monsters into men.

It would have to be so, for the men who waited for them prided themselves on being the slayers of souls, the spreaders of fear—the Four Horsemen, as their survivors proclaimed, some even thinking it was the very same spoken of in the holy text they persecuted. They were a robust force of nature that made even the boldest men shake in the presence of their trepidation. Worst of all, in all the things they did, they now only had one goal: to capture and break Leonardo.

CHAPTER 9

For Whether Thine Heart Be of Lamb or of Lion

 day's travel had come and gone, and it was long and tiring. The blizzard's wind had beaten upon the traveling men as its snow fell with a fast and steady thrust, the wind continuously picking up its force. Night had fallen over the land, and the trees that surrounded the three were tall and thick, only to be compared to fortress walls that Man could only dream of making. They were impenetrable, formidable, and ultimately unbreakable, though thankfully, they were easy to sneak around. The night provided excellent cover to those who rode between the trees, and the blizzard covered any light the moon might shed. The pines were forty feet high, and their branches were broad, which made it easy for snow to collect rapidly.

The soldier, the hunter, and the preacher all rode their horses cautiously, each one's hooves crunching through the snow that bunched up around their ankles. Michelangelo held his lantern in his left hand, his double-barrel shotgun in his right. His lantern lit the front of his face and body, providing light to the snow-covered trail. He gripped the weapon by the barrel, holding it pointed to the sky, loaded with no finger on the trigger, ready to be fired at any who might come from the darkness. William and Leonardo followed in the same accord, attaching their lanterns to the pommels of their mounts and looking through the forest with equal vigilance. Leonardo's light shone dimly on his stolen steed, revealing the pale complexion of this olden horse. What appeared to be white fur once was now made grimier by the horse's years of age, with the mane and tail following in the exact nature. His horse was a skinny and bony creature that seemed to have been ill-cared for in its life. However, with Leonardo, it was ensured that the horse would be treated with the dignity and respect it deserved, for as long as he had it.

Truthfully, the preacher had not stopped thinking about the well-being of his brethren and whether they were alive or dead. He wanted to believe that they were alive, but deep down, he could not be sure. All he knew with certainty was that regardless of how his brothers were found, the soldier would see them and avenge them, regardless.

He looked over at Michelangelo, who continued to gaze out into the forest, lifting his lantern slightly higher as he peered deeper into the woods. Leonardo noted the redness in Michelangelo's cheeks that had been given to him by the winter's wind. He looked over the stitches that sealed his nose and eyebrow shut, noticing that each one had bled over slightly, protruding forward into frozen and frosted icicles. He went on from that and noted the bruises that were spotted around his face, now seeming to have faded slightly. He considered the look that the soldier had and found that it matched what he had been told before about the vengeful soldier on his quest for retribution. Up to this point, he was more of a ghost story than anything. Still, now, seeing the beast up close—in reality—he began to finally consider the finer details, the less glamorous aspects of Michelangelo's doings. In the stories, the soldier was a man likened unto a knight, a glamorous fantasy of a man who defended the defenseless. No, after what Leonardo had seen the night before, in all its bloody brutality, it was more than that. He was a killer who murdered the unjust, which was not as incredible as it had been painted or as he had imagined. He pondered the concept of taking a man's life and how it was such an immoral act. He wondered how someone could do it so easily and viciously, wondered how many lives the soldier had taken so far. He couldn't comprehend it, and in that moment, he felt the fear that followed him. He looked away and back out at the pines. Though he did not know how many men Michelangelo had killed, others did, and if they were to stack the bodies of those Michelangelo had killed, they would be stacked as high as the surrounding pines, six times over.

Leonardo tried to understand how one might conclude taking another man's life; he tried to know if it was best to put wicked men in the grave or to save their souls. He wondered why such actions had been thoroughly prohibited by the Bible he knew so thoroughly. These thoughts ran plentifully in Leonardo's mind, especially given the recent run-in he had with Icarus. Leonardo began to weigh the reality that he may be forced to give Icarus a second chance, to do the right thing and offer him redemption, as God's word instructed him to do—to impart new life. To continually believe that, regardless of how lost one is, they still deserve a second chance. As the only believer in the mix, potentially one of the last alive in Northern Arizona, he knew it was his job to be the one to do it, if the moment came.

But then he thought further: *If second chances made way for greater injustices, like the continuation of wickedness through wicked men, then how was the act of 'soul saving' the believer's victory?*

Wickedness seemed to flourish constantly, regardless of what believers had done in the past and the present. Then there was Michelangelo's way, bringing an end to these wicked sects, men, and monsters that struck fear into the hearts of their lesser. Although Michelangelo's methods were morally questionable, even biblically prohibited for the believer, they did produce conclusive results. *These conclusive results,* Leonardo thought, *could save my brothers.*

In the end, he knew one thing: whether Icarus' men should be killed or not, the soldier was going to do it regardless, and he wasn't entirely opposed to it. The more he thought about it, the more the thought enticed him.

"How much further?" Leonardo asked loudly, the wind and snow blowing loudly.

"Shouldn't be too far, now," Michelangelo replied loudly in return.

"How do you know about this place?"

"I knew a platoon of men who scouted this place out for a fortress, years ago. It was more work than it was worth to tear it all down, so we never followed through." He smiled. "It appears that, naturally, an unoccupied place would have a rat infestation."

"Right... so, what's our plan?"

"There is no 'our plan.' Once we get closer to whatever this place might be, Bill and I will take care of it. You'll hold back in the shadows."

"And what if they come for me?"

Michelangelo looked over at Leonardo with a look of brutal coldness. "They won't."

Leonardo gulped and looked over to William, who tilted his head to the side and nodded. He looked back at Michelangelo. "Alright, well, if I'm going to be forced to hold back, should I not at least have a weapon for self-defense?" Michelangelo looked over to Leonardo and raised one eyebrow in interest. "You? Defending yourself? Isn't that somewhat ironic?"

"I may be a believer, but I am no fool. Obviously, with you around, I doubt I'll have to do anything, but I am only asking just in case."

"Just in case, huh?" Michelangelo reached backward into his horse bag to pull out a spare hunter's knife. The metal of the knife was thick, made of stainless steel, with a black wooden handle. The blade was slightly dulled from its previous use and the lack of Michelangelo's sharpening. The pouch it was in was brown in color and made of thick leather, tied together with hardened leather string around the edges. The back of the knife pouch had a belt loop that was stretched and worn from its previous uses. "You understand what it means if I give this to you?" He said, holding out the blade, handle first. Leonardo looked at the blade handle, then back up at Michelangelo. "You know," the soldier continued, "that you might have to kill a man. Stab him to death."

"Yes... I understand. Still... we are to avoid violence to the *best of our ability*. That does not mean that we avoid violence entirely. Besides, unless you think that you can take down every single one of Icarus's men, in the dead of night, in the middle of a blizzard, then by all means, do not give me a way to defend myself."

Michelangelo looked over to William curiously. William looked back. "Kid's got a point, Mike." The soldier looked back. "You got a belt?"

"Of course I have a belt."

"Put this on it."

He tossed the knife to Leonardo, who caught the pointed blade and looked at it in his hands, pulling it from its tiny sheath and examining the glint of the blade in the lamp's light.

"You think this will be enough?" Leonardo asked.

"I think it's about all you can handle," Michelangelo replied.

He looked up, offended. "I can handle more."

"Sorry, I'm just confused. Here, aren't you all about 'thou shalt not kill' or something like that?"

"Again, I have no intention of killing someone."

"Intention or not, kid, the fact remains: killing a man is still killing a man. Self-defense or not."

"I can seek repentance if it comes down to it."

"Repentance? You want repentance? Read your Bible. Don't go looking for it with a gun and then plan on your religion to be your insurance policy."

"Listen, I know the Bible. All I do is read it. Every day, scripture after scripture relentlessly plays in my head. Don't tell me what I do and don't know about my faith."

"What do you mean by 'plays in your head?' Like a moving picture?"

"It means I have the entire Bible memorized. I can find it like looking through a picture book or something similar to that."

"Huh."

"Yes, so in case you were ever unsure, I do know the Bible, and I'm more than fine with my choice on this matter."

Michelangelo sighed. "Okay."

The soldier knew it was an almost impossible task to protect Leonardo amid the chaos. Self-defense, as much as it could scar him, was better than losing him entirely. After all, the mission was to keep him safe, and in this instance, that wasn't entirely possible. That understood, it wasn't the idea of Leonardo killing a man that made Michelangelo hesitant; it was how comfortable he seemed to be with it as a man who was supposed to be far removed from the act. So, he agreed to a happy medium, one that could both work without compromising the young preacher. To Michelangelo, saving him meant more than just keeping him alive; it meant preserving his art. He had to keep the light inside alive as well.

He scooted forward on his saddle and reached into the back top of his pants, pulling out Icarus's revolver. He turned to Leonardo and tossed it to him with a gentle chunk. The preacher caught the revolver with an awkward clamor, his hands fumbling to hold the heavy piece. He looked over the revolver, examining its grime and poor state, and more than anything, its apparent lack of bullets. Leonardo looked to Michelangelo, then back at the revolver, making a fluent motion to open the cylinder. To Leonardo's irked confirmation, there were no bullets loaded within the piece, rendering the revolver nearly useless.

"What good is a gun with no bullets?" Leonardo asked.

"It can make a good hammer," Michelangelo joked.

Leonardo was not amused. "You know that's not what I meant."

"Yes, I do. I'm no fool, but I would be a liar if I said that you weren't acting as one." He looked forward on the path ahead. "You have a gift, Leo. It's what's made you somewhat of a celebrity. After what happened yesterday, I have no doubt your name will only go further. The question is, for better or for worse?" He looked at Leonardo.

"I don't know," he replied.

"Exactly." He looked ahead. "The truth is, it's entirely up to you, but my goal is to do my best to make sure that I do not put you in harm's way. That revolver in your hands is an invitation to trouble. Trust me. However, if worst comes to worst, you can aim the revolver at whoever might get the jump on you. Then once they're stuttered, run in our direction. It'll give you just enough time to get our attention so we, the killers, can do what we do." He looked over. "And like I said, it does make a good hammer."

"Yeah, like the grip is going to do anything."

"You'd be surprised," William and Michelangelo said at the same time.

They looked at each other, then forward again. Leonardo placed the revolver between his back and the top of his pants. "So what is it? You don't trust me?" He asked.

Michelangelo looked back at Leonardo. "When you look at me, what is it you see?"

"A soldier?"

"Right. Now look over to the man on the other side of you. What is he?"

"A hunter."

"Correct again. Remember those stories you were telling us about earlier?"

"Yes."

"They're romance. They're not the full story, as I'm sure you know now. In reality, men like us are just boiled down to killers. Not a knight in shining armor or a hero: a killer. We're both professionals at it, good, even, but we are not heroes. What we do is unnatural and unhealthy. It hurts people, harms people. We're not myths or legends, we're just cold-blooded killers. We are takers of lives and removers of men, and we do such things with the same relative ease that you might preach a sermon." He looked at Leonardo. "Which is a good thing."

Leonardo listened intently and seriously to what Michelangelo was saying. He gained a new sense of understanding, as well as a more profound fear. "I understand what you're saying." He paused. "You're both fighters. I see that, I want that. I want to be that. Maybe not a killer, but a defender. Of freedom, of faith. I want to put my life on the line for those who are in need."

"And who's that?"

Leonardo hesitated. "My brothers." Michelangelo looked over and nodded. "I get it, but you don't need violence to do that. Do it in the way you've been trained and let us do it in ours."

"But I feel as though you oversimplify yours."

"How so?"

"You say you're not heroes defending the faith or the people, yet what you do defends them and their freedoms. Even now, you're escorting me to save my brothers."

"Everything that's happened for your people is nothing more than a byproduct of my main goal, Leo, including you and especially your brothers. Don't get this idea in your head that I'm here to defend your people or defend your freedom and faith. I am not here to fight your war, I'm only passing through it."

"I just don't believe that."

"Well, believe it. Icarus has information I need. That's why we're here. You and your brothers are a distraction, if anything."

"No, you're lying to yourself. I know there's more to you, Saint Hart, you just refuse to accept it."

"Like you refuse to accept my advice on killing."

Leonardo smirked and shook his head. "My point is your actions speak louder than your very grumpy words. You didn't have to do any of this; you chose to. You could have killed William earlier, from what I gathered, yet here he is still alive."

"Yes," William interrupted. "Thank you for that pleasant reminder."

"You made a decision, and whether you agree or not, you are more than a killer. You are a soldier; William is a hunter. You're both like knights, and though you may not have the cleanest armor, you help people, my people."

Michelangelo's guilt ate at him a bit. William noticed.

"Our fates," Leonardo continued, "have been swayed by what you did. We owe you our lives."

"Kid," Michelangelo sighed, "you just don't know what the hell you're talking about."

He tilted his head slightly back, took a deep breath in, and considered the thought. Although the perspective was interesting, it was not one Michelangelo believed in, and due to recent events, he felt it was an ignorant and untrue notion. He looked forward again.

"But it is an interesting point," he conceded. "That said, you should not use your perception of me to justify your actions that, in my best opinion, would not be good for you. Whether or not I am a soldier or a killer makes no difference in comparison to the fact that you are a preacher. Maybe in your eyes, I am doing a good deed so that this war might not leave all things torn in its wake, but that is my deed to be done alone. It requires more death than any man should ever have to endure. This act of killing is a work reserved for men like myself who have faced the decision to take a man's life before, and have chosen to go down that path." He looked at Leonardo. "You can be saved from that fate. The one from which there's no coming back. You believe me on that." He looked forward. "There is no life as it were, or return to what was. You're just changed forever. Broken in a way. Divided from your humanity, as if a part of you has died. And, sure, maybe over time you make your peace, but you can never undo what has been done. Never take back the bullet." He looked at the preacher again. "You, Leo, you are not a man who should be cursed with such actions, but are a man made for something far more special; something worth preserving. You've got something that nobody else in this nation has, and whether I believe in it or not, it inspires people around you. I can see that. I'm not blind to it. You give people something to believe in; you give them hope. People need a whole lot of that right now... people need something to believe in. That is something I could never give, nor even attempt to. But you? You can." He looked forward, pain in his eyes. "Heed my warning, preacher: do not kill another man. There is a precarious light that flickers within you, much like a candle in the breeze. Do not let blood douse your flame; do not do work meant for men like us."

Leonardo gulped at the point and the warning that came along with it. Though thoughts of violence had crossed Leonardo's mind, they had not crossed in the capacity Michelangelo was referring to. Thus, there was still hope, still light, inside this dark world, one that seemed as bleak as the blizzard raging around them.

"That said, I guess it's pretty safe to say you do care at least a little bit?"

Michelangelo turned with an annoyed smile. "Yes. I guess I do."

"Well, thank you. I appreciate it."

Michelangelo nodded. "I failed to protect someone innocent once. He wasn't much younger than you at the time. I won't be making that mistake again."

William looked over at him and understood what he was saying, sympathizing with the guilt and grief that haunted them both in their ever-waking moments. The only difference was that William's ran much deeper, encouraging him to make a better tomorrow rather than try to fix the past. He understood, now, why Leonardo, to Michelangelo, was so important: it reminded him of Thomas, and if he could save the preacher, he could save his younger brother. Thus, William determined that saving Leonardo might be the solution to saving Michelangelo, and that this act could change the terrible fates that awaited them. He could stop Michelangelo's vengeance that would inevitably make him exactly like the hunter. It was from that point forward that William determined that he,

THE PRICE OF RETRIBUTION

too, would join the soldier in his cause to save the preacher. *This might be my redemption,* he thought. *Innocence for innocence.*

This was William's honorable and worthy fight. It gave him hope, and he smiled at the thought that this fight was one he and Michelangelo could fight together. So, he strategized. *To save Leonardo, I gotta save the Brothers' Six. How exactly do I do that? Where are we even going to be fighting—*

"Whoa, easy," Michelangelo commanded Bleu in a low and firm tone, putting his right arm out to the side, halting Leonardo. The others followed in his lead, the three stopping and looking forward in between the pines, noting the evidence of life that walked in the distance before them.

Between the interwoven pine trees, light shone from within a building, which flickered in the not-too-far distance. In front of the building, multiple lanterns flickered and rotated in the hands of the guards, who watched vigilantly in the blizzard-ridden night. They walked the path leading up to their shelter, a tightly kept base that let its light dance across the snow-covered ground, outlining the silhouettes of the men who sank in it to their shins.

"Lanterns out," Michelangelo ordered, the winds howling.

The soldier, hunter, and preacher all lifted their lanterns and pulled up the glass that covered their lantern's flame, letting the winter's wind blow out the light. Michelangelo placed his doused lantern upon the pommel of his saddle, then held his double-barrel shotgun with both hands now, inching Bleu forward into the darkness with a slight hit of his heels against her sides. The three made their way to a closer viewpoint, while the soldier analyzed the battlefield before them and determined the best way to attack. William performed the same calculations he had done on many battlefields during the Civil War, but now he was out of his element amid the storm, and as nervous as he was frozen because of it.

The soldier halted the three fifty feet away from the nearest patroller. "A penny for your thoughts and a dime for your acts," William quipped.

"Darkness is on our side. Not to mention the forest. I figure we use them both to our advantage," Michelangelo shared.

"You want to go the silent route? That's uncharacteristic of you."

"Not as much as you might think. Using these elements can send them into a panic if we scare them well enough. Not to mention, we need Icarus alive, and the best way to ensure that happens is by keeping the situation under control, which tends not to be the case with guns blazing. The fewer guns we have to fight head-on, the better."

"When are we saving my brothers?" Leonardo interjected.

Michelangelo looked over to Leonardo momentarily, then grabbed Bleu's saddle pommel as he stepped off into the white ground. The snow swallowed his boots to the middle of his shins, crunching and smooshing under his weight. William did the same and landed in the same manner, then waded over to the front of Leonardo's horse with Michelangelo. "Kid," the soldier started, "I'm going to be straight with you: there's a good chance your brothers won't survive this. It's important you make peace with this." Leonardo's eyebrows dipped in concern as his mouth tightened at the thought of his brothers being dead. Michelangelo sighed. "Look, if they're alive, I will do everything I can to see that it stays that way," Michelangelo reassured.

"Okay," Leonardo accepted.

With a quick and consenting nod, the soldier turned to the hunter. "You take the ones on the left, I take the ones on the right?" He offered. "Sure," the hunter accepted. "Where are we meeting?"

"By the building. If all goes well, we should be able to take out the horsemen quietly, then make our way in to get Icarus."

"Makes sense to me."

The two crossed in front of one another and slipped away into the dead of night while Leonardo looked between the two, sitting upon his horse. Michelangelo stopped for a moment, then slowly turned around. "And kid," he started. "No matter what happens, stay put." Leonardo clenched his jaw and nodded. The soldier nodded back and continued.

Leonardo was now alone, the wind swiping bitterly against his cheeks, his hands freezing to a stinging numbness. The snow seemed to fall larger and faster, though the wind had not increased its speed, and to Leonardo's understanding, he had determined that the blizzard was nearly here. He looked over to Betsy and noted a strange object he had not seen before. It was the blackened repeater that Michelangelo had used in Little York, now attached to the side of William's steed. He stared at the repeater for a moment, gazing upon its black scope and metal, wondering how many lives it had taken and how many more it soon might. Leonardo shook his head and broke his gaze, then looked to Bleu, noting the saddlebags that lay across her rump. He reached over calmly and lifted the frozen leather lid. He remembered that Michelangelo had a pair of binoculars and searched for them with his numbed hands, fumbling and stinging as he did his best to find them. He clamored, his face wincing at the pain, until finally he felt the bite of a cold, metal pair, nipping at his fingertips. He gripped the frozen metal and pulled it out, opening it up and lifting it to his eyes. He peered forward through the pines at the fortress before him.

The settlement solidified within a vast, circular, natural opening that was surrounded by hundreds of pines. The pines shielded the settlement from being spotted. It was a decaying structure, with the roof nearly missing, having caved in due to years of weather and neglect. Despite this, the second story still held firm and had not fallen to the bottom. The walls were made of old wood, and the four corners of the building were made with hundreds of stacked rocks cemented together. The first floor appeared to be relatively intact. Even the windows weren't cracked, though the same could not be said for their covers. They clashed violently with the wind, swinging and slamming against the settlement as the gusts of wind blew against them, their nails barely holding on. As the gusts blew, the front door held on almost the same, though far more sturdy. Little bits of snow would get in through the bottom, along with plenty of cold, but that was what made the fire from within so helpful. The interior glowed with a hot burn as a fire raged within the fireplace at the back center of the building. The light flickered with its oranges, yellows, and reds, shaking as it warmed its inhabitants. Leonardo looked up at the front door, noting the porch roof, which was dangerously worn but remained intact. Below it was the porch, featuring a set of stairs that led down to the ground below, covered in a foot of snow like everything else.

The preacher looked at the side of the settlement and saw a barn, more intact than the fortress in front of it. He looked back at the center of the Hillberry Settlement, right at the center of the circular opening filled with snow and surrounding the settlement. He saw the massive rock walls that stood three feet high, remnants of the Civil War. These remnants seemed to sprout out of the snow all over the settlement, providing what Leonardo assumed to be cover in those times. They weren't much to look at, now, and seemed to topple over more by the minute, so Leonardo decided to shift his sights over to the left, noticing a large pile of wood that was stacked in a neat and orderly manner, covered by a large white canvas that flapped wildly in the wind. It was held down by rope and anchors, though the snow atop the tarp seemed to be more secure than the rope and anchors, which didn't do much good to keep the snow off the wood. It was because of this that Leonardo noticed the strange shape the canvas had taken. Although wooden logs could be made out, something different protruded from the side, like a mass or clump, that did not fit with the rest.

Light suddenly fell over the white-surfaced snow as silhouetted figures stepped forward onto the porch, casting their shadows before the lights reached them. Leonardo whipped around and focused on the front door, seeing the three men who had exited the building. They stood upon the porch armed with anger and a revolver; their clothes as dingy as any other civilian's, having not seen society in months. It was then that the preacher realized that these men were the horsemen—the men beside Icarus in Little York. He noted their agitation, each one flustered and lacking the same confidence they had when Icarus was beside them. They were talking to one another, looking around the settlement, unable to see further than a few feet in front of the light coming from the building. The forest around them was pitch-black and dauntingly vast, which was only worsened by the raging snowstorm.

It was then that Leonardo realized that something, or someone, was missing. *Where's Icarus?* He thought. Leonardo continued to look at them as they pointed around frantically, assuming they were talking about the forest that had now been filled with lantern-holding men. *Did they see our lanterns? How do they know we're here? Do they know at all?* He thought. As his mind raced and suspicions rose, he stopped looking through the binoculars, only to realize that the lights had come far closer to him than before. His eyes widened as his body tensed, wondering what the soldier and hunter would do next. There were thirteen of them, all unaware of what watched them from the shadows.

Michelangelo crouched in the snow, pushing through it as quietly as he could, using the pines to cover him further in the darkness. On the left side of the forest, William was using the same tactic, looking over the approaching lanterns and calculating his next move.

Three men approached the soldier unawares, trudging through the snow in a broad search group. They began to spread out about six feet, hoping to come across the sneaking soldier. "Can you believe they sent us out here?" One guard started. "Like we stand a chance against the soldier."

"Hey, don't be talking like that. We're gonna be fine. It was probably nothing," another replied.

"Yeah, the flickering lights over the ridge were just 'nothing.' Look, the fact of the matter is we're expendable. It's just as Icarus says: some are made leaders, and others are made fighters. Not all men are created equal," the last guard added.

One of the men drew near to Michelangelo. He holstered his shotgun over his right shoulder and pulled his hunter's knife from its sheath, holding the handle firmly and pointing the blade down below his palm. He lifted the knife in front of his chest as he prowled closer.

"At this point, I'm to think even the leaders are expendable. The way the soldier has been taking us down, it's hard to believe anybody is safe," the first guard reiterated.

"Yeah... you know, you might be right. Still, we should focus up," the second guard added.

The men were now directly behind Michelangelo's pine. He clenched his jaw, looked down at the snow, the light from their lanterns shining around the pine, moving the tree's shadow as they walked forward.

"That's true. He could be anywhere," the third guard agreed.

Michelangelo whipped around the tree and rushed the third guard. He looked at the scene of commotion as an expression of horror overtook his face. The soldier slammed his left gloved palm upon his mouth and squeezed. The guard let out a muffled scream for only a second before the soldier's blade swiped across his throat. He gurgled under the glove as he gripped his throat, dropping his lantern in the process. The other guards turned around quickly at the commotion. Michelangelo, figuring this, flicked his knife around in his hand and gored the man, repeatedly thrusting the knife into his lower belly, causing him to shake and wiggle. The other guards stepped backward slightly in horror as they watched their friend get brutalized, and in this moment, Michelangelo turned and tossed the third guard's bloody body toward the two, sending it through the snow with a trail of red forming behind it. Michelangelo flicked his hunter's knife in his hand, grabbing the bladed end and then launching the knife through the air directly into the first guard's right shoulder. He screamed in pain and terror as his partner looked, fumbling for his revolver. Michelangelo charged the first, noted that the second had drawn his weapon, then slid on his knee into the first guard, grabbing him by the knife's handle and aiming him toward his partner as a shield. The other pulled his revolver and rapidly fired off six rounds, Michelangelo moving the guard's body around, dodging the bullets, the blood splattering shots onto his face.

The rest of the camp was alerted by the shots, particularly the three horsemen, who now stopped talking and looked to where the shots had been fired. Leonardo flinched and looked to the right, noting that they had stopped and changed course.

"That who I think it is?" Bo asked rhetorically.

"Yup," Roger answered.

The four men in front of the horsemen on Michelangelo's side now made for him as well, following the flashes of light and the screams.

The first guard twitched and slowly fell to his knees as the bullets penetrated his body, relying more on Michelangelo's strength as the other guard's cylinder ran dry. Suddenly, the revolver clicked, the second guard's eyes widening. Michelangelo stood tall, ripping the blade out of the first guard's shoulder, tossing him to the ground to his side. The soldier grimaced as the second guard put up his shaky hands in surrender, his face contorted in a whimper. Rage filled Michelangelo's heart, and with one quick fling, he launched the knife through the air, piercing the second guard's right side, kicking his head back, and dropping him backward to poof into the snow, a horrified expression left frozen on his face. Michelangelo looked over at the four approaching lanterns to his left, and as he did, he heard the faint sound of blood being coughed up from the first guard beside him. He looked over at the guard on the ground, somehow still alive despite having more lead than lungs, then looked back at the guard with the knife in his skull. He casually walked over, grabbed the knife, then put his boot on the lifeless chest and pulled out the blade with a quick ease.

"Come on! Hurry up!" The fourth proceeding guard said, charging in the darkness.

Michelangelo turned to the guard gurgling on the ground and made for him. Seeing this, the guard weakly reached his left hand up, begging as blood spattered forward from his mouth. He tried to speak, but nothing came forward, as the bullets had turned his insides to shredded meat. His clothes continued to dampen with his crimson flow as Michelangelo arrived above him. The first guard looked up as Michelangelo lifted his left boot above the dying man's face, then slammed it down on his right cheek, twisting it with a deep, crunchy snap. The guard went limp. Michelangelo looked over the body, then leaned down and unsheathed the first guard's knife, slowly turning and looking toward the four approaching men as he slowly slipped into the shadows and pines.

William stalked his six unaware targets quietly, picking up the pace since they had been alerted to Michelangelo. "So much for not going in guns blazing," he complained to himself. He was a mere thirty feet away from the left side and knew he had to act fast. He squatted and walked up behind his furthest target in the back, reaching up behind him, covering his mouth, and slitting his throat. The blood poured forth as he flung his arms quietly and manically, gurgling. William ducked into the trees, letting his first target thud to his knees, gripping his neck as blood spurted out, his gurgling just reaching through the winter's wind, alerting the five other men who were before him. They turned at the sound and looked down at him as he reached out, pleading for help.

"It's The Soldier! He's here!" A man said, hysterically.

"How? I thought he was over there?" Another one questioned.

"Is he in two places at once?" the third one asked.

"Oh, *why! Why did he have to come here?"* The fourth one regretted in fear.

Each target drew their weapons and pointed them at and around the one bleeding out on the ground, finally falling face down in the snow, motionless, his blood filling the white. The targets shakily looked around, aiming their revolvers in every direction as they tried to catch a glimpse of the soldier. William twisted around his tree, ensuring his targets could not hear or see him, then rammed the blade into his second target's ribs, covering his mouth so that his scream would not alert the others.

His muffled yell did not.

In that moment, he reached down, stole the knife from his gun belt, and looked up at his third target. He flicked his arm back and tossed the knife forward into the now turning third target's throat, sending him stuttering backward in a painful reaction, gurgling and reaching for the blade. William ripped the knife from his second target's ribs. He rolled forward powerfully, the remaining three targets turning and firing at nothing, only catching glimpses of the dark shadow, the hunter. *"Where are you?!"* His fourth target screamed in fear. The second target reached for his bleeding ribs as he fell to the ground, and the third grabbed desperately at the blade in his throat, falling backward and bleeding out into the snow.

The guards on Michelangelo's side halted at the sound of the gunfire. They turned back, then forward, then back again, also confused as to how the soldier could be in two places at once. Up to this point, the assumption was that the soldier was acting alone, and thus, terror gripped them as the thought of the tales of the soldier became more real, more horrifying, and now even more supernatural.

"Hell's been loosed upon us," Blanco exclaimed, afraid.

"Keep your wits! Icarus saw this coming; it's all a part of the plan." Roger calmed down.

"Is being slaughtered a part of the plan as well?" Bo questioned.

Roger looked over at Bo, and though he wanted to scold him, he knew he couldn't, that he felt the same doubt and fear that Bo felt. "He's just a man. He dies the same as we do."

"Not yet, he hasn't." Blanco actualized.

The three horsemen stared forward at the darkness before them as the lanterns of their men continued to go out, and Michelangelo vengefully dispatched them.

William launched his knife into his fourth target's center chest. As his target reeled back, William leapt from the shadows and rammed into his fifth target with his shoulder, slamming him into a pine behind him, rendering him unconscious. This target was right beside the fourth, and as William pinned the fifth to the tree, the fourth fell to his knees, leaning forward as he began to drool red liquid. The sixth target aimed his revolver as the fifth slid down the pine slowly. William ducked and rolled underneath his sixth target's aim. He fired and missed, sending the bullet just above William's head into the pine. William stopped on his left knee, pulled his right revolver from his holster, hammered in a round, placed it under his armpit, aimed backward, and fired a round blindly into his sixth target's heart. The target toppled backwards as his legs fumbled beneath him, his arms going as limp as his legs as droplets coated the snowy ground behind him. William stood to his feet and turned around to see his targets as the sixth one fell backward into the snow. The hunter saw the surrounding carnage, then saw the one with the knife in his chest still somehow alive, taking deep breaths on his knees as he tried to breathe through the knife puncturing his lung. William looked at the knife protruding and then walked over to retrieve his weapon. He grabbed the hilt of the blade and ripped it from the flesh, pulling his fourth target forward, falling face down silently. He poofed in the snow that was stacked around him, prompting William to look over to the waking fifth target on the pine. He saw him placing his hands on the ground, trying to regain his bearings, and as he did, the hunter slowly raised his revolver forward as he pulled back the revolver's hammer. His fifth target dizzily reached for his gun that was buried deep in the snow, making eye contact with the Brother of Grim. Anger filled the fifth target's heart as he tried to find a weapon to finish off the hunter, knowing the soldier's fable had deceived him. "Of course. It was always the two of you," he remarked. "Not always," the Brother of Grim corrected.

The fifth target chuckled. "So you say, Grim. So you say." He said, shakily and slowly lifting his revolver.

Grim fired, blasting a hole through the center of his last target's head, smacking backward into the pine as his body went limp, brain and blood coating the frozen wood. In seconds, his head flopped forward limply as William shook his head, holstering his revolver and looking over to where Michelangelo was fighting, waiting for the right time to move forward on the horsemen.

The three horsemen stared at the last seven lanterns that shakily shone through the forest, hoping one would remain, letting them know they had driven off the soldiers. The last lanterns continued to move, with each one sharing a sporadic yet focused directional change. Roger watched as one lantern stopped and shook violently, lifting upward with a slow, rigid progression, then crashing down, igniting over the top of what looked to be a head that eventually became an evident body. His wild and painful screams echoed through the valley as he twisted and flailed his arms in the lantern's flaming oil, running through the forest as he clawed at his face, then fell to the ground dead as the other men screamed in fear, blindly firing rounds into the darkness that surrounded them. The flashes from the gunfire gave a slight flash of light, showing a quick streak of red and blue, but nothing was able to make a shot on. He was a blur, and not before long, the last lantern fell as the fifth guard screamed until he was abruptly silenced. The sixth guard ran, but was stopped; his lantern slammed to the ground along with him as he screamed, *"No! No, please,"* before being silenced with a quick crunch.

The last guard sprinted from the forest. *"Help! Help!"* He screamed as the remaining men watched in horror. His lantern showed him fearfully running toward the edge of the Hillberry Settlement's light, then suddenly, just before, a loud thud sounded out, his lantern dropping. It slowly rolled through the snow and into the three horsemen's sight, the three staring at it, then the darkness behind it. To them, it was silent, the flying and flicking snowflakes racing before them. They listened in, hearing the sound of a fist savagely breaking and smashing the man's face as he pleaded and squealed for mercy. Though they could not see what was happening, they visualized it all as the crunching and meaty thuds echoed through the night until the man's faint screams were silenced as the crunching turned to a splat. Then, silence. The wind blew, and the three horsemen watched in terrified anticipation, their hearts racing. Each one slowly raised their hands to their revolvers, leaving them hovering over as they waited for the soldier to make himself known.

Leonardo's heart pounded just the same as he continued to look for his brothers.

Faint grumbling and spitting of blood was heard from the darkness around Michelangelo. The horsemen squinted their eyes as a silhouette came forward with a slow momentum. The seventh guard stepped out into the lantern's light, a hunter's knife firmly pressed against his left jugular.

"How is he still alive?" Roger asked in disbelief.

Over the seventh guard's left shoulder, a blue-coated arm and black glove aimed a navy revolver directly at Rogers' forehead, as Michelangelo used a majority of his hostage's body as a human shield. The horsemen drew their revolvers and aimed them towards the shadowy figure, with each one moving nervously, their boots shifting on the porch. Their eyes glanced between the hostage and the shadowy figure behind him. The soldier's hostage was over his lantern now, revealing his nose that was blended profusely, his mouth and eyebrows puffy and busted, blood all over mixed in with the tears that flowed from his eyes, though nearly swollen shut. Roger looked behind him and saw a face begin to take shape, though it was hidden in the darkness. Blood was splattered over his face, sleeves, and gloves, resting in the forms of little thick droplets like rain, but red. Roger looked into Michelangelo's eyes and froze in horror: He saw that his eyes were glowing unnaturally, reflecting the light of the lantern from his. It was in the same way a predator might be, only it was unnaturally seen in Michelangelo. This struck fear into Roger more than anyone else. *What if,* he thought, *he is more than human? What if he is a revenant of retribution?*

Michelangelo stepped into the light and revealed his face, his eyebrows curving down ferociously. His mouth curled down the same, as he stared Roger down with murderous intent.

"Major General," Roger opened. "Might I compliment you on the proficiency of your skills?"

Michelangelo said nothing.

Roger blinked nervously, then gulped. "You know, we've heard stories about you... a lot, recently. We've heard about all you've done for folks like us and then got a little taste of it back at Little York. I didn't believe much of it, if I'm honest. I didn't think you would survive, but... here we are." He smiled nervously. "You have made me a believer."

Silence again.

"Where's Icarus?" Michelangelo finally called out.

Roger's smile slightly faded as he began to think over his current situation and the advantages he had left. "Okay. I guess we're skipping over introductions today." He looked around. "Look, I don't want to be that man, Major, but if you haven't noticed, you're a bit outnumbered. One against three isn't exactly good odds. You may want to think about that before we get going down that road."

"That's where you're wrong, horseman," William interrupted, stepping forward from the darkness, his revolvers aimed at the other two. "There are two men with three guns, two of which I hold, facing off against three men with the same firepower. 'Way I see it, I'd say we've got some pretty good odds. In fact, I'd wager we're just about *even*."

The other two horsemen now divided their attention between the soldier and the hunter, shifting their aim to William. It was then that Roger realized this was the Brother of Grim. "As I live and breathe. Is that the Brother of Grim?" William said nothing and instead stopped a distance away from Michelangelo. They looked at each other slightly, both curious about how Roger knew his name, given that the Brother of Grim, around here, was mostly unknown.

"I can't believe I didn't see it before. *Of course,* that was you! Now, it makes perfect sense," Roger went on.

"My hands are getting mighty shaky, horseman," Michelangelo interrupted. "You take much longer, you and your boy will both be dead." The soldier pressed the blade into his hostage's throat. The man gritted his teeth and cried as Roger looked back at the two of them.

"Please! Tell him what he wants!" Michelangelo's hostage cried.

Roger looked between the young man and Michelangelo, pondering how he might save his skin.

"Well. I can't argue with that, Major. I gotta say... killing my men in the dark. Taking a hostage. Even having the good ol' Grim back up your play? I don't know if we could've done any better." He laughed nervously. "Well, only slightly."

Roger let out a whistle, and within an instant, a door on the side of the settlement, behind the horsemen, flew open, slamming against the wooden walls of the building. Five men, armed with rifles, ran out of the settlement and over to the woodpile. Michelangelo didn't break eye contact with Roger; he nervously forced a quick smile on his left cheek. William glanced between the men at the woodpile and his horsemen.

"We got hostages, too, Major. Some we intend to use, all the same as you," Roger continued.

"What are they doing, Bill?" Michelangelo asked loudly.

"They're going over to the wood... and they're armed," William yelled back.

Leonardo directed his attention towards the tarped log pile and noted the five riflemen who approached it. One removed the right peg, the others aimed their rifles at the canvas, as Leonardo's heart raced in his chest. His hands shook as he held the binoculars, though they did not tremble from the cold, but from the fear and rage that had begun to grip his soul. The canvas ripped off rapidly as the wind carried it over. His eyes widened, for underneath it, huddled together, freezing in the cold, were his brothers.

Leonardo's emotions twisted in his chest, ones of relief, bitterness, and sorrow, all coming out in a shaky breath as a smile spread across his face. Each rifleman picked a member of the Brothers' Six and hoisted them to their feet, then pushed them forward with their rifles aimed at the back of their heads. The riflemen forced them to march toward the three horsemen. "No," Leonardo let out to himself. "Come on! *Do something!*"

"Mike... they're coming this way," William informed.

Leonardo glanced between Michelangelo and his brothers, waiting for the soldier to make a move as he held his ground. "He can't win this. *He can't win this!*" He doubted, looking up from his binoculars. As Leonardo's mind raced, he began thinking of his solution. He looked over to the black repeater on William's horse, tied to the side of Betsy's saddle, and stared at it for a moment. He reached for it, then, just before grabbing it, thought about what Michelangelo had said. He remembered that he had instructed him to stay back and out of this world of violence. He looked at the rifle again, clenched his jaw, tossed the binoculars to the ground, and unsheathed the repeater, jumping from his horse into the snow and making his way down the path toward the conflict.

Michelangelo glanced at the approaching brothers. He understood that the situation had changed, more than likely for the worse. The brothers arrived at the front right of the horsemen and waited to be dealt with. The riflemen lifted the stocks of their rifles and smacked their heads once, dropping each one to their knees, encasing their legs in snow. Roger eased his shoulders a bit as Bo and Blanco did the same, relaxing into a newly acquired safety. William looked over at the Brothers' Six and noted the torturous state they were in. His face twisted in disgust, as it was a state that no man should ever see, nor be subjected to live in.

Lucas's eyes had been beaten shut, with his face bruised and coated in frozen blood. His body was weak, and he was looking around as lightly as he could, using sound to determine where everyone was.

Javier's right cheek was large and blackened, his chin busted open from what appeared to be the stock of a rifle. His lip was busted as well, apparently recently, for it was bloody and dripping, and his eyes were nearly swollen shut.

Lee appeared to be the second most beaten of all; his left cheek had been left agape with crimson. It was busted open by fists and assorted objects. His right eye was swollen shut, similarly to his brothers. His face shared more blood than it did the color of skin, forcing him to hold on to every inch of whatever life he had left.

Judah's lips protruded forward in a puffy and mashed state. Bruises and blood froze all over his face, the only additional beating being an extra hard crack to the top of his skull, made clear by a frozen streak of blood that ran from the top of his head to the bottom of his right cheek.

Lastly, Jordan had been ripped to shreds. His arms had cuts like the ones on his face, which were knife gashes that were carved into both of his cheeks, while his left eye was covered in a bloody, ripped cloth. William knew Jordan was now lacking an eye in that socket, for he had seen, even done, knife torture that ended up looking like that at the end. He was shocked that he endured it. William examined the bruises from punches as well, and how his energy was drained just as much as the rest. But he held on, for reasons that William could not understand.

It was then that William looked under the gashes on Jordan's face and saw something that he had yet to notice on all the others: an upright cross was burned into their cheeks, fresh with pink and white flesh, shiny flesh. He shook his head as he looked over them and noticed the purple in their fingers and the paleness of their skin, wondering what quality of life they'd have to live if he and Michelangelo did manage to get them out. At this point, it seemed more like an act of mercy to let the brothers die. This troubled him, and as he looked back at the targeted horsemen, that image and those thoughts replayed in his mind relentlessly.

"Now... let's be honest with one another, Major. This fight doesn't concern you. I know you want us all dead. I understand that. Hell, I might even sympathize. But between you and me, we know that what's going on here is none of your concern."

"I already did this dog and pony show, horseman. I'm not interested in your offers," Michelangelo interrupted.

"Yes, yes, I know that... but allow me to be direct with you, even more than Icarus. See, Icarus prefers you alive. He's told you once, and I'll tell you again: an outcome where you are *not* alive proves to be most unfortunate for us. I know that might sound shocking, but truly, despite all the surprises you've brought us and the drop in the number of our men that followed, Icarus does want you, even needs you alive. Truth be told, he, along with us, wants Caine dead probably as much as you. So, Icarus *drastically* sped up his plan and changed with the times, so to speak, but things are still going to plan." He paused to gauge Michelangelo. The soldier only got angrier. Roger gulped and let out a sharp breath through his nervous smile. "We know you want blood. We know that it's Mr. Kingsley's, specifically, that you thirst for. We can assure you that if you let Icarus finish his work, you will get it. You'll be well on your way to your sweet, sweet retribution, and we're free from Kingsley's hand. Just give us the boy and walk away. Let Icarus finish what he started, and shortly thereafter, we'll meet you at Guarida Del León and tell you *exactly* where the king rules. Everyone wins! Everyone's happy. Additionally, the amount of blood spilled is significantly reduced. I'm not sure if that last bit appeals to you, but it appeals to any other man in any other war, so I'd wager you, at the very least, can understand that."

Michelangelo mulled it over. "So blood for blood. The boy's for your men's?"

"That's about the size of it."

"Explain to me how, after everything you and your men have done, you deserve to live? How is that justice? How does 'everybody win' in those circumstances?"

"Oh, come on, major. Let's not confuse justice with vengeance, though I will admit you have walked that line nicely. Instead, let me appeal to your battle-hardened wits: is not cutting off the head of the snake better than working your way through its body? Is it not safer, and strategically more effective?"

"Sure, but even still, do not mistake me for a man without principle, horseman. There is more to me than you've perceived, and that is intentional. Besides, though your strategy may be true, you all aren't exactly the trusting type. How do I know you'll keep your word?"

"It's as I said: Icarus wants Caine just as dead as you do. We all do. We benefit from one another, and we have something to offer each other. On top of that, he wanted me to tell you he is currently waiting for you in Guarida Del León. He wagers that even if he weren't, it wouldn't be long before you tracked him down anyway." He raised his hands in a surrendering fashion. "That's the truth, take it or leave it."

"Mike," William interrupted, "you and I both know that we need to act now. Though that all makes sense, and I see the reason in his thinking, he is still a murderer at the end of the day."

Roger slowly looked over to William, a wicked smile gracing his face. "Rich, coming from you, Grim." William's eyebrow lifted slightly, confused. "Oh, you don't recognize me? We've crossed paths before. How have you been?" A firm tension filled the air. Roger let out a condescending whistle. "Look at how far you've come! From soulless bounty hunter to unwavering defender. Or, is that just the story you've spun our poor major general, here?"

"If you like that mouth of yours, I suggest you close it."

"What, like you? Willfully keeping your mouth closed for whatever selfish reason it might be?" He smiled. "At least that's what I assume, given Mr. Hart's continual search for Caine Kingsley despite you knowing his location?"

Michelangelo clenches his jaw, staying focused on the horsemen but solidifying in his mind what we already knew. He hung on every one of Roger's words, while simultaneously thinking of how he would kill him and the horsemen beside him.

"And who are you, exactly?" William questioned, controlling his anxiety.

"Aw, you don't remember? Either that or I assume you're playing dumb as to set me up as a liar." He adjusted the grip on his revolver, the cold etching away at his finger muscles. He looked between the soldier and the hunter, worried, but collected. "I guess you didn't care to mention that you and I used to work together, at least in some capacity. Now, he may not have done exactly what I was doing, but the fact of the matter stands that we were both employed by the same man. When Mr. Kingsley sent his outlaws out to eradicate believers, he had to ensure that the business would continue uninterrupted.

This meant that if any opposing bounty hunter got any bright ideas, the Brother of Grim was sent to hunt them down at Mr. Kingsley's command. It was good to be an outlaw in those times, at least for a while. We easily made our way around Utah before dropping down here into Arizona, and as we made our rounds, we started to notice that, though the bounty hunters were dropping dead, outlaws were doing the same. Mathematically, it doesn't add up. So as we went on, we noticed that, once the outlaws that Mr. Kingsley used had been used to their entirety, the Brother of Grim was right there behind them, ready to collect the bounty. And he did for every single *one*. Kind of like right now."

William clenched his jaw as a volatile expression overtook his face, no different than Michelangelo's, who had now side-eyed the hunter.

"I wonder," Roger started again. "Did you lie because you were scared, or lie because you were hunting another bounty? Like the Brothers of Boudiclare, for example! If memory serves, and the story is true, did they not also work for Caine Kingsley? Was that not the very gang that harbored your younger brother? What was his name? Thomas. Yeah. *Thomas St. Hart*. The same legend that he so calculatedly hunted down. Strange how that works, isn't it? How *small* the world can be. A world where a man such as myself can meet the Brother of Grim countless times, and only survive because we were once on the same payroll."

"You don't know the full story!"

"No, but I know enough. Now the soldier does, too." He smirked. "Tell me, brother, did Caine send you to clean up his mess, or did you set this whole thing up on your own?"

"I'm here to help my nephew, *that's it!*"

"Oh, cut the bullshit, Grim. Come on: what's the payout for even one of the Four Horsemen these days? Two thousand? Four thousand?"

William's heart raced as Michelangelo's breathing increased angrily. Roger looked at the soldier. "The good news is, Major General, that Icarus, being the man he is, figured out Mr. Kingsley's plan long ago. That's why we need you alive, we want you alive because we *want* Mr. Kingsley dead, if not more than you. Honestly, I feel as though your fight is not with us, but with Grim. We, Mr. Major, are on diverging paths that have just so happened to cross on their way to their natural conclusions. But the Grim? He's only in it for himself and will bring you more death and lies to accomplish whatever his goals may be."

William glanced at Michelangelo, the soldier gripping his revolver and pondering what decision he could make. Despite the final pieces to the puzzle coming together, shooting William now may not be the wisest choice, and whether the horseman saw it or not, Michelangelo was here for more than revenge. He also preferred that every one of them die. "You've misread me, horseman," he started. "I'm here for the Brothers' Six. I'm also here for Icarus. I would be a liar if I said I wasn't here for vengeance, either. In all, I find it amicable that Icarus would be willing to give me his location and that you would be so forward and honest about my partner... but the fact is, I prefer you all dead, anyway."

A look of angry fear overtook Roger's face.

"Give me the brothers, horseman, and I'll allow you to die like a man rather than a monster—with dignity and not with reproach, like the rest. "

"This isn't your fight!" Roger exclaimed. "Don't be a fool! You got nothing to do with this holy war."

"No, but your holy war has got *everything* to do with me! You made sure of that when your king killed my brother, when your men killed innocent people. Now, why don't you stop the nonsense and *die like a man!*"

Roger's hands shook in fear as his heart pounded in his chest. He shook his head and looked down briefly. "I wish you had seen things differently, Major General." He looked up. "Might've played out better for all of us."

"I doubt it."

Roger chuckled. "*Leonardo!*" Roger shouted over the wind, not breaking eye contact.

Leonardo froze as he looked through the scope of the repeater, which was now primed and aimed at Roger's chest. Leonardo's heart pounded within him; he was befuddled that Roger knew he was there.

"*The kid isn't here!*" Michelangelo defensively lied.

"Oh, of course he is, and you'd be a fool to think he did what you told him to."

"*Regardless*, you're not getting the boy, and you *best not* make the mistake of thinking you're getting his brothers either!"

"Oh, I know that, Major. I just want to make sure he understands what that means."

Michelangelo was still trying to save the brothers' lives. In truth, it was somewhat of a stalemate. He couldn't trade Leonardo for his brothers the same way he couldn't let the men go. The only good outcome was the one where Roger chose to die like a man and not give in to his monstrous appetite.

"Since the soldier cannot seem to be reasoned with, I would like to open this dialogue to you, Mr. DelMuerto. You are a passionate boy, as far as I know, and thus, I know you are somewhere close enough to hear me. I want to make it clear to you that if you do not present yourself, your brothers *will* die. Icarus wants *you*. Everyone else that's died has only died because you have not taken their place. Every believer branded, every casualty of war, has been because of your negligence to face the music. This is all about you, Leo, and thus, you can stop this *right now*. All you have to do is come forward."

"Don't forget I can still *kill you*, horseman," Michelangelo growled.

"Yes, I know, and much like you, I am willing to die for my cause, which is what I wager will happen to all of us any minute now. Whether I'm dead or alive makes no difference to Icarus. He only needs one of the nine of us here to deliver the preacher."

"Don't forget who I am, horseman. I've killed far more than nine men in far shorter a time, and had greater men than you attempt on my life. I'm not just a soldier: I am the one sent to rain vengeance on *all of you*. Not *one of you* is getting out of here alive!"

The air was thick, the cold biting, and the muscles in every man's body stiffened to an instinctual focus. It was silent as they all made peace with what could happen, glancing between one another.

"Hold... to God's unchanging hand," Jordan spoke in tune, weakly. "Hold to God's... unchanging hand."

There was a short silence. All the men in the standoff looked over at Jordan, taken aback.

"Build your hope on things eternal," the brothers sang weakly, their puffed lips sputtering.

The brothers weakly spit up blood, barely able to keep themselves up on their knees. Leonardo looked over the top of the rifle's scope, tears filling. He looked at Jordan helplessly as Jordan stared at the snow-covered ground beneath him, breathing heavily. "Just hold... to God's unchanging hand," he finished. He slowly looked up at Leonardo. He couldn't explain this; it seemed his brother knew exactly where he was. Still, they looked at one another, somehow making eye contact in the darkness.

And Jordan smiled.

The men all went back to looking at each other in their standoff, gripping their revolvers, Roger's jaw clenched, and Michelangelo completely at ease. William's heart raced as he darted between the riflemen, the horsemen, and the soldier.

Roger let out a fearful smile, shrugging his shoulders. "Que sera, sera."

The riflemen raised their rifles and fired through the back of the brothers' heads, flicking them forward and toppling them into the snow. Leonardo's eyes widened in shock, everything playing out slowly before him. His sight began to fade as a blinding, bright red overtook it; his rage overtook him as his disbelief began to shatter his mind. *"No!"* Leonardo roared. Michelangelo sneered as he went to pull the trigger, when suddenly a repeater fired from behind him, skewering the left side of Roger's neck and sending him sideways to his right knee. Michelangelo's eyes widened as Roger's open left hand reached for his now bleeding neck wound. William wasted no time and fired off both of his revolvers, hitting Bo in the left spleen and Blanco in his right leg. He dove to his left side toward the rock wall as he fired four more shots out of his revolvers. Two of his rounds sliced through a rifleman's gut and skull, the other two shattering through the third one's thigh and knee. The remaining riflemen and horsemen reloaded, then fired. Blanco shot a round toward Michelangelo, who was still caught off guard, sending it through the front of his hostage's head. It jerked backward as it coated Michelangelo's hat and face in a red spray. Disgusted, he threw off the limp body and looked at Roger, leaning against the wall of the settlement, as blood flowed between his fingers.

Leonardo sprinted for his brothers from the tree line, rifle in hand, as the blizzard crashed down in full force behind him. The snow whipped viciously around the men at war, limiting their vision to a mere ten feet in front of them. Michelangelo loaded and raised his revolver as he aimed it at Roger, but Bo pulled the trigger and launched a bullet into the center of Michelangelo's chest. The bullet clanged and ricocheted off, launching into the snow with a light poof as Michelangelo was thrust into the snow. He hit the ground forcefully as the air in his lungs shot out of him, forcing him to try to regain it. Roger looked at his gun in confusion, then at the soldier in disbelief, his fear overtaking him as he pondered the idea of being immortal. Terrified, he aimed his weapon again, firing off shots at Michelangelo, as he lunged and crawled over to the rock wall to his right, opposite William. Snowflakes flicked and raged as bullets exploded into the rock. Michelangelo looked to his side and saw Leonardo running past him toward the riflemen, who were now disbanding and relocating. Two of them stayed to lay cover fire on William, who was reloading his revolvers. Uncontrolled and off-balance, Michelangelo rose from his cover and trudged toward Leonardo, simultaneously angling himself toward Blanco and holstering his left navy revolver and unholstering his right one. He aimed at Blanco's chest and yelled as he flicked his left hand back rapidly across the hammer, firing six rounds into Blanco's chest, sending him backward and slamming him into the porch wall. Blood emerged from his wounds as he slowly sat in a slouched position, his eyes agape and his arms twitching after death. Michelangelo tackled Leonardo just beside the settlement's wall, launching them to the ground as they dodged the bullets Bo had fired that flew by Michelangelo's head.

"Let me go!" Leonardo commanded, fighting Michelangelo in the snow.

"First, you give me the repeater!" Michelangelo ordered.

"Fine!"

Leonardo tossed the repeating rifle to the ground. Michelangelo released him, grabbed the weapon, and cocked the lever once as he rose to his feet. Leonardo rose to his feet as the two took shelter beside the wall.

"How could you let this happen?" Leonardo blamed.

"There wasn't a way to save them, kid. I'm sorry," Michelangelo replied.

Leonardo looked around in panic, his eyes wide with shock.

"All right, kid, here's the plan, I need you to—" Michelangelo began as Leonardo ran around the corner of the settlement. *"Leo! Wait!"*

Leonardo didn't listen and flew around the corner. Michelangelo let out an angry sigh as he shook his head, holstering his revolver and gripping the bigger weapon. "I've just about had enough of all this nonsense," he concluded, rounding the corner while aiming the rifle from the hip. *"Come and get me, you blood sucking parasites!"*

The men on the battlefield looked as the soldier walked atop the porch, fired into the winter's night, as the bullets allowed for suppressing fire just above Leonardo. Each shot blasted in a flash of light, followed by a crunchy reload as Leonardo ran thoughtlessly toward his brothers' bodies. He slid through the snow, stopped directly beside Jordan's body, and hopelessly grabbed at his lifeless shoulders. *"Jordan! Jordan, get up! Jordan!"*

William stood from his cover and raised his newly loaded revolvers as Michelangelo continued his slow walk-and-fire strategy on the porch. The hunter fired shots at the riflemen, who retreated to the woodpile but missed, unable to see due to the blinding snowy wind. He continued to fire, nonetheless, suppressing the men. As he did, a rifleman who was hidden on the left side of the building took notice.

Michelangelo stepped quickly for Roger, flipping the rifle in the air and grabbing the barrel-end of it like a baseball bat. Roger looked up at the soldier as he cracked the stock across the side of Roger's face, knocking him to his side as he continued to hold his throat. Swiftly, the soldier kicked Roger's revolver off into the snow as Bo turned and noticed him. He sat upon the base of the porch with his body leaning up against the building, then weakly pointed his revolver with a somewhat accurate aim. Michelangelo turned and swung the rifle's stock into Bo's hand like a golf club, launching the revolver into the air and darkness, breaking Bo's hand.

Before Michelangelo, a rifleman's weapon flashed, a shot firing from it, zipping through William's left leg. He let out a yell of excruciating pain as he dropped to his knee, then over to his shoulder. The soldier dropped the repeater, letting out a loud thud on the frozen porch, and unholstered his shotgun, holding it firmly in both hands. Bo looked at Michelangelo and noticed the change in weaponry, as he held his broken hand with the other, blood leaking from his spleen. Michelangelo pulled back both hammers on the double-barreled shotgun and aimed it down at a defeated Bo. "Oh, come on," Bo complained. Michelangelo pulled one trigger, firing a round through the center of Bo's chest, the shockwaves thrusting his arms out to the side as his body slammed backward into the porch wall, splattering blood against and through it via the freshly made hole.

An effeminate scream let out from inside the house, signaling Michelangelo to look in its direction with a predatory quickness. He looked through the window and saw a shadow running before the fireplace. Michelangelo listened more closely and heard a most peculiar sound: a baby crying. Michelangelo's attention was redirected to the rifleman to the left of him as he stepped out from beside the settlement's wall, inching his way out towards Leonardo. The soldier looked at William, who was now motionless in the snow. He paid no mind and, in part, hoped the hunter was dead. He looked forward at the rifleman, reached out, and grabbed the exposed repeater. The rifleman was taken by surprise, but before he could react, he was pulled toward the soldier. His eyes widened as the stock of a shotgun lifted and slammed into the bridge of his nose, knocking him backward and leaving Michelangelo with the rifle in one hand and a double-barreled shotgun in the other. Michelangelo holstered the repeater on his left shoulder and placed his left hand back on the shotgun's double barrel, as the rifleman stumbled to his feet quickly, holding his busted and bleeding nose. He aimed his shotgun between the rifleman's shoulders as he tripped and stumbled backwards through the snow. He pulled the second trigger and blasted the slug through the center of the rifleman's back, spraying red through his front and onto the snow before him, which he shortly thereafter launched into. A rifle shot rang out and clanged against his left armor plate, flicking him sideways to tumble backwards onto the porch. Almost instantly, a shot rang out from where William was lying, sending a revolver round into the head of the rifleman shooting by the wooden pile.

Michelangelo looked up and noticed William had been playing dead, his left arm perfectly hidden underneath the underside of his belly, pulling off a crack shot. The rifle-man fell backward to the ground with a snowy crunch, the woodpile before him toppling forward. The soldier looked over at the falling logs and saw another rifleman rise. With a quickness, he dropped his shotgun and pulled his navy revolver from his left holster and blasted a shot forward to skewer a bullet through the side of the second-to-last rifleman's head. It wobbled side to side as his arms dropped with looseness, leading William to look at him as he fell to his knees, his eyes still locked on William as he died. The two retained eye contact as he slowly tilted to his left side, fluffing up the snow beside his fellow rifle-man. The hunter breathed a sigh of relief as he slowly rose to his feet, applying pressure to his leg wound and limping his way to Michelangelo, who stood slowly as well. The impact of the rifle bullet, though non-deadly, still kicked with full force into his ribs. He looked down at his jacket and leather covering that held his armor, noting the holes that were now present.

Leonardo kneeled over Jordan, his head lay on his back as tears fell from his eyes.

He confronted the reality he was in. He blamed himself for it. He looked over to the bodies of his fallen brothers beside him, their blood seeping from the bullet holes in the back of their heads, and the brands upon their faces that burned over their other injuries in the shape of a cross. His brain could not handle it.

"Is that everyone?" William yelled to Michelangelo.

The soldier holstered his left handgun, bent over, picked up his shotgun, holstered it across his shoulders and back, and stepped off the side of the porch and walked up to William, taking note of his injury on his leg, only to stare up at William blankly. He squeezed the rifle in his hands and considered the different ways he could kill the hunter. As he did, a woman burst through the side door of the settlement and rushed toward the forest, the faint sound of a baby crying drifting through the blizzard wind. Michelangelo and William whipped around, aiming their weapons. They both saw her and were able to make out her clothing because of the lantern she held in her free right hand. She was dressed in white pajama clothing that showed underneath a thick men's leather jacket she had thrown on. She had on untied boots that collected snow more than they kept it out. Michelangelo recognized the top, remembering that Roger had worn it back at Little York. "I guess not," he answered, hammering another round in.

"*Michael, stop!*" William halted, grabbed the revolver, and aimed it down, throwing the gun to the ground

"*Damn it, Bill!*" Michelangelo said, unholstering the repeater on his shoulders and cracking in another round as he aimed it at William.

"*Hey!* Hey! Whoa! Easy!" William calmed, raising his hands in surrender.

"She's with them, William!"

"She has a child! I know you heard it's crying. So did I!"

Michelangelo grimaced.

Leonardo looked up at the fleeing woman, and then at Michelangelo, seeing the soldier's blinding rage and coldness. He wondered if this cold-blooded mentality was what some men truly needed. He considered that, if he had been willing to shoot Roger sooner, perhaps his brothers would still be alive. He knew that his fight was against principalities, but in this moment, it had seemed as though his fight was more with man than monster. He internalized what Roger said, that blood had been shed on his behalf by the gallons, and the weight of a thousand souls began to crush his guilty conscience. Leonardo looked at his hands and saw Jordan's blood, wondering what he would tell Sophia, how he would explain that he stood idly by and let her uncle die, all so he did not fall into Icarus's hands. Truth be told, he was scared to come out. He didn't know if Michelangelo did the best he could, but from what he could tell, the overall situation was inescapable. As Leonardo looked over his brother's bodies, he remembered that it was Jordan who had told him to avoid Icarus at all costs. This gave him some peace, knowing that it was for the best, that their sacrifice was the best move.

At least, that's what he had once believed.

Now, he fancied himself avenged. He wanted blood for blood, and as he thought this, movement caught him from the corner of his eye. He turned and looked at the shadows of the forest, created by the pine trees and the blizzard's darkness. He squinted and saw a shrouded figure. It scared him at first, but as the figure reached out its hand, motioning for him to come forward, he dropped his guard. It was the last rifleman who had gone and taken cover in the tree line, firmly holding his weapon in his right hand. Leonardo looked at the man's face and saw something that could only be seen as otherworldly. His eyes were likened unto a snake's, and they seemed unnaturally wide in the darkness that fell over his sockets. His mouth was twisted into a wide and unnatural smile—a strange thing to see, to say the least. He knew what the rifleman wanted; the Red Horseman had stated it: the rifleman wanted Leonardo because Icarus wanted him. It was then that he wondered if, by facing Icarus directly, the bloodshed would finally cease. After all, the war that Icarus waged ended with him. Leonardo pondered the paths before him, as he began to doubt the trust he had placed in the soldier and the hunter, just as he started to doubt his beliefs. He questioned the choices that God was making and why this was His sovereign will. *If this is the fruit of my faith,* he thought, *perhaps it is not a faith worth believing.*

Leonardo stood to his feet, determined to pave his path, approaching the rifleman quietly. The rifleman glanced between Leonardo and Michelangelo, making sure that the soldier did not notice the preacher leaving. As Leonardo got closer, the rifleman's face took on the appearance of a man once more, and in a flash, he gripped Leonardo and took him into the darkness.

The mother dashed into the woods, and Michelangelo regained her attention. He aimed in her direction again and fired the rifle, honing in on her back. William grabbed the gun with both hands and pulled the soldier and it in close, the weapon going off and blasting a bullet into a pine beside them. The woman flinched, picked up speed, and kept on running.

"Mike!" William stopped again.

"If the next bullet isn't in her, I'll make sure it's in you!" Michelangelo threatened.

William was mortified by what he said. *"I'll handle it!* You deal with Leonardo!"

William released and limped quickly after the mother, her lantern barely giving way to her direction. Michelangelo gripped the repeater and considered shooting William, slowly aiming it at his back, but eased with an angry sigh, given that it benefited him to leave him alive for the time being. He turned around and looked at the Brothers' Six bodies. They were there, but Leonardo was not. He looked from left to right and quickly searched for any clue of the preacher, and as he looked forward once again, he noticed bootprints in the snow that were quickly fading by the falling snow. The boot prints led into the forest, getting washed away by the blizzard's wind. He followed them forward into the darkness for a moment, hoping Leonardo had not done what he thought he did.

"Leo!" He called out. There was no reply. He sighed as he realized that, more than likely, Leonardo was a dead man.

In the absence of a reply, Michelangelo looked out into the bitter, dark emptiness, hoping he would see the preacher or that he would return. He knew there was nothing he could do, at least right now. Worst of all, he knew he had failed, which was the most discomforting thought of all.

"Boy j-just left a minute ago... you might st-still be able to catch him, if you try." Roger choked out, his face contorted in pain.

Michelangelo turned around slowly, his anger burning within him. Roger had just enough blood in him to stay alive. He was impressed by the horseman's persistence and made for him in a slow and heavy walk. Roger stared at Michelangelo, his head lying against the front wall of the settlement, his hands resting at his sides as blood continued to flow down. His throat oozed red onto his clothing and the porch beneath him, as Michelangelo tossed the rifle to the side and unholstered his right revolver. He flicked open the chamber and loaded a single round, then closed it and looked down at the gun, thumbing the cylinder around to the hammer slot. Roger looked as he approached, flicking the chamber closed and powerfully stepping across the porch's surface, creaking the wood with every step. Before he knew it, Michelangelo stood above him and stared down at the horseman coldly. Roger looked up at Michelangelo and accepted his fate, waiting for Michelangelo to do what he had done to so many.

"Guarida Del León, you said?" Michelangelo clarified.

Roger smiled and looked to the right. He was impressed by the soldier's unending thirst for blood. "You haven't figured it out, have you?" He caught his breath. "You can't win this one, Major. This war wasn't meant to be. You can't beat, Icarus... everything you-you've done, everything you will do, he has seen and he has planned."

"That's not the same story you told me earlier."

"True... but that was before. This is n-now. Still, you don't get it. He didn't see you before, but he *sees* you now. You are a mystery unveiled that is a mystery no more." He sputtered up blood. "He knows your name. Icarus knows... he always knows... he has professed all that has come to pass... and it has come to pass as such."

Michelangelo chuckled. "So that's what this is. You all think he's some kind of prophet?"

"*We know he is.* We have seen it."

"You haven't seen shit."

Michelangelo whipped the navy revolver's barrel across the right side of Roger's face, throwing him to the ground on his left side. His face pulsed with pain as he reached up and held his broken cheek in a bloody and dying mess. Michelangelo pressed his boot firmly into Roger's ribs, pushing him over onto his back. He then slowly raised his left boot and placed it upon the bullet hole in the side of Roger's neck, smooshing down slowly, a painful, wet squish sounding out as blood slipped out over the sides. Roger gritted his teeth as more bubbled through his mouth, the soldier pressing down harder, slowly. "Like I said earlier," Michelangelo started, "you can die a man or you can die a monster; either way, today is the day you die." He moved his boot to the side, mushing the flesh slightly. Roger screamed, the sound of liquid coating his vocal cords. "Why does Icarus want the boy so bad? You answer me that and I'll make it quick." Roger said nothing as he gritted his teeth and groaned underneath Michelangelo's boot.

Roger said nothing.

"Suit yourself," Michelangelo said, pressing his boot down harder.

Roger bellowed in a painful scream as his flesh slightly tore, the pain shooting through his neck as blood shot out of his mouth. "Alright!" He yielded. Michelangelo let up his boot from the wound. "In truth, all we know is Icarus has said Leonardo is the key to the continuance of our mission. He is the martyr, the prophet, and the hypocrite."

"Excuse my scriptural ignorance, but those all sound the same."

"They are, and they are not."

Michelangelo rolled his eyes and pressed down again. *"Quit playing with me, horseman!"*

"I'm not! I'm not! I am only professing his words, speaking as he has spoken to us!" Roger screamed.

"Where is Leonardo?"

"I would assume with the rifleman you missed, Major."

"You all took him through this storm? He'll die! Where's the point in that?"

"You ever hear of a mineshaft?"

"Of course," he said, releasing his boot a bit. "The Hillberry Settlement got its wealth from the mine." He pressed down again. "Where is it?"

Roger smiled weakly. "It's over, Michael. I can feel death taking me. Torture me all you want, but I'm not giving you anything else."

Michelangelo nodded his head slowly as he sighed angrily. He raised his navy revolver, pointing the barrel at the center of Roger's head. He stared into Roger's eyes, slightly tilting his head to the right, letting out a small smile. Roger's, however, faded as he stared back at the soldier, disturbed by his grin.

The mission had been changed once again. Michelangelo thought that if he could find Leonardo, there still might be a chance to save his life. Whether that was in between or at Guarida Del León, there was still a shot. It was this thought that made the soldier realize he may not have failed after all. If he could get to Leonardo before Icarus did whatever he planned to do, there was still hope. On top of this, he now had Icarus's location thanks to the bastard's boldness and could now also attain the information he needed to find Caine Kingsley.

"How does it feel, horseman?" He started. "To know that everything you've done and every sin you've ever committed has led to this end? How does it feel to know that despite your following of a prophetic madman, you still found yourself at the bottom of a boot just the same as all the rest?" He pulled back the hammer on his gun.

"Madman or not... Icarus offered me something I could not have gotten on my own: power. Something that no man nor God could ever give me. I ask you, Major: as a soldier, what has humanity ever offered you? What has its God, its rulers?" Roger questioned.

"You."

Michelangelo pulled the trigger, the round exploding through the center of Roger's head, forcing the skin and skull to blast forward in a bloodily explosive mess. Blood spurted up, the droplets flickering onto Michelangelo's face. His head fell backward to the wooden porch, a puddle slowly forming behind Roger's open-eyed head, as his body went limp. Michelangelo lifted his boot from the dead horseman's neck and wiped the blood on the wood as he stared at another dead monster. It was odd, now, to see the man he had been hunting for months on end finally dead at his feet. To him, it was a surefire sign that the mission was almost over.

He holstered his navy revolver and looked back into the depths of the forest, and thought upon Bleu and Betsy, who stood in the blizzard, freezing. Michelangelo walked back through the snow, picked up his other revolver, and heftily lifted his knees as he trudged through the deathly cold to his and William's steeds.

William limped after the mother, as she continued to run through the forest, her feet freezing as her shins did the same, both stabbing at her with every step. It was a slow, stabbing pace. Her and her baby's body temperature continued to fall as the wind ripped at what little clothing they had on, though the baby fared slightly better, having bundles of warmed cloth around it as it held tightly to its mother's chest. It cried as it felt its mother's panic, especially and primarily when the mother could go on no longer. She stopped, breathless, looking around frantically at the vast darkness around her, the forest seeming to consume her whole as the blizzard relentlessly tore at her flesh. She looked down at her baby in her arms and began to cry, just before William rounded a pine tree and halted abruptly, looking at the mother. She whipped around and looked at him, his breathing heavy as oxygen puffed forward in the light of the mother's lantern. He raised his left hand toward her slowly, his right hand hovering over his revolver. He tried to make out the features of her face, but all he could see was that she was pale and wide-eyed. She was afraid, her lips shaking violently in the cold, and in terror, as she stood frozen in fear.

"Miss," William opened. "I don't want to hurt you, truly. I'm not like the rest." She began to turn around, facing away from William slowly, her movements slow and oddly deliberate. This took William aback. "I have principles. I'm not like the soldier. If I'm being honest, he'll probably kill me just like he's killed the rest of your men just for talking to you."

"If he's going to kill us, then what's the point of my returning? I might as well take my chances with the snow."

"You'll *die* in the snow. With me, you have a fighting chance."

"You have no power here, hunter."

William was quiet for a moment. "Don't make the mistake of underestimating me."

"I think it is you who underestimates him."

"I can keep you safe!"

"Safe beside the man who betrayed the Saint of Retribution, the same bounty hunter who killed the very same's younger brother? I fear it is only you who has not seen just how dead we all truly are, hunter." She turned toWilliam again, each making eye contact with the other, the baby continuing to cry.

"Those are all fair complaints, but what you fail to see is that he only kills those who are corrupt, who are wicked—those who *need* to be held responsible for the killing of the innocent, in his eyes. But you? You aren't wicked, you're just a mother."

She smiled. "That's where you're wrong, Grim." William stared silently. "Roger is my husband, William... normally that wouldn't be much cause for concern, but Icarus doesn't allow wives unless they believe in what he preaches. The horsemen all had wives before they met Icarus, but I'm the only one who's left alive. Do you know why that is?"

William's heart raced. "Why?"

"Because I agreed with what Icarus was saying. I participated because I liked it. I *chose* to believe it."

William stood motionless as he watched the mother's eyes gloss over, the fear being replaced by otherworldly possession. He tensed, as did she, each staring at the other down in the bitter cold, the baby wailing. "We can make Michael understand," he pleaded. "We'll say it was an act of desperation, of survival! For you and your child!" She noted his desperation and decided to use it against him. "That would work, and all, if he hadn't seen me torturing some of those hypocrites himself." William's heart dropped. "Funnily enough, they all seemed just about as desperate as you."

William's eyes widened as she dropped her lantern and reached behind her pajama pants to go for her revolver. *"No, don't!"* He yelled. She aimed the weapon at William's chest, and within a second, a shot was fired, leading to her head flicking back as the rest of her body followed. William stood stiff as his revolver barrel smoked, perfectly aimed from the right side of his hip. She fell into the snow back first and dropped the baby into its cold depths, it rolling and crying in a manic wail as snow covered its body and face. The infant was buried, and William stared at the mother's body in disbelief as he tried to reconcile what he had done. His morals had finally been broken along with a portion of his mind, for this permanent action he had done, though he had sworn he never would, could not be reversed. William clumsily holstered his revolver as he looked around in shock and uncharacteristically stared into oblivion as shock overtook his sight. William looked around in a daze, his mind refusing to accept what he saw, as he searched for every possible avenue to remove the guilt that already, unrelentingly, plagued his conscience.

William had killed a mother of one, and to him, it was as though he had killed his mother.

The cries of the baby grew louder as William came back to reality, realizing that it would freeze to death in a matter of minutes. He limped over to the sound of the crying and found it in the snow, picking it up and quickly wiping away the white from its face and the blanket that wrapped its body. He looked over the baby and saw that it was a white one, a girl, appearing to be no more than four months old. This was the youngest child William had ever seen, and it shook him in ways he could not yet explain. He opened his jacket and placed the baby within, holding her on his right shoulder as he closed the coat tightly. "It's okay... It's okay... I got you," he comforted.

William limped toward the Hillberry Settlement, his blood crystallizing on his leg. The mother's body behind him was already half buried by the snow that quickly flowed over her, knocking out the lantern's light. He walked out of the forest and made his way to the side of the settlement, looking at the door that led to the warm interior. He glanced over to his right and made out a shadow of Michelangelo with Bleu and Betsy, marching with his head down as he made his way to the barn. William breathed heavily, gripped the knob, and pulled on the door, thrusting it toward him as he stumbled into the heated shelter, quickly drawing his revolver with his free hand and aiming it around hysterically, the snow flying in behind him and melting on the wooden flooring.

Once he saw there was no life inside, he holstered his weapon and began looking around. He saw the rock and cement fireplace that had a fire burning wildly within it. It was at the back of the room, and provided a deep warmth that fought brilliantly against the winter's cold. It was at the center of the Hillberry Settlement, its interior wood flooring creaking with every one of William's steps. The wood was a dull, dying grey, only lightened by the orange glow from the fireplace. There was an old wooden table at the center, stacked with varying forms of canned goods. They were piled three feet high, enough for the members that stayed within. Thin blankets were spread around the fire like a carpet, and appeared to be the place where the people would sleep. There was a set of stairs that were caved in, built in the left corner of the room, which led to the second story. William traced the stairs with his eyes, leading him to the ceiling, only to notice a very uncomfortable bend of the roof that he stood under. Some spots on the ceiling were broken entirely open, giving sight to the heavens above, where sheets of white snow flew with the wind, while others were slightly more sturdy. He looked at the walls of the settlement and noticed they were built of the same wood and roughly the same shape, for they too had holes that gave clear sight to the outside world, letting snow fall through and instantly melt. William looked at the front of the fireplace and noticed a steaming pile of wood, stacked in a perfect triangle and placed only a few feet from the fire's heat to dry the frozen fuel. This wooden pyramid was an ideal means for thawing and drying frozen wood.

William's breathing started to slow, though the baby's crying had not ceased. He limped over to the fireplace and removed her wrapping, then placed her down in the blanketed area surrounding it so that she might warm at a safe distance from the fire. He sat beside her with a hard fall, straightening out his injured left leg with a painful stretch of the skin. He looked at the bullet hole that ran through the outer sides of his jeans. At the same time, the snow dripped from the crying baby's face as it turned from ice to water. He noticed the bullet had run through the outside of his leg and only penetrated the outer layer of skin, leaving a bloody bullet hole in the front of his jeans that matched the bullet hole in the back from the night prior.

The bullet had gone right through.

He didn't think about it much further as he looked around the fireplace for a cauterization tool—any familiar objects he had seen before that could help him with this. It was then that he saw three branding tools with iron crosses, stacked promptly beside the fireplace, beside him. He sighed and reached over, grabbing the metallic branding device, then chucked the iron end into the fire.

Suddenly, the front door of the settlement swung open with a powerful force, and Michelangelo stood in the doorway. He stared for a moment as William stared up at him, then quickly limped in and slammed the door behind him. He rubbed his arms with his hands as he moved forward, his movements stiff, the flooring creaking beneath him. Snow stuck to his jacket and hat, while thin pieces of the same frozen follicles made a home on his eyebrows. It was on his shoulders and all over the brim of his hat, and from the tips of his rider's boots up past his ankles. With every stiff step, Michelangelo moved forward, and the frozen flakes fell off his clothing, melting on the floor. He was beaten and tired, not just from the blizzard, but from the men who had done their best to take his life. He made his way over to the opposite side of the fireplace clumsily, parallel to William, then sat down weightily. The two looked at each other, then down at the wining baby, now no longer crying, but calming to a restful quiet. Michelangelo stared in silence as the heat from the fire began to warm his frozen body.

"You kept the baby?" He questioned.

"You'd prefer I let her freeze?" William responded coldly.

"Not necessarily." He looked up. "But the mother, yes," he said, looking at William.

"She's dead, Michael. You can be sure of that."

Michelangelo looked down at the blanketed floor beneath them and thought about what William was forced to do, the lengths he had gone to save the mother's life, only for her to die at his hand, regardless. He knew the principles William had and the feeling one gets when they have to violate them. "She was a killer, William," he comforted. "She was no different than the rest."

"So was Rosa," William commented back.

"In action, maybe, but nothing in comparison on principle, and you know that. That's why you saved her."

William nodded. "Yeah. I suppose you're right."

"No, I know I'm right. You're beating yourself up about this, but you have no idea who that woman was. I do. Her name was Harley Wilcox, Roger Wilcox's wife. The only survivor of the Four Horsemen's wives, by the way. Anyway, to retain her vows and inherit the Reds' position of power, she was ordered to torture a believer at one of the towns I had come across. At least, that was what they told me. By the time I found that poor believer, all that remained was a mutilated corpse that was covered in blood from head to toe on separate sides of the room. He was tied in the middle of the chamber, and the only part of his body that was not coated in blood was the part with a cross branded into his cheek. It's one thing to torture a man, but... to do what she did? It was clear she didn't just torture him, but enjoyed it. She *wanted* it. These 'people'... they're more animals than they are human... they enjoy what they do and the power it gives them as they lord over these believers. To them, it's intoxicating. Addicting, and much like any addiction or intoxication, it begins to poison you... and it's poisoned every one of them to the core." Michelangelo shook his head and looked forward at the table of food. "Apparently, these fools view Icarus as some kind of a prophet. Some divine seer of futures worthy of worship. That is what you don't see, Bill, in a way I can't quite understand. You think everyone out here is trying to survive in a world that doesn't want them no more, but it's more than that. This is no longer a game of survival, but the prospering of evil. Wickedness for wickedness's sake. This is the way things are, now. This is what happens when monsters take the place of men." Michelangelo spoke honestly. "We are the natural response to that."

William turned, and the heated metal from the fire lifted his coat to his mouth and bit down on the jacket, and hovered the bottom end of the cross over the top of his bullet wound. He pressed down on his skin through the hole in his jeans, causing it to sizzle and pop. He thrust his head back as he bit down on his jacket. Michelangelo looked over at him, then up at the ceiling to see the winter's snow continuing to fall. The hunter pulled back the iron and felt the immediate relief of pain as he released the sleeve from his mouth and breathed heavily.

"I don't want to be a monster, Mike. I'm *not* a monster! This will no longer consume me! If this is what it takes to save your life, to stop these fanatics, then I have concluded that I want no part of it." William rejected.

"Yes, Grim. You are. Whether you want to be a part of it or not is neither here nor there, anymore," Michelangelo said, looking over coldly. "If that were true, you should've made that decision a long time ago."

William breathed in heavy silence as he listened to what his nephew was saying. "Mike, I get what you mean, I even get where you're coming from... but how many more innocent lives are we going to hurt?"

"How many more are they? Don't get me wrong, the life of an innocent made harder is a tragedy, sure, but the hundreds of lives her mother has ruined are a tragedy more."

William pressed the heated iron to the bottom of his leg and bit down on his jacket once again, this time letting out a suppressed, grunted scream as the metal burned against the sensitivity of his underleg. Michelangelo thought about killing William right then and there, about finally doing what he knew he would have to do not so long ago. As he did, his attention was drawn to the baby, whose crying had resumed. This got on his nerves, but also reminded him that if he killed William, he would have to either leave the baby for dead or take it with him. Neither of these options sounded good, and truth be told, Michelangelo was tired and even injured at this very moment. Thus, he lay down and rested, the heavy metal armor on his chest being heated by the raging fire that roared beside him. William removed the iron and tossed it to his right side while he leaned his head back and took in a breath of relief, for the pain and bleeding had come to an end.

"Can you shut that baby up, please?" Michelangelo requested.

William breathed a heavy breath of annoyance as he glanced over to Michelangelo, already nearly asleep. William's arms extended forward and slowly lifted The Infant, only to bring it into his chest and lean back as he patted her, slowly rocking her side to side, softly shushing her to calm. Within moments, the baby girl was resting and quiet again. Michelangelo looked over, surprised. "You're pretty good at that," he commented.

"So it appears," William replied.

William continued to look forward as he did his best to ignore Michelangelo. His guilt was too great, and he was more concerned for the child than he was for anything else. This baby had no mother and was doomed to be left in the hands of a hunter and a bloodthirsty soldier. It was what he sought to avoid, what he thought he was better than, yet despite it all, in the end, he became the very source of his trauma to another, as another had become for him. Michelangelo saw this, and though he didn't care too much for William's life or well-being, he cared a little, though he didn't want to. More than this, he was curious about William's principal, this cardinal rule that he forced upon himself, regardless of how foolish it might make him.

"Why do you have that rule, Bill?" He asked.

William looked over, then down to the child again. "My mother... she was a good woman. She did everything she could to help me stay on the right path. To 'keep me on the firing line' as she would say. I remember back when they were looking for men to fight in the war, she said that if I went to fight, it would ruin me. It would make me into something I would never want to be, something she couldn't bear me to be either. The only problem was that I didn't see it that way; I didn't see it as 'ruining me', I saw it as the next stage of my evolution as the person I was meant to be. I *wanted* to be this ruined version... to be a monster. I wanted to feel that feeling of taking the oppressor's life, the same oppressor who stood above me and my mama and whipped us relentlessly. I wanted to kill an objectively heinous evil, and fight for my people of today and tomorrow. I wanted to fight for my mama and all likened unto her, to ensure they could see a better day, and every time I walked onto that battlefield, I thought of *them*. Every time I walked onto that battlefield, I thought of *her*. Every time I ripped a man's soul from his body... I remembered the horrendous things they did to her, to *me*. I remembered what it was I was fighting for: the beatings, the lashings. My mother would work the fields for long hours so that she wouldn't get whipped again. Some days, she wasn't even able to clean herself after a day as long as hers, and she would go to bed smelling worse than any human should ever smell. But regardless of that, what I found most surprising was how she never harbored even an *inkling* of hatred. It wasn't in her. Neither was her need to fight... to hit back against the men that abused her. When I realized that, I decided that I would need to fight for her. I would need to fight back, and honestly... I enjoyed it. Every throat I slit and every head I dismantled brought me great, *deep* satisfaction. I took pleasure in what I did. I fought for the people who could not fight for themselves, and with that tenacity, we won the war. It was only after we attained victory that I realized my mother was right: that war cost me everything. Not just who I was or what I could've been, but it cost me those I loved. After it was done, I traveled to her plantation and found out she had died long before I arrived. Long before she got a taste of her freedom, a freedom she *undoubtedly* deserved. I fought for many people in that war... but above everything, I fought for her. Or, at least I thought I did. In the end, I couldn't help but feel that I was only fighting for myself, and that it was I who killed her. Maybe because I broke her heart or because I wasn't there to protect her. Maybe without me, she lost the will to live, but I can never say. All I knew was that without her, I-I couldn't figure out who it was I was fighting for when I needed someone to fight for the most. All I had done for years was fight, and for the life of me, I could not understand what it was all for. Maybe both were true; maybe not." He sighed and looked ahead, a deep darkness taking over his eyes. "It only got worse from there. Most of my people couldn't leave the plantations they worked on... they were freed, but still enslaved. And myself? The only way I made it out was by doing more killing, becoming the 'legendary bounty hunter.' The *Brother of Grim*. So I went on killing, but regardless of the number of outlaws I put in the ground or the fights I fought, I could not find my way. I came to realize that without her... I was lost. I had no home, and when one does not have a home, it is hard to find reasons to keep on fighting, especially a good one, knowing there's nothing to come back to. I was a man in a position just the same as you: no north star to guide me, no God to take hold of me, just a hunter wandering the roads in search of his next distraction." He chuckled painfully. "I tried to tell myself that every outlaw I killed got me another step closer to redemption, but every outlaw I put in the ground only seemed to take me deeper into guilt and dehumanization, until I was nothing but a shell of who I once was. Now, I feel like I'm that old William again. That scared, confused, angry William that just needed his mama." He clenched his jaw and looked at the floor before him. "I developed my form of moral compass to make sure I never crossed that line

I could not come back from, which was clearly the source of what traumatized me, now that I'm hearing it. I wanted to set *one standard* to make my mother proud, to prove to her that I was not *all gone*. That somewhere in here, I'm still me. I'm not the man who killed her. That line separated me from the rest." He slowly looked up and over to Michelangelo, his eyes red with sorrow. "So I ask you, Saint Hart: what do we do when we cross the line that keeps us from evil? What do we do when we cut the rope that tethers us to our humanity? That places us among men and removes us from monsters, which proves we are more than savages; we are human. You found it, yet, '*soldier?*' " He looked forward again. "This war has required that we cross the lines of the wicked and cut ties with the just, and I don't think I can fight it. Not anymore. Not when all I am, at the end of it all, is a killer of mothers." William monologued.

William reached into his jacket and touched his canteen with no water inside that was wrapped in a multicolored and frayed bunch of string, a bullet hole blasted through its side. Michelangelo said nothing and instead stared at the ceiling, thinking over what Roger had spoken about the Brother of Grim as well as what William had just told him. However, it was true that the man who sat beside him seemed genuinely intent on helping him, on saving him from these haunting actions that tormented him. He had finally perceived who William was, underneath it all, and finally got what he meant by the two not being so different. He considered the possibility that William wanted to collect the bounties of the horsemen, but could not shake the thought that William might also, truly, be seeking redemption.

However, the more alarming information he was reconciling was that two people were saying William had known where Caine was all along, only one of them having an immediate gain to lie about it. Rosa gained nothing from lying. If anything, it only put her in danger when it came to the Grim. So, if this were true, why didn't William tell him where to begin? If William was trying to help him purely, why did William withhold the information? What did he have to gain? Was it truly all about the money? Could both be true? Was none of it? He couldn't ignore the extent to which William had gone to help him, for as many bodies as Michelangelo had stacked, William had stacked almost half of them. Then again, William had killed thousands before these men. Killing wasn't much of a sacrifice for him.

More than this, among the thousands William had killed, Thomas was among them. It was a confessed fact that William had set Thomas up, that it was foul play. It was admitted by two people other than William that he was involved directly with Caine Kingsley to a specific degree when it came to Roger's submission. Though his evidence was easily the least reliable and more than likely being used to turn them against each other, the more he thought about it and compared it to Rosa's, the more it made sense. Michelangelo breathed heavily through his nose, for in his heart of hearts, he knew what was true, but still he found himself choosing to disbelieve it. His heart was torn between what he wanted in all of this, though he wondered, *What if my heart isn't ripped, but I am healing?*

He looked over at William. "Maybe you should just be honest with yourself, Bill. Come to terms with the fact you're a monster. What was it you used to say? 'Acceptance is the start of a long and tiresome trial?' Perhaps it's time to start taking your advice and stop playing the part of a man built on a flimsy, moralistic foundation so that you can improve. Maybe it's time you understand that you are just some twisted old man who's too afraid to admit it like the rest of us, and needs help getting untwisted."

"Yeah... maybe you're right," William agreed. "Maybe this whole men and monsters rhetoric is a tired conversation."

Michelangelo nodded. "I'm starting to figure out that these days they're all the same. Calling them monsters just makes it easier to do what must be done."

The two looked forward and thought. Michelangelo considered the idea of William being a father, particularly of the child he held. He thought about what it would take to heal William from his long and painful walk through life. Furthermore, he considered the thought of letting William live, forgiving him, as he asked, and giving him a second chance.

"You know," Michelangelo started, "you got that baby just the same way I got the kid. Serves to tell us that we're not all evil, that there's something other than war that we can fight for, keep going for. Men like us were born to be soldiers; you, being one from a time long gone, now—but maybe we can be more. Fight for something more just than what we were told, for something more valorous. Like the kid said, we're like knights in a time with no chivalry. We are soldiers who fight in the darkest of all wars." Michelangelo nodded. "And I accept that."

William nodded slowly as he looked down at the baby and thought about what life he could offer her, if he applied himself to it. With even three of the four horsemen bagged, William would have more than enough money to retire and care for the baby he had fatefully adopted. As William thought upon it more, he quite liked the idea of taking care of her and had determined, with great responsibility, that this was what he would do.

"I think you're right," he agreed. "I think that might be caring for this little youngster, here. I think I'll fight for her."

He rested his head upon the warmed wall behind him and closed his eyes to drift into the night.

"Yeah," Michelangelo agreed.

Michelangelo laid his head back down and confirmed he had no doubts as to who he was, nor the purpose he had been given. Michelangelo believed he was the one sent to destroy men of evil, and though the reason had a personal motivation, it was still something far greater, as he always knew it would be. William may have reached his limit for blood, but Michelangelo was not satisfied. More than this, he needed to save Leonardo, and at the end of it all, kill Caine Kingsley. In truth, Michelangelo took great pleasure in the purpose he was given. He enjoyed being the Saint of Retribution.

"So, your plan," William opened. "Does it have any more details other than 'save

Leonardo?' "

"Nope," Michelangelo answered.

"And you're still gunning for Caine?"

"Yup."

William's heart beat heavily as he realized something; Something he had not considered before this moment: he determined his conscience would not be clear if he didn't tell Michelangelo the truth, yet the truth is often a taxing contender, and is hardly taken well by those who hear it. With the baby as his new responsibility, he wondered if he should risk revealing the whole truth about his involvement with the kingpin, for he knew if Michelangelo knew the entire truth, his vengeance would fall upon him. But the hunter was willing to wager that the soldier would be merciful, despite him deserving every bit of his vengeance. Thus, William determined in this new venture of guiltlessness that it would be hypocritical, even impossible, to leave things unsaid. It was only fair to Michelangelo that he knew the whole truth of what happened to his younger brother.

With this newfound heart, it was clear that William Davidson was alive once more, and the Brother of Grim was dead.

Michelangelo opened his coat and slowly removed the brandy bottle, popping open the cork to take a mighty and long swig. He stopped drinking and exposed his teeth while closing his eyes and swallowing down the numbing liquid. He proceeded to pull out his canteen and place it in front of the fire, now waiting only for the frozen water within to melt. He lay back once again, the alcohol taking effect, allowing Michelangelo to dull the thoughts that plagued his racing mind temporarily. He often thought about his failures, the horrors of war, the slaughter of all involved, and his dejection and retribution for such. He felt hopeless and angry, yet encouraged by the new purpose that had grown within him.

Shortly thereafter, the hunter, soldier, and the baby drifted to sleep with a wavering trust among one another. Although they slept on the same roof, they were not in agreement. William and Michelangelo had changed paths and hearts, and behind it all, lies and deception still plagued their unity. Still, on this bloody and blizzarding night, the truth would be dispelled, but only for so long, for William knew that the truth constantly cometh as the clock ticketh forth, and the truth would indeed arrive in the morning.

CHAPTER 10

The Unworthy Shall Fall At the Foot of Orion

aybreak had awoken Michelangelo. It was silent and calm, the blizzard having passed many hours prior. Dried blood was left smeared over his face, allowing for the olive of his skin to peek through under the hand-wiped, brown flakes. He had used the water in his canteen to clean his face the night prior, leaving it empty on its side on the wooden floor. The settlement was quiet in the early morning, save for the fire that was dying, lightly puffing and crinkling as it let loose its dying embers. There was no wind, no conversation, only the silence that one might find in the presence of death, made evident by the dozens of bodies that lay in the surrounding forest.

Michelangelo looked over to where William had been sleeping and noted his absence. He slowly and steadily stood to his feet, his body aching and shaking. His upper body was bruised and beaten, mainly by the impact of the bullets slamming into his body armor. Though they ricocheted, that didn't necessarily distribute the force, which shot straight through his body each time. He touched the tenderness of his chest under his armor and winced at the tenderness. As he did, he looked down and noticed the baby, swaddled and sleeping with a pleasant rest, unaware of the world surrounding her. He scoffed and shook his head as he began to assume the worst of William, that he had left them both behind. He was quick to come to this conclusion, but as fast as he finalized his thoughts, the first sound of the morning came into earshot: a horse blowing air through the lips of its mouth.

Michelangelo looked toward the sound, then leaned down, picked up his empty canteen, and turned toward the front door, walking steadfastly as the noise of the horses grew louder. The sound of hooves digging at the freshly powdered snow, light whinnies huffing out underneath their breath. He opened the front door to the settlement and was greeted by small and quiet snowflakes falling from the light grey sky. The snow had risen above its initial foot of height, and the bodies that were outside were now barely visible through the coverage. It had built up to the porch now, covering all the stairs that led up to it. He looked down to his right and saw the outlines of the bodies that belonged to the three horsemen.

Their bodies had been removed and placed somewhere else.

Michelangelo looked to his left and finally saw the commotion he had heard before: four horses tied together with a rope. Betsy led the front of the string, and the others stood behind her in line. The horses behind her had belonged to Roger, Blanco, and Bo. He recognized them, given that he had seen them stashed in the barn the night prior. They were impossible to miss or mistake: one was red, one was white, and one was the darkest black. The soldier looked upon their backs and finally saw their most important feature: the three horsemen, lying across their saddles as dead as they were the night before. Each was tied down to their respective beast, their bodies frozen blue and their limbs stiff. Rope wrapped around them, under their saddles, and holding them in place. They were now nothing more than a caravan of cadavers, despite all they had set out to accomplish. Michelangelo found this to his liking, but only slightly. He could not take much pride in an outcome that they were all more than willing to have. Icarus had convinced them that this was something worth dying for, though he could not yet place just how.

Bo's body nudged and jerked a bit, leading Michelangelo to look toward the body. He watched the pair of black gloves, which matched the black jeans, just below the black horse in vision, move and adjust the corpse. It was William finishing up his packing. The soldier stared, wondering how long William had been up to accomplish such a feat. More than this, he started to see the complete and genuine picture as to why William was here. His heart twisted as he began to feel a vile mixture of sadness, bitterness, and hatred. William walked around the back of the black horse with a tread through the snow that was now up to his knees, as he examined the work he had done to make sure no bodies would fall on the journey. *Was the horseman right? He thought. Was this all just an act to get the bounties?*

William wiped the crystallized blood from his gloves and looked up at a now-watching Michelangelo. This stopped him in his place, for the way Michelangelo stared at him was enough to prevent any man. It was apparent what he was thinking, though the scene was not entirely how it seemed. Regardless, William knew that for his valid absolution, he would need to present the truth forthrightly, warts and all. This was his conviction, his acceptance, and with it, he found the courage to make his way to the porch.

He casually limped up the stairs as he pressed his good leg down for support, lifting his wounded leg with the bit of strength he had left. His bullet wound had grown quite sore overnight and was made worse by the treading in the morning's snow. The frozen powder shot forward onto the porch as he stood atop it, just before Michelangelo, who remained motionless, watching his every move. He tensed as he came forward, though William had not approached in a threatening manner. The soldier eased as he looked into William's eyes, noticing the darkness that crept into his deep and regretful lids. To his surprise, they seemed to be filled with guilt and sorrow. He could make out a frown through

William's beard, despite it covering the entire lower half of his face.

From what he could gather, it appeared that, for once in William's life, there was no facade, no Brother of Grim. There was only William Davidson, as honest as he would ever be.

"Morning, Mike," he greeted.

"Morning, Bill," Michelangelo returned.

They stared at one another in a moment of silence, reading the micro-expressions of the other.

"I'm not gonna lie to you anymore," William proceeded. "Though there are reasons for doing such a thing, maybe now more than ever, I cannot attain peace leaving your side with a heap of lies." He sighed. "It's time you knew." He looked at the bodies on the horses. "I want you to understand that though I may be taking the bounties, that is not the only reason I'm here. At this point, it's more a matter of necessity than desire, but on account of you paying me half a bounty's fee, yes, I would like to collect on these men to end out my life peaceably." He looked back at Michelangelo. "I know you must feel that's not deserved, and maybe it's not, but if it's any consolation, I'll be taking the baby with me, raising her as my own." He nodded gently as he sighed. "The reason why I'm here, Michael, is because I care for you. Truly. That's what I've told you from the beginning, and that hasn't changed. I came here in hopes of helping you, of saving you. Of making right my wrongs, but... I see now there is no one to help. I—... I see everything more clearly. The war raging around and within you is a war I cannot fight, though part of me wishes I could. I know you think I'm here to help myself, and that is partially true. I wanted the money. I want absolution, redemption. To remove the guilt I can no longer carry. This guilt that weighs me down, and it makes my old bones more weary. I see that now... and in light of seeing the truth... I realize I must share it with you, entirely." He clenched his jaw. "The truth is, Mike... I did a horrible thing. And I can never change it. I don't wager that I can fix it, only move on. No matter how hard I try, it will always be what it is." William paused a moment as his breathing quickened. "It's true—all of it. Every word you've heard spoken about who I am or what I've done is nothing but the truth. I worked with Caine. I was on his payroll. I hunted every outlaw just as he wanted, and I killed every one of them all the same. I used those kids as bait. I-I set up the Brothers of Boudiclare, I set up Tommy, and honestly... whether I'd like to admit it or not, I would've taken down Caine all the same as the rest if granted the opportunity. Cashed in on his head, too, all for a comfortable retirement."

Michelangelo turned his face away from William as his hands rose to his hips. In his heart, he already knew all of these things, but something about hearing his uncle say it finally made it real, made it actual. Still, forgiveness was on the table, despite all the pain and death William had caused and the suffering he had inflicted for his own selfish needs. Michelangelo's nose twitched as his jaw clenched and unclenched, the sheer disbelief of the betrayal and honesty coming forth from his uncle being too painful to hear.

"After what happened to Tommy," William continued, "I just couldn't take it anymore. I figured... maybe if I could save a life rather than take one, then it would make everything right."

"Nothing you could ever do could make things right." Michelangelo rejected, as he turned his head sharply."How long did you know?" Michelangelo interrogated. William's heart jumped. For the first time in a long time, he felt afraid and vulnerable.

"You'll have to be more specific than that," he replied narrowly, though genuinely.

"How *long* did you know about *Tommy*? If you worked with Caine and you knew about the Brothers of Boudiclare, then you must have known about him, so *how long*, William?" Michelangelo continued, his voice shaking.

William's heart sank as he debated telling the truth. "Two years." His eyes saddened. "I knew about him for two years."

Michelangelo's heart broke more. "*Two years?* You knew where he was, what was happening, and *you didn't do anything to help him?* You didn't think once, then, to save him?"

"I was a different man then, Mike. You gotta understand that."

"Oh, I understand *perfectly* well."

"*I know no number of apologies can make up for that!* I know! *God,* I know! But I am trying to be better, to go forward better, to live better. I hope that in this truth, you will see that. It's only fair."

"*Fair?* None of this is fair, Bill! It would have been *fair* to prevent any of this from happening! It would have been fair to *save Tommy's life*! That's what was right! That's what was *fair*, yet here you are in his stead, asking for a peaceful retirement and a life to 'make things right.' "

"I'm a changed man, Mike!"

"You're still the same selfish man I met at the beginning."

"What can I do to prove to you that I'm changed?"

Michelangelo looked at the bounties. "Dump the bodies." He looked back. "If you're so different, unstack the bodies you aim to replace your rightfully robbed payday."

William looked at the bodies, his heart racing. He looked down, thought about it, then looked back up. "I have the baby, now, Michael."

"*Really?* You're going to use the damn baby to justify what you're doing?"

"It's not like that!"

"Then what is it like!?"

"You know *damn well* what it's like! That child's mother is dead! I killed her! How do you expect a black man to take care of a white baby with anything other than a boat-load of money behind him? She's not even mine, Michael. *Think about it!*"

Michelangelo clenched his jaw as his breathing through his nose intensified. He looked down, shaking his head. "What you're saying is reasonable, and I want to believe you." He looked up. "But I can't, Bill. I just can't. When I look at you, all I see is the Brother of Grim: a corrupt bounty hunter who kills his own for money. The liar, the cheat, the

339

manipulator, the 'legend' who only seeks to better himself regardless of the hell it brings down on others."

William shook his head, his eyes begging. "Michael, please, I... I know that I've given you no reason to believe me, but I *swear to you* I am telling you the truth! This once more, just *believe* me! Listen to reason!"

Despite everything and the potential for it all, Michelangelo, in this moment, could not believe that men such as William could change. He didn't believe he could change, and frankly, no longer wanted either of them to.

"You know what I think makes this all worse?" He started. "The fact that I wanted what they said about you to be a lie. I wanted it to be a hoax, a bad rumor spread by evil men that wanted to divide us. I wanted the man I once called uncle to be my uncle again. I wanted to feel less alone, and I let that loneliness, that misery, let me make excuse after excuse for you... But the truth is, I knew the whole time, and I chose not to believe it because I didn't want to. I wanted to remember the feeling of having a family instead." He shook his head and looked out at the forest. "Reality is far less appealing and often unforgiving, isn't it? It's as ironic as it is cruel, and the greatest example of this is found in my willful ignorance toward you. The hoax was not coming from those who sought to defeat us." He looks back. "It was coming from me."

William shook his head, desperate. "I cannot change how you perceive me, Michael. All I can say is that people can change. They *can* be different. Thomas taught me that. He taught me that I can be Uncle Bill again. I can be there for you so that you're not alone."

"Yeah? And what's that gonna require?"

"Forgiveness, Mike."

"Of course," Michelangelo scoffed.

"Let go of the anger," William continued, "the vengeance. Let it all go."

Michelangelo looked away. "You and I both know it's not that easy, nor is it that simple." He looked back. "That we don't just forgive and forget and go back to sunshine and rainbows. You made good and sure to burn it down, to burn our family down. Hell, you wouldn't even be here if you hadn't gotten caught. "

"But I *did* get caught, and I *am* here now."

"And yet, justice has yet to be served."

"There is more justice in letting all this go and turning away from Caine, from retribution, than going down this warpath that you and I know ends in your destruction! I know you know that. I know you know where and how this ends, and you feel as though you deserve it... But *you* deserve better. You deserve more, you do, Michael. I know it's hard for you to see right now, but so do I. We all do. Don't let this *eat you* from the inside out. Build, don't destroy." He took a moment to control his breathing. "We may never have what we once had, but we can have something new. Something *better*. That's what Tommy would've wanted."

Michelangelo's heart burned with anger.

"Don't hold onto this," William continued. "Let it go... before it kills you."

The soldier looked out into the woods. He thought over everything William had said, and even still, after it all, contemplated forgiveness, of letting go. Releasing the grief and bitterness that drove him toward his final destination. He weighed the thought of both outcomes in the balance, as the fire and fury from within him grew. He remembered burying his younger brother and how the actions of the Brother of Grim had caused it. William Davidson had set so many events into play, had caused so much death and suffering, sorrow and bloodshed, that it seemed almost incomprehensible for him to walk away with a reward for it. Whether he used Michelangelo, actually wanted to help him, or did a little bit of both, the fact remained that he was still profiting from it. As this thought continued to fan his flames, he remembered one final truth that, in his mind, would seal William's fate. He looked over to William as a vengeful rage filled his eyes, William's heart freezing as he looked back, waiting for the soldier's decision.

"You say you came here to help me, not to use me or benefit from this in any way." He nodded. "Yet you also say you worked with Caine, and even Rosa places you in his office. Roger would attest to that, if he had the mind to do so." He stared quietly. "So answer me this last question, truthfully: do you know where Caine is? Have you known this whole time?"

William's heart beat wildly in his chest, his throat closing as his hands began to tremble slightly. He clenched his jaw, his breath shaky, as he let out a quiet and fearful "Yes." Michelangelo looked away, his heart broken for the last time, and his anger filling in the cracks where it once bled.

"You said for me to let this all go before it kills me," he started.

"Michael, please don't do this," William begged.

He looked back. "The problem is, I've been dead for a long time now."

"No—"

"So has Tommy."

"Stop!"

"And whether you realize it or not, you have been too."

"Michael! *Make the right choice!*"

"I already have, Bill."

They stared at one another in silence.

"And I'm sorry, but you killed my brother."

Michelangelo let out a loud and deep yell as he lunged forward and grabbed William by the jacket collar. He whipped him to the side and slammed him into the wooden wall of the settlement, forcing snow to fall violently from the porch roof behind William, who was grabbing Michelangelo's arms. He finally attained a hold on both of them with a tight and powerful squeeze, as Michelangelo pulled him forward and slammed him back into the pillar, his hat flying from his head. The hat landed on the porch as William slammed down his fists on Michelangelo's forearms, making a quick window of

342

opportunity. He rammed his forehead into Michelangelo's, knocking both off balance but allowing William to counter. He reeled back his right arm and flung his fist into Michelangelo's left cheek. He flicked to the right, only for him to quickly look back at William, unfazed but more enraged. He pulled his right arm back and rammed his knuckles into William's nose. He stutter-stepped back as Michelangelo continually punched his face. He absorbed the shots, his head repeatedly flicking back, until finally, he raised his hand and caught Michelangelo's fist. William quickly countered with another right hook that landed in Michelangelo's eyebrow, letting out a bloody squish from the popped stitches. He flinched back in extreme pain, grabbing his eye, as William launched a punch into Michelangelo's ribs. This forced him to slightly wince, letting William recalibrate with a punch to Michelangelo's chest. However, instead of flesh, he was met with metal, a painful crunch sounding out from his hand. William pulled back his right hand and grabbed at his shattered knuckles as Michelangelo stumbled back into the front door, leaned on it, and looked up at William. He saw the painful expression on his face, the groaning that came from his mouth. Quickly, he interlocked his fingers and lifted his hands high into the air, stumbling forward and slamming them down across William's face. The hunter fell heavily onto the porch, trying to recollect himself on all fours, though his fuzzy head and blurry vision would not let him. Michelangelo quickly followed up with a sharp boot to William's ribs, punting him forward off the porch and into the snow. He rolled through the powder sideways as Michelangelo let loose another blood-raged yell, fueling his anger through the pain, his eyebrow once again dripping with blood. He charged forward at William, as William regained some of his bearings, the snow covering his entire body. He pulled his revolver from his holster and quickly aimed forward with a synonymous pull of the hammer, firing a bullet into the center of Michelangelo's chest. He stutter-stepped back into the front door of the settlement as the bullet bounced off with a metallic clang. He gasped for air as it left his lungs, while William quickly rose to his feet. He let out a yell of fury as he sprinted up the porch and rammed into Michelangelo's lower body, throwing the two through the front door and slamming them both into the ground, dropping his revolver in the process. It skid beside them upon the wood as he rose to his left knee, planting his right leg beside Michelangelo's left side and grabbing him by the collar, rapidly wailing ferocious punches into Michelangelo's face. The stitches on his nose popped as well, the blood spurting forward with every punch William dealt. Michelangelo's hat fell from his head as his face continued to take the hits, each one bruising and busting a new part of his face. He countered with a well-aimed punch into William's bullet wound on his leg, stopping him as he lifted his head in pain. Michelangelo quickly slammed his fist down on the wound again, forcing him to reach for it. Michelangelo pushed William off to the side and placed his left elbow on the wooden floor behind him, using it as support to help him gain bearings, his blood continuing to seep from his mouth, upper lip, nose, and eyebrow. His vision was blurry, his face and body feeling all the damage as he did his best to breathe normally. Michelangelo placed his right elbow behind him, leaned back against the wooden floor, and focused as a revolver hammer clicked, loading a bullet into the chamber. The soldier slowly shifted his gaze up to William, who was now holding his other revolver in his hand, aiming it between Michelangelo's eyes. He breathed heavily as his nose and mouth bled, the injury on his leg now bleeding through the white cloth that wrapped around it. They looked at one another and breathed exhaustedly, knowing their relationship had come to an end. William looked at Michelangelo and remembered who he once was, as tears began to form in his eyes. Michelangelo stared at him, broken and angry, but accepting that he had lost the match. The baby cried in the house as the fire had smoldered to a chill, the ashen wood barely holding together, with small spots of orange heat shining brightly in the burnt wood but dying with every passing moment. William's aimed revolver shook in his hand as he continued to aim at his nephew. He knew what he needed to do with the soldier, and his lips quivered as a single tear fell from his eye. He pulled the trigger of his revolver while holding the hammer simultaneously, unloading the revolver as he lowered his aim to the floor. He dropped his revolver, letting it hit the wood with a loud thud, leading Michelangelo to sigh and spit blood from the left side of his mouth, as he leaned back onto the wood, resting in his moment of defeat. William limped to the baby, slowly and painfully, as she continued to wail. He leaned down with a calming and comforting demeanor, picked her up, and cradled her on his shoulders with a slight shake.

Michelangelo stared at the ceiling, closing his eyes as he tried to process the pain. "You're a coward, Bill," he said. "A liar. Your legacy is nothing more than deception and betrayal of the ones who loved you most." He spat blood onto the floor. William placed the baby under his jacket and upon his chest as he turned and limped toward the front door. "You're a killer for Caine just like the rest of them," he continued. *"You don't deserve a second chance."*

William stopped in the doorway and looked at the forest in front of him, readying himself for the end. Tears dripped from his eyes as he thought upon the final image Michelangelo would have of him, one that could best be summarized as the relentless, ruthless, Brother of Grim. To Michelangelo, William was no longer Uncle Bill, nor was he family; to Michelangelo, he was nothing more than a monster who deserved to die. Regardless of how hard he tried, he ultimately failed. Failed to be the same man that he was to that eighteen-year-old boy that he had met many years ago, and had loved as an uncle would. *This is my punishment,* he thought, *for all I've done. Remembering him as family, knowing he will not remember me the same way.*

This, above all, was what pained William most; this, above all, was what hit him the hardest.

"I may be a killer, Mike," William agreed, "but I won't kill you."

He unbuckled his gun belt and dropped it to the floor, letting out a light thud as the holsters hit the wood.

"You'll pay for what you did," Michelangelo replied. William limped out onto the front porch as Michelangelo raised himself to his left elbow weakly. "One of these days, I'll find you, and when I do, *I will finish this!*" Michelangelo promised in return.

"No... You won't," William replied, stepping out into the snow and limping toward Betsy. He grabbed her saddle's pommel with his left hand and held his baby tightly in his right. He painfully raised himself atop Betsy as carefully as he could, then nudged her forward into the forest, the horsemen's horses following behind him.

Michelangelo watched William leave, which seemed to last an eternity. He breathed heavily and reached into his jacket to pull out his canteen along with his bottle of brandy. He sat upright and began pouring the brandy into his canteen, which filled the liquid canister to the brim. He chucked the glass bottle to the wood floor below him, bouncing it across the floorboard. He took a swig from his canteen and did his best to dull his reality, as something caught his eye: it was William's gun belt and revolver, lying stiffly on the floor in front of him.

Michelangelo sat alone for half an hour in the dim and lifeless Hillberry Settlement. Despite his having been defeated, he was not too beaten to keep going. He determined that he still had a mission, regardless of whether the hunter was present or not. The Soldier could still save Leonardo; he would only need some extra firepower. Thus, he stood to his feet and made his way toward the gun and its belt. He leaned down and picked up the revolver by placing his left hand on his left knee to support his pain.

He lifted the revolver and proceeded to walk over to the gun belt, hovering above it, gathering his strength to pick up the leather. He leaned down and lifted the belt with a firm grip in his right hand, examining its leatherwork. He holstered the blackened revolver in it and looked at the belt's width and customizability. With a quick adjustment via loosening its straps, he widened it to fit around his chest, using it as a makeshift bandolier. He removed his jacket and let it fall to the floor as he slid the bandolier over his right shoulder. Before he tightened the bandolier down, he adjusted the holsters upon the gun belt so they lay right beside each other, in front of his lower ribs. The grips of the revolvers faced away from one another, and the buckle of the bandolier was placed above them to the left, at the center of his chest. After adjusting them, he buckled the blackened belt together, letting the revolvers rest just below his metal-plated armor. This gave him agility and weaponry, which he concealed under his jacket that he had picked up and was now pulling over his shoulders.

He was ready for his mission, determined to see it through to the end. He looked through the open doorframe and gazed upon the forest as the snow continued its slow fall, wondering where the preacher was and if the bastard was with him. He decided that helping Leonardo was his primary objective, now, for this one was running on borrowed time, and in his experience, time did not wait, especially for Man. Alas, neither did he, and he had decided that they both would continue forward, regardless of how long it took.

A long and bitter two days had passed since Leonardo had left the Hillberry Settlement during the blizzard. His presence came as no surprise to the occupants of Guarida Del León. They were expecting him. He sat on his horse riding behind the last rifleman in complete silence, both making themselves ready to meet with Icarus. The sky retained its light grey complexion as light snowflakes continued to fall and steadily built up towards another blizzard. He was acclimated and focused on his goal, while his horse was tired and walked with its head down, its mouth agape, taking deep breaths that came out in the form of white, cloudy, and frozen air. He pondered the gravity of his situation and what it was he was doing on his current venture. He thought upon whether his venture was divinely inspired or if he had chosen a path of his own making. Surely if he had walked a path God did not want, he would have been killed by the blizzard that had passed previously. Maybe it was an exemplified miracle that the last rifleman had known of a mineshaft, strong enough to hold up against the winter storm. This was a justification Leonardo had given to himself to further his flight forward to Icarus.

The two walked over the top of the same hill he had walked over countless times before, only now, he rode over it with a deadly stranger rather than his brothers walking beside him. He looked over Guarida Del León, which was once brimming with life, his home; now it was nothing more than a desolate remnant from the past, blackened in smoky, war-torn rubble. In place of villagers who once made merry, some villainous soldiers laughed and hollered with one another. Fifty men occupied this fallen village, and fifty men stood in large groups around the camp.

In the houses that often held two villagers, the occupiers managed to fit six to eight men instead. Leonardo likened them to wolves that slept in a pack, for they huddled together in a warm bunch, making great use of the space they had, leaving no room wasted. The bonfire at the center was still lit, though it was not as controlled as the firestoker used to make it. It was large, chaotic, and roared with a wild dance, for the occupiers constantly threw whatever they had to throw into the fire to keep it burning. From furniture that once belonged to the villagers to handfuls of clothing, everything was fuel that helped them toward their intended goal: to fuel an ever-consuming fire.

Leonardo looked around at the horses that stood aimlessly in the village, the ground within becoming a muddy circle full of bookmarks and excrement. It was clear the men didn't care for the town. What was unclear to Leonardo was why they were waiting there, seemingly for him to arrive. The last rifleman kicked his horse onward, and Leonardo followed, the two trotting down the hill in the direction of Sophia's cabin, which was the only building that wasn't destroyed or occupied by the surrounding men. Leonardo looked upon it and darted his eyes around it for any sign of life, though sadly, to his dismay, she was nowhere to be found. His chest tightened uncomfortably as his worried thoughts raced through his mind. He wondered what had become of her and whether or not she was safe.

The attention of the occupying soldiers had shifted to Leonardo as the two drew closer, each one watching viciously with faces as dirty as the clothes on their bodies. Leonardo noticed that the soldiers were wearing warmer clothing that they had picked up from the villagers' homes. Each of the soldiers smiled wickedly at Leonardo as he passed between the groups, taunting and mocking him, which only fueled the anger building within his heart. Their teeth were yellow, and their hair was waxy and uncombed. The grime on their faces was the same as the versions of it underneath their fingernails. Their clothing was covered in blood and soot, and they were broad and tall, similar to the ones Leonardo had preached to in Little York, only now they were visible, in all their disgusting presentation. Still, he tried not to pay them too much mind and stayed focused on the mission: *Sophia. Icarus. Sophia. Icarus,* he thought.

The rifleman stopped in front of her home. Leonardo quickly did the same. "We're here, preacher," The last rifleman informed.

Leonardo wondered who or what might be inside, as he nodded his head once and hopped off his horse, his boots splatting into the mud. He looked around Guarida Del León once again, taking note of the soldiers who watched his every move, gazing upon him like an uncaught meal in a den of wolves. He turned and looked at the front door of Sophia's cabin, noting the light that flickered underneath the doorframe. He walked toward it and smelled the pine that burned in the cabin's fireplace, the crackling and popping of its warmth. His heart beat viciously in his chest; he debated turning back and running away. *If I run now,* he figured, I could hide forever. *Never be seen or heard from again.* This was, of course, assuming he could escape fifty men and live guiltily with the thought of dooming Sophia along with countless believers. Despite his struggle with his faith, he still determined that running away from Icarus was an act of cowardice that would result in more believers dying in his stead. It was all too much, too heavy, and as his hand froze just before the cabin door's handle, his hands shook, afraid, unsure, and out of place.

He slowly pulled his hand back, the rifleman watching in intrigue. He turned to him, letting him know with his eyes that he couldn't do it, didn't want to do it. He was trying to run. The rifleman smirked and slowly raised his right arm, pointing out just beyond the village's borders. The other men watched and smiled as Leonardo followed the finger's point, tracing it to something he had not seen before: just past the left side of Jordan's home, there was an unfamiliar pile. As he fully turned to it, squinting his eyes and focusing, he realized what it was: a pile of bodies left in the snow, branded with up-side-down crosses, frozen, and unceremoniously disposed. He looked at the faces of the bodies and saw the people he had once known and cared for, some of whose mouths were agape, almost all with their eyes open, their skin pale, grey, and purple, and a thin layer of snow covering them, keeping them slightly preserved.

Leonardo's breathing intensified as his nostrils flared and his eyebrows bent down into a piercing anger. His emotions raged within him, taking control once again and forcing reason and fear out of his mind, replacing them with fiery impulsivity. He turned and burst through Sophia's front door, rushing into her cabin as he looked forward in a manic and wild expression. *"Show yourself, you coward!"* He screamed, seeing who sat before him.

Leonardo halted in place as he saw Icarus sitting in Leonardo's wooden chair, his muddy boots propped up on Sophia's table, carving a little wooden figure in his hands with a Bowie knife. He looked up from his wooden carving and, at Leonardo, under the brim of his stampede hat, his smile slowly grew. Leonardo glanced at Icarus's wooden carving: it was a lion that Icarus held up just a bit and rotated in his hands. Leonardo looked back at Icarus as he placed the carving back in his lap, both reading one another. Up until this point, neither had met the other, yet both lived up to the stories they were told. *Bullet hole through the right side brim, sheepskin vest, gun belt with no ammunition, worn material,* Leonardo thought.

Prideful preacher, Icarus thought as well.

The only difference between the stories Leonardo had heard and now was that his face was bruised, and his lip was slightly busted. He figured this must have come from the beating he had recently taken from Michelangelo in Little York. Meanwhile, to Icarus, the only new and notable feature was the blood that coated his jacket, hands, and sleeves. He didn't have to take too many guesses as to whose blood it was, but either way, the thought of it being his brothers' made him glad.

Leonardo noticed this and clenched his jaw along with his fists. Icarus placed the handle of his knife on his thigh and held his carved lion in his hand on the other, the black steel reflecting the fire's light.

"Leonardo DelMuerto! As I live and breathe. I am glad to see you!" Icarus opened, honestly. "Though you are a lot shorter than I imagined."

"Where's Sophia?" Leonardo asked sternly.

Icarus chuckled. "You got a fire in your soul, Mr. Muerto. I respect that. In all honesty, it's because it reminds me of me." He lifted his boots from Sophia's table and placed them firmly on the wooden floor, leaning forward in the chair as he continued to whittle away at his lion. "I suppose that is the crux of the human being. We are always so... shallow. So surface level. We rarely dare to see what's *really* underneath."

"Where *is she!*"

Icarus looked up with his eyes just underneath his brim, smiled again, then went back to whittling."Easy there, valiant one. The girl's fine." He examined the carving. "In fact, before we get started, why don't we make sure that everything is in order. For example," he said, pointing to Leonardo with the tiny idol. "I believe you have something that belongs to me. I'd like it back."

Leonardo was confused. "What are you talking about?"

"You know what I'm talking about. Come on. Don't play dumb."

The preacher froze as his mind raced to figure out how Icarus knew about his revolver, for Leonardo had not told a single person, nor shown Icarus where it might be. Regardless, he slowly pulled the handgun from the back of his pants and placed it on Sophia's table. Icarus looked at the revolver and was surprised by what Leonardo had produced, but was nonetheless pleased with his compliance.

" 'Appreciate that," Icarus thanked, grabbing his revolver and placing it back in his holster. He looked up at the now more put-off Leonardo and smiled out of the corner of his mouth, pointing over to the open chair opposite him with his lion idol. Leonardo looked at it, remembering it was the same one that Sophia liked to sit at.

"It don't become any more of a chair the longer you stare at it. Have a seat," Icarus commanded.

Leonardo walked over to it, taking the opportunity to look around the cabin's main room, then to Sophia's, noticing that it was bound shut tightly with a rope around the handle. He sat in the chair and looked at Icarus as he went back to whittling. The fire crackled and danced in the darkness as the laughs and conversations of fifty occupying men were heard outside, their horses hooving and neighing amongst them.

"The soldier didn't come with you?" Icarus investigated.

"No," Leonardo replied.

"Really? That's surprising. What about the huntsman?"

"Not sure."

Icarus stopped whittling and looked over to Leonardo. "You mean to tell me that you came to a den full of men who are all ready to kill you at a moment's notice, alone?"

" 'Appears that way."

"... Well, I'll be damned."

"One can only hope."

Icarus laughed. "That's a good one, preacher. Very good." He squinted his eyes in confusion, slowly shaking his head. "But why?"

"What do you mean?"

"I mean, of all the plans you could have planned, this is by far the worst." He spread his arms and gestured around the two of them. "Where do you even go from here?"

"What makes you think I plan on going anywhere?"

"Oh! Is that right?" Icarus dropped his hands, his eyes widening with his smile. "So what is this, then?"

Leonardo thought about the question. Truth be told, he didn't entirely know the answer; he only knew he wanted to come here. "I came here to confront you. To stop the bloodshed. No plans, no anything, just a man-to-man conversation."

" 'Man to man?' "

"I like to think so."

"Well, at least one of us does."

"Look, you wanted me here, so here I am. It's as simple as that."

"Hm. So, come to end the war then?"

"Something like that."

Icarus laughed in his throat. "How noble." He went back to whittling. "If only wars could be ended in one night. Wouldn't that be something? Unfortunately for both of us, that is never the case and will not have its first occurrence here." He pointed his Bowie knife at Leonardo and looked at him as he rested his elbow on his knee. "No, this war, Mr. Muerto, will not end with me, and it certainly won't be ending with you." He continued to whittle.

Leonardo contemplated what he meant. "Why? From what your men say, and what you have made clear, you want me. You've been hunting me for a long time now. I can only assume you started this war by those means, so why? Here I am. You've got me. Why not end it? If you started it, why can't you finish it? What makes you think that I can't, or won't, for that matter?"

Icarus laughed. "See, that's your problem, Leo." He looked up, vaguely pointing the Bowie knife in Leonardo's direction. "You think the whole world revolves around you. You think that all this is because you're some great central figure to America. Truth be told, the world as it currently turns would rather forget you than remember you ever existed. Yet, despite that fact, you still place yourself at the center of God's creation." He smiled. "Do you want to know why that is? Because He gave you gifts, right? At least, that's what I've heard you preach. He made you the 'walking Bible that's sent to save the oh-so-common sinner!' Correct?" He nodded a few times to the side. "Yeah. That's enough to give even the most humble man an inflated ego. A god complex, if you will. You and the rest of all them God-sent believers." He lifted his head, pointed his knife at Leonardo, and looked off to the side. "The only thing I can't quite make sense of is why." He looked at Leonardo. "Why did you come here, truly? I mean, forget the codswallop about the whole 'talking to end the war' nonsense, I mean the *deep* truth. Why would a preacher confront a bastard such as myself?" He leaned back in his chair, tapping the tip of his Bowie knife to his head. "That just don't make sense to me." He pointed the blade again. "Unless you came all this way to save my poor, old, wretched soul." He laughed. "Is that it? You come all this way to pave my path to Jesus?"

Leonardo smiled angrily, letting out a single huff of forced laughter. "If that's what it takes."

"Ah, right, right. The whole 'virtue' thing. You actually believe that? You believe I can be saved?"

"I would be a fool to believe that you can't be, and unfaithful to pass that judgement."

"Really? That's interesting. You know, the truth is, I'm already a believer. Really, if you wanted to accomplish your mission, all you'd have to do is change the way I believe, assuming I don't change yours first." He smiled wickedly. "That is, of course, assuming that is *truly* why you're here. No other reason."

Leonardo sat, rage building within his heart, burning like a nearly uncontrollable fire. Icarus nodded and pointed his blade with one quick flick. "See! There he is! That's who we're after! That's the reaction I was looking for from a man who's seen as many of his loved ones die as you have!"

Leonardo's breathing pressed through his nostrils. "What do you want from me?

"Again with all this me, me, me nonsense. See, you're still not *gettin'* it. I don't want anything *from* you, Leo. You have nothing to offer. Your gift, your information, what you stand for. It's worthless. 'Matter of fact, I couldn't care less whether you live or die, though, in all honesty, I would prefer it if you lived. It makes my job a whole lot easier." He leaned in. "No, what I want, Mr. Muerto, is to break what you stand for, for what people believe in. I want to destroy their symbol of hope, which, whether you realize it or not, is you. You have become somewhat of a legend, a hero to the common man. To those who watch, you appear to be the epitome of a believer. 'God's chosen man of this hour,' if you will. You're living proof to the ordinary fool that there is a reason to keep believin', keep goin'. Which is a shame because, truly, as inspirational as your preaching may be, it was never legitimate. It was never goin' to prepare people for the wickedness that was comin' their way, and I hope you see that now. No, it was far worse than you could have ever imagined, much less let on, and still, the people were willin' to face and fail against such odds, such evil. All because of your ramblin', your self-praise, and mockery of what you said you believed in. See, if you had put their hope in God, you could've saved everyone, though they would have died. But now? Now they're as dead spiritually as they are literally." He nodded with approval. "That's why I need a man like you workin' for me."

Leonardo chuckled nervously as he processed the audacity of the statement. Icarus squinted, unamused.

"You're serious?" Leonardo asked. "After everything you have done? To me, to my family, to my *people*, you think I would just start working for you?"

"Uh, no. That's never how it's worked. There's a lot more talkin' and walkin' we gotta do before it comes to that. I'm merely elaborating on your situation."

"And what situation is that?"

Icarus continued whittling. "That the moment you walked through that door, you lost. I want you to understand that; I *need you* to understand that. With the soldier gone and the huntsman presumably dead, or worse, all that remains is you." He looked from his whittling. "And here you are, sitting exactly where I wanted you to, facing off against an adversary that you are not readily equipped to beat." He whittled again. "Your odds of survival are not looking good. Your fluffed-up preachin' and big-headed tomfoolery never stood a chance, and the sooner you realize that, the sooner we can move on and get to workin' on fulfillin' your *true* purpose."

"My purpose is in Christ—"

He looked up from his idol chipping. "My God, man. Will you give it a rest? Who are you trying to convince? You and all your programmed razzmatazz that you don't even believe." He held up his index finger. "That is the first rule of evangelism: you must first believe what you speak, or people, the *real* people, who got more than two brain cells in their heads, are going to see right through it." He gestured to himself. "People like me. I mean, my goodness, your preachin' is about as shallow as you. They're those 'messages for the broken,' as I call 'em. Broken minds and broken hearts that look to be exalted as though they are gods, which is what makes them so willing to believe your con." He shook his head and shifted his body backward in the chair. "And they call me evil? Let me ask you somethin', and for the love of God, answer honestly, but do you actually believe *anything* that you say?"

Leonardo sat back in his seat, initially offended by the question, but unable to answer.

"Silence, I see," Icarus said, expecting. "I'm not surprised." He leaned forward. "Look, I'm not askin' as a non-believer, I'm askin' one believer to another: do you really believe what it is you say? Do you believe that 'the Lord's goin' to save you?' Do you believe He's goin' to 'come over the hillside and swoop down and pick you up out of the jaws of evil?' Those are your words, not mine." A certain darkness fell over his eyes. "Did you believe He was goin' to save your brothers? Save your people?"

Leonardo retained eye contact with Icarus, though his ability to answer such simple questions was stuttered by the absurdity of the points Icarus was making. "I believe that God always wins in the end," he replied, unconfidently.

Icarus rolled his eyes and shook his head. "Ah, that ain't no answer. That's barely faith. That's surface-level." He crossed his arms. "You do realize that you can answer me honestly, correct? Just so we're clear, I am the only man alive who will reasonably hear you out and appreciate your honesty. That's what I'm trying to get *you* to see. These people that you fight for, these 'believers?' " He gestured outside to the pile of bodies. "They couldn't have cared less about you. They only cared about themselves, and that's why your preaching worked so well, because they were drawn to it like birds of a feather. That's also why they have those upside-down crosses on their face. That's why I had my men retrieve their bodies, to *show you* their hypocrisy. They betrayed their God, they said they loved, and then came to kill me. I mean, how make-believe can you get?" He shook his head. "If they don't care, why do you? Why do you try to help these people who don't even want it? Why put yourself through all this torment so that they can 'be saved?' It doesn't seem fair to a man with your capabilities."

"Nothing is more rewarding than the Lord's work—"

"Seriously? Dig deeper, Leo. Come on." He leaned forward and pointed at Leonardo's heart. "See, I know deep down you're nothing but a make-believer. You may have fooled everyone else, but not me. You want to know why?" He leaned back. "Because I'm a professional liar, and I know for a fact you can't lie worth a damn. So, let's try this again: why do you help these people?"

"I am answering you honestly!"

"No, you're not."

Leonardo looked at Icarus in silence, his face telling the bastard everything he needed to know. He let out a half-cheeked smile. "See, not even you believe that. You may be a very charismatic preacher, but you are no liar. Deceiver, sure. But a liar? No. Not yet, anyway." He examined Leo's expressions as Leo looked away. "Let's try this exercise." He leaned forward. "Look at me." Leonardo did. "Ask it out loud: 'Why do I help these people?' Can you do that for me?" Leonardo hesitated. "Come on, now," Icarus continued.

"Why do I help these people?" They said together.

"Very good. It helps to hear it out loud, don't it?"

Leonardo thought to himself about the question he had never quite got around to asking, pondering why he had committed himself to this life. He couldn't quite place why he had trudged miles of muddy and snowy land for little to no reward, or lived a life of poverty when he could have had fortune. In his life of obscurity, he craved fame and could never understand why it was not afforded to him. He couldn't place why he had given so much to God's people, when in return, God and His people had taken so much away from him.

"So, what's the answer?" Icarus asked.

"I don't have an answer," Leonardo replied.

"Mm. Not havin' an answer is still an answer, Leo. In fact, it's quite a reavealin' one." He clicked his tongue. "You wanna know what I think? What I think you are and why I think you do what you do? Because you love what it *could* offer you. Yes, fame, fortune, and material possessions, all of that is splendid. It's enough to tempt any man to damnation. But really, what you want is *power*. That's why you do it. Nothing is more *potent* than when an audience cheers and beckons at the sound of your voice, when they heed your every command and call and do as you command." He chuckled. "Yeah. You know, my men have been watchin' you preach for quite some time. Months on end, really. The one thing they consistently report is how much you *love* that *praise*. All those women flutterin' their eyes while you preach the good Lord's gospel. 'Makes me wonder if they're serving God or serving you. Are they serving the 'patron saint,' or the One who sent him?" He shrugged and went back to whittling the lion on his lap. "It makes a man wonder where a fella like you gets his sainthood from, where you lead these people. Whom they follow: a man or Christ." He looked up, pointing his knife. "Now, if it were up to me, I would say a majority follow you much more than God. The ones who don't end up dead, and that is mighty rare. Of your 'converts,' a majority, if not all, have died or denied their faith, their God." He continued to whittle. "They were never worshippin' Christ, just themselves, or you, even. In fairness, you are a very gifted young man. Arguably even divinely inspired, if you'd apply yourself to it. But, as we know, gifts and callings come without repentance," he pointed his knife at Leonardo's chest, "and you, Mr. DelMuerto, are unrepentant. You know why? Because you don't know what you're fighting for or if you even should be, which is a question you should have asked yourself a long time ago."

Leonardo thought about the real reason why he had come to confront Icarus, what the bastard was saying. He considered what it was he was after. Leonardo could not place it, not entirely because he didn't know, but because he didn't want to admit it.

"The thing is, Leonardo," Icarus continued, dropping the point of his knife, "you're guilty. Guilty as sin, and I know why: you blame yourself for all that's happened. The dead, both spiritually and physically—the ones you 'saved' from damnation." He chuckled. "The damned and the dead are all that remains of your ministry. Now, you can blame many people for that, as we know you have: you can blame God, which is reasonable; blame yourself, which you did; or blame me. All are good blames, in my opinion, but it doesn't change the fact that your ministry, God or not, and me excluded, was an empty one. I think you know that." He went back to whittling. "Yeah. I think you know that I was just a catalyst that exposed the fraudulence of your evangelism. I'd argue that's why God allowed it. Your people are dead, more than half in Hell, and all because you never got your 'act' together." He looked up, smiling proudly. "See what I did there?" Leonardo was not amused. Icarus shrugged and continued to whittle. "Your brothers are dead because of you, too, you know. You could never just stand on your own two legs—be a man, for once. You always had to have everyone else there to support you, and why?" He looked up. "Because you're 'a troubled teen.' " Icarus laughed. "Lord help us for what's to come next for humanity if you are its savior." He shook his head and whittled again. "You feed off everyone you love like a cancer, because you *crave* that attention like a desperate whore, insufficiently attended to by her father, and thus, seeking any form of validation elsewhere." He looked up. "You're pathetic. What's worse is that even with all the support you could have possibly had, you still couldn't save a one. Not your brothers, not your people. Hell, it's arguable you can't even save yourself." He laughed. "You had not just one, but two bloodthirsty killers ready to protect you, and you came here for what? To kill me? Save me? You don't even have a plan, and the one solution you had, you left behind!" He shook his head, laughing harder. "Oh, gee. My, that's funny." He wiped his eyes with his hand, wielding the Bowie knife. "No, it's the guilt, isn't it? It's all this put together. See, only guilt makes the coward less cowardly and the heroic herculean. The only difference is that a coward faces his guilt to save his skin, while the hero faces his to save others." He started whittling again. "So what are you, Mr. Muerto? Who do you face your guilt for? Who are you here to save?"

Leonardo's mind raced as he searched for an answer, digging through his mind and soul to decipher why he was there. The consequences of his compulsive, passionate decisions had finally reared their ugly heads, and he was now faced with an existential crisis: he was being forced to discover his true self, and Icarus had successfully begun guiding him to the one he truly wanted. He watched out of the corner of his eye as Leonardo looked down at the floorboard, defeat weighing on him. He smiled, having successfully trapped Leonardo in the confines of his mind. He looked at his whittled lion, turned it gently, then gripped it in his hand. "Well, who the hell am I to judge?" He stood to his feet. "I'm sure whatever conclusion you come to will be the best one. After all, all things work for good, and so on." He sheathed his blade. "Ready when you are."

Leonardo looked up at Icarus, far more defeated than when he walked in. He slowly stood to his feet, realizing then that he was the same height as Icarus, as he looked at the smile that formed through the side of his mouth. He let out a whistle, and in the instant, a stagecoach could be heard coming around the back side of the building. "You know," Icarus started, making his way over to Sophia's door. "A preacher's power is good and all, but if you want real, *tangible* power, you don't use love." He removed the rope that had tied the door shut, only to look back at Leonardo in antagonistic enjoyment. "You use fear."

Icarus opened Sophia's door, revealing her wide-eyed expression as she looked at Leonardo from the shadows. Leonardo was released, his heart filling with joy as their eyes connected, her smile spreading in the darkness. "Leo!" she cried in relief, rushing forward into the cabin room's light, embracing him, sinking her face into his chest. They smiled, the two squeezing each other tighter than they ever had before. "I thought I lost you," she revealed. "I thought he killed you," she cried, burying her face deeper in Leonardo's chest. "No, it's okay," he comforted. "I'm here." Sophia slowly pulled away, her face coming into the light as Leonardo looked down, seeing the upside-down cross branded into her face. His smile began to fade, his eyes widening as the realization that she had survived came with the fact that she had been damned. She noticed him looking at her injury and quickly reached up to cover her cheek. Her eyes filled with worry and dread as his eyes filled with morbid guilt and sorrow. "No, no, Leo, it's okay! I'm here, that's what matters!" He started to look away from her. "Look at me! Look at me!" She exclaimed, grabbing his cheek and turning his head toward her. He looked back at her, then slowly began to distance himself.

"You know, this reminds me of a metaphor I came up with not too long ago," Icarus began. "I had seen this piece of ashen wood burned to a crisp. Still, it held its form sturdily despite its emptiness. I remember when I kicked it, it burst into ash and crumbled to the ground like nothin'." Leonardo and Sophia looked into each other's eyes, Sophia clamoring gently for Leonardo, tears falling down her face. "I remembered saying to my-self, 'This is like a lot of believers. They present this illusory sturdiness, this unbreakable image, but the moment you hit them with the slightest push in any direction, they crum-ble to pieces.'" He smiled. "Ashen wood is all a majority of you are."

Sophia grabbed Leonardo by the arms, forcing him to stop. "Leonardo, *stop, please!*"

"Why did you do it, Sophia?" He asked brokenly.

"For you! I-I did it for you, so you wouldn't be alone!" Sophia cried. "Can't you see that?" She gripped his leather collar as he began to walk backward toward the front door, his face now a broken mess, his guilt overtaking him.

"You hear that, Leo? She chose *you* over God. She chose *you* over her eternal life.

She valued this moment more than the infinite ones she could have had! Now, what does that say about *you*? For as a man is, so is he reflected in his wife, and here I stand before two cowards, one of whom is a spineless bastard, and the other, his fiancée, set to be wed to a man-child that cannot stand on his own, requiring his woman to stand up for him!"

"Leo! Say something! *Please!*" Sophia sobbed as he removed her hands from his jacket.

Icarus walked behind him and opened the front door.

"*Leo!*" She pleaded, tears flowing from her eyes as she cried bitterly.

He stepped backward fearfully as Sophia fell to her knees in front of the door, reaching for him with her right hand as her left hand balled into a fist in front of her heart. Icarus smiled, looked down at his lion, and then tossed the tiny idol forward into the fireplace. He turned and walked out the front door, leaving Sophia, as Leonardo did the same, walking backwards into Sophia's front yard.

"Leo, just say something, *anything! Please!*" She begged, her voice trembling as she spoke, attempting to control her tears. He stared blankly as what he felt was the weight of a thousand boulders had been placed on his shoulders, rendering him unable to speak. Icarus grabbed the front door handle, waiting for Leonardo to say something as he looked between the two. "Well? Come on, lover boy. Say somethin.'" Leonardo shook his head, unable to speak, and instead, turned his back, looking at the snow beneath him in shock. "Damn," Icarus commented, looking at Sophia. "And I thought I was heartless."

Sophia's face tightened brokenly as her tears flowed in full force. She held her face with her dirtied hands and lurched forward, squeezing her hands to her chest as she sobbed uncontrollably. Icarus slammed the door and began walking towards the coach in front of Leonardo. "You, Leonardo DelMuerto, are one cold-hearted son of a bitch." Icarus affirmed, walking to the stagecoach. "That's good. I can work with that," he said, opening the door and ushering Leonardo in. He looked up and walked over and in without saying a word, still in shock from what he had seen. Icarus stepped onto the foothold attached to the light grey coach and looked out over his platoon of men within the village. *"Gentlemen, we have got our lion!"* Icarus hollered with a smile. The men cheered as he shut the door with a hefty slam, the driver whipping the two black horses forward. Icarus looked to Leonardo, who was staring out the window, unsure of what would happen and where he'd go next. Icarus, however, knew exactly where they were going and was content with knowing all was going to plan. "Just remember, Leo," he started, "this war doesn't end with me. It doesn't end with you. It's one waged on principalities that have fought on for millions of years before us and will continue for millions after, God willing. All that matters, all that you must ask yourself and answer, is are you willin' to die for it? Are you willin' to die for them?" He finished, pointing to the pile of bodies outside the window.

Leonardo looked at the bodies out the stagecoach's window, buried in the snow. He stared at them, his shock intensifying, as the stagecoach wobbled and thudded through the ground. Icarus did the same and was pleased to realize that his efforts were coming to fruition. He and the preacher were off on a seemingly unchangeable fate, and within minutes, his men had cleared out of the village and formed one large battalion around the stagecoach, standing guard as they made their final leg of their journey. But above them in the hills, hidden away, was a man stalking them through a pair of cracked binoculars, watching and waiting for the right moment to strike.

It was the one sent, the one fearfully known as the soldier, Michelangelo Saint Hart.

CHAPTER 11

Taketh Wide Birth of He Burned by the Son

reaking from the uneven ground filled the stagecoach's interior as it made its way through the ground. The road was filled with bumps of earth and rocks underneath the snow, squishing and sloshing under the carriage's weight. Leonardo had determined that the coach had been sitting for a while, or that this one had once been thrown away altogether. It creaked and ached with every motion, for the wooden frame was old and shaky, along with the wheels that barely rotated. An army of fifty men walked about, some on horses and some on foot, all making their way up the steady incline that led to the place Icarus often referred to as home. His home, though broken, was an old and abandoned structure that was built during the time of the Civil War. It was at the top of a far-reaching incline that rose higher in elevation as the trail continued. The snow fell lightly from the sky as the day started to darken, for the sun had begun to set once again in this war-torn land. Leonardo continued to look out the stagecoach window, staring at the passing land and soldiers that moved by him. He noted the whiteness of the

pine trees that sporadically sprouted from the vast, white hills that surrounded them. He looked up and saw the backdrop of the land: an extensive and imposing mountain, consisting of black rock and fresh-snow-covered peaks.

This was Mt. Sorrow.

The sky remained clouded, though now the clouds had taken on a lighter grey that hinted at the winter soon relenting. Leonardo saw this, sighed, and looked forward again, having not said a word since he and Icarus had stepped into the stagecoach. Icarus hadn't said a word either, but thought many thoughts as he shifted his gaze between Leonardo and the pines outside. Leonardo had many questions and doubts that began to form in his mind, much like the clouds that formed above, tormenting him with guilt that weighed upon him, getting heavier as time passed. He tried to distract himself by looking at the interior of the stagecoach and its simple designs. It was a faded red and black, and the seats were made of old, worn cloth that shed cotton from its holes. Rips and tears had been made in the seating, making the seats fairly uncomfortable. The stagecoach's interior was made of redwood, except for the doors, which were made of black. It had three windows on each side, separated by thin wooden pieces, and was covered by old, ripped, and ragged curtains that had tufts of dirt all over them. The windows shared the same dirtiness, as did the coach's interior, with a dusty and unclean presentation that smelled of old, musty wood and cotton. Leonardo sat in the seat that was at the back of the stagecoach on the far left side, allowing him to peer out the windows towards Mt. Sorrow in a lost gaze. Icarus, mirrored Leonardo, sitting on the front seats on the right, now peering out the opposite window at the pine tree forest that surrounded them.

Leonardo thought about his brothers and wondered what Jordan would do in a similar situation. Jordan always had an answer to every scenario, and he always looked out for him. Alas, Leonardo was now on his own and had little understanding of how to handle the situation he was in, nor the grief and guilt that came with it. It was in a moment of light that came from the setting of the sun that he pondered a peculiar thought. *What if I answered Icarus's question?* He thought. *Could I save the devil's soul?* He considered the path of good rather than evil, the one Jordan wanted. It was the path of nobility, not selfishness, requiring one to live for others rather than oneself. He continued to look out the window as he thought about the dialogue one should have with someone whose soul was supposedly absent.

"Why is it you do what you do?" He asked Icarus.

Icarus calmly looked over to Leonardo, instantly catching onto the thought he was having. Icarus noted the preacher's line of questioning and was impressed that Leonardo had learned this trick from him quickly. He wanted this, this attempt to get into his mind. Thus, he smiled and bobbed his head, impressed.

" 'A broken man's mind is a one we should explore, save the ones that would first break thee.' " Icarus quoted.

Leonardo looked at him, then fully faced him, calmly, though with a look of disdain. "Your mind does not scare me."

"Behold!" Icarus said, raising his hands. "The great miracle! The river of man doth floweth forth!" Icarus humored, smiling. Leonardo stared blankly. "What?" Icarus asked, dropping his arms. "You don't get it?" There was silence. Icarus sighed. "Fine. Let me try a different way: 'and he shewed me a pure river of water of life, clear as crystal, proceeding of the throne of God and the lamb.' " Icarus recited.

Leonardo remained unamused.

"Shame," he continued. "I figured if anyone were to get that joke, it would've been you."

"I'm not in a joking mood."

"And reasonably so, I'd wager."

Leonardo rolled his eyes. "You asked me earlier why it is I do what I do; why I help these people. So I'm asking you, why do you do the opposite? Why do you kill them? Why did you start this war? Why have you done what you have done?"

Icarus nodded, then clicked his tongue once. "Trust me on this, Leo: there are some questions you don't want answers to."

"Yes, but to me, this is not one of them. I do want answers."

"Why?"

"I feel after everything I've been put through, it's something I'm owed."

"First of all, you ain't owed a thing in this life. You of all people should know that. A homeless man asks for money on the street; do we owe him that dollar? No. If the homeless man were owed anything, it would be a bullet in the brain to remove his worthless existence."

Leonardo gulped. "That seems a bit harsh. You don't know the homeless man's circumstances, any of the homeless people's circumstances, what if— what if he can't get a job? What if he's broken and cannot go on?"

Icarus leaned in. "Well, then it's better he's put out of his misery."

Leonardo scoffed. "You cannot generalize like that. Every person is different, all their stories are different."

"Are they? Are we not all a part of the same story? Catch my meaning: I can tell you're not readin' what I'm writin': every time you go to the Lord in prayer, does God owe you what you've asked for? Does He owe you a response to every beck and call? Did He owe you your brothers' lives? Think on that for a minute. I believe you'll find the answer is an overwhelmin' no."

"So that's it then? This is all about God and what He owes and what He doesn't owe. And you're what? Some kind of bringer of revelation who shares the 'gospel truth' with people?"

Icarus smiled at Leonardo's persistence. *Look at him tying his own noose,* he thought. *It's almost admirable. He leaned forward.* "Well... looks like someone is finally catchin' on. Though I would argue that I am only a bringer of revelation, a match of sorts that starts the fire meant to burn this whole thing down. I am not the only one. No. Regardless, I believe you're beginnin' to see that we are part of some story... some plan. We are all believers and disbelievers in a universe ruled by God. We are like His ink spots on a page written before the dawn of time. Now I know that you have every scripture of the Bible in your brain, so you know that what I speak is true. This whole scene, event, and story you're livin', and the stories of countless others are all pre-planned. Predestinated! To work towards God's will. Now, whether or not things play out perfectly is up to those with free will." He leaned forward.

"For example, say the shepherd is tending to his sheep on the grassy knoll—that beautiful grass that was made just for them that he has provided. Most of the sheep follow the shepherd's lead. They eat the grass they are given and live a simple yet livable life. But one day, this one sheep decides, in his permissive wisdom, that he would like to find the greener grass. 'Surely,' he says, 'the knoll isn't all there is. Surely there's more!' So, he leaves and searches, and eventually finds something that resembles a patch of grass, maybe even has a perfect view, but it comes with a problem: it's outside the fence. It's unsafe. It's un-protected by the shepherd, and the wolves, oh, those *hungry* wolves, they hunt. And they *eat*. Later on, the shepherd goes to check on his sheep and discovers it in its messy state. If it's alive, it's starved. If it's broken, it's bleating. But most cases? It's just bloody chunks—remnants of what was." He smiled, chuckled a bit, and laughed lightly. "Imagine the irony of the permissive sheep dying just the same as the perfect one, only it suffered far more than the other? But they all die, don't they? They all go out the same and inevitably are all a part of the same flock on the same field with the same shepherd." He paused and pierced Leonardo with a sharp look. "We are all part of the same story, playing a part that we have been sentenced to in this life of servitude that we cannot escape or control. Therefore, we owe nothing and are owed nothing by anyone. We all just get what we deserve, playing out the parts of the individual elements that make up the broader story. It's all neither here nor there. What matters is what choices we make and what we do with our circumstances."

"But is that not contradictory? The sheep made a choice, though it was the wrong one... but he still made a choice."

"Yes, one that God already knew He would make. Therefore, what point was the choice?"

"The choice is the point!"

"And you don't find that problematic? That these choices that people can make are all okay and pre-acknowledged by God, and He just lets them happen?"

"I do not pretend to understand God's infinite wisdom, the same way I don't know how a man such as yourself, doing such horrible things, can continue to believe in Him. How does this connect to why you do what you do?"

"You haven't figured it out yet, have you?"

Leonardo stared, dumbfounded. Icarus smiled and continued, nodding slowly and looking down. "You probably think I'm the sheep in the story. That I'm the believer that believes in God the same as any other." He looked up underneath the brim of his hat menacingly. "But I am not. I'm the wolf who killed the sheep and left its dismembered corpse for the shepherd and the other sheep to find." He looked up full-faced. "And I watch the other sheep from the shadows as they look at what the shepherd allowed, what the permissive will can create, and I scare them. I get them to leave. I get them alone, and then I *eat,* and I *eat,* and I *eat,* one by one, until all of them are dead." He smiled wickedly. "I understand my place far more than they do."

"So, in this story, you've accepted your place as the villain?"

Icarus shrugged. "Every David needs a Goliath. Every Moses is a Pharaoh. The necessity for good is only made present by the presence of evil, all understanding and recognizing the existence of God, though we oppose Him. This is also why most people only need God when they are in the presence of the Devil." He smiled and stared out the window. "Isn't it interestin' how people can get religious but only when they're at their worst? And even then, it's only if it conveniences them." He looked back. "But, then, once God delivers them from their sufferings, they forget about Him just like they did before.

I'd be offended, personally, if I were God. Imagine disgracing the all-powerful being of the universe, and despite all of that, He still comes back. He still puts up with it." He shook his head at Leonardo.

"Which leads me right back to you, because, in a way, they have an excuse: they don't have access to the whole Bible, yet *you do,* in that photographic cranium of yours. You have the entire thing memorized from front to back, yet you don't understand a single word of it. 'Matter of fact, I think I know it better than you. I looked in it and I saw who I was. I accepted that. *I know who I am*, and who *they* are. You, however, have no idea. You are as much a David as I am a Moses, which is to say, not at all. I am the one who is forgotten. I am evil among the darkness that stalks them in the night, hunting God's sheep, devouring some flesh and soul, while sending the few who keep their souls to the Son." He smiled wickedly. "I'm only waiting to see if you'll discover that you are the very same, only worse."

"I am nothing like you!"

"You are *exactly* like me, you just refuse to *see it*!"

"I would never kill believers!"

"Haven't you already?"

"No! That is you putting ideas in my head! You killed them, you did this by some sick and twisted way of getting them closer to Christ, but it is not the way!"

"You sure? I believe that's the whole point, is it not? If you die a believer, you get to spend eternity with God? Even more so if you seal your testimony with blood. It's a golden ticket, really. If anything, I'm doing them a favor."

"You are a sick man... one who confuses radicalism with revelation! The reason a believer believes is not so that they may die and go to heavenly places, but that they would live here as they will live there! They are to live a life of the gospel, and they are rewarded for such!"

"And they have gotten their just reward, have they not? Have I not given that to

them? Are those who were truly 'living the life' not there now?"

"So that's it, then? You exist to challenge believers? To send them to their earned end by determining who lives and who dies? That's why you do this?"

"I do this to challenge believers, yes, but also to challenge *God*. He's the one who's in charge, right? It's not the Devil; we know this. So it can't be me, I'm just a tool He's using. I'm a challenger He's allowed on the scene, so who's *really* responsible? Who *really* allowed this?" He crossed his arms. "Wasn't it you just a few days ago that stood before an audience and claimed, 'Hear me, hear me: God will not allow any of these evil men to do evil things! They will not enact any violence on you people!' " He laughed. "Yet, here we are. Here *I am*, very much alive, while everyone you've ever loved is either branded, dead, or a mixture of the two. I mean, your fiancé turned out to be nothin' more than a yellow-bellied make-believer, just like yourself. Yet you sit here and wait for the very same fate as those before you without asking once who is responsible for that?"

"Yes, and I recognize my mistakes in that. I also hear what you're saying and understand that they are good points, but free will is necessary for God to be just, and the bad that happens is going to happen as a product of that. However, that doesn't mean we have to be a part of it. Instead, we should love Him and serve him in the good times and the bad."

Icarus forced a gag. "Oh, give me a break with that nonsense. Do you even believe that? Legitimately, after everything that He's allowed to happen to you? Do you *honestly* feel that way? I mean, you sit here, lookin' at me thinkin' that I am the face of evil while you quote scriptures you don't even believe, while ignoring the fact that God is lookin' down on us, watchin' this all happen and is doing nothin'!"

"Stop!"

"He did nothin', and why? Don't you want to know why *He* allowed *me* to bring death upon this land? Why has he allowed me to bring death upon this land? Why has He let me cleanse out the filth and strengthen the real? No, you're more concerned with tryin' to convert me with your memorized scriptures, which, as admirable as that might be, is only an example of how effete you are as a preacher!"

"Shut up!"

"Oh, Leonahdo DelMuertow, you make me sick with how much of a hypocrite you are, *no closer to bein' a son of God than me!* Some mighty 'Lion of the Dead.' You are not a mighty roarin' lion, you are the deceiver who walks about as one seeking whom he may devour, having hopes that one day he might be worth the blood that's been *spilt to save him!*"

Leonardo screamed and lunged forward, gripping Icarus's collar as he pulled his right fist back, his left hand holding Icarus in a tight fist. He tensed and reddened with an angry and violent bend, his body furiously shaking. The stagecoach stopped abruptly as the surrounding soldiers aimed their rifles at it, waiting for further instructions. Leonardo continued to shake with an angry fist clenched harder than ever before. He blinked, un-clenched, then pushed Icarus back into his seat while his hands slowly raised in a sarcastic surrender as his face formed a smile. "It's alright, boys," he said, slightly laughing. "We're just havin' a passionate discussion. Nothin' to be concerned about."

The men dropped the aim of their weapons, and the stagecoach whipped forward. Leonardo eased his anger and sat back in his seat, controlling his breathing. His mind cleared as the emotion slowly drained from his body, all while not breaking eye contact with Icarus as he continued to smile proudly.

"We're all chosen to fulfill some form of purpose, Leo. Some of us were meant to be Goliaths and Pharaohs, while others were meant to be kings and prophets. I accept that I am who I was meant to be... I only aim to see that you do, too." Icarus manipulated.

Leonardo looked to the stagecoach's floorboard as he thought about what was said. Leonardo thought about how he would always be part of an overarching story, re-gardless of the choices he made or didn't make. He figured he could not change the out-comes of the events leading up to this, for they were predetermined and foreordained. He wagered that his brothers would have died regardless of the location, and Sophia would have chosen damnation just the same as the remaining villagers. He determined that Icarus made good points, and though he was callous in his methods, he made clear the motivations that drove them.

"Besides," Icarus started again. "It's easy to say what you said, having grown up without knowing true evil," He looked out the window. Leonardo slowly looked up. "What do you mean?"

"I mean, you've never seen the full extent of what God will allow."

"So there's more to what you do? It's not just targeting hypocrites and shaking faith in God... Is it something more? Something that would make you want them to denounce him, to damn themselves or die vindicated."

Icarus nodded.

"What are you not telling me?" Leonardo questioned.

Icarus's right eyebrow raised as he noted Leonardo's genuine interest in him. This was the first time in a long time he could remember someone having an actual concern for him. It felt good. It made him feel human.

"The depths of my actions are simple, really. I believe people should be aware of what happens to believers. Real ones and fake ones. I want them to look at them and see Him: a fake and a fraud." He looked at Leonardo. "I want them to look and see that in you, too. I want them to see who you exemplify. I want them to see the preacher who said they would be safe, bring them harm because of his arrogance and ego that produced deception." Icarus answered.

"So you're trying to destroy God's plan?"

"I'm trying to destroy God. I believe the best way to do that is to destroy you and all these remnants of faith that are scattered about."

"You're presenting an incomplete picture of who God is. That's dishonest; it's not the full truth."

"The full truth is subjective and dependent on perspective, Mr. Muertow. From where I'm standin', my understandin' is clear: is there a God? Sure. Is He all-powerful and all-knowin'? I would say so. Should we buy into the justice and power that He brings? Should we believe He is not evil? Why believe in such a harsh God? To that question, I answer 'no', and honestly, Leo, all that aside, you may put on a good face, but I believe you feel the same. I believe you are wonderin' how your God can sit you here, to look the killer of your brothers in the face and make you save his soul. At least, that's the idea, right? To save my soul? Or are you just here to find peace in your comin' demise?"

Leonardo sat quietly as his wheels turned, for Icarus' words grew ever more convincing and enticing. "You never answered my question," he redirected.

Icarus smirked and let out a huff of a laugh. "Yeah. I was gettin' to that." He looked out his window and thought about his dark and distant past. "What could make me hate these people so much, right?"

Leonardo shrugged. "If I am going to die, what would it hurt to share your reasons with a dead man?"

Icarus looked at Leonardo, perturbed. He shook his head, scoffed, and looked back out the window. Though he made it look like he didn't care, this legitimate care from Leonardo shocked him. He detected no lies and saw something different in the hypocritical preacher he had not before. Something genuine. He had never shared what happened to him with anyone else before, and was almost comforted by the idea that he finally could. After all, Leonardo was right: they were both reaching the end of their time.

"When I was a boy, I lived in a village much like yours. I lived with my parents. He was a preacher, a good one, too. Very inspirin', very charismatic. We lived many happy years together and were, as many would say, 'the perfect family.' " He chuckled sadly. "What they didn't know was that my father was a troubled man. He struggled with things that he found far too unpleasant to share, or couldn't share, really. It would ruin his reputation and, frankly, would have gotten him ostracized as a heretic. He knew it was wrong, and he tried to resist it, but eventually his temptation overcame him, leading him to betray my mother. When she found him having an affair, she left, leaving us both behind and never looking back." He sighed. "I'll never understand why that woman never took me with her. She knew how he was, how bad he could get. Who knows. Maybe she thought I was goin' to be like him, that I was more trouble than I was worth. Regardless, as a young man, I wasn't capable of understandin' such complex things. So, I took on the creed of 'Why worry? It's all in God's hands. We have no reason to fear, nor to question why He does such things!' " He chuckled. "Who knows, Leo. Maybe I missed my calling. Maybe I could've been a great charismatic like you." He paused.

"Anyway, after my mother left, my father was very understandin' of the matter. He did his best to raise me in the good and right ways of the Lord, and for a while, I was raised to believe in such things, and had strength in knowin' that there was hope for a better tomorrow. At least at first... see, my father, as strong as he was, he could not overcome his frustrations. His struggles only increased, and his reputation was comin' to a destructive demise when the local townsfolk started to notice a thing or two here and there. He eased the rumors through his lies and manipulation, mostly from behind the pulpit, but that also meant he had to stop his nightly engagements or public flirtations. He had to face his demons on his own, and day by day, that demon grew stronger, making him more frustrated, more tense, and more stressed. Eventually, his frustrations became unbearable, and no amount of preachin' or put-on salvation was goin' to save him anymore. I trusted that God would take care of it, that the demon would be conquered." He took in a deep breath.

"It wasn't. That night, just as sure as the moon rises, he came into my room and relieved his frustrations on me. Afterward, he blamed me. For everythin', mostly. For my mother leavin', for his frustrations. I recognize now that wasn't true, given he was the one whom the devil possessed, but that didn't matter then, and frankly, it doesn't matter now. I wasn't the same after that. After my childhood was ripped away from me as my world burned before my eyes... the same world that God created and sat above, doin' nothin' to stop what happened to me. He never did. Despite it happenin' again, and again, and again, until finally I decided, 'If the Lord won't protect me, I will protect myself. If God couldn't care less about what happens to me and my tiny, insignificant life, regardless of how good a believer I am, then I will do what I must." Icarus unsheathed his Bowie knife and held it up to the sunlight. Leonardo scooted back. "He always came in a certain way," Icarus continued. "My father. I could tell when he was goin' to come in and do what he did. It always started with the same words. 'This is your fault, you know. Your mother left us, and now I have to do this. How could you make me do this to you?' " He let out a blank-stared smile. "It's funny. I could've run, you know." He looked at Leo. "I could've left. Just run away and never look back." He looked back at his knife. "But then I thought about his position of power as a preacher and all the other young men in that church. I couldn't help but think about what he would do to them if he couldn't do what he was doin' to me. I knew he needed to be stopped. I wanted to stop him." He looked at Leonardo. "And I did, and as he came in toutin' his usual nonsense in his unaware manner, I pulled my bowie knife out from under my pillow and jumped from my bed and onto his chest, plunging the blade deep into his chest, slamming his wretched body to the ground, and I stabbed, and I stabbed, and I stabbed, until blood coated everything I could see. My face, my hands, my clothes, my arms, the floor, the walls, the ceiling." He looked at his knife.

"That changed me, obviously—that moment where I became the bastard son of a preacher. Mostly because I realized that I not only didn't regret it, but I *liked it*. Unfortunately, none of the other believers would believe anything I said, regardless of how much I explained, especially considerin' how much they blindly loved him. He could do no wrong in their eyes. So, I ran, and for years I hid and never stopped thinkin' about that moment. Never forgot the moment I plunged that blade into my father's chest, over and over and over. It didn't feel wrong. Didn't feel unjust. It felt *right*. The world had finally made sense, and I had done somethin' that needed to be done; I had found my true religion." He sheathed his knife and looked back at Leonardo. "I tell you all this, Leo, because you have seen many attributes of God, but you have not seen them all, for I have seen God behind the faces of wicked men and their lustful passions and how they can use God to pursue them, and how He will do *nothin'* to stop them. I do not doubt that men like my father will pursue it again. Therefore, I must ensure that they are not given the opportunity."

Leonardo looked to Icarus in horror as he took in the story that had been told, while Icarus looked to Leonardo without a smile, nor a laugh, nor a joke.

"I... don't know what to say."

"I didn't expect you to. In fact, it was never my intention that you did. All I want you to do is listen." He leaned in. "The people deserve to know the truth, Mr. Muerto. They deserve to live in reality, untainted by religious men. They don't deserve deceivers who stand before them and charismatically spew lies atop a soapbox. Most of these 'preachers' are not worthy to stand above ground, let alone a pulpit." He leaned back. "The crazy thing is, as believers, we know that God will come out victorious. We know He always wins... but hell," he said, smiling wickedly, "can you blame a man for tryin'?" He leaned back comfortably, easing his tension. "Still, even when he does it, it won't change the fact that the people will never forget what happened here. They'll never forget what'll happen to you. It'll haunt them for all their days, and serve as a reminder that when you 'serve the Lord,' that does not mean that he serves you. He don't owe us nothin'. Maybe that'll make some stronger, but for the most part, it'll only show them how foolish they *truly* are." He looked out the window. "I have done my best to scrub the works of God's men from this plane of existence, and I wager will continue to do so successfully. Maybe then the nightmares will cease. Maybe then, the nights will bring sleep, not terror. Regardless, I will finish what I have started."

Leonardo thought about what Icarus had said and mulled over the dark thoughts that plagued his mind. He understood what he was up against—how twisted Icarus's mind truly was, and could empathize with how a man could become so vile. Yet, even then, it wasn't this that scared him the most; it was that he did more than empathize with Icarus:

he was sympathetic. He even found himself agreeing with some of the points, although not entirely in agreement with the execution of the philosophy. *Maybe he's something more than a mad anarchist looking to destroy God,* he thought. *Maybe he is the answer to the God problem.* The God problem is not being God, but being self-righteous, deceptive, and cunning men. He understood Icarus's form of justice, of revenge, doing what he felt was right because God would not do it for him. He sympathized with this as well, still having a slight thirst for Icarus's blood while doing his best not to shed it. *Maybe we are the same,* he thought again. *All that separates us his how we were raised.*

Regardless, destroying the faith was not the solution. Leonardo knew this and knew that what Icarus had done and was doing, along with whatever he had planned, was not the proper approach. With this in mind, he wondered if Icarus would complete his plan, regardless of how much he insisted on it.

"What about the soldier?" Leonardo asked.

Icarus looked over. "What about him?"

"What if he comes for you? What if he tries to stop your plan?"

Icarus nodded, looking back out the window. "He was a great surprise, I'll give him that. Very unpleasant, I might add. Still, I believe he will not succeed."

"Why? Because you're a 'prophet.' "

Icarus smiled cheekily and looked over at Leonardo. "You don't actually believe all that shit, do you?"

Leonardo let out one single laugh and smiled. "I believe in the gift of prophecy, yes. It is scriptural. But you, a prophet? No. Clearly, no."

Icarus nodded with an upside-down smile. "Turns out someone does know his bible." He smiled and looked down at his clasped hands. "No, I'm afraid I'm no prophet. I'm just the guy who saw a bunch of desperate fools and sold them something they thought they needed." He looked at Leonardo. "I learned from the best. You'd be surprised how far a little charisma and intelligence will get you with morons, particularly if they're male. I just said all the things they wanted to hear and used spiritual mumbo-jumbo to back it up. You want the truth: I know how the human mind works. I know how to plan. You learn how to do those two things well enough, you can 'prophecy' anything."

Leonardo nodded in agreement. "So what's your plan then? I'm assuming you want to kill me like the rest. Make me a martyr. That seems like a pretty effective way to 'destroy God' as you would have it."

Icarus shrugged. "It's one way, sure, though it is the least preferable. There are many ways to destroy a man, Leonardo, and physically is only one of 'em." He leaned forward, holding up his balled-up hand, the back of it facing Leonardo. "You can destroy his body." He lifted his index finger. "Destroy his mind." He lifted his middle. "Or destroy his soul." He lifted his ring, then leaned back, resting his arm. "And you, Mr. Muerto, are in line for any one of those three. Whether you see it or not, as I've told you, you've already lost. By the end of this, you'll be one of three things: a martyr, a follower, or a successor. That choice remains yours."

The preacher and the bastard stared at one another in a moment of morbid silence, the lanterns of the army around them beginning to light the caravan while the sun slowly set behind the mountain. Darkness quickly enveloped the land, covering the snow, the men, and the pines of the forest. Leonardo considered the outcomes as he slowly lost sight of a fourth possibility: being rescued or escaping. He didn't want to admit it, but Icarus was right: the soldier was nowhere to be found, and even if he was, it seemed highly unlikely that he could take on an army, alone or with the hunter. So, Leonardo leaned back, accepting his situation.

"I will never follow you. Never *become* you. You're sick, and that's what separates us." Leonardo repented.

Icarus smiled wickedly. "Don't be so sure, preacher."

A look of remembrance came across Icarus's face as he raised his index finger and reached into his pants' pocket, pulling out a small piece of ripped and crumpled paper, tanned from the many miles of travel it had undergone. He folded it in half and held it out to Leonardo, waiting for him to grab it. Leonardo stared, confused. "Go on. Take it." Icarus encouraged. Leonardo hesitantly reached forward and took the piece of paper, then carefully unfolded the message:

Caine Kingsley
Kingsland Enterprises
Heddlebrook, Arizona
USA (obviously)

Leonardo looked up, confused.

"The words on that paper don't mean anything to you. I know," Icarus started. "I gave it to you because I want you to give it to the soldier, whenever he finds you, as I'm sure he will."

"Why?"

"Because I sympathize with the soldier's efforts. I find them compellin'. That and I hate Caine. He annoys me."

"Okay, but why me?"

"Because regardless of how he finds you, be it a corpse, a servant, or my replacement, it is you who is most likely to give it to him. Not me."

"So you do think he'll come."

Icarus smiled nervously as he looked out the window of his stagecoach, glancing between the pines as they became less visible by his men's lanterns. "You never know."

Leonardo's eyes widened. "Are you scared of him?"

Icarus looked back. "*You're not?* After seein' what he's done to a number of my men and how quickly he'd do it to you if you got in his way? That man's warpath has no mercy for the cruel, including but not limited to *you*. That man is as persistent as he is deadly. That would put the fear of God into anybody with a target on their back." "So you're afraid of death?"

"I'm afraid of dying and not finishing what I was put here to do. Dying and knowing that everything I went through was for nothin'."

"Maybe you don't have to die for nothing. Maybe there is a different way to accomplish your mission."

Icarus looked out the window. "I think you and I both know that we're well past that now. Not just for me, but for you too. What happens next is a natural consequence of the failures of the generations that came before us. There ain't no changin' that."

Leonardo put the paper in his pocket. "So be it, but the Major General doesn't come for my blood. He comes for yours."

"For now." Icarus looked back at Leonardo, menacingly. "Nobody escapes the hand of God and the retributive saint He has sent."

"So you're willing to die for this? For your cause?"

"Anyone who truly believes in anything should be."

As Icarus looked back out the window, noting that they had made their way into a forest and were now almost at his home, Leonardo thought about the soldier and whether or not he would end up in his crosshairs. He figured not, the same way that another thought had become clear: he didn't need the Saint of Retribution. If this truly was the way things were meant to be, and this was his destiny, then he felt as though he should face it on his terms, not by being saved by those around him, once again. He could take matters into his own hands, even if it meant he would become Icarus's servant, replacement, or sacrifice.

Leonardo wondered if all those who had been sacrificed, killed, were worth the outcome. He wondered what would happen if he let Icarus kill him and complete his task, if God could sort him out. Then again, he could stop everything right now, or at any time. He could kill the bastard before he had any chances to hurt anyone else. No one knew if Icarus would stop here, but Leonardo could make sure of it. It was then that he remembered Michelangelo's words about being changed forever, about potentially losing his calling as a preacher if he went through with it. He agreed with Icarus that odds were the soldier was on the way, but he didn't know for sure. Leonardo didn't fully trust him after what happened with his brothers. He couldn't. Therefore, Leonardo wagered that it was up to him to stop Icarus, either by being publicly executed or executing Icarus.

But that's the thing, isn't it, Leonardo thought. I want you to die. I want to kill you. You deserve it. God knows you deserve it.

The stagecoach began to climb a steep incline as Leonardo considered the situation further. A part of him wanted to help Icarus. It was what he was trained to do all his life. It was what would make Jordan proud. *But Jordan's dead*, he continued thinking. *They're all dead, and I'm all that's left.* He felt the hunter's knife on his side, the very same Michelangelo had given him for self-defense, as the fear, anger, regret, and sadness all began to overwhelm him. He had felt them stronger than he ever had before. *I get what happened to him. I know it was horrible, but what he's done is worse. Maybe it's up to me to do what must be done. Avenge my people, my brothers... Sophia. Stop this psychopath where he stands. Maybe that's my destiny.*

The coach came to a stop at the top of a gently sloping hill. Icarus opened the door and stepped into the snow, only to wait for Leonardo outside. He walked out and looked up at the building before him, an old and decrepit three-story one, a fire burning inside. Icarus made for the front door as Leonardo slowly followed behind him. As he thought about everything more, even after trying to learn why Icarus did all the horrible things he had done, he couldn't find any mercy or grace for him. It made it worse.

So that's it? We were all just your punching bag for your trauma? Your vessels for vengeance? His heart questioned as it burned with rage, as the faces of those he lost flashed before him.

The time to act was now.

Icarus opened the door and held his arm out with a smile, welcoming Leonardo in as he entered, then closed the door behind them. The only light that remained outside was the fifty lanterns that were held by fifty men, all of which were scattered about the hill of Icarus' homestead resting at the center of a small mountain. It was surrounded by pine trees and larger hills that circled and rose to equal height. The small mountain sloped down a hundred feet and created a circular pit at the bottom, where the hills and Icarus's small mountain met.

The pine trees on the hills reached to the snow-capped sky. They had grown thinner than most, but still concealed all that hid within their shadows, including one formidable figure, who stood in the shadows, atop the mountain in front of Icarus' homestead, watching through his cracked binoculars as he thought about the best way to unleash fury, to kill Icarus and his men.

CHAPTER 12

Or Findeth Thy Soul be Quickly Undone

 qually elevated with Icarus's homestead, Michelangelo stood in the darkness. He examined the home, which was more of a fortress than the former, and noted that it was situated in an open area, surrounded by snow, at the top of a hill, with a rim of forestation surrounding it. The climb down Michelangelo's small mountain was as steep as the climb up Icarus's, with fifty men spreading across the hillside with lanterns and weapons aplenty. Each lantern moved down and around, slowly filling the forest at the bottom of Michelangelo's hill as instructed. He looked over the men through his binoculars and considered his next plan of action, thinking about what he could use to make it work. He examined the slope that led up to Icarus's homestead, noting the few scattered remnants from the Civil War: walls of rock stood toppled over by years of war, while two old cannons lay worn down and broken, sunk into the snow. The snow filled every inch of the hillsides and continued to fall in slow, yet large flakes, covering every footstep and stagecoach wheel mark made in the ground.

Michelangelo noticed that the top of the building had caved in, but it made for a functional watchtower, though nobody appeared to be within it. He looked at the stage-coach, which was parked beside the building, wobbling side to side and positioned on the left side of the building. He lowered his binoculars to his chest, which filled with wrath, readying himself for the coming bloodshed. He was not afraid, nor was he ill-prepared.

He was ready for Icarus to die.

He reached over to Bleu and chunked his binoculars into her saddle bag, then used his free hand to ease her rising tensions, patting her on the left side of her neck. He flopped the saddle bag's lid closed, then reached down and grabbed the blackened repeater that once belonged to the Brother of Grim. He pumped a round into the barrel with a crack of the repeater's lever, then grabbed the leather strap of his double-barreled shotgun lying diagonally upon his back, giving it a quick shake. He adjusted William's gun belt, strapped across his chest like a bandolier, only now it was filled with revolver rounds in the divots across the front. William's revolvers were holstered across his chest within easy reach just below Michelangelo's left ribs. He reached down and felt the tops of the bullets in his gun belt, counting twenty-five revolver rounds. He then unbuttoned his winter jacket and tucked the coat's bottom behind his navy revolvers, ensuring there was nothing in his way.

He breathed heavily with angry breaths, building himself into his rage as he reached up to the brim of his navy hat and pulled it down tightly. Snow fell heavily now all over the land, and drifted in front of Michelangelo's eyes as it grew upon his clothes. Bleu grunted softly at Michelangelo, gaining his attention, leading him to turn to her slowly, and lean over to her to give her a few soft pats. "If I don't make it back here, you make sure to find yourself somewhere safe to rest," he ordered gently.

Bleu made no sound and instead only stared at him, feeling his uncertainty.

"It won't be long. I promise," he comforted, beginning his trek down the hillside, silently sneaking in between the pines and wading through the shin-high snow.

In Icarus's home, Leonardo looked up at the large homestead upon the porch and noted the dark, grey, and black wood that made up the structure. The porch, the doors, and the wooden windowsills were all made of the same rotting wood and were barely in any shape for someone to live in, seeming to be mere inches from destruction. He was in a large room that was ten feet wide and twelve feet long. There was plenty of room for those who would huddle in front of the concrete fireplace at the back of the room, with two wooden chairs in front of it. The chairs were made of finer, more modern wood and were stained to a mahogany red. There were two tables in this room, as it was the main room, and they were stained a deep mahogany red, contrasting with the light green lanterns that sat upon them, unlit, unmoved, and covered in a thin layer of dust. A dozen sheepskin hides were at the foot of the fireplace, each overlapping one over the other, working as a resting place for those who want to sleep and get warm in the presence of the fire. Beside the fireplace was a set of stairs made of broken wood.

He looked around and noticed the six massive beams built into the walls, their thickness supporting the weight of the building. The beams were placed at equal distances from each other, with four in the corners of the room and two in between the corner beams at the center of each wall. Six lanterns hung lit on them, one on each beam, supplying light to every section that the fire could not.

He walked upon the sheepskins just before the fire and stared into its orange and yellow light, dancing across his face and the broader room. The fireplace had a large, rock-like chimney fortified with concrete and a substantial opening at the bottom. Icarus stood a safe distance behind Leonardo, leaning against the table.

"Oh, how curious is the fire that burns within us," Icarus poeted. Leonardo continued to stare into the flames, his jaw clenching. "They say you look into a fire long enough, you'll end up lookin' into your soul," he continued. "I wonder... what happens when a man doesn't have one? What does he see then?"

"Why don't you tell me?" Leonardo bit.

Icarus chuckled. "Oh, there he is! Finally! I was wonderin' when you were gonna stop mopin' about, makin' a fuss of all this."

Leonardo turned around slowly, tensely, making his way to the table opposite Icarus, with a walk that was as methodical as it was furious. The fire cracked in the silence as Icarus stared calmly.

"What do you think the point of the believer is? Why do you think believers are here?" Leonardo asked morbidly.

"To suffer, mostly," Icarus replied. "Believers are meant to be put through trial, as far as the Good Book is concerned."

"Do you believe they have suffered enough?" Leonardo asked, stopping in front of his table and facing forward to Icarus.

"If they are still alive, then they have not found the limit to their sufferin'." He thought for a second. "Why? You wonderin' if I'm gonna make good on my promise and make more suffer after I kill you?"

"No. I just wanted to know if *you* still suffer, if *you* can still feel pain, being a believer and all."

Icarus smiled as his eyes glinted from the firelight. "Sure... if God were bold enough."

Leonardo sat upon his table the same way Icarus was seated, both six feet apart from one another, each holding their stare. Leonardo clenched the lip of his table with his hands, squeezing and releasing.

"Is that what you're planning on doing to me? Making me suffer?" Leonardo asked.

"For you?" Icarus began answering, unholstering his revolver and aiming it at Leonardo's chest casually. "I'd give you the preacher's discount: nice and quick, but violent enough."

Icarus pulled back the hammer of his gun, rotating the cylinder, his hand holding firmly to the base. Leonardo glanced at the barrel of the revolver, then back to Icarus, not moving an inch as he did. "It's not loaded," he stated. "For the moment," Icarus replied. He pulled the trigger, letting out a click, not phasing either the bastard nor the preacher. He slowly re-holstered his weapon and crossed his arms. "Honestly, it would be quick. 'Wouldn't need a lot from you, given that the people would see your corpse and get the message. They've seen enough tortured folk already; now, all they need is that final nail in the coffin."

Leonardo was offended that such a belittling act would end his life, that there would be no grand blaze of glory, no final act of resilience to fight against a tyrant. Instead, he would end as little as Icarus thought of him, as nothing more than a measly nail. His life was reduced to a forgettable hunk of metaphorical metal, which made him even angrier. His rage roared within him.

"That is, of course, if you decide to go that way." Icarus smiled wickedly. "You can always join me... or kill me."

Leonardo smiled back. "You know, my brother used to say that some people are so broken they're beyond a man's saving. For some people, it takes an act of God Himself to truly save them. It is like when you are lost in a storm at sea, and you wake up on the beach after having crashed. He used to believe that, though we may be His chosen vessels, it is still only Him who does the saving, and sometimes he saves without us. He would say, 'Man cannot save Man, but the Son of Man can.' "

"How pretty. I'll be sure to tell that to my daughter when I tuck her into bed at night, just after the fantastic tale of the pretty princess who rides her unicorn to save Rainbow Land." Icarus mocked.

Leonardo nodded once, then looked at the ground. "I know it's not very gritty." He looked up. "But despite that, I understood what he meant: Man cannot save man because Man fails. For example, I tried to save you, but it didn't work. I thought that if I tried, demise and all, if I did what I was *supposed* to do, that I could. I thought that maybe this was the moment where I would prove I am a great man of God, that I would prove that I am meant to be something more than a nobody from nowhere." He laughed. "And that was the problem! I never wanted to save you. You were right." His body tensed. "No, the truth is, I want to be the one who *beats* you. I want to be the one who destroys you, who *proves* that you *failed*. That you *lost*, and that everything you did was all for nothing." He shook his head, looked down, then back up.

"It's been made obvious to me the plan that God has for me. It's what I have feared for all my days: dying as nothing more than a nameless, meaningless martyr that will be forgotten by history, when *I could have been* one of the greatest evangelists of our time!" He stood from the table. "*I could have started a revival!* I could have saved so many, but the Lord has *refused* to make a way for it! Instead, here I am, looking into the face of my killer rather than the faces of the *hundreds that I could have converted!* Some plan... what kind of a plan places the survival of the faith into the hands of a killer? Why is it *you*, when it can be *me!*"

Icarus smiled slowly.

"If this is God's plan," Leonardo continued. "If this is God's will, then I would rather take the permissive route than whatever form of 'perfection' this is." He slowly pulled his hunter's knife from its sheath, holding the blade firm at his right side, angling it toward Icarus. "I will not stand here *while you continue to win! I will beat you!*"

Icarus slowly came off the table. "Version three, then," he said to himself. "What can I say, Leo, that God of ours is quite the conundrum. I'll never understand why He'd never trust you." Icarus stated sarcastically, gesturing to Leonardo's knife, laughing.

Leonardo's nose pinched, his teeth showing, and as he readied his body to lunge forward, a repeater round cracked off in the far distance. Both he and Icarus looked in the direction of the sound as a second and third firing of the weapon went off. The mountain range lit up with forty-seven men calling each other to arms at the location of the sound. Gunshots were fired out individually and blindly as Icarus's men rushed to the scene, doing their best to identify the shooter.

"The soldier... he's here," Icarus said fearfully.

Leonardo looked back at Icarus, the first sign of worry on his face. Icarus looked at Leonardo, composed himself, then stood tall, holding eye contact with the preacher as he strategized again. "If you were a gamblin' man, what would you place on a man facing a one in fifty odd?" Icarus questioned legitimately.

"I wouldn't know, I'm not a gambler," Leonardo disregarded.

Icarus noted that Leonardo had not changed his approach or mind. " 'You still plannin' on killin' me?"

"What's it look like, genius?"

Icarus smiled. "All the same to me."

The two began to walk in a circle, not getting any closer to each other.

"You want to know why I asked if you can still suffer? If you can feel pain?"

"Why don't you tell me, parson?"

"Because I want this to hurt. I want you to feel every inch of this blade ripping into you."

"Well, come on then, preacher," he said, raising his arms to the side. *"Do your worst!"*

Leonardo yelled as he rushed Icarus with a blade in his hand, as Icarus pulled his Bowie knife from his sheath, back in front of his table.

In the forest, Michelangelo slid into a crouch within the shadows as forty-seven men came barreling towards him. Each man came from a different direction and was only visible by the lanterns they held in their hands. He took cover behind a pine as twelve men approached his position, each aiming their weapons at the tree, and strategically circling him. He flipped around the left side of his pine and fired off three rounds from the repeater, shredding through one man's heart, kicking him backwards, and slamming him to the ground. The second round shot through the second man's right lung, forcing him to lean over, grab his chest, the blood oozing from his mouth and hand as he dropped to all fours.

The third round zipped through a third man's head, stopping him mid-run and toppling him forward with his momentum, filling the snow where he face-planted with red liquid.

Revolver rounds rang out and exploded into Michelangelo's tree, forcing him to take cover once again, quickly holstering the repeater over his left shoulder and unholstering his right navy revolver. Nine men finished their circle around him, a small bit more following close behind, with each one yelling and firing off rounds for suppressive fire. He twisted around with a loud and deep roar, his left hand flicking across the hammer of his revolver, firing off six rounds in quick succession. The man closest to Michelangelo, just around the left side of his pine, was thrown backwards into the snow, a bullet blasting through the center of his chest, launching him to the ground in a bloody spurt and leaving his body to twitch in pain. The second man was struck in the leg, immediately dropping him to the ground, as the third bullet caught him in the side of his skull, spraying red mist onto the pants belonging to the men behind him. The bullet that blasted through the second man's skull ran through the spleen of a third one, standing behind him and now dropping to his back on the ground, as he yelled painfully and grabbed his injured side. The fourth man managed to fire off a revolver round that struck Michelangelo's armor, launching him to the ground with considerable force, coating him in snow. He raised his right arm and fired three more shots in rapid succession, leading the first one to land in the fourth man's right leg, and the next in his stomach. The third shot found its way into the fourth man's throat, which sent him backwards into a tree, only for him to slide down as blood leaked through his fingers from his neck. The fourth man's eyes opened fearfully agape as Michelangelo took shelter behind another pine, holstering his empty revolver and unholstering his left one.

Suddenly, a man whipped around the ride side of the pine, aiming a double-barreled shotgun at Michelangelo's face. He threw his left hand up and grabbed the barrel, lifting the gun above his head milliseconds before the shotgun's explosion let out. The shot blew his hat and the pine behind him to pieces, sending pieces of blue cloth and wood into that man's eyes. He screamed, closing his eyes as the soldier kicked in the man's left knee, forcing it to break inwards, dropping him to his other knee. Michelangelo punched the man in the jaw, crunching as he was discombobulated. He dizzily held to the weapon as Michelangelo raised his left leg and thrust it into the man's chest, sending him backward, disarmed, the soldier retaining the shotgun. He leaned against the tree, slid up to his feet, and flipped the gun around in his hand, aiming it at the man. He pulled the trigger and launched the other round into his chest, exploding blood all around as the shotgun kicked back, nearly dislocating the soldier's shoulder. The remaining shavings of Michelangelo's navy hat fell from atop his head, leading him to look down and notice the lantern's light that shone behind him, around his pine tree. He noted the shadows that made themselves present, one approaching his right side. He looked forward and to his right, and noted that more men were now coming from the distance.

Quickly, Michelangelo flipped the shotgun in his hands and held the barrel end with both hands, rendering the stock end of the gun as a bat, waiting for the fifth man. The fifth man walked around the pine tree with a revolver in hand, as the soldier smashed the stock into the fifth man's nose, cracking his head back with a meaty crunch, quickly disarming him. He flew backward to the ground in a quick fall, reaching for his nose that was busted and bloody. Michelangelo tossed the shotgun into the snow, holstered his revolver, and unholstered the repeater, aiming it at the three men to the right of him, taking on the forms of silhouettes behind their lanterns' lights. The bullets soared through the snow-filled air, one making contact with a lantern, bursting it to the ground as a bloody scream quickly followed. The second shot missed entirely as the third shot made its mark, a groan of pain sounding out from the darkness as a bullet lodged itself in the hidden man's left chest.

A defensive round exploded into Michelangelo's pine as the fire from the five men remaining behind him began. He ducked behind his pine entirely and redirected his attention to his left, another quickly approaching from the front. Michelangelo saw him, raised the repeater, and fired a single round that plunged through the barely visible, left man's right eye, jerking his head backward and dropping him quickly. His lantern fell to the ground, grabbing the remaining thirty-seven men's attention, prompting them to realize that their numbers were quickly dwindling. The fifth man, who had recently had his nose smashed, slowly rose to his feet, leading Michelangelo to turn in a quick reaction, flip the repeater in his hand, raise its stock high and to the left, ready to swing down with skull-cracking force. Suddenly, a sawed-off shotgun shot out from the darkness, obliterating the stock of the repeater, catching Michelangelo off guard while the repeater bits launched through the air. He chunked the repeater and immediately took cover behind his pine, more gunshots continuing to light up his cover, as the fifth man stumbled to his feet. He unsheathed his hunter's knife, breathing heavily as he looked at the repeater bits that lay dismantled in the snow before him. He noted the direction the sawed-off shotgun was fired from, then twisted around to the right side, attacking from that angle instead.

The shotgun man's eyes widened as he corrected his aim, as Michelangelo launched his hunter's knife through the air, planting it sharply in the left side of the man's neck. He stumbled backward and slammed into the base of a tree behind him, frantically reaching for his neck and gripping the blade of the knife, gurgling and twitching as his blood quickly drained. Michelangelo stopped just before him as he sat down, yanking out the knife in a panic, gushing blood onto him and the snow below. The soldier looked at the sawed-off shotgun that lay motionless in the shooter's hand. Instantly, the four remaining men fired rounds at Michelangelo, leading him to roll over to the man who had just stood to his feet, twist around him, and use his body as a shield while simultaneously grabbing his revolver out of his holster.

The soldier crouched behind the man, as bullets splatted and splotched through his shoulders, chest, and legs, his face staring at the soldier in horror. Michelangelo raised the borrowed revolver towards the sounds of gunfire and aimed it underneath the man's armpit, firing blindly at the sound of gunfire. He shot four bullets, all but one making its mark: one man attained a fatal shot to the chest, another was shot in the leg and groin. Michelangelo held the human shield in his arm as the last man, whom he had previously almost knocked unconscious, stood before him. All but one of the rest dropped dead in the snow. He shook from fear as he squeezed his trigger, the revolver clicking, leaving him to stare at the soldier. Michelangelo stood up straight and tossed his meat shield aside, holding firm to the borrowed revolver's grip as he stared at the man in front of him. The man clumsily pulled a bullet from his gun belt and attempted to load it into his revolver, dropping it in the snow. He glanced up, then back to his gun, then up again, continuing to fail to load bullets into his weapon as Michelangelo approached. The soldier flipped the revolver in his hands and grabbed the barrel of the gun, the man looking at him again, dropping the weapon and raising his hands. "Please," he whimpered.

Michelangelo whipped the revolver across the top of the man's skull, launching him down to the ground as he screamed in terror. The soldier knelt on top of him, gripping his collar and smashing the grip down with meaty, hollow bludgeons. The screaming stopped as Michelangelo roared viciously, smashing the man's skull in, his head turning into a red, mushy, and meaty pile. Blood and brain splattered and spurted in every direction as the soldier continued to beat down on the head, the cracks and smacks turning into mushy splats, as the man's hands and legs twitched with every hit.

Michelangelo stopped, then stood breathing heavily, staring upon the crimson slop at his feet. He slowly turned back to the sawed-off shotgun, then walked over to it, his entire self coated in meat and blood. He reached down with his free hand, grabbed his knife, wiped it, sheathed it, then grabbed the sawed-off double-barreled, the lanterns that were once moving toward him now stopping their charge. He felt the eyes of the men who stared at him in fear, and noted how they were all too afraid to shoot or move. He stood in the light of the lanterns around him, which began to fade slowly in the cold and snow. He heard the sound of painful grunting and looked over, seeing that the man he had shot in the groin was still living, grabbing his bleeding crotch and crawling backwards, pitifully attempting to escape. He saw that the soldier had seen him and began clawing at the snow behind him faster, as Michelangelo slowly walked over to him, a borrowed revolver in his right hand, and a sawed-off shotgun in the other. The escaping man raised his snow-covered hand to the soldier as a bullet blitzed through his skull and launched his head backward into the blood-stained snow behind him.

Michelangelo tossed the borrowed revolver to the ground, calmly reached into his pocket, pulled out a single shotgun shell, and slowly turned around, looking at the faces of the terrified men that stood before him, each holding their weapons in hand, though too afraid to lift their aim from the ground. He cracked open the sawed-off shotgun, thumbed in the shell, and flicked the weapon closed, pulling back the hammer. He reached down and pulled out his left, navy revolver. The lanterns behind him finally faded, leaving him to stand in shadow, with both weapons at his side, as the five remaining men retreated backward.

They stopped a mere thirty feet away from Icarus's homestead on the treeless hill. Michelangelo noted the retreating men, leaving only twenty-seven more to face him, and as the light from the last lantern flickered out, Michelangelo was enveloped in darkness.

Back at the house, Icarus threw Leonardo into a support beam, shaking the lantern above him viciously. He struggled to stand on his feet after the blow and leaned against the wood for support as he felt his freshly busted lip. His hand graced over his cheek, feeling the bruise that had formed, then down to his upper body, where he had taken some well-placed punches from Icarus. He stood breath-bated, then looked at Icarus as the bastard paced in front of him, untouched and unharmed. Leonardo's head and body were weak, but still, he lifted his knife slowly, holding it close to his chest.

"You're weak, Leo," Icarus antagonized. "You don't have what it *takes*! You can't take me down; You can't *kill a man*! You can't bear the weight of *retribution*!" He laughed menacingly. "You're in over your head, just as you were before! Just as you've *always* been!" He stopped pacing. "You know, your brothers died knowin' that. And you? You will die the same!"

Leonardo yelled, grabbed the lantern above his head, and launched it towards Icarus in a hate-filled fury. Icarus side-stepped the flying lantern, narrowly avoiding the flaming metal, as the lantern blasted open on the other wall's support beam, igniting it into flames through the oil's fueling. The fire rapidly grew, the old wood quickly being engulfed as Icarus turned and looked at it, letting out a humored smile. Leonardo wasted no time and sprinted towards Icarus, who turned, smiling, but was quickly stabbed in the lower gut just above his hip. He let out an angry grunt of pain as he grabbed Leonardo's hand to hold the blade in place. He gritted his teeth, somewhat surprised, as the pain surged through his lower body. He grabbed his bowie knife and lifted it into the air, then plunged it down toward Leonardo. He dodged to the right, pulling his hunter's knife out with him, forcing Icarus to let out a teeth-gritting yell, his blood quickly seeping out. The fire continued to grow rapidly as it spread up the wall and promptly consumed the old wood, the only saving grace being the wood's wetness from the snow. White clouds of steam emerged as the snow and cold exited the homestead's infrastructure, as Icarus angrily squared up with Leonardo again, impressed but furious.

"You know," he looked at the blood on his hand, "I was goin' easy on you before... now?" He put his hand down. "But now? I say we really let the demons out," he gritted through his teeth. He flew forward at Leonardo, forcing the preacher back toward the fireplace. Icarus swiped his Bowie knife left to right, Leonardo dodging every slash. "What?!" Icarus exclaimed. "Can't take me in a straight-up fight?!" He taunted as he unsheathed his branding iron with his other arm. He reeled back the iron over his left shoulder and smashed it into Leonardo's right side, lighting his ribs up with pain as he promptly dropped to his knees. Icarus dropped his iron and grabbed Leonardo by the collar, pulling him to his feet, only to reel his head backward and smash his forehead into Leonardo's nose, jerking his head back. Icarus threw Leonardo across the floor, sending him into a painful tumble over the wood, the solid surface letting out loud and hollow thumps and thuds as the preacher rolled five feet away from Icarus. Icarus leaned down and picked up his iron, the fire upon the homestead's wall now moving up to the ceiling. Smoke began to fill the air as a bright red flame engulfed the room, bathing the individuals inside in a red hue as Leonardo groaned, feeling the bruised bones in his body as he gritted his teeth. Icarus moved his iron in a circular motion as he walked towards Leonardo slowly and methodically.

"You know... You never stop hearin' the screams. The painful cries of the people as their skin sizzles at the end of an iron. The sound, the smell... it never leaves you." He pointed his iron at Leonardo. "But strangely enough, I am *thankful* for that." He stopped pointing. "Do you want to know why? Because it would be a *shame* not to remember the pain your fiancé felt when I burned this cross into her pretty little face," Icarus antagonized.

Leonardo stood to his feet, cautious and tired, but unrelentingly vengeful. His blood dripped from his nose over his gritted teeth as Icarus got closer.

"But you know," Icarus continued. "Regardless of all the pain I caused her, that was *nothin'* compared to what you did. Leavin' her to die after she gave up *everything* for *you?*" Icarus laughed. "Only the Devil himself could do such a deed."

Leonardo's flame burned at its brightest red, as Icarus's did as well, burning bright orange in the center of his eyes as he was just about to set on Leonardo. The lion in the preacher roared as he threw his hunter's knife at Icarus, lodging it into his left shoulder, forcing him to stumble backward as he grabbed the blade in pain. Leonardo ran forward and slammed into Icarus's ribs, twisting him to the left and then pushing him toward the fireless, right side wall's beam. He smashed Icarus's back into the beam and positioned himself in front of him, only to quickly wail his fist into the bastard's face. The homestead crackled and creaked as the support of the burning side began to bend, the wall splintering and bursting while the weight of the homestead buckled in on itself. Leonardo continued to punch repeatedly, forcing Icarus's head to jerk back lightly. His fists were bloodied as his knuckles busted open, with Icarus taking every hit to calculate his counter. The fire had consumed the entire ceiling and now reached down towards Icarus and Leonardo, the preacher continuing to beat the bastard blindly. Icarus dodged the coming punch with a quick flick of the head to the right, sending the fist into the beam in front of him, and forcing Leonardo to reel it back, clutching his hand in pain. Icarus pulled back his right elbow and cracked it into Leonardo's face, completely dazing him. He then grabbed him by the collar and twisted around in a circle, slamming Leonardo into the beam, allowing him a moment to regain consciousness painfully.

"Feels good, doesn't it?" Icarus questioned. "All that fury? All that rage? *Aaall that passion*, that *fire!* Oh, how *dangerous* it can burn!" Icarus lifted his Bowie knife and aimed it at Leonardo's right shoulder. "It's ironic, really. You got all this passion for blood yet no passion for Christ!" He smirked. "How disappointin'."

Icarus plunged the knife down as Leonardo's vision came back. He lifted his hands to grab Icarus's arm, holding it with all his strength just inches from his shoulder's flesh. Icarus continued to press, gaining inches with each second. Leonardo gritted his teeth and pushed mightily, refusing to die as anything other than the victor. Blood oozed from Icarus' mouth, chin, and nose, all busted open and bruised. "You've lost, Leo! The sooner you accept that, the sooner this can all be over!"

Leonardo looked at his hunter's knife that protruded from Icarus's right shoulder, the bowie knife now hovering above his own. He glanced between the two and, with a painful decision, released his grip of Icarus' right hand, sending the blade into his fleshy socket. He screamed in pain as the knife sank deep into his right shoulder, all while he quickly pulled his hunter's knife from Icarus's, forcing him to let up slightly. Leonardo plunged the blade through the air towards Icarus' head, leading Icarus to pull his head back to avoid the hit, the blade slicing through the center of his left eye, cutting down to his nose. He reeled back in agony, pulling the Bowie knife from Leonardo's shoulder, blood dripping from Icarus's eye and skin. Leonardo's shoulder bled the same, making it nearly immobile. Icarus dropped his weapon as he walked backward, pressing the palm of his left hand against his eye. He tried looking at the blood on his hand, but was only able to see through the right eyeball. His face twisted in an angry snarl as Leonardo stepped away from the beam, the flames quickly consuming the wall behind him. "You blinded me!" Icarus yelled out. *"You blinded me!"*

The homestead creaked heavily as Icarus looked around at the flame-filled room, the wood viciously bursting and crackling as the homestead's weight became nearly un-bearable. Leonardo walked forward and reached down, picking up Icarus's Bowie knife, his own blade in his other hand. He stood, angling his face forward as Icarus turned around and locked eyes with him. "Let me kill you now, and maybe you will not burn." Leonardo threatened.

Icarus smiled and dropped his bloodied left hand to his side, revealing the bloody gash in his eye socket. "There ain't no savin' me from burnin', Leo. How about you?" Icarus damned as he picked up his branding iron from the floor. He flurried his iron once, raised it into the air, and waited for Leonardo as he yelled, both knives angled forward, and plunged.

In the forest, Michelangelo watched from the darkness as the homestead went up in flames, its firelight bright and shining across the forest and hillside. It glistened on the snow of the hill, the snow closest to the homestead melting away into a muddy and watery mess. The snow that fell from the sky melted around the flaming homestead, and the re-maining men's confidence, though once shaken, had now grown a little, given the darkness of the forest no longer aided the soldier. This factor did not faze him. His only focus was on saving Leonardo. "Don't worry, kid... I'm on my way," he said to himself.

Michelangelo was crouched behind a pine that barely hid him from the twen-ty-seven men who remained. He huffed a few quick breaths, working himself up as he controlled his fury. With an animalistic growl, he walked from behind the pine with his navy revolver in his left hand and the sawed-off shotgun in his right. He aimed at the men before him, letting out a deep and booming yell. It was monstrous enough to send any well-armed man running for the hills, and of the ten men that stood before him, most of them did. The ten men turned frightfully to the soldier as he fired his weapons at the adversaries.

A shotgun bullet launched into a man two feet away, obliterating his right shoulder and detaching his arm in the process. The soldier shot his revolver at a man in the farther distance, sending a bullet through his chest, forcing him to wobble forward and fall into the snowy ground. He shifted the sawed-off shotgun's aim to a closer man who charged him from the left with a machete in hand. He fired another shot from the sawed-off and sent the metal beads into the man's upper chest, spraying crimson in every direction as a fleshy, bloody hole exploded from his ribs. Blood splattered across Michelangelo's left side as he fired another revolver round into another opponent, jerking that man's head sideways, his jaw exploding open. The soldier dropped the shotgun and swiftly brought his left hand to the hammer of his revolver, repeatedly flicking the hammer back, firing four bullets into the men in front of him. Three bullets punctured through one man by first hitting his hip, then the center of his gut, followed by a shot in the center of his chest. The fourth bullet found itself in the skull of a man beside him, jerking his head sideways and throwing him to the ground.

Fire opened from the remaining twenty-three men, the pine trees bursting with bullets. Michelangelo hid behind the very same pine he had taken cover behind before as splinters launched in every direction. Michelangelo clenched the bridge of his nose and closed his eyes, gritting as heated metal flew around him. He was overwhelmed until the firing of the weapons stopped. A few of the remaining men reloaded their guns. Michelangelo holstered his revolver.

"Come on out, Major. Ain't no sense in prolongin' the inevitable," a man mocked.

Michelangelo breathed in one slow and angry breath, pulling William's revolvers from the holsters on his chest and flipping them around quickly, positioning them across his chest. He breathed out, then whipped around the tree, aiming both weapons in the direction of the ten men and firing one after the other, filling five men in front of him with deadly lead. He yelled angrily at the men before him as the men fired back, their bullets whizzing and zooming past him, bursting into the trees and snow-covered ground. Michelangelo marched forward, continuing to rain fire upon the men, flicking back the hammers of the revolvers one by one as he alternated the shots. A bullet twanged into his left side of his armor, kicking him slightly over to the left as another bullet made contact with the center of his breastplate, stopping him in place. He gritted, yelled again, and continued to march forward, firing the few bullets he had left. The bullets bloodily connected with the five other men, leading each one to wiggle and twist as their bodies became corpses. Crimson flow squirted out of them, shooting forward, backward, and sideways onto the snow as thirteen more men rushed toward Michelangelo. He took cover behind a pine beside him, their bullets flying forward as they stepped over the ten bodies of their fellow men. Their focus did not shift from his last known position. He holstered William's revolvers in his bandolier, then unholstered his double-barrel shotgun from off his back, pulling both hammers back as he waited for the men. They marched forward powerfully, each firing as the homestead lit ablaze behind them. As it groaned loudly, Michelangelo twisted out from his pine and aimed his weapon at the men, pulling the trigger and sending a slug through the taunting man's face. Bits of his head flew in every direction.

The men around him flinched in fear, some dropping to the ground in a panic while others stared in horror. The body slowly fell to its knees, then fell over sideways, horrifying the men and sending all of them running away. Michelangelo lowered the placement of his shotgun to his hip and fired off another shot that blasted through a tripped man's ribcage, throwing him to the side and sending him rolling down his hill. He cracked open the barrels, flicking out the steaming shells, then reached into his pocket, grabbed two more slugs, and rapidly thumbed them in. He snapped the barrel shut and looked up at a running man who had looked back and aimed his revolver at him. The soldier lifted his shotgun faster and fired another slug out into the man's back, throwing him into the pine before him, and painted the very same pine with red. The man smacked into the tree and flopped into the snow, as death and snow covered him. Michelangelo aimed at the remaining men who continued to run, all of them dropping their weapons and running to the bottom of Michelangelo's hill, as he drew ever closer, getting ready to start his march up Icarus's.

"Go on and run, you rats! Run as far as you can! But no matter how far you run, there is no pit of hell for any devil to hide that is safe from my retribution!" Michelangelo yelled.

He smiled as he watched, almost proud of himself, as a rifle round fired in the distance, sending a bullet through his left leg. Pain immediately lit Michelangelo's leg ablaze, dropping him to his left knee as the bullet wound immediately began to bleed. He looked in the direction it came from, noting that it had come from the side of the flaming homestead. He looked at his leg and saw the blood coming through the top of his pants, but also dripping out through the bottom, meaning it exited out the other side. He gritted his teeth and slowly stood, huffing in a painful anger as he limped toward the closest pine. He angled himself away from the trajectory of the shot as the running men turned around, noting the sudden change of energy. Michelangelo slid down behind the pine as another rifle shot cracked off from the homestead, zipping into the snow beside him, launching up a violent poof. He leaned against the pine and clenched his jaw in pain as he straightened out his leg, the blood continuing to ooze from his wound. He angrily felt his leg, then removed his winter jacket while carefully doing his best to keep his limbs hidden from the last rifleman. His jacket flopped out from behind the pine, leading to another rifle round cracking off, slicing through the sleeve.

"Alright! You got me already!" Michelangelo yelled out.

He chunked his jacket into the snow in front of him, then shifted his focus to the right sleeve of his button-up, rolling it up to reveal the white union suit underneath. It was a white, thick material reaching down to his wrists. He pulled out his hunter's knife and cut the cloth at his elbow, then carefully removed the sleeve. The men who had run away continued to look at his last known spot, noticing that he had not moved or attacked, and more than anything, had appeared to have taken damage.

"He bleeds... just as any other man!" A man said.

"It might be a trick!" Another responded.

"No... no, you heard him! He's hit! He's weak," a different one interjected.

"Can we kill him?" A fourth one questioned.

"How? We dropped our guns," a fifth questioned further.

"We don't need guns to kill a man who's been shot!"

The men all nodded in mumbling unison as they debated and pressed the conversation further.

"We got the rifleman up top watching over. We can finish him!" A sixth agreed.

"No... I'm done with this. You all can go on ahead, but I'm finished takin' chances!" The seventh man said, and then ran away.

He ran along with another to meet up with the five men who had left and created a defensive line far out front of Icarus's homestead. This line was now seven men strong—all that was left to defend Icarus's hill if all else failed. The other seven men were left to face Michelangelo, along with the last rifleman who watched from above. "If you want me," he called out. "Then *come and get me*!" He challenged, tightening the white cloth on his leg.

The seven men looked at one another, then began their slow walk toward Michelangelo, slowly trekking through the shin-high snow, believing they had the advantage. He looked at the white cloth that quickly absorbed his blood, then leaned his head back on the pine behind him. He breathed heavily, then looked up at the silent sky above him as snowflakes fell lightly upon his skin. He peered into the grey, clouded heavens that the burning homestead had lightly lit. He stared into them, admiring their beauty as he waited for his death.

"It's a beautiful night tonight, Tommy," he said, making peace.

Back in the homestead, Leonardo stood to his feet as Icarus attempted to balance on his. He had been thoroughly beaten, just like the preacher. Smoke filled the air with a hot suffocation, the fire consuming the inside of the homestead, continuing to crack, burst, and creak. The ceiling snapped as the wooden beams destabilized, Leonardo jumping to the side, his hunter's knife and Bowie knife still in opposite hands, waiting to attack Icarus. The bastard held tight to his branding iron and flurried it in a circle once more, this time weaker, giving the preacher a moment to regain his strength. The two continued to stare one another down.

"What's wrong, Leo? Havin' trouble beatin' a half-blind man?" Icarus mocked as he walked before the fireplace. Leonardo limped forward as Icarus braced for the coming impact, leaning forward while pointing the iron cross in the preacher's direction. He threw his hunter's knife again, only this time Icarus struck it out of the air, opening up his left leg for an offensive strike. Leonardo slid on one knee and sliced the Bowie knife across Icarus's left calf, forcing him to reel his head back in pain, and immediately look down at Leonardo. He swung the branding iron down onto Leonardo's back, causing him to fall to the ground. Icarus slightly gimped away as Leonardo slowly stood to his feet, grabbing at his spine as he turned toward Icarus. He violently swung at Leonardo's head, missing by a mere inch as he ducked underneath. He raised the Bowie knife above his head and went down for a stab into Icarus' right leg, but was immediately stopped by a furious Icarus, who slammed the iron into Leonardo's right ribs. Leonardo flinched in pain only to be hit again, his entire right side lighting up with pain. He used this opportunity to grab the iron with the pit of his right arm, then raised his Bowie knife high, and then plunged it clear through the center of Icarus's right forearm. He reeled back in painful agony as blood gushed forth. He stumbled and looked at his impaled arm, holding it up to the firelight as he took note of it coming in one side and out the other. He looked at the blood that glided down, forming droplets at the end of the edge that splatted upon the smoking, wooden floor. He looked at Leonardo and smiled, resting his arm at his right side, his streams of blood dripping down his fingertips. Leonardo grabbed the hilt of the branding iron from under his armpit and held it firmly in his hands like a sword, readying for yet another offensive strike. Suddenly, a massive snap of wood exploded above them, exploding debris from the ceiling as an enormous pillar smashed through it and onto the floor beside them, bursting into red embers that raced through the air. The two reactively flinched away from the crash, the floor lighting up with the unquenchable flame, coming closer to consuming them. Leonardo looked back at Icarus, who was already looking at him.

"You wanna know somethin' kind of funny?" Icarus asked distortedly, Leonardo cautiously watching him. "I always imagined I'd go out exactly like this," he informed, smiling. "Except with a little more of a foe than the one I got."

Leonardo yelled as he slammed the iron down towards the top of Icarus's skull. He raised his left arm and stunted the blow of the iron, but only slightly blocking it as he took the full force of the metal. Leonardo continued to wale, fracturing the bastard's arm, then striking his left shoulder as he dropped it. He followed up by hitting Icarus in his left ribs, then his arm again. The slugs were rapid and vicious, and ended with Leonardo slamming the iron down once more, cracking Icarus in the head. He fell to the ground in a beaten and bloody mess as Leonardo slowly raised the iron for one final hit, Icarus rising to his right knee and debating whether or not he was done with this fight. Leonardo held the iron for a moment as the heat from the fire seeped into each member's skin, heating their bodies to a sweaty mess as the fire grew greater. "No," Leonardo rejected. "You don't get to get off that easy." He chunked the iron to the floor beside him. "That's the spirit," Icarus encouraged.

Leonardo grabbed Icarus by the collar and lifted him to his feet, then quickly marched him over to the right wall beside them, lit ablaze. Icarus stumbled, unable to resist, for Leonardo's strength had grown all the greater. With a final twisting motion, Leonardo shifted to the right side of Icarus and grabbed his right side of the face, holding it tightly, and then grabbed his right shoulder, slamming the right side of Icarus's body into the wall, which set the left side of his face and shoulder on fire. He let out a horrific scream as the left side of his face and body popped and sizzled, the flame quickly consuming them. In a panic, he mustered a survivalistic strength and raised his right arm, smashing it down on Leonardo's arm and quickly following it up with a punch to his nose with his burning left arm. Leonardo stumbled backwards as he held his nose while Icarus slowly stepped away from the wall and looked at him. He looked to the bastard and backed away. He was scared, for what he saw was far more horrific than anything else he had ever seen: it was Icarus's inner form made manifest on the exterior.

Icarus hobbled toward Leonardo, then toward the front door as Leonardo watched. He looked at the left side of his sheepskin vest and noticed that it was still slightly enflamed, along with whatever remained of his left sleeve. He looked down at his pants that were also somewhat on fire, and then examined his arm that had been burned thoroughly. Icarus' arm shone red, pink, and black, for his skin had been burned nearly to the bone, from his shoulder down to his hand. He ripped his sheepskin vest from his body and tossed it to the ground, clear into the burning flames that were now merely feet away from the two. He chucked his flaming hat from his head, revealing his skin was bubbled, hairless, pink, and mushy, complemented by slight shades of maroon. Leonardo looked over it all, then gazed at his own face, which stared back at him, its flesh the same black and red, while his left eye stared wide, having no eyelid, just as his left lip was also absent. They were both burned clear off, and his teeth had shown through where his left lip once was.

And he smiled.

He retained eye contact with Leonardo, grabbing the Bowie knife's handle with his left hand with a firm grip. Leonardo watched in horror as Icarus slowly removed the blade from his arm, shaking and groaning as he pulled the blade from his arm, his blood oozing and squirting out. Leonardo clenched his jaw in an uncomfortable terror as he gazed upon the devil before him, Icarus pulling the blade completely from his arm with one final, great yank. The blade flicked outward, a final spurt following it, leaving him there to hold the blade in his burnt left hand. Leonardo's eyes were wide with fear as he stared in disgust, Icarus forcing a disturbed and manic smile on his face.

"Cursed is he who hath been burned by the son... wouldn't you say, Leo?" Icarus said with a raspy and deep voice, the fire flickering upon his clothing. Leonardo's breathing turned angrier than fearful as he tightened his fists, his shoulders moving up and down slowly. "You can't kill me, preacher... You can only *transform what I am!* I am an idea to be possessed, or a devil possessing! Can you bear that burden, Leo?"

"No... I can be *so much more.*"

Icarus spread his arms to the side. "Then come on, preacher! Take it!"

Leonardo yelled as he ran towards Icarus.

"Take it all!" Icarus shouted, smiling as he prepared himself to get hit.

Leonardo slammed into Icarus's chest with a full force dive, launching the two straight through the front door of the homestead and into the muddy ground where snow used to be. Leonardo slid and rolled through it, as Icarus did the same, while both were coated in the dark, brown, and wet earth. The Bowie knife landed blade-first into the mud after being flicked in the air, the flames from the homestead flickering on the bloody metal. Leonardo got to his knees and looked around, noting the snow had melted in a loosely identifiable circle around the home. He shook his head as he tried to remove the mud from his face. Once he did, he looked down the hill, seeing the seven men who stood guard against what he presumed was the soldier. He looked past them at the tall pines in the forest, the dark shadows that formed five feet behind them. He turned his head back to Icarus, who was now standing to his feet, coated in mud, blood, and burns that ran all over his body. Leonardo stood to his feet as well, in the same bloody and muddy manner, limping sideways to face Icarus head-on. The bastard breathed with a tired heaviness as the preacher did the same, the two staring at one another with no words spoken. The homestead beside them creaked and snapped viciously, finally buckling under the pressure of its own weight.

The building leaned to the left and exploded, shooting flames and embers in every direction, exploding into a heavy, flaming mass. The last rifleman looked up from his scope and saw the flaming debris that came crashing down above him, a hundred pounds of brick and wood that was being throttled down with a wild flame. The last rifleman let out a morticious scream, as the debris smashed down on him, squishing him to a fiery crisp. Leonardo balled his fists one final time, Icarus copying him, the two facing each other, each limping forward.

Down the hill, Michelangelo looked around his pine and saw the explosive execution of the last rifleman as the homestead lay crumbled atop him. As it turned out, he was under the stagecoach. The soldier painfully stood to his feet as quickly as he could, using the pine to support his upper body. The seven men who were charging the soldier stopped just a few feet away from, looking at the fallen homestead that burned ablaze, high and mighty.

"I think we just lost the rifleman," one man said.

"You're about to lose a whole lot more than that," Michelangelo reminded.

The seven men looked at the soldier standing out in the open beside his pine, thumbing another slug into his double-barrel shotgun as fear consumed them all.

"If we run, will you kill us the same?" A man questioned in hopes of hearing a no.

"You're already dead," he answered.

The seven men looked at each other, then rushed the soldier, who let out a bellowous roar, standing his ground. He raised his shotgun and fired a round into the man to his left, launching him backwards into his own red spray. The man poofed into the snowy ground as Michelangelo turned to his right, the other one rushing him. Michelangelo adjusted his upper body and did his best not to put pressure on his left leg as he whipped the stock of the shotgun across the right side of the man's face. He dropped to his knees, allowing the soldier a moment to refocus and aim his shotgun in front of him, firing a shell inaccurately into another charging man. The slug obliterated his left hip, blowing meaty bits and sprays of blood into the air as he twisted to his right side. He fell face-first into the snow, as Michelangelo raised his shotgun and smashed the stock down on the back of the recently face-smashed man beside him. He repeatedly smashed the stock of the gun into the back of the man's head, yelling ferociously as he beat him relentlessly. Brain squished and skull cracked as the white of the snow turned red, the fourth-to-last man tackling Michelangelo into the tree. He quickly removed his right hand from his shotgun and unsheathed his hunter's knife, raising it high and slamming it down into the center of the tackling man's spine. He twisted the blade with a resounding crunch, paralyzing the tackling man. Another man running stopped and pulled back and tossed his knife at Michelangelo's face, which he saw at the last moment, throwing his head to the left and dodging the blade by a matter of inches. He removed his right hand from his own blade and let the paralyzed man fall, then lifted his hand to the blade beside him, lodged in the pine. He pulled it out with one thrust and, in the same movement, launched the knife forward into the third-to-last man's right eye. He dropped to his knees and then slowly fell to his face, only a mere two feet away from Michelangelo. The second-to-last man raised his knife a foot away from Michelangelo and sent it plunging towards his head. He gripped his shotgun with both hands and swung it forward, smacking the second-to-last man's wrist, launching the blade from his hand. He followed up with a quick crack to the side of the man's cheek, sending him stumbling to his right, in a slow, near-unconscious wobble. Michelangelo cracked open his double-barreled, tilted the weapon upward, reached into his pocket, and grabbed one last slug as the shells fell from the gun and into the snow, with a sizzle. Michelangelo thumbed in the shell and cracked the double-barreled gun closed, aimed the gun at the side of the discombobulated man's head, and pulled the trigger, blasting his skull wide open.

The last man stopped and looked at Michelangelo, who slowly turned to face him. He looked at the bleeding, blood-coated, injured soldier and realized that the soldier had indeed fought without end. He determined he was an unkillable creature, as the legends foretold. This sent terror deep into his soul as Michelangelo stared at him, the firelight of the homestead dancing across him and reflecting off his eyes. He stared back and looked upon the blood and fleshy chunks that coated one half of his face, the other half hidden in the darkness. Michelangelo cracked his shotgun open once again and flicked the shell through the air to plop into the snow. The shell hit the snow-covered ground and melted deep within, releasing smoke and steam from its heat. The last man looked to the shell in the snow, then quickly back at Michelangelo, for fear had taken him over entirely, knowing that all he could do was wait.

"Tell me, stranger: do you wish to die a man, or to die a monster?" Michelangelo questioned, thumbing in another two shotgun shells, buying himself some time as his vision slightly blurred.

The last dropped his knife from his hands and thought about all he had witnessed and done, as he looked upon the Saint of Retribution, who had come to enact his vengeance. "I wish to die as a man," he answered. Michelangelo smirked, flicking the double-barreled shotgun closed and holding it at his hip, aiming it at his chest. "It's a trick question, in my opinion. Men like you are barely men. They're more monstrous in all. I wonder if they're any different these days. All men, I mean. Maybe there isn't much of a difference."

"And what are you?"

"I'm the one sent to damn us all."

He pulled both triggers of his shotgun and lacerated the last man's chest open, flinging him backwards to the ground to tumble lifelessly to his side. Blood poured forth from the reddened and chestless center, as Michelangelo looked up to the flaming homestead, seeing the seven men that stood before it, blocking his path to Icarus and Leonardo. He looked up at Icarus's hill and saw Leonardo and Icarus fighting viciously atop it, their darkened silhouettes swinging violently at one another. He sighed as he painfully limped forward, and with whatever strength he could muster. He tossed his shotgun into the snow at his side and pulled his left revolver from his holster, then reached up to Williams's bandolier, flicking out a handful of rounds into his palm. He flicked open the navy revolver's loader and pointed the weapon upward, letting the shells pour out to the ground. He then dropped the aim of the firearm and thumbed in the new bullets.

Atop the hill, Leonardo pushed Icarus off of him, which forced both fighters backwards to a seated splat in the mud. The two struggled to stand on their feet as each one's arms tried to stay functional. The two retained spatial awareness of the other in an attempt to ensure they would not lose focus. Leonardo tried to stand and fell to one knee, smooshing in the mud with a splat. He rested a moment, no longer able to stand consistently. Icarus noted this weakness and decided to look around with his one good eye. He noticed the Bowie knife lodged in the mud, two feet in front of the preacher. As shakily as he could, he stood to his feet and stumbled toward the blade. Leonardo saw where Icarus was going and tried to gain as much energy as he could.

"You don't know when to quit, do you?" Icarus asked weakly.

Leonardo stood to his feet tiredly, his right knee wobbling while his right hand pressed against it. "No... I don't," he responded breath-bated.

He clumsily stumbled toward Icarus and dropped his right shoulder into a charge, as Icarus leaned over to pick up the knife slowly. Leonardo bumped into him and forced the two to fall beside the weapon, then quickly climbed atop Icarus, pinning him to the ground as he climbed atop him. He raised his right fist high and brought it down upon Icarus's face, hoping that the blunt force would be enough to end Icarus's life. He repeated the attacks slowly, as Icarus took the beating, smiling, and having no strength left to fight back.

In the middle of the hill, the seven men stared downward at the lit forest before them, waiting for the soldier to make his presence known. The homestead roared, and as they looked for any sign of life, all they could see were the shadows between the pines.

Each one stood there with a firm tension in their bodies, their hands hovering above their revolvers at their sides, waiting for the slightest move to force their fire. Faint footsteps could be heard in the darkness of the pain as they crunched through the snow. The men listened as the sound of a revolver loader could be heard spinning, followed by the immediate loading of six bullets. Six slicks of metal sounded out through the night, followed by a quick flip and a metal smack.

Leonardo continued to lay down his beating on Icarus, echoing through the vast hillside. The men stared forward fearfully as a silhouette limped toward them. Each one's breath began to bate, their hearts pounding in their chests. Their hands shook from the fear that had infected them as their eyes bore witness to the soldier who finally stepped into the homestead's firelight. Michelangelo limped forward in his tread up the hill, his body beginning to feel colder and weary. Though his vision slightly blurred again, he looked up at the seven men and stopped walking eight feet away from his opposers. They looked down at him, wondering and waiting for what he would say. The soldier breathed heavily, then looked behind the men, seeing Leonardo lost in his fury. He looked back at the men, eyeballing each one of them. "You're in my way," he called out.

The seven men paused for a moment, considering their next move and weighing the risks.

"I don't know if you've noticed, but you have the disadvantage, Saint Hart," a gunman answered back.

The gunman looked at the men at his side, putting his arms out casually to mask the consternation that grew within him. Michelangelo humored the statement the gunman made and took a moment to breathe. He hovered his hand over his right side revolver, the snow falling around him.

"You're outnumbered," the gunman continued, "outgunned, and bleeding. Hell, you're at the bottom of the hill with nowhere left to go. We have the high ground. What exactly can you do to overcome such—"

Michelangelo flicked his navy revolver forward and fired six shots by running his left palm against the hammer, blasting the six-gunman from right to left. Each shot made its mark in their chests and dropped them instantly with limp flops into the snow. He unholstered his left revolver and quickly thrust the aim forward, accurately targeting the seventh gunman and pulling back the hammer. A revolver shot rang out and echoed through the hillside, only Michelangelo flinched at the sound, the impact blitzing through his lower abdomen.

The last gunman stood untouched, as Michelangelo's lower left abdomen began to bleed, forcing his arm to shake. He dropped the aim of his revolver and looked down at his stomach, only to drop the revolver in his right hand into the snow. He slowly reached down to the wound and felt the area just below his armor, feeling the tender pain. He lifted his right hand to his eyes and noted the blood on his fingers as he slumped to his knees.

Leonardo slid off of Icarus, exhausted, leaving his face in a mushy mess. Icarus' face was bloody, puffy, burnt, and cut.

Yet, he breathed.

Leonardo looked over, noting the gentle breaths, then rested in the mud as he turned to look at the commotion behind him, seeing Michelangelo on his knees, and just before him, his Bowie knife. He looked past the weapon up at the last gunman, who stood tall and breathed a sigh of relief.

"So you do die after all," The last gunman mocked, firing off another round.

The bullet clanged against Michelangelo's upper right chest plate, flipping him backward and onto his left side, his right arm flopping underneath him as he landed atop it. Michelangelo lay motionless as he faced towards the woods, his body sideways and his right arm promptly pinned, but hidden in the snow. Leonardo looked to the soldier and saw that he had fallen. He then angrily rose again, the last gunman looking back at him. He looked down at Icarus, then back up to Leonardo, who was pulling the Bowie knife from the mud, slowly and exhausted.

"I won't lie to you, kid," the gunman started, "I liked Icarus's plan." He raised his revolver at Leonardo's head. "Or all three, really. But I think I would much rather prefer to live on as the 'Saint Killer.' There's a lot more sense in that. I don't need you telling me what to do. I couldn't care less how prophetic Icarus is—"

A revolver boomed through the hillside as a bullet flew through the air and ripped through the last gunman's chest. He looked down as his blood oozed out, his mouth filling with the taste of iron. Bloody drool began to seep forward as he clumsily turned around and looked in the direction of the gunshot. He looked at what he thought was the dead saint, as Michelangelo slowly rose to his knees, while the gunman fell to his. His eyes were wide with fear, disbelief, and utter horror as he saw the Saint of Retribution surviving again. He could not comprehend how he was surviving such an injury. In truth, no one there could. Michelangelo looked up at the gunman as he dropped his revolver in the snow. The soldier breathed heavily as a pale anger overtook his face, his eyebrows curling inward as his mouth frowned shut. The gunman coughed up a splotch of blood. "What the hell are you?" He asked. "What you deserve," Michelangelo replied, raising his navy revolver and firing another round directly into the last gunman's head, flicking it backward as his life left his body. His arms dangled limply at his sides, his head and body falling backward into the snow.

Michelangelo looked at Leonardo dizzily and noted that he held his Bowie knife in his hand, readying himself to take his vengeance. He turned and stared at Icarus, as Icarus looked at him, letting his good eye peer through the preacher to see Leonardo in his final form. He was bloody, bruised, and full of mud and cuts, but most importantly, he was relentlessly filled with retribution. "Finish it," he said. "Do what you want to do."

Leonardo breathed heavily. His newfound strength entered him. Michelangelo rose to his feet painfully by mustering all the strength he had left to offer.

"Leo, don't!" Michelangelo called out, slowly limping forward to the best of his ability. Leonardo stayed focused on Icarus.

"You gonna listen to everyone else your whole life, DelMuerto? Or is it high time you finally make your own decisions?"

"Don't listen to him!"

"The soldier failed you once... he'll do it again. They all do."

"Let me do it, Leo!"

Icarus smiled. "Do what must be done."

Leonardo lifted the Bowie knife slowly as he knelt beside Icarus, the fire from the homestead illuminating his wide-eyed expression. Rage had possessed him entirely, as he bore his teeth and angrily furrowed his eyebrows.

Michelangelo fell to his right knee, his strength continuing to fail him as his vision darkened and blurred. He continued to lose more control of his body with every drop of blood.

"Leo," he called out, "remember what I said." He spat out blood. "If you do this, you will never be the same."

"Never the same? You really want to continue to be the man you are?" Icarus argued.

Michelangelo gritted his teeth. "This ain't the way, Leo!" He stood to his feet and stumbled toward Leonardo again. Leonardo clenched the Bowie knife in both his hands now, as he lifted the blade high above his head.

"Come on, preacher. Do it."

Michelangelo stumbled again, a mere five away.

"Do it, you make-believin' coward!" Icarus roared.

"Leonardo, no!" Michelangelo said, pulling his revolver, hammered a round into the barrel, and aimed it at Icarus's forehead.

Leonardo yelled and plunged the Bowie knife deep into the center of Icarus's chest, sinking every inch of the weapon into him. He tensed as the blade punctured him, his blood pouring out and around the blade. His mouth oozed blood, too, as he stared into the clouds above him. Leonardo clenched his teeth and blade as he looked at Icarus's dying face, his arms and head shaking with fury as his face turned red. Michelangelo dropped the aim of his revolver, losing the weapon in the mud as he huddled over, coughed, and spat out blood into the dirt beneath him. He breathed deeply as snow fell gently from the sky, gracing his hair and sticking wetly to his skin, freezing his blood.

"This dies with you!" Leonardo yelled at Icarus. "All of this dies with you!"

Icarus looked at Leonardo slowly. "No, Leo... it doesn't."

He smiled bloodily as he looked at the fallen preacher. He had done what he had set out to do and had completed his mission. His gaze slowly slipped from his eye as he looked up at the falling snow, his muscles loosening as his last breath released, his body resting, motionless.

The one they called Icarus was dead. His war was over.

Icarus's eye remained open, though his body was lifeless, leading Leonardo to rise and slowly remove himself from his corpse. He looked at Icarus's body, and in the silence, it finally hit him. He looked at his blood-stained hands as he thought about what Icarus said.

"What did he mean?" Leonardo asked, looking at Michelangelo.

Michelangelo stayed hunched over. His body lost the ability to hold him up.

"It never ends, Leo. The cycle continues." He looked up at Leonardo. "It'll continue in you. You're his, now."

Leonardo looked at the soldier and remembered what Icarus said about him.

"Are you... going to kill me?" He asked fearfully.

Michelangelo looked up to Leonardo with eyes of sorrow, doing his best to contain his emotions. "No, kid... I'm not gonna kill you."

Leonardo breathed a sigh of relief.

"I won't have to," Michelangelo clarified.

Leonardo's smile slowly faded. He looked around, his eyes welling up, realizing he had no idea what to do, where to go, or who he might turn to. It was then that he saw five shadowy figures approaching up the hill. "Major General Saint Hart!" A soldier called out. "This is the US Army! If you live, make yourself known!"

Leonardo looked closer at the men and saw their blue US Army uniforms. Each soldier held a Flintchester repeater and scanned the battleground for Michelangelo.

"Mike, there's... men here for you, for me!" Leonardo whispered hopefully.

"They ain't here for you."

Leonardo looked at Michelangelo, confused. He began removing the Brother of Grim's bandolier from his chest.

"They'll kill you. Whether here or somewhere else, they'll prosecute," Michelangelo said.

"W— well, what do I do? Where do I go?" Leonardo asked, frightened.

Michelangelo dropped the grim's gun belt in front of Leonardo, having the two black revolvers holstered. "Go home, Leo. Get away from all this. You find that girl and— and you take her somewhere where nobody knows you. You hide... and you start over. Live the best life you can with her. The world will think you're dead or remember you as a killer. Either way, you can live." His breathing began to shake. "They'll treat you the same, regardless." He began to taste iron.

Leonardo looked down at the gun belt Michelangelo placed in front of him. "Why the guns?" He asked.

"You might need them," he answered.

"Hey, I see movement!" The soldier informed. Leonardo quickly draped the bandolier over his shoulders. *"You, over there! Don't move!"* Another soldier ordered.

All of them aimed their weapons. Michelangelo raised his arms in surrender as Leonardo ducked behind him.

"Mike I— I don't know if I can... I don't know if I wan't—" Leonardo lamented.

"Kid," Michelangelo said, looking up at him. "Do the goddamn right thing. For all our sakes."

Leonardo leaned back and prepared to make a run for it, looking out at the pines that surrounded him. As he looked, he remembered something he had been given an hour prior that he was tasked with delivering to Michelangelo. Leonardo reached into his jeans pocket, pulled out an old piece of paper, and handed it over to Michelangelo, shoving it into his front pocket behind the leather-covered, metal armor. "For you from Icarus." He stood upright. "You'll want to read it."

"This is your last warning! Do not move or we will fire!" The soldier repeated.

"You need to go, kid." Michelangelo reminded.

Leonardo nodded. "Thank you for trying. For everything." He began shuffling away. "I'm sorry... I'm sorry."

He sprinted down the hill, making way for the forest of darkness that circled him.

"He's moving!" A fourth soldier called out.

The repeaters fired from the hillside and launched bullets at Leonardo's body and head. The metal poofed into the snow beside him as he ducked and weaved through the darkness, only to fall down the hill and roll uncontrollably. He rolled through the snow to the bottom of the hillside, then lay there coated in snow and cold.

"Wait, I think I see The Major... he's surrendered!" The other soldier discovered.

"Forget the other guy! He's gone! Get the Major General!" The Last Soldier commanded.

Leonardo caught his breath, only to stand to his feet gently and disappear into the darkness. Michelangelo's arms fell to his sides as his eyelids fluttered shut. He slumped over on his left side and splatted into the mud below, his body, now, too bloodless to carry on.

"Lord above... he's dying!" A Soldier called out.

The soldiers ran over and holstered their rifles over their shoulders as they waded through the snow to make it over to the fallen soldier. Michelangelo's body grew increasingly numb. The soldiers now stood above him, looking him over.

"Like hell he is. Where are the horses? *We need to get him out of here!*" The third soldier commanded.

The soldiers whistled frantically as they called out to the forest, the group leader hovering over Michelangelo, staring at him blankly. "It's okay, Major. We're gonna get you home." He reassured.

"What in the world happened to that guy?" The other soldier questioned, looking at Icarus' body.

"The Major General happened, that's what. Now come on, we need to get him out of here."

Michelangelo's eyes lightly opened as he looked at Icarus's body, realizing that Icarus was right once again. Icarus stated Michelangelo would fail Leonardo once more, and he truly felt he did. Whether it be by manipulation or prophecy, this had crushed him. He closed his eyes and stopped fighting his wounds, as death's presence warmed over him in the cold. The soldiers worked on him in a panic, while Michelangelo fell deathly limp, drifting away from reality as his life slipped from him.

Leonardo ran further into the forest that surrounded him. Both the preacher and the soldier were dying, albeit in separate ways, but both ran closer to their final destination, unaware of where they were going. In this moment, there was only one certainty, one absolute truth for both of them: from this day forth, they would no longer be the same. They had gone too far into the darkness.

CHAPTER 13

Tales Like this Told Must End in Much Sorrow

arely, rest was in the cool of the air of the woodland lands, still and soft. Today, however, it was. Today, the pines stretched high into the sky, and their green bristles glistened in the sun's shining light. Droplets of water dripped from them and sprinkled upon the ground every so often, their faint pitter-patters clicking and tapping upon the wet soil. The ground, for the first time in four months, was present and pretty, revealing itself to be a dark, rich brown, coated in tiny twigs and browned pine needles. Pinecones were scattered around the muddy land, and rocks came forth from it in alternating sizes. The ground was mushy, wet, and faded in appearance; the snow had now reduced to small piles, which remained solid in the shade of the pines.

It was also located underneath the cots in the camp, as well as beside the tents and wagons that housed the soldiers' supplies. There were tan canvas tents, pitched in a triangulated, angled fashion in a mid-sized circle, sporadically. Each was built high with metal poles and rope, their stakes firmly spiking the ground at the front, sides, and back.

The soldiers walked about their camp, attending to their own business, with one sitting beside the fire pit, stirring a stew that simmered in a large, black pot. The fire released a smoky, pine-scented aroma into the air, along with a meaty and garlic scent from the stew that boiled within.

The burning wood in the campfire popped and snapped, waking Michelangelo up from his sleep. His eyes jolted open as he came to, looking around at his surroundings, his heart racing, for the sound the fire produced reminded him of an all-too-sinister recent event. He looked around, moving his head slightly, noting that he was no longer on a hillside, but somewhere else.

Somewhere else completely.

He looked down at his cot, then to the wide-open forest around him, noticing the season had noticeably changed. He felt the warm cool of the morning on his chest, then looked down and realized his shirt and union suit were not there. His upper body was laid bare to the nature around him, wrapped in bandages and ointments. He looked over his vessel and took note of the punishment he had taken. Large circular black, blue, and purple bruises coated his chest and arms. He looked at the wrapping that was tightly wound just above his hips, which covered the bullet wound he had taken to his lower abdomen. The gauze extended to just below his ribs, wrapping around his back and stomach, and also covering and wrapping over his right shoulder. It was laid on thick, but despite this, his blood had, at some point, still seeped through the material, leaving a large, dark brown circle in its wake.

Below the wrap was the cut remains of his union suit, which were snipped down the center and left to rest at his hips. He looked at the dangling sleeves that wilted down beside the cot, seeing the union suit's uncut back was barely holding them together, which was now crumpled and flat beneath Michelangelo's lower back. He noticed the loss in weight he appeared to have taken, only in his muscles. They were leaner, and his body was noticeably thinner, which, for a man as broad-shouldered and tall as he was, was an alarming sight to see. This told him that he had been resting for quite a while—a few weeks, at the least.

He moved his face and winced at the tight, pulling pain in his left eyebrow and bridge of his nose. He lifted his hand and felt the areas that pinched, finding new stitches in place of the busted ones. He slowly slid his hands over his face, and for the first time in a long time, he felt the softness of his skin, which was no longer caked in dried blood that flaked off of him. He touched his chin and cheeks, the slight stubble pricking his hand. His beard had grown to a moderate stubble, which further confirmed to him that he had been resting for some time. That said, he was surprised that he didn't smell, but was clean, with a fresh water and soap scent.

With this information, he rested his hand on his chest and lifted his head to look at his left leg, the other part of his body he remembered had taken a bullet. The same white gauze was wrapped firmly around his thigh, where the bullet had appeared to pass through. His union suit was cut open from the ankle up to the injury, and his navy man's pants were not upon him. In fact, save for the union suit covering around his groin, he was without any clothing. He took in a deep breath and felt the cool, brisk air upon his skin, embracing the feeling of the changing season and the warmth that radiated from it. He squeezed and relaxed his muscles in his black and blue legs, then opened his toes to feel the springtime air. He felt the cool of the morning after winter upon his sore but healing flesh, then sat up with a painful and sore groan. This grabbed the attention of the soldiers around him, who were surprised to say the least. The soldier by the stew stood to his feet quickly, "He's awake... the Major General is awake!" He exclaimed.

The other, by the ammunition wagon, turned around slowly. The wagon was loaded with rifles and ammunition and was a large and spacious vehicle designed for long-distance transportation. The wood it was made of and the ammo boxes within it were wet, dark brown, and faded. The ammo wagon was parked between two of the five tents placed nearby. Michelangelo looked closer and noticed a Captain's insignia on this soldier's clothing.

He was their leader.

A few horses of black and brown stood on the outside of the camp, walking behind and around the five canvas tents standing. Michelangelo turned and looked in front of him, and seeing the medical tent, which was also a tented wagon, parked just in front of his feet. It had a white canvas top supported by a wooden wall, which was part of the wagon, and wooden beams that extended outward and connected to the wagon in the same manner. *This must be where they got their supplies and ointments from,* he thought. He noted the empty medicinal glass bottles scattered on the ground, and as he looked underneath the makeshift medical zone, he saw a few stools and tables, all placed in a strategic position for him.

The stew soldier, noticeably younger, walked over to him quickly as three other young men exited their tents, looking at Michelangelo with the same excitement. The ammo soldier stayed in his position, continuing to load the weapons with ammunition, cleaning the rifles, repeaters, and navy revolvers. The ammo soldier stared at Michelangelo while he looked at the rest of them, unsure of how to act, given that he presumed they had all come to kill him. He sat up in his cot slowly, his injuries squeezing and straining his flesh, his muscles shaky, his body exhausted. He plopped his left leg over the side of the cot and immediately followed it with his right, firmly planting both in the damp soil beneath him, cooling his feet as the wet earth embraced them. The young soldiers stood in front of him, wide-eyed and excited, as they looked upon the unkillable, the legendary, Saint of Retribution.

"Man, he's even more intimidating in person," one said.

"Incredible. Absolutely incredible," the other replied.

"You know, you really shouldn't be sitting up, Major General," the stew soldier started. "The injuries you've sustained are... severe, to say the least. For all intents and purposes, you should be dead, but since you're not, resting is the best policy."

Michelangelo looked up to the young men as his wits started to come to him.

"Who are you boys?" He asked groggily.

"The ones sent to take you in," the captain interrupted, looking up from the revolver he was loading as he thumbed one final bullet in. "Or kill you, if it comes down to it."

The young men, now determined to be no more than eighteen or nineteen, in Michelangelo's opinion, cautiously backed away. He looked at the captain. "You're all they sent?"

The captain chuckled, ignoring the comment. "Name's Captain Mathews."

The captain was far older than the young men—twenty-eight, to be exact. He flicked the chamber of the weapon closed, then looked over the revolver.

"Hm. I'm assuming you all know who I am?" Michelangelo asked.

"Yeah. We know who you are," Captain Matthews replied.

"Then why have you decided to leave me alive?"

"It's important to note, Major General, that we actually saved your life," the stew soldier clarified.

Michelangelo looked at the soldier curiously, realizing that it was true, then looked back to the captain.

"Congress has determined that they would much rather have you alive than dead, particularly for your execution," Captain Matthews informed.

"Right," Michelangelo agreed, annoyed. "And what say you on that matter?"

The captain aimed the revolver forward at the ground, checking the sights. "There's a great promotion involved for the man who captures you dead. There's an even greater one for the one who takes you in alive." He stopped aiming and looked up, hammering in a round. "And that's precisely what we intend on doing."

The soldiers were confused; Michelangelo was too tired to be defensive and too dead to care. "Captain, with all due respect," one soldier interrupted, "you said we came out here to save him." Captain Matthew began to walk toward Michelangelo. "And we did. You boys are so caught up in your petty fantasies that you forget the mission to which you were assigned. Michelangelo Saint Hart is no hero... he's a criminal, just the same as the rest of them. In fact, he's the last one standing. Congress would like to ensure that the public is aware of this. We need to exemplify that these lands are no longer lawless; that men like him are dying... or dead altogether," Captain Mathews finished, stopping in front of Michelangelo.

He looked up at him, breathing tiredly and without a care. With a quick motion, Captain Mathews unhammered the weapon, flipped it over in his hand, and held the grip out to the soldier, revealing a grizzly bear carved into the yellow and brown wood. Michelangelo looked at the familiar handle. "Unfortunately, we never found Major General St. Hart. In fact, as far as we know, he's as good as dead."

The soldiers breathed a sigh of relief, smiles gracing their faces. The soldier looked up at Captain Mathews with an uncertain, yet gracious, expression, halfway thankful and halfway curious. He raised his aching left arm and grabbed the handle of his weapon, then brought the gun to his knees with a heavy drop.

"You boys go clean up the camp. We're leaving," the captain ordered.

They did as they were told, but not without first saluting the soldier proudly. They then walked off, excitedly talking among one another. Both Captain Matthews and Michelangelo watched them as they walked away.

"You're a hero to them, you know. In some circulations, you're a legend." Captain Matthews turned back. Michelangelo sighed as he thought about the title in full context. "I'm no hero."

"Mm. Yeah. 'Michael the Merciless' and 'Saint of Retribution' don't necessarily give hero, do they?"

They both chuckled.

"I guess not."

The captain looked at the young men again. "After seeing everything, or everyone that you left behind, I had half the mind to put you down, mostly out of fear for my own life."

"What changed your mind?"

The captain stopped for a moment. "I don't know if it is, fully, but I get it." He looked back. "Not to mention that, whether you believe it or not, there is still mercy in you. I saw it when you let the kid go... what was his name? Leonardo DelMuerto?"

"How should I know? It was dark. I was dying. It could've been anybody."

The captain smiled. "Don't worry, Major. You don't have to mince words with me. I can also understand why it is you'd want to protect him. I can also see that those rumors of you going to help an evangelist were true."

"How so?"

"Well, whoever that kid was, you let him go. He couldn't have been one of Icarus's men because clearly you would've killed them."

"So what's your point?"

"My point is, there's more to you. A lot more. This is just... who you are now. The man you *had* to be."

Michelangelo took a moment of silence to consider this.

"So," he started, "any reason why Congress sent a couple of young men and a captain to take me down?"

"Oh, you mean the ruthless, bloodthirsty, violent, and experienced killer that has made national news because of his murder spree?" He chuckled. "In my opinion, because the public agrees with you, and Uncle Sam doesn't want them to. Yet, it's hard to hate a man who does what the government won't. Who fights against evil so heinous that it makes his questionable methods pale in comparison."

"Really?"

"Oh, yeah. The paper has had a heyday with you."

"So you think they sent you all out here on a suicide mission?"

Captain Matthews shrugged. "It would be a good way to twist the narrative... if you had been everything you said you were, that is."

Michelangelo looked up. "And how am I not?"

"We're still alive."

Michelangelo raised one eyebrow and nodded silently. "Well, it wouldn't be the first time Congress was wrong." Michelangelo looked at the ground beneath his feet and pondered whether or not he would've killed the soldiers if they had gotten in his way a moment prior. "But in all honesty, I just don't have any fight left in me anymore, Captain. That's all."

"Well, true or not, a lot of innocent people died because of those men. They died horrifically, some in ways that I didn't know were possible. We learned about them long before it got this bad. We knew about those men going about, torching churches and believers alike. We didn't do anything. Not until you got involved. Even then, we weren't sent to hunt *them*; we were sent here to hunt *you*. So many innocent people have been lost. I feel that we, Congress, and the public share some responsibility in that, but not you." Michelangelo looked up. "You made it right. You did what none of us could." Captain Matthews sighed, then looked down, ashamed. "They say justice is blind, but— I just— I just never thought that meant turning a blind eye... I thought justice saw the wickedness in men and would not succumb to the fragility of humanity. I thought that's what I was fighting for: a better tomorrow... for the innocent and the guilty." He looked out at the open pines. "But if this is what's in store for tomorrow, if this is 'justice'... I'm not sure it's worth fighting for." He looked at Michelangelo. "But, I suppose... as long as there's men like you... Maybe tomorrow is worth it all. Maybe there is hope in bringing justice where justice cannot reach; to fight in a land where darkness is so palpable that no matter what a man does, it still leaves the darkness unaltered. To avenge those who need to be avenged, and bring vengeance to those who deserve it. If that's what it takes, and you are the necessary response to what evil we have created... then so be it." He clicked his tongue and looked at his men. "Is this what it takes? Is this justice? Or is this just... humanity—who we are? Killers, seeking to kill the un-killed."

Michelangelo thought about what was said as Captain Mathews walked over to the medical tent, leaned over, picked up a pile of clothes hidden underneath the wagon, and walked back. The clothes were Michelangelo's, and they were riddled with bullet holes and blood, though the blood had now been cleaned off to the soldiers' best abilities. He looked at his brown gun belt with two holsters, flopping weightlessly as they waited for their revolver. Captain Mathews placed the clothing beside Michelangelo on the cot, who then reached over, pulled up his button-up, and analyzed the caked-in blood stains.

"Unfortunately, it's very rare that blood actually comes out. In your case, it's a miracle we were able to absolve as much as we did," Captain Matthews informed. "You've been in and out for a week and a half, now, maybe two. We tried to clean your uniform in between trying to keep you fed and alive, but... there's just no way you can get out that much blood."

Michelangelo looked over the clothing and remembered something he had been given: a paper that was placed in his upper right chest pocket.

"We couldn't find the other revolver. I'm afraid all that's left is the one on your lap." Captain Mathews informed again.

Michelangelo sifted through the chest of drawers and felt the paper grace his fingers. He gently pulled it out and unfolded it. Captain Mathews watched, intrigued, as the soldier opened the paper and read the words on it. His eyes slowly darkened as he realized what was on the paper. He slowly placed it aside, then slowly but willfully stood, though his leg was pierced with an angry stab as his bullet wound screamed in pain. He slowly put on his button-up shirt, sliding his arms through it with a painful ease. Captain Mathews saw this newfound life in Michelangelo and leaned over, grabbed the tiny paper beside him, and read it. He looked up from the paper, confused. "Caine Kingsley? As in

Brigadier General Kingsley?"

"The very same," Michelangelo answered.

"He a friend of yours?"

"He was."

He buttoned his buttons gently, avoiding as much pain as he could. He redirected his attention to his gun belt on the cot. Captain Mathews looked down at the paper once more.

"Heddlebrook? We all thought the old man just retired and died, but I guess Heddlebrook's as good a place to live as any."

"Yes, Captain Mathews, it is indeed a good place to live... and die."

Captain Mathews looked up at the soldier as he slipped his left pant leg over his leg, clenching his teeth in pain. He then did the right side, Captain Mathews taking on a face of concern, as the other soldiers watched as well, having heard what they were discussing.

"You know, Major, if Kingsley is involved in this in any way, we might be able to swing this in your favor. Give Congress a bigger fish; give people a better demon to focus on. We could change the story and make Kingsley swing rather than you. If you know something we should know, if you could testify—"

"The law didn't work before, Captain." He stood upright, towering over him. "What makes you think it's going to work now?"

The captain felt a bit of fear. "All I'm saying is we might be able to save your life."

"I don't want to be saved, Matthews."

Michelangelo pulled his knife from his gun belt and began cutting his Union suit from around his waist. He ripped the material off his body and slowly tucked the odds and ends into the bottom of his button-up shirt, which he then tucked into his pants, noting the bullet hole in the thigh, showing the gauze underneath.

"So that's it, then? The only way the legendary, un-killable soldier could be killed was by his own hand?" Captain Matthews questioned. He shrugged. "Kind of poetic, I guess."

"There is no un-killable man, the same way there is no law that can go without corruption." He looked at Captain Matthews. "There is only the certainty that we all must face, which is that we all must die. I am a man of personal vendetta, Mr. Mathews, and this is a matter of personal concern. Caine Kingsley's involvement is a burden that I must bear alone. I've expected from the beginning that the shadow of death would be brought upon me for such actions. If I am a legend, then let that live on, but I have no desire to live along with it," Michelangelo clarified.

The soldiers looked to him, their perception of him shifting, as they realized that though they had been told many great tales, the soldier might have been just a man, one with weaknesses as deadly as any bullet, and comparable to any individual. They realized that legends died just like mortal men, and wondered if that made legends legendary at all.

Michelangelo sat on his cot and pulled his socks over his feet in a swift, yet painful, motion. He grabbed his black riding boots and pulled them over his socks, letting his navy pants drape down to the top of them, clearly showing the yellow strips along the sides of his pants, unbloused.

"Will you let them take you?" Captain Mathews questioned.

Michelangelo looked up at Captain Mathews, then the surrounding soldiers.

"What's truer justice? To let the killer live in hopes he might be redeemed, or kill the killer so others may survive? Is it better to live in a realm of brutal reality, or to be fine with our justified illusions? Do we take vengeance into our own hands or leave it in the hands of something higher? I've heard these questions so many times in various places... It'd be impossible not to ponder it. I've heard it from different people in various situations, as if God Himself was trying to speak to me, yet I cannot determine what it is that's being said. I, in my own understanding, would rather kill the killers so others may survive, yet in doing so, I then become the killer, and am now owed the same justice." He shook his head. "It's a hard thing... exchanging one life for another. To end the wicked so the innocent will not be in our inaction." He smiled, thinking about Leonardo. "I understand why some people prefer God to make that decision, because as a man... I have been broken by it. My mind has been torn and my heart has been tortured; my thoughts torment me as they reflect upon my actions and those whom I have ended haunt me and never leave my memory. So, yes, I desire that the torment would cease, for though I have found myself in a war for the innocent, I have not been granted the righteous reward of death, like my brother before me. Instead, I have been cursed with the reward of life in all its infinite pain. Perhaps it is due to my failure, and thus this is my punishment; perhaps it is because I succeeded, and this is my reward. Either way, I figure, if this is my fate, and this is how I am judged, then this is how I wish for it to *cease*. Perhaps, in my penance, will I find release. Regardless, I have determined the life of legends is not the gift of eternal life: it is instead damnation whilst you are alive and wait to be damned again. I have been a vessel of vengeance; I have been the one sent, but I am not saved from the one that will be sent to me. I am not spared vengeance, whether of God or self-regulating actualization; repayment is due whilst I live." He stood to his feet slowly. "This story must end somewhere, with someone, and I believe that someone is me."

The soldiers bore witness to the heaviness of Michelangelo's tolls that his mission had taken on him: the soldier who could not be killed; the soldier who could not die, not because he didn't want to but because he was not allowed.

Not yet.

Michelangelo pulled up his gun belt and buckled it tightly at his hip, then leaned down and picked up his revolver, holstering it at his right. He finished dressing himself by rolling up his sleeves to just above his elbows, now wanting to feel the cool of the spring. He looked at the soldiers who stood in silence, taking in his dark words. He had thought, for a moment, that maybe he should comfort them, but knew that he had no time to waste, given he had already lost so much of it.

"Did you get my horse?" He asked firmly.

"Yeah… she should be with the other mares, somewhere around here," Captain Mathews answered.

Michelangelo limped to the center of the camp and blew a whistle, calling Bleu to his current location. Bleu let out an excited whinny as her hooves pounded through the softened soil. The ground vibrated under her heavy steps, and Michelangelo smiled at the sight of her trotting up to him. She shook her head and lifted it into the air, equally as excited to see her old friend. She stopped beside him heavily as he reached up and patted her side, looking her over and making sure she was okay. She was unharmed, unbroken, with spirits as high as they had ever been. He looked back at her saddlebags and saddle, noting the empty shotgun and rifle holster. However, next to it, he noticed his leather-covered armor, dangling from the side. It was attached firmly to the saddle, ready for use at a later date. The leather on the armor had six bullet holes, revealing a silver-looking metal underneath. Nodding a few times, he reached his hand up to Bleu's pommel and pulled himself atop her with the bit of strength he had, using his right foot to balance in the right side stirrup, and gently lifted his left leg over. The soldiers stared at him as he sat atop his steed. He looked back.

"We anywhere near Little York?" He asked.

"About a day's ride. 'Can't miss it once you hit the trail." Captain Mathews responded, gesturing behind him with his head.

Michelangelo nodded, looked, and then grabbed Bleu's reins and comfortably held them in his right hand as he looked to the south of the Arizona Territory. He slightly looked back at the soldiers. "Thank you. Each of you. I appreciate everything you've done for me." With that, he tapped Bleu's right side, which set them off with her calm gate, carrying them on their last legs of the journey, as she had done many times before. The two arrived at the rim of the camp and stopped as Michelangelo had a thought. He turned to the soldiers, who were all sharing a collective thought on what they had seen and heard.

"Captain Matthews," he said, turning them around. "You understand the discretion of this situation, correct? I would greatly appreciate it if you did not breathe a whisper of the name Caine Kingsley to anyone. He is mine, and rest assured, justice will be served. I would hate for you to get in the middle of that."

Captain Matthews's heart pumped a little harder. "Of course, Major General."

Michelangelo nodded as the soldiers took heed of the threat, and from that day on, never spoke a whisper of Caine Kingsley's name.

Michelangelo turned Bleu forward and heeled her into a gate, beginning their day's travel.

The two had arrived in Little York by midday, which was as bright and beautiful as Michelangelo had imagined. Without the snow covering it all in white-washed bleakness, it shone in the sun, its infrastructure gleaming. Little York was bright and beautiful, but empty. He found this to be an odd contrast: a wondrously small city with only a few to enjoy it. Bleu clopped upon the brick-laden street as a few carriages with their drivers walked beside them. Wagon men prodded and creaked by, as their supplies wobbled within their wagons. It was silent, eerily silent, letting every slight sound be heard.

Michelangelo looked down at the brick that lay upon the ground, shining with a colorful and fascinating black. Only this time, there were no bodies, no blood; just the stony road and the buildings that surrounded it. They stood in the same way in which they were left. Aland's Theatre was bright and shining with all its beautiful bulbs atop it, save a few that had been shot out or exploded. Regardless, this did not stop the beauty of such a modern town, for upon the top of said buildings, working away, were men who had been paid to replace the bulbs and restore the theatre to its former glory. Bullet holes riddled the entire building, though they were hardly noticed if the sunlight had not shone upon them. Michelangelo, however, caught them almost immediately, for he remembered why they were there and who had shot them.

He looked back at the Sheriff's Office, still standing with its fancy cut granite and perfectly stained white wood, untouched as the day it had been placed, and as prestigious as the day it was founded. He looked forward again and took note of the buildings that stood along the street of Little York, mostly left unchanged, with only the General Store and Aland's Theatre needing extensive repairs due to their damage. He looked to his left at the store, noticing that it had been closed permanently due to the owner's passing. He stopped to look upon it for a moment, examining its interior, which was completely dark. He stared through the broken glass windows, now boarded up by two large pieces of two-by-fours, nailed together in an X design.

From there, he felt eyes peering at him, and turned to look at the few people who were once walking the clean concrete sidewalks, all dressed in their fancy attire, which was complete with fine linens and monocles. He did his best to remain anonymous, though the few who walked these streets knew who he was. At this point, he was unforgettable. Once they saw him looking at them, they scattered, fearfully averting their eyes and going about their business.

Michelangelo rolled his eyes, then tensed as the pain in his lower body struck him quickly, forcing him to reach down and feel the spot where a bullet had run through. Though the wound had been cauterized, it was still deep, and his blood would break for air at the slightest pinch and twist. This blood was the only blood that was fresh upon Michelangelo's clothing, for it had accumulated in a little spot, and was now upon the tips of his index and middle fingers.

"Major General!" The sheriff called out. "I'll be honest, I did *not* expect you to come back."

Michelangelo turned his head toward him, equally as surprised to see him. He turned Bleu to the right, wiping his blood on his pants, which grabbed the sheriff's attention further. He saw Michelangelo was beaten and broken, more of a skeleton than a soldier. Michelangelo was not the same man the sheriff had met two weeks prior. Now, he was a far different creature, acting as more of a remnant than an animal. No navy jacket puffed him up, no navy hat to add to his authority; there was only a man, bashed and bloodied, just managing to stay stitched together. Remorse overtook the sheriff's eyes as he remembered what had happened on Michelangelo's last visit; he remembered what he had seen in the morning light.

"Sheriff," Michelangelo greeted.

"I... feel it's only fair you know that a group of soldiers came through looking for you. Came almost two weeks ago, shortly after the journalists."

"Yeah. I met the soldiers."

"I see... and are they well?"

"They're well."

The sheriff nodded and looked down, then back up. "Did you get him? Icarus, I mean."

"Yeah. I got him."

"What about Leo and his brothers?"

Michelangelo hesitated. "They didn't make it."

The sheriff sighed; his heart saddened. He didn't want to hear this terrible news, and truthfully, Michelangelo didn't want to give it, but they both accepted it, nonetheless. The sheriff shook his head as he looked at the ground, thinking about the times the Brothers' Six had come to visit. "You at least kill all those bastards?" He asked.

"All but one," Michelangelo foreshadowed. He turned Bleu in the direction of Hotel Emilda, the sheriff continuing to look after the soldier. "Be well, sheriff," he hollered out. "To you the same, Saint Hart." The Sheriff hollered back.

He turned and made his way back to his office as Michelangelo arrived in front of Hotel Emilda, then carefully hopped off Bleu, slowly and gently landing on his right leg. He hitched Bleu to the fancy horse posts out front of the hotel, then shifted his attention to the large, glass front doors. He stared at them a moment, mentally preparing himself for what was to come, for the promise he had to keep. He opened the doors to the hotel with a slow and gradual ease, allowing the people inside to enjoy their meals. The fireplace was no longer lit, and the room was bathed in the midday sun's light. It glistened through the front windows and doors, onto the wooden floor.

The people in the hotel looked up at Michelangelo and stopped their eating and conversing, for he was very distracting. They looked upon the battle-scarred soldier, who stood out wildly against his surroundings, yet he continued to try to blend in. Rosa looked up from her work, her eyes widening in an expression of hopeful joy. "Michael? *Michael!*" She greeted, splitting the attention of the guests.

He smiled out of the side of his mouth and raised his right arm to a hip-high wave. He thought it was nice to have someone excited to see him.

Rosa gestured her head to an empty table. "Come on over, soldier. Don't be shy. I got a seat for you, right here." He raised his hands in a surrendering motion, then limped towards the table as the guests within the hotel continued eating their afternoon meals; the aroma of potatoes and bread filled the air, making for a pleasant smell in Michelangelo's nostrils. Meat and potatoes had come together in a light, gravy soup, complemented by celery and carrots. The people slurped away at their dining as he sniffed hungrily, but could not bring himself to eat.

He limped past the mahogany red tables, filled with people, but a lot fewer than before. Rosa walked around the corner of the bar, then over to Michelangelo, which was a surprise to him. He hadn't had help like this in a long time, or someone who seemed to care, for that matter, legitimately. She crouched underneath Michelangelo's left arm and lifted on his left side, allowing him to walk just a little less painfully, as they made their way to the table. Rosa pulled out the mahogany chair and helped Michelangelo sit, who did, carefully and slowly, placing his right arm on the tabletop. She pulled out a chair for herself that was right beside him and sat at his side, looking him over, then into his pain-filled eyes. She saw that the torment they had in them, not just from bullets and cuts, but from somewhere deeper. "What happened, Michael?" she asked, worried. Michelangelo took a moment as he thought about his answer, for he was slightly unwilling to be honest, but knew that honesty was what was best. "I lost the kid. His brothers. I lost them all."

She slowly placed her left hand on his arm, her eyes growing sad. She let out a painful sigh. "I'm sorry, Michael. I'm so sorry," she comforted.

"I killed every one of Icarus' men... but it still wasn't enough. I couldn't save any of them. And Bill—"

He choked down the lump in his throat.

"You were right about Bill... everything you said. It was all true. More than you know, and it was far more malicious than either of us could have imagined."

Tears began to fill Rosa's eyes as her heart lit ablaze. "Did you kill him?" She asked vengefully. "I tried," he replied. "But no. He's gone. I don't know where to."

She sighed and looked away from Michelangelo, releasing him as a tear rolled down her cheek, leading her to wipe it away as she did her best to control her crying. Of all the men Michelangelo could have killed, William was the one she wanted dead the most. Michelangelo looked down at her, sorrowfully. "I guess gone is as good as dead, for our sakes," she determined.

"He won't be coming back," he reassured.

Rosa cried a little harsher. Michelangelo, unsure as to how to handle this, reached out his hand to her. She looked over and smiled, letting out a slight laugh at the gesture, not because it was silly but because it was sweet. She took it and looked up at him.

"When, uh— " he tried. "When we first met, you told me that this all had to mean something. That, Tommy's death, and you being alive... Tomás' birth... it all had to *mean* something. I've been thinking about that a lot lately - about what all this means. For a while there, I thought, you know, maybe it does. Maybe this holy war, maybe Leonardo... maybe it was all worth fighting for, that this was all building towards something bigger than me or any of this. It all started to make sense, you know? But after what happened, all I can think is what could it build toward now? Why wasn't what I did *enough*? Why did I lose Leo? If this is all supposed to mean something, I don't understand what. And worst of all... I am the only one left alive to think about any of it... and I can't figure out why." Michelangelo shared.

Rosa looked between each of his eyes as he did to hers, each one sharing a look of compassion for the pain that the other felt.

"I don't know if there's an answer right now, Michael. I don't know if there will ever be, but I *do* know one thing: sometimes, living is far worse than dying, and sometimes saints are meant to suffer. It's kind of like the saying, 'no good deed goes unpunished,' yet many forget that no punishment goes without reward. If you are alive, and this is your punishment, then there must be a reward out there... somewhere."

"Killing is no good deed, Rosa—"

"But trying to save innocent people is! You're more than just the 'Saint of Retribution,' like these reporters want to call you. You're more than 'Michael the Merciless.' You're a fighter! A soldier, who, though he may be harsh in his practice, may even be slightly misguided, ultimately fights on the side of good. Now that *alone* cannot save you from your sins... but it shows you are a man worth saving."

Michelangelo thought about what Rosa had said and pondered his own worthiness and redemption. He wondered whether that was something possible for him, or visible in his future, despite the current road he was on. Still, in the end, Michelangelo could make no sense of his fate and saw no other end to his tale, for a soldier bent on vengeance was absolutely bound to be found guilty of bloodshed.

"I appreciate the sentiment, Ms. Felina, but even if second chances were to be given, they won't be given out to a man like me anytime soon. I have yet to reach the end of my road."

Rosa's eyes hardened in a state of concern as her grip on his hand slightly tightened. "What do you mean?" She asked hesitantly.

"I found Kingsley. I know where he is, or at the least, a place he's been. He's in a town called Heddlebrook."

"Really?" She chuckled with a slight laugh of disbelief. Michelangelo smiled. "What?" He asked. "Well, I could've told you that. He hasn't moved an inch from where I saw him, where William was standing right behind him." Michelangelo sighed and chuckled a bit as well. "Isn't that ironic?"

"It's coming full circle, is what it is."

"Yeah... seems to be a lot of that these days."

Michelangelo looked out the front door of the hotel and thought about the coming trip home. Rosa, on the other hand, continued looking at him, more comfortable than she had been for a long time. Rosa gently caressed his hand with her thumb. He looked at his hand, then to Rosa, feeling the same comfort. He gently squeezed her hand with his thumb, with each sharing a moment of calm and comfort.

"Are you sure you have to do this? Are you sure you can't stay?" Rosa attempted.

He thought about it for a second. "After everything that he's done, that *I've* done... I feel as though I have to."

Rosa nodded her head slowly, then looked between each of Michelangelo's eyes. "My offer is still on the table." She looked over at the bar counter. "Tomàs and I could use someone to look up to."

He thought about taking on this role, about leaving everything else behind, but just as soon as those thoughts came, they were overrun by his failures and flaws from before. He didn't think that was something to be looked up to, something he would want passed on to a son that he raised. He thought about his biggest flaw of all, being that despite all of this, he could not bring himself to spare Caine Kingsley's life. He wouldn't be able to live in peace if he did so, even with someone as wonderful as Rosa in his life.

"I appreciate the offer, Rosa, but... You and I both know I can't stop until Caine is dead," he decided, removing his hand from Rosa's.

"I know. I know," Rosa understood.

He lifted himself with a fragile care from the table. Rosa didn't move, but stayed there in her sadness. He stood and turned.

"See you around, Michael," Rosa let go.

Michelangelo looked over his shoulder, taking in one more moment of peace before it was forever gone. "Michelangelo," he corrected.

"Oh?"

"My name, in full... It's Michelangelo."

She let out a sweet smile. "Like the painter?"

He turned around. "Yeah. Like the painter," he said, smiling back.

"Well... in light of sharing our real names, I guess I should share mine. My name is Rosaline."

"Like the outlaw?" Michelangelo joked, sarcastically.

"Yeah. Like the outlaw," she agreed, rolling her eyes with a smile.

Each shared one final look, now candid and fully known.

"It was a pleasure to meet you, Rosaline," he smiled.

"All the same to you, Michelangelo," she said, smiling back.

He nodded his head once, then turned around and made way for the door, his heavy and steady limp continuing. She watched as he left, tears forming in her eyes as a bittersweet smile spread across her face.

He looked to his right and saw another familiar face as he stopped in front of the front doors. It was Bozco. Michelangelo gave him a content and thankful nod. Bozco nodded back, as the two remained grateful that he kept his word. With that shared glance, Bozco had felt that it was as though, without saying a word, he should continue doing it. Keep keeping his word, forever, if possible.

And he would.

With that, Michelangelo limped out the front door and made his way over to where Bleu was stationed. He unhitched her carefully and climbed atop, turning her in the direction of Heddlebrook and clicking his tongue to get her into a slow gate. Just as soon as he arrived, he left, off into the forest and held by his determination as he traveled back to the land of Heddlebrook, knowing that no matter what came next, Caine Kingsley was going to *die*.

CHAPTER 14

Take Note of the Lesson, Ye World of Tomorrow

eddlebrook, once a dying and outdated town, was now brimming with life, its travelers and locals enjoying their modern way of living. It was June, and in the eight months that had passed, the city had grown exponentially. The train station was located at the outskirts of town, where it had been before, but now it was flowing with people in their bright and fluffy clothing, flashing and waving their colors in the sun. The road had transformed from an old, dusty path to a red brick-built road, shining due to its polish. The sun highlighted the black cement that filled the space between the laden blocks, complementing the grey concrete sidewalk, which was neither freshly paved nor well-kept. Telephone poles were erected around the exterior of the town, extending behind the beautifully crafted buildings of Heddlebrook. One of them was a bank, made of fine white granite, complete with two large pillars on each side of the front, each supporting a large white curved top. The people walked in and out of the Heddlebrook Bank's freshly carved stairs, pulling and depositing their funds to live their

life of luxury. Beside the bank to the right stood the Hotel Heddlebrook, complete with bar and brothel. It was receiving a new coat of black paint, and working men were fixing the town's lights by hammering away atop their wooden scaffolding. To the left side of the bank, there was a gun store: Carlos Gunman, named promptly after the owner, who had opened the business and sold to the local community. It was a black, wooden building with a freshly stained coat, the name of the place just above the front door, in big, bulging letters colored with white gold.

Heddlebrook Transit, the train station, stood across from the gun store, in all its now freshly painted white wooden glory. The ticket master's booth was now covered by a long rectangular roof that covered the entire station. The area as a whole was improved with a fresh set of white wooden stairs, featuring wonderfully carved handrails to pair. The station's platform was filled with white benches and people, while the white guard rails surrounded the platform of the elevated building.

On the street, a few vehicles tooted and bumped their way down the road, catering to those who sought more luxurious transportation. They were clunky, large, and slow-moving machines, painted black in all their mechanical glory. Tailors and barbers now worked in the tailor's shop and barbershop, ready to give premium measurements and premium cuts. In front of these buildings, light posts stood tall in a large Y design, sprouting lights that drooped, evenly lighting the sidewalks at night. Oddly, and to most who toured there, the nights at Heddlebrook were a wonderful experience, even better than Little York's, especially given its controversy.

Heddlebrook was pristine, modern, and *glorious*. More importantly, it was all made possible by Caine Kingsley, the man who lived and fulfilled the American dream.

Toward the front of the town was a large, unoccupied building painted a dark brown, two stories high, that seemed similar to the dying west. Although it had an old-western look, it fit in with the modernized town and added to its overall charm. At the top of the building, where the words 'Kingsland Enterprises' used to be, there was nothing. It had been that way for nearly a year now, and with the time, wind, dust, and manpower that worked to destroy it, there was nothing left. Two large windows were built on each side of the front door, coated in dust, making it difficult for those walking by to peer in. The building's walls had two similar windows on each, as dusty as the interior and exterior. The windows were blocked with grey, woolen curtains, closed with the draft occasionally opening them a little. Out front of the building, built within the sidewalk, there was a set of horse hitches, custom-made and fancily crafted. They were an interesting creation, featuring a wolf's head hitch design atop the black poles, which were held firmly at the base and nailed to the ground.

To the left of Kingsland Enterprises, a heap of unfinished construction lay, consisting of wood planks stacked high in piles upon piles, with workers scattered about, reviewing their plans and discussing the best course of action. Some lay on the concrete beside the red-bricked street, getting some needed rest in the shade, while others continued their work on another new building. The workers' sweat beaded down their heads as the summertime heat radiated upon them, much like all Arizona weather surely did. Regardless of the changing seasons, the ever-marching waves of progression did not cease nor bend the knee.

Inside Kingsland Enterprises was Caine Kingsley's office, promptly placed on the second story, down the hall, away from the staircase. The staircase took the shape of a zigzagging Z, which made its way up and back on itself to fit within the tight building parameters. Caine's office was barren, now, with only the large wooden work surface, a wooden chair, and a leather rolling chair behind his desk. There was no fire lit within the fireplace, no trophies hung upon the walls, no men to watch over him for his protection from outlaws, nor outlaws in general. There were no cooked business deals or corrupt bounty hunters. There was nothing illuminated by the sunlight that came into the great Caine Kingsley's war room via the white rays that shone through the office window, the dust particles floating through them.

His office walls and floor were made of wood, with a grey, death-like, peeling paint. The desk and respective chairs had the same wear, the leather facing toward the front door, tucked neatly behind his desk.

"If you notice, you'll find everything in the shape you left it, given your abrupt exit," Caine's assistant assured, the door to Caine Kingsley's office unlocking.

The keys jingled and rattled against the wooden doorframe as she made her entrance into the office, opening the door with a gentle and calm motion, pushing air into the room. The dust in the air swirled outward and moved around the door in fluttering, dusty waves. She walked through the office door, holding her notebooks in her hand, each one neatly stacked on top of the others, keeping records of all the nearby properties owned by Kingsland Enterprises. She wore a grey sports coat, paired with grey men's slacks and grey dress shoes, accompanied by fancy black socks to match. Underneath the sports coat, she wore a white, men's button-up shirt that was neatly buttoned all the way to the collar, complemented by a thin black tie. The suit and button-up fit her loosely, despite coming in the smallest size. She was a slender, petite woman, resembling a young teenage boy, which inevitably worked in her favor when she conducted her business dealings, as the situation required. Her hair was blonde, cut short to her head, with trimmed sides that resembled a young man's haircut. The blonde of her hair was complemented by the white of her skin, which paired ever further with the blue of her eyes. Atop her head, she wore a grey bowler's hat.

Caine Kingsley slunk in behind her the way he had done many times before. He was still a heavyset man, wearing a custom-tailored pinstripe suit that fit his body neatly. The suit was colored with black and white stripes, head to toe, in a vertical pattern. He wore a fedora that matched the striped design, completed by a white, shining wrap and bow that tied pleasantly around the base. His face was pudgy, with a constant look of disgust everywhere he went. He had a thin, groomed, and black mustache that extended out from his face in a pointed and combed manner. His button-up shirt, worn underneath his sports coat, was a white one that matched a loose, black tie around his neck, tucked into his buttoned coat, effectively hiding his protruding belly.

He stood at a whopping five feet twelve, making for easier distribution as he walked. His feet heavily creaked on the wood as his black and white dress shoes, now covered in a slight layer of dust, made every step. The dress shoe featured a blackened toe, paired with a strip of white that encircled the top and sides of the foot.

He stopped at the center of his office and gazed upon the old room, which contained far too many memories to count, all of them good from his perspective. He thought about all he had accomplished, one final time, and the memories he had made in there.

"Is there anything else I can help you with, Mr. Kingsley?" His assistant asked.

"No, you have done a remarkable job, Ms. Rosenbaum. Remarkable job," he replied. He weightily turned around and faced her, then looked her up and down. "Are you still wearing men's clothing?"

"Uh... yes, sir."

"And to those that I've instructed you to disclose that you are a woman? How have they responded?"

"On the simpler ones, they tend to complain, but on the not-so-simple, they rarely care."

"I see. And how do you feel about this?"

"About not being able to express that I am a woman?"

"Of sorts. I myself would not appreciate it if I were forced to trod about as a teenage girl, dressed in a dress."

"I imagine so."

"That's why I ask, are you comfortable and willing to continue with this agreement?"

"Do I have a choice?"

Caine Kingsley put his arms behind his back and walked toward his favorite window. "My dear, with me, you will always have a choice." He stopped before the window, looking outside at his kingdom. "There is an overwhelming understanding that these people have of me, both through their indebtedness and experience. The people of Heddlebrook know that without me, none of them would have the jobs they hold today. I know this includes you as well. Therefore, in joining in that sentiment and recognizing that their families, homes, and futures are dependent on me and what I say—the civilization I have created, free from the lawless hand of the West, they will do as I say. They will accept what I say to accept, and *that* is their debt to pay, metaphorically, and they will never pay it." He turned back. "I am proud to call you the smartest of my crew, and I will gladly oblige your desires to be recognized as you are, not who they want you to be."

She smiled, breathed out a single breath, and thought about what Caine said. "Well, Mr. Kingsley, uhm. Yes! A million times, yes!"

Mr. Kingsley nodded his head as a proud smile fell upon his face. "Then it's done." He looked back out the window. "You know, Ms. Rosenbaum, as stated, you are the smartest of the men and women I work with. You have been a great deal of help to me and an even greater success, to boot. You are a woman who possesses a level of skill that is, quite frankly, *wasted* on these matters." He turned and walked toward her. "Perhaps it is time for a promotion. We're beginning our expansion of the business affairs in New York. I need someone who can effectively manage the company. You've done an excellent job here, but how would you like to handle *more?*"

"Mr. Kingsley, I—I don't know what to say."

"It is entirely up to you. After all, someone needs to manage the barber shops and gun stores. Of course, if you were to accept the position in New York, your salary would greatly increase, which I believe you, as much as anybody, would want. With this, you can drop the theatrical acrobats of a manifested manhood in exchange for being able to act as yourself: a woman of great intellect and responsibility. You'll be more readily accepted around sophisticated individuals rather than these cowpokes. Again, as a woman of the free nation, this is your choice."

Ms. Williamson smiled from ear to ear as she thought about the idea, containing her excitement within her professionalism.

"Why, Mr. Kingsley, that sounds quite fine! I'll pack my stuff and head there in the morning."

"No, no, you'll go there now," he stated with a smile, removing a billfold of ten-dollar bills from inside his sports jacket. "Big things are happening, Ms. Rosenbaum. I'd prefer it if you were there rather than here, as soon as possible. I'll have my men ship you whatever attire you've left here, although I encourage you to buy something new and nice for yourself. My men will be expecting you at the train station, at your earliest."

She smiled as she reached forward and took the money, her face overwhelmed with glee as she held the bills in her hands. "Thank you, Mr. Kingsley, I'll get right on it!" She excitedly walked out of the office and closed the door behind her with a professional shut, making her way to the train station.

Caine smiled as he turned around to look over his office once again, pondering over what his success had brought. He walked behind his desk and felt the old, familiar piece, thinking about the decisions he had made to reach his current position of power. He grabbed the leather rolling chair and rolled it backwards as he had done thousands of times before. Then promptly sat himself down as fluffs of dust shot out from underneath him. He rolled forward in front of his desk to where he had always sat, and reminisced with a slight lean back, resting in the reflection.

He had won. At the end of it all, he was the victor. He was the king left on the throne.

In a way, Caine was sad that he would be destroying his office. It was where he had worked many hours and burned many midnight oils to get where he was today. In fact, if the office and all it stood for hadn't meant as much to him as it did, he would have never come back from New York to it to see it off, but he had to. He had to bask in the glow of his success and all his accomplishments. It was his pride and joy, and it deserved to end with the one in which it began.

And Caine grinned.

Then there was a slow, heavy footstep, creaking in the wood. He looked up at the faint sound and listened. More proceeded. Creaking, weighty footsteps made their way to him, drawing closer.

"Ms. Rosenbaum? Is everything alright?" He called out.

There was no response. He looked to his office door as the footsteps drew closer. He listened closely as he looked at the white light shining underneath the door frame, now hearing the clunks of riding boots stepping against the wood. They were closer now, and as he continued to look at the light, it disappeared as the figure stepped in front of it. The doorknob slowly turned as Caine watched, unsure, his heart beginning to pick up speed. Then, slowly, it opened outward, revealing a shadow—a ghost that he thought was dead, or at the very least, a remnant of the past. "...Michael?" He asked in disbelief.

Michelangelo stepped forward from his silhouetted state and revealed his aimed navy revolver in his right hand, pointed at Caine's head. He looked at the weapon, then back at Michelangelo, whose left side of his face was now lit by the window's light, revealing his expression of anger, sadness, and betrayal.

"Hey, Caine," Michelangelo greeted.

He walked forward, the revolver held firm, remaining as calm as a summer's breeze. Caine calmly put his arms on the armrests of his chair, then slowly sat upright to face Michelangelo better, while he took a seat in the wooden chair just before Caine's desk. Caine looked at Michelangelo and examined his state.

He was lean and had lost much of his muscle mass, but was nourished enough to seem well for his height. His facial hair had grown to a long and bushy length, for his beard dirtily reached down to just above his collar. He was covered in a mixture of red and brown dust that had caked on his navy blue clothes, obscuring the bloodstains. He wore a red neckerchief that hung loosely around his neck, old and worn, with dust still visible, tied together in a rounded knot. The knot rested in front of his button-up shirt, leading down to the front of his shirt. His sleeves were rolled up to his elbows, and the shirt was tucked into his pants, the top button left unbuttoned. His pants were the same faded blue as the rest of his clothing, though they were now slightly torn from bullet holes and travel, with yellow stripes on the sides that barely had any color. They were bloused over his riding boots, which were now scraped, with red dust covering them. His pants were destringed at the ankle, and his gun belt was now a faded brown, with one holster on the right-hand side, as empty as the bullet bandolier it was attached to.

Caine looked at his face and examined the new additions: the scar on the bridge of his nose, which left a large, wide, white line running from side to side. He noticed a similar scar on Michelangelo's left eyebrow, which cut cleanly through the hair and left a white scar that began slightly above it and ended just below it. His hair was longer now, though still wavy and brown as it had ever been, reaching down to just below his ears, flowing back.

The two stared at one another in a moment of silence, as Michelangelo pondered what he would say. He burned inside as he looked at Caine's face: one of a man he had relentlessly hunted for nearly nine months.

"Do you know why I'm here?" Michelangelo began.

"One could assume," Caine responded calmly.

"Then you understand there is nothing you could say that would change my mind?"

"I figured as much."

Michelangelo nodded twice as he continued looking at Caine, feeling every bit of anger and sadness he had felt before, both emotions battling to see which would take hold.

"I'm going to cut right to the chase and say it: the only reason you're alive is because I want you to answer my questions, to try and make sense of... all of this."

Caine sighed. "Ask away."

Michelangelo hesitated. "Why did you kill Tommy?"

"I didn't kill Tommy."

"You know *damn well* you could've stopped it."

"Which is just as bad, yes... I hear you."

"So, then why? Why would you kill him with the same prejudice as you killed the outlaws, the believers?" He paused. "The hell's it worth?"

Caine carefully thought about the question. "It depends on where you're standing. Doing what I have done has been a hard thing to do... but I did it, not thinking of myself, but of the people in this country." Michelangelo scoffed. "No," Caine continued, "this is the way the world is, Mike. This is how things are now. It's a world of powerful men, and if you are not among them, then they will *consume* you. You know that, probably better than any! Everyone knows that this is how and why the men in power stay in power: to do what's best, not just themselves, but for the world. For the country."

"Funny how 'what's best' tends to change definitions, isn't it? Especially if you remove the moral good that most follow."

"Oh, give me a break. You mean the believers?"

"You're damn right I mean them. You really think burning them alive inside their own churches is 'doing what's best' for your country?"

"I can't speak to the methodology of certain criminals, Michael, but the concept is a necessary evil to attain power, to *make way* for the new world. What good did any believer ever contribute to the movement of progression? Think about it, Michael, these 'people,' they hold back the betterment of Man! While they're out there worshipping some deity, the working man is contributing to the economy and providing for his family. They'd sooner live in a world of poverty and pain than in riches and reward, and do you want to know why? It is because they cannot *do* better. They believe they will always *be* worse off, *must* be worse off, because they've been led to *believe* such fallacies. They've been indoctrinated since their birth and share the same weak-minded insolence that their generations before them had! Now, that wouldn't be too big of an issue if the evangelists didn't take their beliefs and spread them like a disease. That's all, most of these people are anyway... a disease in need of a cure, a cancer needing to be cut off! Only then will we have true prosperity."

"You fought for these people, Caine!"

"Ah, hell—"

"I joined the military because I looked up to men like you!"

"Yeah? And 'the hell you find? Nothing like what it seemed to be, right? The damn government doesn't make the rules; they don't 'do what's best' for the country; they fight for freedoms so that *men like me* can."

"But it's their freedom, Caine. It's theirs that you're taking!"

"People don't want freedom, Mike. They want comfort and security. Peace. Safety. That's what the hell they want. Look at what freedom has done to us! Look what it did to the West! It created a bunch of savages and hypocrites!"

"And how is that any different from you?"

"Because I don't destroy what I don't have to, Michael. I progress."

"So that's all Thomas was, then? That's all they are? You truly believe that they were all just a simple-minded disease that needed medication?"

Caine took a moment to think carefully about his response.

"One life does not outweigh the lives of many, Michael. Especially an outlaw's."

"He was more than an outlaw!"

"He made his choice! Why can't you accept that?"

"Because you keep calling it a choice. You keep painting the picture a certain way, but it's still clear what it is: it's an image of a selfish man, as detestable as they come, doing what's best for *his* life. Not the American people's, not the believers', but his. They all seem the same to me, if not worse, given that you also choose which ones live and which ones die." He shook his head. "You say one life doesn't outweigh the others, but tell me, Kingsley: does yours?"

"Don't be mad at me because you're incapable of being a visionary."

"So that's your excuse. You're life is so above the rest, your hand is so highly exalted, that you get to kill and spare?"

Caine chuckled. "That I *kill?*"

"Don't be mad at me because you're incapable of seeing the throne of corpses you sit upon."

"How can you blame me for all the dead? Like you didn't have a hand in all this? There are no more dead because of me than you! Read the papers, Michael. That's what they'll tell you. I may sit atop a throne of corpses, but I am not *alone* in making it. I am a man of vision, of the people for generations beyond me! I am a futurist who knows my dealings are not as clean as many, but they have done what it takes to make the world go around, to make progress, and to bring about *real* change. Look at the people outside this office, look at their lives. They have jobs, homes, a means to carry on... what believer ever provided that? What outlaw ever contributed to what you see outside? In fact, you and I both know those types did *nothing* but pull every single American they met down with them. Yes, I am the main beneficiary! *I deserve it!* After all that I've sacrificed, after all that I've done, my pockets *deserve* to be lined with cash! That is my reward for my risk! *My risk!* My risk provides for these people more than outliers ever could, and I take it so that I may give back. That's why I did what I did, and continue to do what I do, and it's *not* easily done! There are nights when I don't sleep, and instead, I think about what once was, comparing it to what it is now. The faces of those I've used for the *greater good:* they haunt me! But when I look and see the people thriving outside these windows, it makes it *all the easier* to close my eyes and believe it was all worth it!"

"So you're the good guy? After everything you've done, the people you've hurt, and the blood you've indirectly spilt, you're the one *justified* in all this?"

"There are no 'good guys,' Mike. This isn't a storybook; this is *real!* There is no justification for what Man does; there are only tormented souls with means to an end, that we are all striving to reach. I will admit that I am more callous than most, but it takes a man like me to get this job done, just as it takes a man like you to do yours. You've got blood so deeply stained into you that the metaphor can be seen upon your clothes. Yet the blood that's on your clothes is nowhere near the blood on your hands, 'Michael the Merciless'.

According to the papers, how *history* will record you, you are a killer of the guilty and avenger of the innocent. Does the shedding of guilty blood make you the 'good guy'? Is the blood you've spilt any other color than the crimson of mine? Are you justified in what you've done?"

"No!"

"Then why the hypocrisy?"

"Because you made the men I killed!" The ones you killed were *innocent*, Caine! They were innocent! You can't kill the innocent to help the innocent. That's as hypocritical as it gets, and in your hypocrisy, you are found! You say you're not willing to trade lives, yet I've seen you trade the lives of *hundreds!* Hundreds that, as far as you've determined, are nothing but a cancer; A meaningless *waste!* I killed those of *yours* who sought to kill the people, who were undeserving of such 'necessary evils'. I fought to preserve their freedom of practice, while you sought to destroy it! That doesn't justify my actions by any means, but it does make a great distinction between you and I. A distinction that I am at least morally sounder than men like you—"

"That no one will remember! Who's going to remember 'Major General Michael St. Hart, fighter for the believer and liberator of the innocent'?"

"It's not about being remembered."

"Like hell it isn't! You mean to tell me this office, this enterprise, that the people *whom it has given jobs* won't remember that? That's called *legacy*. But you, Thomas? Even

Bill. You are all like dust, fading away, as the winds of tomorrow brush you by. You are forgotten memories that will never be given a second thought. You especially. Your own government wants you dead, Michael, for doing what you say makes you 'morally sounder'. Yet here I sit, not with a warrant for my arrest, but rather, tax cuts and loan agreements from the very same government, because I *benefit* the country. I *grow* the economy, while you run into the night to fight a war for *ghosts*. But I suppose that makes sense... you are 'the soldier.' That's how they see you: a number on a chalkboard that can be easily wiped away, with one swipe of an eraser. Not too different from your believers in the plan of God, whom they follow so blindly. They are nobodies, doomed to go extinct, and you align yourself with *them*? You will *die* as no one; you will die forgotten, and as far as freedom goes, Michael, you should know better than *anyone* that it is only an illusion. Freedoms change with the times, and the times say the believer is no more. So if the times have moved on, and the government has moved on, and, by the looks of it, their *God* has moved on, then *why the hell haven't you?* You act like killing me is going to solve anything; *it won't*! Killing me will only kill the thousands of people who could've been offered a future through *what I do*, and in no time at all, someone will take my place. Killing me kills my legacy, and my legacy provides for thousands, in our generation and the next! You fight against an unstoppable force that, if you were wise, you would either join or *get the hell out of the way!* Yet, instead, you come to me like this, and you ask why I do what I do? It is I who should be asking *you* why you do what you do, given how pointless it is."

Michelangelo nodded painfully, not only realizing that Caine meant every word, but that he also couldn't answer his question as to why

"Now you see my predicament," Michelangelo yielded.

Caine looked at Michelangelo and felt some form of pity for the weary soldier, for he, too, was once a soldier who was at the end of his rope, in a world that did not want him, need him.

"You're fighting a losing battle, Mike. Whether you're fighting for the believer, against progression, or just fighting against yourself... this war: it's one you can't win. Not alone. Trying to make sense of all this... It's impossible. With our own ideas, all we can hold onto is the truth, and the truth is that the world turns relentlessly. Time passes, people die, and all we can do is try our best to survive and make something of it. Help people within it. Eradicate that which tries to destroy it." He slowly reached his hand up to his face as he rubbed his chin. "I remember, back when I was younger, I would read the signs that said 'taming the West is the new frontier!' " He looked back, keeping his hand upright, his elbow resting on his chair's arm. "I always liked that play on words... this idea that great beauty and exploration was carving the path forward for the future of America." He clicked his tongue. "The truth is, it never improved. In fact, I'd say it got worse. The nature of its beast is that it constantly grabs for power, and men who fight for that power eventually turn it into war. That's what it is... that's what it always is. So, if it's all just a grab for power, why not give some of that power to the people? Not through laws or constitutions or religions, but through true, *attainable* power. Self-fulfilling power that you and I can take for ourselves and make something of it. Because no matter how hard we try to fight it, we cannot stop change. You cannot stop progression. This— this is the way things are."

Michelangelo nodded, looking between Caine's eyes as he thought back to a time long before, one that he remembered fondly.

"Do you remember when you and Bill used to come over for Christmas?" He started. "Back when our mom and dad were still around. Tommy and I were young then. Tommy, especially, I mean... he was just a kid. Feels like a long time now. I remember my dad would say, 'Alright, boys, Uncle Bill and Uncle Caine are coming over to visit,' and we would just... light up like a Christmas tree. I remember that you both would come over with a big Christmas turkey, and of course, a dozen war stories from the war, most of which had been told before, but they seemed to feel fresh every time you told them. You would all share how you fought for the 'freedom and right of man'. How you fought for the perseverance of the human spirit... the greater good. You fought without the promise of tomorrow, without the promise of reward. You fought because you knew it was the right thing to do." He stopped, his eyes darkening. "I'll never forget those stories. I guess Tommy did, but me?" He smiled painfully. "It's kind of funny, speaking of stories, I uh... I read Tommy's in the paper. I read about what those kids said about him, and I remember the journalist of the piece had written, 'True freedom is not living for yourself, but it is the ability to lay yourself aside, and live for others.' And then the kid, uh, what's his name? Paul! He said, 'If living for others is eternal life, and the exemplification of Christ can be made known in the body of even the most dastardly men, then we all have the hope for true freedom, for freedom has transcended beyond its current understanding.' So, true freedom is living for others. Living is Christ and dying is gain, or something like that. It's a beautiful story, really. From what I've heard, it inspired a lot of people because they needed something to believe in. Some believe with hope, some believe with faith, some use both, but to be *free* of the grips of the world by living and dying for others, that's— well. That's salvation." His eyebrows furrowed angrily. "But the things you've built, the things you've done: they don't give the people something to believe in. All they do is rob and cheat the people of their ability to see a tomorrow, as they tirelessly work away today with the illusion of one. It beats and bleeds their faith dry, regardless of what it is they believe in. Because of that belief, it's something to look forward to... but you don't want them looking forward to it, because if they did, if they saw even the *slightest* glimpse of what really waits for them, they would *run* from men like you. If it is God, then let it be God; if it is hope, then let it be hope, but the people should be free to choose. It doesn't matter how many bars, barbershops, or brothels disguised as hotels you build; the people will always seek something more. No amount of money could ever pay for the people's true salvation. It can barely pay for the lives they live now."

Caine sighed. "Well. I guess you got me all figured out." He throatily chuckled. "I'd be lying if I said I wasn't impressed. I'd be lying if I said you weren't right. I suppose that is the truth, really, or at least a part of it." He shook his head, sighing again. "But, Mike, I *did* my time, just the same as you're doing yours now. I knew the truth then, and I know the truth now... don't be angry at me because you're barely figuring it out. Yes, we could give people their religion and their hope, but that wouldn't change the world. Even their Bible says this has to happen. Everything is constantly in flux with the distribution of power, and men fight and die for it every day. What you see now is the same as it's always been. The world is a wicked place, only filled with wicked people, but with peace and safety through control, it can be mitigated."

"But not all men are wicked. I've seen wicked men and I've seen good ones. I've seen violent gunslingers turn to loving mothers and unbelieving men turn into believers."

"And I've seen incorruptible bounty hunters get paid off and believing men turn their backs on God!"

"But that doesn't discount the good that's still present, and would remain present if men like you didn't choose to destroy it."

Caine looked into Michelangelo's eyes and glanced between the two of them. "I've paid my price, Michael. I knew what it cost. I only wanted to make sure that you knew what you'd be paying for your retribution."

"I am."

The two stared at one another in the silence, both staring, content and unmoved. Caine's breathing quickened. He gulped once.

"It was good to see you, Mike."

"You too, Caine."

Caine thrust his hand into his sports jacket and grabbed for the pistol that lay stowed away in its hidden holster. Michelangelo fired, blitzing a round through Caine's forehead, shooting blood through the back of his head and onto the wall behind him in a splat. His head quickly flicked back, lying in the chair lifelessly as blood dripped out the back. A tiny droplet slid its way out of the fleshy and bloody hole in the middle of his head. Michelangelo watched it trace down as Caine's right arm hung from his suit jacket, and his left dropped over the side of his armrest, his eyes remaining open, looking up at the ceiling of his office.

Michelangelo breathed a sigh of relief as he thought about his dead uncle before him, feeling that true justice was served, but also that he was now truly alone. He had no brother, Uncle Caine, or Uncle Bill. They were all, literally and figuratively speaking, dead.

He stood to his feet slowly and stood over the body in the same way he had so many times before. He looked at his revolver, then chunked it onto Caine's desk, leaving it and the past it carried as he walked out the office door, thinking about the body behind him. *It didn't matter how rich he was,* he thought, *nor the throne he had built. He ended up dead just the same.* To Michelangelo, it seemed as though all the power in the world could not stop a man from getting a bullet, for no amount of money or power could save him from his own death. Death, to Michelangelo, was the great equalizer. After being its vessel for so long, he determined it was of godly understanding, for after everything, he still could not explain the flippancy of its enactors.

Regardless, with no fight worth fighting and no war worth waging, he was without purpose. Now, he was left with the knowledge of what he had to do, given he was emptied of purpose and somehow still alive. He walked outside and hoisted himself atop Bleu, turning them both toward the desert surrounding to make way for their final destination. He knew it was time to return to Fort Sanction: a home that would be where he'd pay his final price for a completed retribution.

CHAPTER 15

For Though Resting Bones Make Quick Solution

 ourneys from Heddlebrook to Fort Sanction were always lengthy and trying ones, only taken by the very few who know the terrain well. However, it was known that if you were to brave such a natural and dangerous trek, you would be rewarded with beautiful sights as you went. However, for a man such as Michelangelo, the stunning canvas of desert mountains was only desert mountains. The beauty of the red rocks that covered the ground and the canyon's sides was only ever seen as rocks with the color red. Despite the desert glowing wonderfully in the afternoon's sun, there was no beauty to be seen in Michelangelo's eyes, only the empty, barren landscape, hot and unforgiving.

The forests of the northern pines, though wonderfully dark brown and green, were only just pines to him, though they were massive in height and wonderfully wide. The red desert sand sloshed beneath Bleu's hooves as she made her way to the base of Mt. Restmoore, rising high above the land. Once at the top, she and Michelangelo stopped before

Thomas's grave. He stared at the wooden cross, still standing but slightly more worn, now. This was the only item he saw that made him feel anything, and all he felt was sadness.

He sighed and looked forward, then rode down the mountain to the forest that led to Fort Sanction. This fort was a large and formidable structure that resembled a kingdom more than a base. Michelangelo looked up at the sky, noting the grey and white clouds that created a gloomy ambiance. It was the first clouded gloom Michelangelo had seen since the days of the Great Snow, and just as he looked at it, it began to rain, the water lightly pitter-pattering on the ground, making the air cool and the grass and leaves wet. The pines that stood tall trickled water, each glistening and dripping with raindrops. Bleu's hooves sank and sloshed through the thick soil as dead pines and twigs were bent.

The two walked beside the base of Mt. Restmoore, passing by the town of Promise on the path that led through the thick forestation to the well-hidden Fort Sanction. In no time at all, they arrived, and as Michelangelo looked upon the fort in front of him, which was the very same one that he had left eight months ago, he was reminded of how colossal it was. The fortress walls reached nearly as high as the trees, being they were thirty-feet tall, and made of vertically placed pine trees that had been chopped and trimmed with a pointed top. Their wood was a dark and wet brown wood, with the morning's rain seeping in as it dripped down.

He and Bleu rode directly to the fort's front portals, seeing the watchman who stood watch. The massive wooden doors were closed, and he was their guard in the tower, which stood dry as rain droplets dripped off the triangulated roof atop his post. The tower also had a wooden balcony that was built up to waist height for the watchman to stand behind and take cover if needed. The watchman looked down at Michelangelo, then aimed through his bolt-action rifle's scope. He looked over the dampened clothes on his body and noted the navy blue button-up with the stars of a major general on each of his shoulders.

Regardless of his messy and careless state, the uniform still identified him as a soldier, which led the watchman to examine him more closely. He looked at his face, now dripping with raindrops, his lengthy hair damp, the back of his head stuck to his neck, with strands of wet hair streaming down to his eyes. His beard retained its curled yet puffy state, slightly longer, now, and dripped droplets of rain the same. Michelangelo was an entirely different man from the one he was before, a shell in comparison. The watchman pulled back the bolt on his rifle, letting out a loud and recognizable click, loading a bullet with a smooth slide and steady aim. "State your name and business, stranger, and do it fast! This here is a fortress owned and run by the Federal Gover—"

"Yeah, yeah, I know. It's Major General Michael St. Hart." Michelangelo interrupted loudly.

The watchman's eyes widened as the aim of his rifle slowly dropped. He looked between Michelangelo and those in the fortress behind him. He thought about what to do next. Michelangelo rolled his eyes slowly, letting out a heavy sigh, for he realized that the watchman was a bit green for his critical thinking.

"Watchman. Is Brigadier General Peter Slovinski stationed in your command?" Michelangelo asked, annoyed.

"Uh... no, sir. I— well, wouldn't that be you?" The watchman replied.

"Watchman, if I were in your command, would I be asking you who it was that commands you?"

"N-no, sir-."

"So who is in your command?"

"That would be Lieutenant General Stone, sir."

"Then go get the Lieutenant General!"

The watchman nodded quickly and made his way out of sight, shuffling down the stairs. Michelangelo shook his head slowly as he looked down at Bleu, patting her side one last time.

"I think we've reached the end of the trail," Michelangelo thanked.

Bleu gave a low and upsetting grunt as her head shook side to side, flicking rain from her mane.

"I know... I know. We had a good ride, girl, but I don't think I can ride anymore."

She let out an upset whinny.

The tall doors of Fort Sanction began to open as two soldiers pushed them through the dampened soil, leaving a collective pile of dirt, sticks, and leaves before the gates, growing more substantial as they moved. Michelangelo calmly hopped off of Bleu's saddle and squished into the ground below, then walked forward with slow and steady steps towards the open fortress's arms. He stayed looking at the ground as the sounds of two dozen footsteps came squishing and sloshing from the fort. He listened to the sounds of rifles and revolvers clicking. They surrounded him, then continued to aim as he slowly walked into the fortress, looking up at the audience he had attained, all dressed in a uniform. Their rifles were aimed directly at his chest, their eyes glued to his every move, with each face taking on a look of palpable fear. He looked around at each one, seeing some were old and some were young. He didn't recognize the younger ones, but the older ones he did, and they him.

Michelangelo looked around the fortress's interior and saw that it was just as he had left it. The watering well was directly behind the twenty-seven men that stood before him, and the wooden cabins for the soldiers were all still standing. The cabins retained their backward-slanting wooden roofs, with two windows on the front, allowing the man to see out. The housing was made of thick tree logs that were tightly bound together with rope, and had flooring and roofing made of two-by-fours that were imported from distant towns. The horses' stables stood with all four horses loaded, made of the same pine wood that grew in the forest. However, when Michelangelo looked to his left, he saw the quarters that had once belonged to him, only now something was different. The building had retained its rectangular structure, and the roof was still a pointed triangle, but its inhabitant, who angrily marched toward him, was very different.

"You got some nerve showing your face around here, Saint Hart!" The lieutenant general yelled out.

"Of steel," Michelangelo replied, humorously. "Come give 'em a knock and you'll see what I mean."

The lieutenant general marched through the crowd of soldiers to the front, getting a front-row seat to look at Michelangelo. The soldiers shifted their aim around the lieutenant general as he noted the emptiness of his holsters, or any weapons, for that matter, save the hunter's knife that was sheathed on his left side. He shook his head condescendingly as he stared at this soldier of ill repute. At the same time, Michelangelo looked at his lieutenant general.

Lieutenant General Stone was an old and ornery man, with a greyed goatee upon his face and wrinkles around his eyes. Upon his head, he wore a blue navy man's hat with yellow strings, similar to the one Michelangelo once wore. Rainwater dripped off the wide, circular rim that shielded his balding hair, peppered with black and white. He was a lean and smaller man who wore the same attire as his soldiers, only his insignia was far more prestigious. The other notable difference was his stained and faded white cavalry gloves, dirtied from many miles of riding.

"Look at you... Once a proud and promising soldier, and now nothing more than a killer and a deserter! A bad memory, burned into the American people's minds!" Lieutenant General Stone rebuked.

"Ahhh, here we go again," Michelangelo interrupted.

"You're a horror! An uncorrectable stain of American abomination!"

"You know what, do me a favor, Lieutenant General Stone, and save me the judgment. I'd rather not be preached to about how bad killing is, from a killer."

"A killer?" Lieutenant General Stone laughed. "I have orders. What do you have? Some psychotic vigilantes creed?"

"*Psychotic?* Don't be rude, Lieutenant General!" He gestured to the Fort Sanction.

"Isn't the nuthouse where the sick and deranged must go to get better?"

Stone smirked angrily. "Your insolence will cost you, Major General. I'd recommend you take that into account, as I have."

"Why don't you take into account that I didn't come here to hear you run your mouth, or the hole in your ass you've continued to talk out of."

"... You know what your problem is, Saint Hart? You lack *order*. You are a man of chaos in a *world* of chaos, when you are *meant* to be a man of order, making a world of order. Order, Saint Hart, is better for all. For democracy! There is no democracy among *fools* and savages, comparable to the likes of you."

"Fools and savages?" Michelangelo questioned sarcastically, lifting his arms to his side, mockingly looking around at the men surrounding him. "Birds of a feather, Lieutenant General. You all wear the same uniform as me, only you're so blinded by the color blue you can't see the hypocrisy." He smiled.

The Lieutenant General grumbled angrily to himself. "Men like you, Saint Hart... you're a dying breed—men of a time past who fought for moralistic justice that no longer exists. You are a defender of the wagon burners who would rather remove your scalp than defend you similarly; a fighter for the believers that their own God would sooner burn than be saved by the very same One. You are a soldier of lost causes, fighting a losing battle, unable to see the future and understand what is to come! Therefore... you will die as you lived: in the past, the same as your brother."

Michelangelo gritted his teeth as he balled his hands into a fist, wondering if he should beat the Lieutenant General senseless. However, with no anger left to give and hardly a care to provide either, he released the tension in his fists. "Well, go on, Stone. Don't stop there!"

Lieutenant General Stone laughed, madder now. "Oh, you want more? Okay: you and your brother were scoundrels that spread a fallacious gospel as if it meant *anything* to the American people, and all that they *should* stand for. For peace and sanctuary!"

"Yeah, well, I'd rather die a scoundrel that gives people hope than a visionary who would sooner take it from them."

"And you will do just that as soon as we've put you on trial, letting the true justice system take its course. The people will see how a delinquent, who lives by his own laws, is rewarded for such constitutions!"

"Oh, the people will see, alright. They'll see a soldier who fought for a dying people, where their own government would not."

"They will see *you* as a disgrace to their country, and the very men and women that uniform is meant to protect! Congress will make sure of it."

"You know, the more I keep hearing talk of these people, the less I see them. You say people in the general term, but I think you and I both know 'people' is a relative term. People often change definitions as Congress dictates, based on what they need to do to advance in the political sphere. Even a man such as myself, who would sooner damn Congress than join them, found myself working up that ladder the same. 'Oh, Major General St. Hart, how prestigious!' Yeah right. If men like you and I are what's meant to be called 'prestigious,' I'd prefer to be among the disreputable."

Michelangelo reached up to the patches upon his shoulders and ripped each one from the button-up, leaving nothing but black strings from the patch sewn on his right shoulder, and his shirt was ripped entirely on his left. He tossed his Major General badges to the ground before the men and into the mud. The Lieutenant General scoffed as he turned his back to Michelangelo, walking away with less care to give as he went back to his office. "Major General Slovinski, you've been promoted. Do us all a favor and take this fool to the brig," he ordered.

Peter stepped out from the crowd and, with a straight-faced expression, walked through the group of armed soldiers to Michelangelo. Each of the soldiers raised their rifles into the air, releasing the hammers of their weapons slowly. Each soldier disbursed as Peter grabbed Michelangelo by the arm, looking at him to examine all his differences.

"Good to see you, old friend," Michelangelo greeted.

"All the same to you, Major General," Peter returned.

He pulled his navy revolver from his holster and aimed it at Michelangelo, clicking back the hammer and flicking his head forward, toward a solitary location. This was the brig. It was a secluded underground location, used solely for holding lawless soldiers.

The brig's bulkheads were large, outward-opening doors that were held together by wood and steel reinforcement around the border. A solid steel bar, installed as a locking contraption, was attached to the left door and fit into a metal loop that protruded from the proper cellar side. Peter pulled back the steel bar and grabbed the left door's handle, creaking open the dark cellar, revealing cement stairs that led down into the mud-filled den. Michelangelo walked down into the darkness as Peter leaned over and picked up a lantern that had been left inside the cellar on the first step. He lit a match and held it to the lantern wick, which lit it aflame as he walked down a bit into the brig, pulling the right bulkhead shut behind him. The cellar door slammed with a heavy solidity, insulating the sound, light, and temperature within. Michelangelo looked at the prisons before him that were lit in the light yellow glow from the lantern's light that approached behind him. There were two prison cells in this brig, one on each side, and each was modeled the same. The metallic bars reached to the ceiling above, which was a plane, a light wood ceiling buried below the ground, and as old as Fort Sanction itself. Dirt and moisture had seeped through the old wood ceiling. Today, it was especially moist, which further destabilized the wood.

"Any of this structurally sound?" Michelangelo asked rhetorically.

"I don't think they care whether it is or not," Peter answered honestly.

Michelangelo opened the prison bar door on the right by twisting the metal bar's hitches open with a loud screech. The hitches were rusted and old, but they did their best to remain intact. The prison cell bars, steel underneath the rust, held the cell together in an evenly spaced fashion, leaving only ten inches of space between each bar. The wall of the prison and the entire brig were made of the same wood as the ceiling, though the planks had busted and shifted in certain places due to the constant movement of the earth around them. Upon the wall, hooked in with two large metal chains, was what many would call a bench that functioned as a bed. This bench hung about 3 feet off the ground and was designed for sitting, sleeping, and waiting. That was all that was within each of the prison cells, and though it was an empty prison cell, it was not spacious. Michelangelo walked into the cell and sat on the chained bench, causing the wooden seating to creak and bend as the chains strained tightly. Michelangelo raised his right eyebrow as his lip protruded, giving a nod as he wondered if he would die from a bad bench rather than a hangman's noose.

Peter walked up to the door of the prison cell and pushed it shut, letting the metal screech nonetheless, as he reached into his pocket and pulled out an old, rusted key. He slipped the key into the keyhole and twisted it with a clunky click to the right, now assuring that Michelangelo was truly and indeed imprisoned. He sighed as he turned around and opened the prison cell on the other side, sitting down on the opposing cell's bench with an ominous and ill-sounding creak. Michelangelo rested his head against the wooden wall behind him and directed his attention to Peter, who did the same. He placed the lantern beside him and lit up the right side of his face, as Michelangelo's was the same, only on the opposite side. The sound of dripping water onto soil echoed in the brig, the occasional creak of wood and shifting dirt interrupting the silence.

"They'll kill you, you know," Peter reminded.

"Yeah... I know," Michelangelo informed.

"So why'd you come back?"

Michelangelo looked at Peter knowingly, leading him to nod and look down.

"I could get you out, you know," Peter said, looking up. "Wouldn't be that hard. I could just leave the key in the mud and then, under the cover of night, you could slip away."

"Oh, yeah, and then be shot by the jumpy watchman watching at the front gate." Michelangelo agreed humorously.

The two chuckled, then quieted and sat in silence for a moment.

"After all the times you've saved my life, I feel like it's only right I save yours. At least just this once," Peter attempted to persuade.

"I never saved your life expecting anything in return," Michelangelo shot down.

"I see. So, in all your infinite generosity, you rob me of the opportunity to do a good thing at the end of it all?"

Michelangelo chuckled. "You can't save me, Peter."

"Why, Mike? Because you don't want to be saved? Because you 'deserve' this?"

Michelangelo tiredly looked at Peter, the flame of the lantern glistening in his eyes. Peter looked and saw the lonely sadness that harbored within them.

"I've got nothing to live for," Michelangelo said, sighing. "More than this, men like me don't get to do what we've done and not pay for it in some way. Righteous or not, we all get what's coming to us." He took a moment of silence. "Look, if you want to help me, do something kind for someone else. Someone else who needs it. Don't waste it on me."

"This is not a waste, Mike. I think you and I can both agree we understand what *waste* is, given the years we've wasted... but this is different. This is *your life* we're talking about."

"And what's it to you?"

"Michael, you may have always been my Major General, but before any of that, you were my brother in arms, and a good friend."

Michelangelo smiled out of the corner of his mouth. "And I appreciated that," he said, looking down at the flame in the lantern next to Peter, watching it dance in the lantern's glass, brightly in the darkness. "But that's not enough to keep me going."

Peter thought for a minute as he pondered their brotherhood, recalling the many life-or-death experiences they had shared. "Do you remember the Battle at Grizzly Peak?"

He started.

"Yeah... you almost got your head blown off by Burden Von Oppenheimer," Michelangelo remembered.

"Exactly! There were about thirty-three men, right?"

"Pretty sure. Thirty-three men against five Union soldiers on the wrong battlefield."

"Yeah! Yeah, that's right."

They shared a laugh. "I remember, uhm," Peter continued, "I remember that you and the boys were riding out, given that his gang was roosted on the ridge, as a means to ambush us, and as you were, the boys said that you noticed I was missing."

"Yup. You got bucked off your steed in the middle of a firefight."

Peter laughed, "So you remember well?"

"Oh, I'll never forget that."

"The *point* is that you didn't leave me behind. Despite how foolish I was or how dead every single one of us might've been, you came back, and we fought and killed every one of those men, taking down one of the biggest gangs in Colorado." He thought further. "I remember after that, the boys and I put our money together and got you those navy revolvers, the ones with the grizzly bear carved into the handles. That grizzly... he reminded us of you. This ravenous and vicious fighter that, when you looked deep underneath the surface, saw a big heart." He smiled. "You were like an older brother to us, then. In many ways, you still are. You showed us that regardless of the circumstance or what you're up against, you never gave up."

Michelangelo nodded. Peter paused a moment to think further.

"I don't get it," Peter lamented. "No matter how much they preach about never leaving a man behind, all I see is the people we're supposed to be fighting for getting left behind left and right. And our brothers? Us? We're left behind the most. To rot when the war is over. Whether it's in a grave, public execution, or suicide, they use us as examples of what happens when you fight for the people; when you fight for the 'right cause,' whatever the hell that is. We fight so many fights, yet rarely ever fight the one that's worth fighting for, and when we do, *this* is how they treat us... how they're treating you." Peter sniffed quickly as he brushed his sleeve across his face, controlling his emotions. "They're leaving you behind, Mike, and of all of us, you're the man who deserves to be fought for the most, and you won't let me. Why won't you let me?" Peter mourned. "It's not right—none of it. You should be getting medals, not the noose. You should be being served a steak dinner in your quarters, not Stone. Instead, they throw you down here, to be mistreated and left to starve, in this pit of a brig that's two shits away from being a sewer."

Michelangelo smiled weakly as he breathed out a slight laugh at the analogy Peter made. "Now, that's not true, Pete. You and I are here. That's two shits aplenty."

Peter smiled tearily as Michelangelo eased his rising emotions, calming him in the best way he knew how.

"You asked why I won't let you save me," Michelangelo started. "It's because I lived, Pete. In all my days, I was never more alive than I was when I was fighting a fight that was worth fighting... and sure it was a bloody and brutal one, but it was one that I felt I was purposefully a part of. It was like I was fighting a force that was undoubtedly evil, and I did not doubt, for one second, that evil is what I was fighting against. For the first time in my life, when I killed a man... it wasn't an innocent father begging for his family's lives, it was a wicked man who begged for his own. Every man I killed, I did knowing it would help the broader people... and in some twisted way, it helped me. It made me feel like... Tommy's dying meant something. That if there was a divine God who knew of him, then the reason I found him was because every one of those malefactors known as 'men' was soon to face their judgement, and thus, He sent me. Metaphorically or literally... I don't know. But the fact remains: they did... and now it's over. Every single one of them is dead, and I myself am all that remains. I am the one who sits atop a throne of blood that so many others have died for. Stone may be a heartless man, but he is right about one thing: men like me...

we're a dying breed. We're brutal. Justifiably, we are uncivilized. And this right here... this is why. No more are the laws of 'eye for an eye'... now are the laws of Man."

Peter thought for a moment about what Michelangelo was saying.

"So knowing what you know now, would you do it all again?" He asked.

"Without a second thought. If you saw what I saw... you'd say the same. I saw the mouth of hell open and consume these people in the name of progression. I saw the faces of grieving mothers as their children lay dead in their arms. I saw crosses burned into their faces, upside down and upright. I sleep at night now, knowing that those people can be free once again. I sleep knowing that no matter what they believe, they will have a tomorrow. That preachers can preach and not fear for their lives, despite the words they speak, that the believers and the non-believers can walk their light-laden streets, without seeing what I have seen. The oppressive tyrants that walked about as bringers of the apocalypse now lie dead as nothing more than bones in the soil. Everything I've done... it did all mean something, I guess. It has to. Maybe they're what it means. Maybe they're the portrait that I see before me: beautiful, but painted in blood. Like an artist, I will die forgotten, but in death, the works that I have done will be seen for their beauty without any of the bloodshed. But I cannot live on... I must swing, for if I do not, then I am no better than them. I'm a hypocrite, and thus, I am okay with dying. I'm okay with swinging if it ensures that thousands can live freely. That makes it worth it."

Michelangelo lay his head back on the broken boards, closed his eyes, and took a moment to rest as Peter started to understand his thought process.

"They said it was near three hundred men that you killed... is that right?" Peter asked.

"Well, I wasn't counting, but that seems about right," Michelangelo responded casually.

"You hunted down and killed nearly *three hundred men?*"

"Again, yes."

"Good Lord... may he have mercy on their souls," Peter said sarcastically.

"He didn't."

Peter smiled and shook his head, mostly in disbelief as he thought about three hundred men on one battlefield at once. "They said you took on one hundred men from Icarus's army somewhere over by an old fort... is that true?"

"Oh yeah, yeah. I also fought ten legions of bulls that flew on devil's wings."

They chuckled.

"So no regrets?" Peter asked calmly.

Michelangelo opened his eyes and looked at the stairs. "I just wish I could've saved the kid," he informed.

Peter looked up, confused. "Who?"

"Leonardo... he was a preacher."

"The DelMuerto boy?"

"Yeah. The very same."

"Hm... well, odds are he's still alive, Mike. They never found the body, so I'm sure the kids are out there somewhere."

"No. He died a long time ago. Whoever is out there now... it isn't the kid I knew. 9 the kid I knew."

Peter nodded, unsure of what Michelangelo meant, but knowing he was out of time.

"Well, I'd better get going. Don't want to raise suspicion." Peter decided as he stood from his bench and grabbed the lantern.

He walked over to the side of Michelangelo's cell and hung the lantern on a nail, a few inches from the ceiling, which provided a decent amount of light to where he had been resting. He was thankful for it.

"Technically, I shouldn't leave this here, but I also technically don't care," Peter rebelled. "I'd rather you not go mad while there's still time to change your mind."

Peter made his way towards the stairs as Michelangelo closed his eyes once again and eased into this quiet and peaceful moment. Peter turned to him one last time, thinking about all the soldier had done, not just for him, but for many who would not know him. He wondered what he could do for him, even still, though he did not want it. After all, his last request was for Peter to help someone who needed it, and he wondered who this someone might be and how he could find them. He turned and exited through the right bulkhead door, slamming the door to lock it behind him, leaving Michelangelo to his thoughts in the darkness, alone.

The lantern flickered softly for weeks as Michelangelo waited and rested. Occasionally, the soldiers would bring a mushy porridge made from leftovers and old food, with just enough water to quench his thirst, but not enough to strengthen him. Lieutenant General Stone feared Michelangelo, for he had heard the stories of the soldier, and wondered if too much food and water would make him too strong to transport.

On one particular day, Michelangelo stared at the lantern's flame waveringly as his mind drifted away, and the light began to fade, shrinking to a small flame. The flame was yellow and had once shone through the brig in its entirety, but now let the darkness creep in closer to Michelangelo. He lay down on his wooden bench and watched the oil within the wick run dry, as the room was conclusively filled with a lifeless darkness. With this, Michelangelo closed his eyes and decided that his mental state, too, would fade as the light faded.

Suddenly, the bulkhead's right door flew open and flashed bright, sunny light into the brig, alerting Michelangelo. He opened his eyes and looked at the blinding light, which displayed three silhouettes of individuals that he could not see. He raised his right hand in an attempt to block out the sun, as the other bulkhead's door opened with a loud creak, and the first silhouette entered, stepping gently and calmly towards Michelangelo.

"Uh... Major General Michael St. Hart?" He called out.

Before he could answer, a female's voice interrupted with a whisper. "It's just Michael, he's not a general anymore."

"Oh, right, right, uh.... Michael, you in here?"

"... yeah," Michelangelo responded, noting the youthfulness in the voices that came forth.

"You got some visitors, Mike. They're fixing to get you out of here." Peter stated happily.

Michelangelo winced at the individuals as he slowly sat up, and his vision returned. He looked between the two curiously as his eyes slowly softened, for the two brave individuals standing before him were a young black man and a young Native American woman. Michelangelo noted the taller, more grown-out curls that rested upon the young man's head, black in color, and left uncombed but tightly wound. His face had grown a trim goatee and thin mustache at his seventeenth year of age, and he seemed to be standing at a solid five feet and nine inches. Upon his body was a white, loose-fitting button-up shirt with the top button undone, and his sleeves were rolled up to above his elbows. Michelangelo noted the satchel over the young man's right shoulder, which was a light brown, hand-stitched one with a rabbit's skin sewn on as the lid. He wore black jeans that were tucked into dark brown, leather, ankle-high boots.

Michelangelo looked at the young woman, who was wearing a denim button-up shirt that she had newly purchased with her own personal earnings. Her sleeves were rolled up to the middle of her bicep, and had strings with beads at the end that were sewn into the front, coming down from just above the breast of the shirt and dangling down. The denim was a loose fit, which helped with agility, and I wore a white shirt underneath. Her skin was a caramel brown that shone in the morning's sun, along with her hair that glistened in the light. Her hair was long, braided, and black as the night, and fell just above the buckskin tunic she wore over her black jeans. It hung down to just above her knees in the front and back, and connected thinly around the waist. The skirt was finished with buckskin strings and beads that tightly wound together around the end of her skirt, similar to the beads and strings she had sewn onto her denim. Her shoes were calf-high, dark brown, tied-up boots with a wolf's fur tied at the top. Her pants were tucked into the top of her shoes, which were fitted comfortably for long travels.

Michelangelo looked between them, unsure whether he should know who they were or know nothing at all, but as the young man spoke, their identities became clear.

"Mr. Michael, my name's Paul... Paul Freeman. This is Hope Homelight. We could use your help if you've got some time to spare," Paul introduced.

Michelangelo leaned back slowly on his bench as he realized who the young people were. Peter saw his cogs turning and decided to get out in front of any counter he might have.

"Now, before you go thinking your way out of this, I want you to know this is not a request, but an order," Peter stated, reaching into his pants' pocket and pulling out a paper. He handed it to Michelangelo through the prison bars, prompting him to lean forward and snatch the paper to read it. Peter walked forward and pulled the prison key from his pocket to unlock the cell and open the prison door. "You've been pardoned, on behalf of President Roosevelt. You're not to be hanged, nor executed in any manner, but rather act as an army of one in an effort to escort these young people wherever they need to go." He opened the door. "Bibles have run quite scarce out here in the West on account of all the burning and martyring that's been going on, and faith has fallen right along with it. President Roosevelt, Mr. Freeman, and Ms. Homelight sympathize with your vision for freedom and aim to rectify such injustices with a mission: to give the people a fair and illustrious opportunity to serve the God they were told they could not."

"At its essence, we want to return the faith to the people... to help restore people as much as we can," Paul agreed.

Michelangelo looked up from the parchment and at the three who stood before him, as they in turn looked at the legendary soldier. He looked at Peter and sighed, as his head shook with an angry nod. "You just couldn't let me die, could you?"

"Not yet, Mike. Not yet," Peter joked.

Hope examined Michelangelo closely. "I hate to interrupt, but are you *sure* this is the right guy?"

"Pretty sure, yeah," Peter replied.

"Hope... of all the times," Paul complained.

"I'm just saying, they look nothing alike!"

"Once we get that beard trimmed, you'll see the resemblance." He looked at Michelangelo. "Isn't that right, Saint Hart?" Peter informed.

Michelangelo chuckled once, then shook his head and started to muster some newfound energy. "Sure, Peter, that's exactly what I wanted to keep living for, to babysit! Thank you for making these young people my problem?"

"Yup, they're brothers, alright," Hope said, rolling her eyes.

"Mike, come on, this is the good fight! This is helping people. This is fighting so that others can live; it's about protecting the innocent. These young people align with those very same principles. It's a match made in heaven!" Peter convinced.

"Is that what this is?" Michelangelo questioned.

"Look, I know how you feel about this... I know you don't want it. But there's more to the mission. That's all I'm saying." Peter sighed. "Let me save you, just this once."

"I don't know Pete. I appreciate the gesture, but I don't see how I'm the best man for this job. Who am I to be out here doing 'God's work' as it goes? I'd be nothing more than a snake within a garden, guiding those whom the Gardener'd better guide."

Peter sighed and rubbed his eyebrows.

"Mr. Slovinski... can I say something?" Paul interrupted.

"By all means," Peter yielded, frustratedly gesturing toward Michelangelo.

Paul looked at him and saw the blood stains and broken spirit that covered him. He thought back to when he had found his brother and remembered how Thomas was in the same state. "Look, I know who you are. We both do. I know what you've done because your stories have garnered enough attention across the nation to capture the President's interest. What you did... It's in the past... we need you, *now,* in the present, and we are more than willing to accept who that man is if he'll let us." Paul reasoned.

Michelangelo looked at Paul and thought about the statement, though he largely ignored it, given that he believed Paul could not possibly understand what he was going through. "Look, kid, I know you mean well... but I don't think all the painters in the world could paint you a clear picture as to who it is you're talking to."

"You're Michelangelo St. Hart, killer of three-hundred and seventy-one men, including the likes of Roger Wilcox, Blanco Salvador, Bo Liverpool, and Caine Kingsley, three of whom are members of the group known as the Four Horsemen. You killed three of the four horsemen, but not the fourth, who was known as Icarus." Paul retold.

Michelangelo's eyebrows angled down in confusion as his head tilted slightly away, and he leaned back from Paul, for Paul knew things that he couldn't possibly know.

"Wait... you didn't kill Icarus?" Peter asked.

"How did you know that?" Michelangelo asked Paul.

"I saw it in a dream," Paul said.

The room went silent. Hope slowly looked over to him as Michelangelo and Peter stared in silence.

"You saw it... in a dream," Hope restated.

"Yeah." Paul looked around. "Why are you guys looking at me like that?"

"Well, one because that's crazy," Peter responded.

"And two because you're right," Michelangelo added.

"And wait," Peter said, redirecting to Michelangelo, "You killed Kingsley?"

"Yeah," he replied.

"When!?"

"Just hold on a minute!" He stopped, looking back at Paul, not believing Paul could know the secrets he knew. "How do you really know, kid?"

"I'm being honest. You said you've been wondering why all this happened... why you did what you did. Why are you still alive? This is why, Michael. We need your help. What we have to do... where we have to go, we can't go there on our own."

"So 'He' picks me?"

Paul sighed. "Sometimes, God needs more than just a servant... sometimes he needs a soldier."

Peter's eyes widened as Paul talked about Michelangelo's 'why', for it was the very same topic he and Peter had discussed, which he had not mentioned to Paul previously. "This kid's creepy," he commented. Michelangelo looked at Peter. He looked back, and the soldier quickly shared a knowing look, indicating that Peter had not disclosed this topic to Paul or Hope. Michelangelo leaned forward, more intrigued than ever, and looked at Hope to get a second confirmation. "You in on this?"

"There's nothing to be in on. It's not a con." She let out an annoyed breath. "Look, I can't explain everything he does, okay? I can't even say I believe in it, but what I will say is he hasn't been wrong so far," Hope replied.

Michelangelo nodded his head and looked at Paul again. "There's plenty of able-bodied soldiers for this God of yours to choose from... what have I done to gain special privilege?"

"I don't know," Paul replied honestly. "I guess we'll find out, 'sent one.'"

Michelangelo smirked as he shook his head, baffled that Paul knew this as well. "So you need me to protect you as you go preaching to people... my question is, why? Aren't these *your* people? Are believers not innately on your side?"

"To the point that they wouldn't let my skin color be a problem, right?"

"Right."

Paul blew air through his nose as a subtle darkness overcame him. As he thought about his past experiences with Hope over the past eight months.

"Apparently not in all of their eyes. Neither is Hope. She's gone with me to plenty of places before and can attest that despite what the Bible says, they do not all agree when it comes to race, and where we're going, we're going to need someone with a bit more authority to keep the unreasonable from becoming unreasonable." He clenched his jaw. "Though they are my people, believers and non-believers alike, I have found they would prefer the sermon come from a man other than me. When it doesn't, it tends to have violent repercussions. We must have someone like you there to be the protector."

Michelangelo nodded his head slowly as he realized their predicament.

"Evangelism is a tough business these days, huh?" He empathized.

"If there's even any business at all. There's only so far you can go to reach a brother's soul before he notices the color of the hand that's reaching," Paul answered.

Hope let out an angered, quick sigh as she crossed her arms and stared down Michelangelo. "Listen, you've got two choices, Saint Hart: you can come with us, or you can die in a jail cell. Not *great* options, I know, but I think I can speak for the three of us when I say we'd all be better off if you stopped being a fool and *came along.*"

Michelangelo chuckled to himself as he stood to his feet and smiled hesitantly while he took in a long, deep breath and readied himself for the coming challenge that had been given to him. "You make a fine point, Ms. Homelight. That I cannot deny."

"Glad to have you on board," Hope stated proudly.

"Well, it's not like I have much of a choice."

"There's always a choice, Michael," Paul rebutted. "You know that."

Michelangelo shot air through his nose as he smiled and shook his head lightly. He was reminded that the choice he made was his alone, and that, truly, it was he who came and wanted to move forward with the inevitable commission.

"Well... where are we headed?" He asked curiously.

Paul looked at Hope and raised an eyebrow, only to then look back, and up, to Michelangelo. Hope smiled enthusiastically as she made ready for another journey, more excited than she had been in a long time. "I hope you're ready for a long trip, Mike, because we're going *to the South!*" Hope informed with a smile.

Michelangelo stopped, hearing what Hope said. "The what now?" He asked, knowing what lurked in the South's swamps.

CHAPTER 16

Mind the Price Paid for Your Retribution

 nkept, unloved, and un-lived in for four empty months was the village of Guarida Del León. In a few words, it was no more. In the time that had passed, the small town had gained far more greenery than it had in recent history. The grass had grown tall and strong, for the Junetime summer rays had nourished its growth. The lifeless cabins and adobes making up the village were weathered from the constant beating of heat and rain that they had taken. Most were caved in, broken, and consumed by green, much like the bonfire at the center of the village. It had crumbled to ash and rock, for the rocks that surrounded it had tumbled destructively over from the previous occupants. There was no longer a circle of mud around the bonfire where many villagers had once walked. Now, the bonfire was surrounded by solidified soil, sprouting patches of grass. Wood and furniture lay outside of the households, along with articles of clothing and garbage that had managed to remain unburied.

Despite it all, not all was lost in the old abandoned village. There was a groundskeeper who still made weekly trips to preserve this forgotten land of desolation. After all, Guarida Del León was his home, and it was one that he enjoyed taking care of, despite the constant reminder of his peers, now nothing more than tombstones behind it.

The groundskeeper was tending to some flowers outside his house, snipping the buds and grooming the ground to make it look its best. It was then that he felt eyes staring at him from the shadows, feeling predatory but not entirely animalistic. He slowly turned, looking at this peculiarly quiet visitor who stayed unknown in the early morning's shadows. He stared, his eyes unseen, though the groundskeeper could tell they were looking. For what, he didn't know. *Is he looking for someone?* He thought. *But who? And why?* It was then that the visitor stepped forward, making himself known as the one they called Muerto.

Leonardo walked upon the grass that bent beneath his cowboy boots, the same boots he had bought with stolen money a few weeks prior. They were made of black, tanned leather and were scratched and dirtied from miles of travel. His jeans and button-up shirt were a dark black, and he wore a yellow bandana around his neck. It was a long one that hung on his chest, ready to cover his face. His hair was long and stringy, running down to his shoulders since he had not cut it in many months. His beard was now thick and untrimmed, and bushed out from his face with long, voluminous curls that stretched just below his Adam's apple. Around his waist, he wore a black gun belt with two revolvers holstered on each side, the revolver handles facing forward, as Leonardo preferred. The gun handle was stained black, and the metal was also colored black, while his bandolier was filled with two dozen revolver rounds that had recently been purchased. He wore a black gamblers' hat, complemented by a dark grey wrap of thin cloth around its base.

His horse walked into view behind him, the very same horse he had made friends with a long eight months prior. It was an older Tennessee Walker that had a paling, grey complexion. Its mane and tail were the same pale hue, similar to the rest of its skin, with the only contrasting color being the black leather saddle that lay upon it.

This all became the defining features of Muerto, ones that anyone who met him would not forget, and seeing this, the groundskeeper ran, not waiting to find out what he wanted.

Leonardo looked from the running groundskeeper to the surrounding village as he grabbed the black reins of his horse with one hand, examining the nature that had consumed his old home. The town was surrounded by a hill with dark brown and green pine trees at its summit. Grass grew high for miles on end, making up the valley below Mt. Sorrow. The river stream paired wonderfully with the beautiful backdrop, where there was no longer snow on Mt. Sorrow, but rather the rich and vast black rock that contrasted with the sky in all its extraordinary beauty. The sky was an expansive, open, and beautiful expanse of heaven, a lightest and brightest shade of blue. Leonardo looked at these familiar friends, the sun beating down on his face, forcing him to squint his eyes as he looked around.

He walked into the village the same way he had done many times before, gazing upon this forgotten land. He walked around the cabins and adobes he remembered well, seeing their front yards overgrown and consumed by grass, with their fences fallen over. He walked through the center of the village and guided his horse over the many patches of rubble. As he did, he finally mustered the strength to look over to one special cabin in particular: it was the cabin of Sophia Rivera, in a terrible state. The wood had taken on a greenish grey hue, and unlike many times before, there was now no firelight flickering from inside; no pleasant aroma of fresh meat or bread.

Now there was only the remains of a broken cabin that had been overtaken by time.

Leonardo walked into Sophia's front yard, looking at the front door as he waited for any form of life to come forth. He wished that Sophia would come out in a rage, ready to rip him to pieces for the long time he had been gone, but as he walked up to the front door and waited where he had so many times before, he realized there would be no abrupt opening of the door, nor sudden flash of angry brown eyes.

There was only silence and emptiness of a midsummer's day. Clearly, she was not there to greet him.

He pressed the door open with a slow and soft creak, the wood of the door bending and grinding against the floor. It was dark, having only the sunlight that shone through the space in the wood that made up her walls. The fireplace was dark and empty, with only black and white ash to indicate a previous life. Each room within the cabin was coated in darkness, with Sophia's room, especially, darker than the rest. The door had been shut, seemingly to be left that way—for no light came from underneath the door, as far as Leonardo could tell. The table in the center of the cabin was in its exact place, but now it had slight traces of mud on it, and the wooden chairs were left in an outward position, seemingly unmoved since their last occupants had left.

He walked toward Sophia's room, each of his steps letting out a light, hollow thud through the cabin, the wood creaking and the emptiness of the room echoing the sound. The emptiness was palpable, and the silence that accompanied it throughout the entirety of Guarida Del León was even more pronounced. It was unnatural, or perhaps only natural, given it was now hallowed ground. Leonardo pressed his hand against Sophia's door. He slid it open with a slow and cautious motion, even more afraid of what might be behind this door, rather than the first one, but as he pushed it completely open, the light from the front door shining in and around him, it gave way to more emptiness.

The bed was made, and the dresser beside it was organized, completed with a mirror and a comb. He presumed the dresser had her clothing left untouched, as the room appeared to have been organized some time ago and had not been altered since. A coat of dust covered every item in her room. He wondered when the last time someone had entered this place had been. More so, he asked what happened to her, letting out a depressive soft breath as he came to his own conclusions on the answer he felt he already knew.

He closed his eyes and bowed his head. *Another dead end,* he thought, his soul filled with more regret, as he thought about his lost Sophia.

"Leo?" The groundskeeper asked, stupefied.

Leonardo quickly faced the voice and flipped his right revolver out of its holster, clicking the hammer back and aiming it at him. He raised his hands in the air as a look of fear overtook him, immediately surrendering to retain his life.

"Jack?" Leonardo asked raggedly.

Leonardo dropped the aim of his revolver, releasing the hammer and twisting the revolver around, holstering it in his right holster. Jack dropped his arms slowly, his eyes glancing over Leonardo, noting the change he had taken. He was far different from the preacher he had known so long ago. He looked at Jack and examined him in return, for Jack was also different. He leaned upon a wooden crutch that supported his left side. He was partially lame, his left foot angled backward while his leg dragged underneath the grey, ragged overalls he wore. His shoes were a familiar pair of tattered brown leather boots that Leonardo had seen many times before. He wore a white button-up shirt that was buttoned to the top, his sleeves rolling all the way to his wrists. Jack's face seemed to have aged a dozen years in the short four months that had passed. Yet most notable of all, upon his face, there was a mark branded into his left cheek: a burn scar in the shape of an upside-down cross.

Leonardo walked towards Jack, his eyes fixed in a suspicious confusion, as a forgotten peace slowly seeped into his heart, calming him. Whether he wanted to admit it or not, it was nice to see a familiar face that he once complained about seeing so often. Jack looked at Leonardo with a dark droop in his eyes, for they were tired and filled with sorrow, only worsening by the second as he gazed upon Leonardo.

"I thought everyone here was dead," Leonardo breathed.

"So did I," Jack replied morbidly.

Leonardo gestured his head toward Jack's leg. "What happened to you?"

Jack looked at his wooden crutch slowly, then back up at Leonardo at the same pace. "After Icarus and his men came through, those of us who were left went to fight for you boys. We tried to save you and your brothers, but... we failed. I got shot in the back trying to escape, and in place of taking my life, the Lord decided to take my leg." Jack retold.

"I'm sorry to hear that," Leonardo apologized empathetically.

"So am I."

Leonardo thought for a second. "Jack... why are you here?"

"I'm the groundskeeper. It helps me to uh... keep going, in-between evangelizing."

"You evangelize?"

"Sure. Not all of us gave up when this was all said and done."

Leonardo forced a laugh, trying not to be offended but respectful. "Well, that's where you're wrong. I didn't give up, Jack."

"No? How so?"

Leonardo rolled his eyes. "You wouldn't understand."

"Oh, I wouldn't, huh? I wouldn't understand why you abandoned us to play Outlaw? Is that what I wouldn't understand, because the dots are certainly starting to connect to me."

"You don't know the full story."

"No? Did Sophia know?"

Leonardo darted a fiery look at Jack. "Careful, Jack. The ice you walk on is mighty thin," he warned.

"Your threats mean nothing to me, Muerto... much like she never meant anything to you. You abandoned her. You left her to die!"

"I couldn't come back! You understand? After everything I did, I—I couldn't *face her*. Not after what I became."

"And what exactly did you become, Leo?"

Darkness fell over Leonardo's eyes. "A killer." He slowly walked closer to Jack. "I am the man who killed Icarus, and I have killed *many* more since. Despite what the papers might tell you regarding the Saint of Retribution, it was *me* who plunged that knife into his chest! And I enjoyed it. I alone must bear that burden, as I walk in my own truth rather than someone else's as a *hypocrite*," he said, stopping in front of him.

"A hypocrite? Why, because you made a mistake? Does that make me a hypocrite, too? Just some fool who spouts on about the Lord, who has no right given the mistakes he's made? No, Leo... you never give up. No matter how hard it gets, no matter how *badly* you make a mistake, no matter how much you think you're 'saving' other people from your nonsense, you can never just *give up*. The moment we do that is the moment that we discover we are only living for ourselves."

"You ever wonder if maybe I'm not who you thought I was? Maybe I was always just... something else? Something like this."

Jack looked over Leonardo, thinking about how the people of Guarida Del León had pushed a purpose onto him that he may not have wanted, and as he thought about this, his eyes dropped to the wooden floor in a disappointed defeat.

"You were supposed to be the best of us... the one who inspired the people!" He looked back up, tears in his eyes. "We all looked up to you! You were the brightest of all the stars, the greatest of all examples!"

"I was never that! *You all made me do that!* You all wanted me to be something that I did not want to be. I wanted to be *more* than what you hopeless, pitiful fools looked up to! *That* was me! I never wanted this... this life of nothing and no one! So sure, maybe you're right, *Jack*! Maybe, it's not that I couldn't come back, but that I didn't *want to*, because coming back to this *empty, dying place*, brought nothing but *bad memories*, and *misery!*" Leonardo breathed heavily. "I'm not your chosen one... so stop trying to make me that."

They stared at one another as a slow and defeated gaze continued to spread across

Jack's face. Leonardo sighed as he realized the harshness of his confession.

"Look, Jack, bottom line: are you all that's left here?" He redirected.

"I'm the only one left alive. Everyone else is buried in the grass behind the village. Except your brothers, of course. I... never found them."

"No need. I buried them myself."

Jack nodded quietly.

"Listen," Leonardo continued, "I know you may hate everything about me after what's been done... but you are the only man I feel I can talk to about Sophia... and where she might be."

Jack's heart sank despite the feeling of resentment he had for Leonardo, knowing that the truth would destroy any humanity Leonardo had left.

"About four months ago, I was well enough to move and bury our people. I packed up the bodies in a wagon at Little York and rode it here. When I arrived, there was not a soul left to be seen... only to be heard. It was Sophia. I heard her crying or... sobbing more like. She was waiting for you to come back. She was troubled by the response you had given her when you saw her in the state she was in, but she believed that, circumstantially, that's all it was. Just a reaction of circumstance." He choked down tears. "In between my burying of the people, I would go and check up on her. Feed her, give her water, keep her well. That worked for a while, but after a month she just... stopped trying. She stopped crying. Stopped eating. I don't know if she ever slept, or if sleeping was all she did, but she was quiet... and her face, when I went in to try and feed her, and I looked at her, it was as though her will to live had just... vanished. It was like her body lived, but her spirit had died. I discovered soon after that the human body can only go on for so long with a dead spirit, or a broken heart, if you will. After she realized you weren't coming back... it only got worse. Two months had gone by, and you still hadn't shown, and as much as I wanted to believe that you would, I just— I knew you wouldn't. I feel like she knew that, too. After seeing your face, she knew you would never come back." He laughed painfully. "But isn't fate cruel? Because here you are, having returned." He wiped the tears from his eyes. "One day, when I walked in, she was as silent as she had been before... only this time she was not asleep. She wasn't breathing. She had died in her bed of a broken heart, after two months of punishment." He looked at the graveyard. "She's buried now, just the same as all the rest: in the graveyard where you can say your goodbyes, if you care to do so."

Leonardo's heart broke as he let out a breath of pain, his body physically reacting to the news. His left arm went up to his left hip as his eyes blinked rapidly, looking around at the cabin as he took in Jack's words. He looked at the wooden floor, a small puddle of tears welling. Still, as the emotions he felt were quick to arrive, they were squandered, for Leonardo's heartlessness had taken over fully, shielding him with the guise of an outlaw.

"Why did you come back?" Jack asked bitterly.

Leonardo looked up with a cold, blank expression as he regained complete control of his emotions. "Truth is, Jack, everything me and Sophia were; everything I was... that's not me, anymore. Whatever it was we had is no longer here. At the time, when it all first ended, I thought, 'What good would it do for me to come back to something that's gone?' To come back to a woman who's been damned to be a husband, damned the same. And as shameful as it is to admit, the only reason I'm here now is because of the emptiness within me." He looked out the window. "There's nothing out there this world has to offer that could ever replace her... she was... everything." He looked back. "I only realized that after I lived among the dead as a dead man all the same. I realized that Sophia... made me feel alive. I came here because I thought that if she was still alive, maybe she could make me feel something like that again... make me feel what it's like to be alive again. But I see now that she could never have fixed that; she could never have fixed what I am. She would have never changed what I wanted to be, because the truth is... this man: the selfish and destructive one, *that* is who I am meant to be. And her death? It is all the more proof of that."

"And the world mourns knowing that it was her and not you," Jack ended bitterly.

Leonardo nodded in small nods as his eyes looked to the ground, for he was no longer able to look Jack in the eye. He knew that his welcome had been spent, and thus, he had begun his walk out of the cabin, forcing Jack to limp backward and out of the front door entrance. His eyes filled with tears as Leonardo walked away from the village, toward his pale steed, knowing there was nothing left for him in Guarida Del León.

"She didn't deserve this!" Jack yelled tearfully. "None of us did!"

Leonardo ignored Jack as he continued his walk to his mare, Jack's head dropping as large tears formed in his eyes. Leonardo stepped into the stirrup and sat upon his horse, kicking the steed onward and making his way to the nearest bar that he could remember. Leonardo listened to Jack sobbing to himself as he placed his hand upon Sophia's cabin, leaning upon it for support. Truthfully, Jack mourned the loss of his loved ones, who had all now been confirmed to be dead. Leonardo thought about what Jack had said: how he wished Leonardo had died rather than Sophia, and oddly, found himself in agreement with him, for he figured that if he had died in place of her, the world would have mourned far less.

There was no longer a shred of doubt in Leonardo's mind about who he had become, and Leonardo thought that if he could do anything to ease these terrible thoughts, it would be to fill his emptiness with the sweet serenade of liquor. To him, there was no longer any sense in prolonging the inevitable, much like a soldier before him had determined. There was no reason to pretend he was anything other than what he had turned out to be, and this was a fate that he had gladly accepted.

The remainder of the day was as lonely as it was long, with Leonardo making his way to Little York. He had ridden the same trail he had walked many times before, staring at the grassy path beneath him until it gave way to dirt, thinking about the many miles he had walked it with his brothers. Eventually, the pine trees that reached high into the heavens ended where the black brick began, prompting him to look up from his slouched and seated position and see the town of Little York.

The town was as brightly lit as ever, its lights shining in the late-night sky as he stealthily rode past the sheriff's office, simultaneously looking over Aland's Theatre: a shining, repaired building that gave life to this small and modern town. The stars shone brightly in the heavens above, and were clearly visible through the cloudless sky, while the buildings, now fully illuminated, shone nearly as brightly and as colorfully. The brick-laden road glistened beneath him, presenting a different image from the one he had in mind—a scene of blood and bodies. He looked at the General Store that was now refurbished and renewed, owned by a new individual whom Leonardo had never seen before. He spotted him through the windows that had been freshly replaced, gazing down on this man of an unfamiliar yet familiar sort, for though he was a different man, his silhouette was the same as the other owner had before. He then looked at the Hotel Emilda, continuing his ride down the center of Little York's empty street. Only a few people walked on the sidewalk, and of those few, none paid him any mind.

Leonardo stopped in front of Hotel Emilda, tied his horse to the horse hitch, and looked over his back, checking his surroundings. With that, Leonardo entered Hotel Emilda quietly, immediately making his way to the bartender to find a drink that would make him forget.

Bozco looked up and was startled by the unrecognizable young man, this ominous fellow that appeared to be nothing more than a bundle of trouble on legs, sitting beside a line of drinking men at the bar counter who were leaning forward drunkenly against the counter. Bozco placed his hands upon the counter as Leonardo looked up to him, the two eyeballing each other suspiciously. Leonardo recognized the suspicious gaze and quickly pulled out two dollar coins, gently clicking them on the counter. "Brandy, please," he asked nicely.

Bozco's right eyebrow raised in a state of intrigue as he picked up the coins and slid them down the bar counter to a hard-working Rosa. Rosa grabbed the coins without a second thought and walked over to the register. Bozco turned around and grabbed a bottle of fine brandy for Leonardo, placed the bottle in front of him, and continued to watch him suspiciously. Rosa looked up at the stranger, then immediately to Bozco, ensuring that the situation was as safe as it appeared to be. Bozco looked over to Rosa and gave her one calm nod, which eased her worries, allowing her to go about her business. Leonardo grabbed the bottle and turned to his right, rolling his eyes and making for an open table in the crowd of people eating. There were very few tables open, for the late-night diners and gamblers were here making good use of their time. The room was filled with cigarette smoke, made visible by the electric lights above. Rambunctious ramblings and the smell of booze filled the rafters, as everyone within paid Leonardo no mind, mostly because they couldn't recognize him.

Leonardo sat at a cherry-red table towards the back of the dining room, out of sight and unassuming, calmly blending into the crowd. He found it ironic that he was forced to be just another face, a nobody in the crowd that blended into the forgotten multitude around him. *Or maybe it's my punishment,* he thought. *My Hell before Hell.* He leaned forward and popped off the bottle's cork, then smelled the fumes of rigid alcohol, burning his nose. He scrunched his nose, making a face, only to lift the bottle to his lips and sip the liquid down as gently as possible. It burned and scratched as it clawed its way down his throat, forcing him to grit his teeth and close his eyes, an expression of pain falling upon his face.

"I take it you've never had a brandy before," a cajun voice said from across Leonardo's table.

His eyes shot open as the familiar accent shot anxiety through him. Quickly, it was eased as he looked at the young woman who had joined him. She appeared to be the same age as him, and was as beautiful as she was mysterious. He stared at her, bewildered by her looks and taken by the amount of interest she had shown in him. He looked at the clothing she was wearing, then her body, his eyes moving over her figure. Her left hand was placed on the table, its softness and delicacy contrasting with the crispness of her white button-up shirt, leading to her left collar, left unbuttoned. It was unbuttoned two buttons down, revealing a fair amount of her cleavage, proving to be very distracting. Her right arm rested beneath the table upon her black jeans that hiked up to the middle of her stomach, which covered her hips that were magnificent as well.

Her lips were a thin, yet perfectly pale pink, and her skin was a glowing, light white. Her face was lean and perfectly complemented the thinness of her figure, while her hair fell in beautifully smooth waves past her shoulders. She was fit and lean, from what Leonardo could tell, and appeared to be in great shape. He looked up at her hat, noting it was a black Reno hat, complete with a perfect, circular brim that slightly bent upward on the left and right sides, and a straight, oval-shaped top. Beneath it, he saw her eye, examining the light brown color, with an orange yet yellow hue at the center, burning in the light.

He smiled at her. She smiled back, and each looked the other over, examining each other's features and enjoying each other's company.

"Is it that obvious?" Leonardo answered, smiling.

"You wan't someone to help you wash it down?" She flirted.

Leonardo slid the drink to her. She lifted it and took a small drink, immediately smacking her lips, then placed the bottle on the table, the alcohol slightly dribbling through her smiling lips. He chuckled as she raised her left wrist to her face, cleaning the droplets from her chin.

"I take it that was your first time, too?" He humored.

"First time with one that strong," she corrected.

The two held eye contact once again, now far more at ease and engaged than before. She leaned toward Leonardo with a sweet smile. "What's your name, stranger?" She asked.

"Why do you want to know?" he redirected.

"Isn't it obvious?" She flirted, batting her eyes.

He chuckled. "Where are you from?" He asked again.

"Oh, I see," she said, leaning back, reserved. "You're a man of secrets, huh? A man of *mystery*." She sarcastically raised her hands and waved them. "Or were you just born with a lack of manners?"

"I'm only cautious. That's all."

"So you're gonna make me go first?"

Leonardo shrugged. She rolled her eyes, then looked back at him and bit her bottom lip, leaning forward and resting her palm. She stared flirtily at Leonardo as she looked him up and down, examining every detail of the outlaw.

"My name's Lily. To answer your question, I'm from Louisiana. Me and my father," she said.

"That explains the accent," he joked.

"Yes, that would explain the accent," she laughed.

He thought about revealing his identity to her, for though she was a stranger, she was the first friendly face that he had shared a conversation with in a long time. He breathed calmly through his nostrils as he decided to lighten up just a bit, looking between each of her flirtatious eyes. "My name's Leonardo DelMuerto. I was born and raised here in Arizona."

Lily smiled as she sat upright, adjusting herself to rest her arm upon the table once again.

"You see? Was that so difficult for you? All that bush beatin' just for you to say a name like it *means* somethin'," she poked.

"It means more than Lily," he poked back.

Lily smiled as she looked between each of his eyes, tensing slightly.

"So," Leonardo continued. "Are you here with your father, or are you on your own?"

"Why? You fancy meetin' him?"

Leonardo laughed as he looked down at the table, caught off guard by Lily's forwardness. "No, no. I'm just making conversation."

"Well, Mr.Muerto, we know two things: one, you are an honest man, and two, you are quite the disrespectful one." She laughed. "Either way, it seems like you are a man worth baggin' nonetheless."

Leonardo leaned in. "If that be so, one thing you can be sure of is it'll be the best bag of your life."

He smiled seductively.

"Oh, absolutely," she smiled back, her eyes straining.

She looked at the table and feigned a sigh. "It don't matter, anyway. You'd never be able to meet him."

"Why's that?"

"He died a few months ago," she shifted, her eyes darting up at Leonardo as she thought about the last image she had of her father.

"Oh, I'm... sorry to hear that," he forced.

"No need for empty apologies. Mr. Muerto... they won't get you any further in the sack that you're already going to be in."

Leonardo's blood began to rush. "Okay, sure, but condolences are condolences, no?"

"Not empty ones." She looked down at the table and began picking at the wood with her index finger. "Besides... I'd be lyin' if I said he wasn't bound to die sooner or later." She looked up. "He was a man of many complexes."

"I see. Well, to assure you that the condolences are true, I want you to know that I understand what you are going through." He interlocked his fingers. "I lost my parents at a very young age. The people who took care of me in their place... they've all died, too."

"I'm sorry to hear that."

He shrugged, looking down at the table. "I think they were bound to such a fate as well, long before they died." He looked up. "We all must face the consequences of our actions."

Lily nodded slowly, thinking about the truth in his statement.

"You know, my father was a vengeful man. He was always plottin' to destroy the world since the world destroyed him. At least, that's how he saw it. He was a nobody without a penny to his name, fightin' the world like the Devil. I suppose we can all find some relatability in that... sometimes we all want to coat the world in oil and throw a match atop it." She shook her head. "The world he wanted people to see was a world he lived in every day. One of anarchy and chaos; a godless world headed by a godless nation, filled with lies and deceit. But his methods... once I discovered what they were... I couldn't believe it. I never could get behind such ideas of a dark and harrowin' world that he had tried so many times to convince me existed, or at the very least, he had created. He wanted to create a world where men became monsters and monsters became *killers*. Where wicked men were revered as heroes and preachers were viewed as villains. Every one of them just *huntin'* and *preyin'* on one another like animals. Come to find out, in the end, he succeeded." She looked into Leonardo's eyes, hers straining.

"The truth is," she continued, "a vengeful anarchy can only end in pain and bloodshed. It is chaos let loose upon the face of the world that destroys all who dare to step in front of it, and I can't understand why a man would want that—what good any of it could produce, though I know that's not the idea. That's just how I'm tryin' to make it make sense in my head, is all." Her mouth straightened, nearly angry. "Gone are the days of godly men, and heeyuh are the days of the forgotten and the wicked, destined to live their lives in misery and sorrow as men of darkness who take vengeance into their own hands as opposed to leavin' it in the hands of the Lord." She clenched her jaw, forcing a smile. "I only wonder... what happens when we run out of godly men? What happens to us now?"

Leonardo slowly tensed as he noticed Lily's tone shift. He leaned back in his chair gently and adjusted his hips to better position himself in front of Lily defensively, staring into her eyes with a newfound wariness. "Yes," he agreed, "the tragedy of man and all his downfalls... much like your father, I assume?"

"Exactly like my father." She looked down, shaking her head. "His death was a terrible thing." She looked off into the crowd of people. "I was under a carriage that had been parked off to the side of my home, hidden away from the winter's cold while my house lit ablaze. I had my father's gun, which I had found on the floor as I just barely escaped with my life."

Leonardo's heart raced.

"See," she continued, looking back at him, "my home had caught fire in a wild fight that my father was having with a young man. It was a deadly tussle, and for the record, I'd wager it was my father's fault, given his radical tendencies. Nonetheless, as the buildin' crumbled and nearly crushed me to death, I saw him fightin' with every inch of his life, brutally beatin' and defendin' himself in the muddied snow... but he couldn't fight... not in the state he was in." Her face started to get angrier. "I saw the man he fought plunge my own father's knife *deep* into his chest, and was forced to watch his corpse as I waited for the Union soldiers to leave. Once they had, I ran up to him and looked him over, seeing his burned and bloodied remains. I watched him die, like I have watched so many others after him."

"Who the hell are you?" Leonardo asked, panicked.

"Uh-uh-uh," she said, raising her finger and wagging it with each tut. "I'm not finished." She tensed. "See, I know my father was a wicked man, but he was still my father. I know he was filled with evil, but there was more to him than that. There was good in him, somewhere; otherwise, why didn't he just abandon me? He gave me more than my mother ever did, that's for sure." She forced out a laugh. If only there were someone who could have steered him in a different direction, right?" She sighed. "Anyway, what he did was more than enough, as a *father*, but after all that, I thought to myself, 'Why must we do this? Why must we fight and kill? What could it be that takes a man to such a level that he would soon stack bodies and be coated in blood, rather than save his fellow man, to attain his vengeance, to satisfy his bloodlust? Why must we bring such pain and misery to each other rather than peace and mercy? And then it occurred to me," she snapped her finger, pointing at Leonardo. "That's just it! It's all for nothin'! It all means nothin', because it leaves everyone and everything *with* nothin'. Vengeance empties but does not fill; it takes but does not give; it bloodies but does not clean; it burns but does not wash. This retribution... it does not restore." She slowly placed her hand on the table. "As time goes on, I find myself siding more with God on the matter than any other, for how can *anything* Man does ever be justified? What else is there for man to do, other than destroy?" She smiled. "I have heard it said that the best revenge is livin' well, at least that's what the believer down the road says. You know: turnin' the other cheek. And, honestly, after all I've seen, I have to say... I agree. I would much rather be alive and livin' well than dead after livin' low, especially if I was dead and didn't know it yet; if I was a *nobody* walkin', talkin', killin' and takin', just the same as all the rest of those who died before me." Her arm tensed. "And that's it, Mr. Muerto? That's just it. That's the price of retribution."

Leonardo reached for his revolver as Lily's hammer clicked under the table, halting him in his place. She slowly leaned back in her chair, her eyes piercing through to his soul. "Put your hands on the table, Muerto. We're not done talkin' yet."

His face twisted angrily as he placed his hands on the table, glancing at her right arm that held the weapon.

"I want to make myself clear," she continued, "I'm not here to take part in your cycle of violence; I'm not here to further the objective of my father. I am here, Mr. Muerto, because in the four months you've had to choose to be somethin' better, you have chosen to be a *monster*. You could've been a husband to your fiancé, a preacher to the lost, but *instead* you have blackened your heart, racking up a bounty in the most innocent of towns, for the very acts you once preached against." She scoffed. "My... how rotten the fruit becomes once it has fallen from the tree, wouldn't you say?" She adjusted in her seat. "I am not here for retribution because it is an act reserved for *fools*. I am here to end it and bring peace upon these lands. I will do what you 'men of God' have failed to do, and maybe, once all is said and done, we can all begin to heal from the *nobodies* that have left it in turmoil, that contribute to the chaos." She smiled and gestured toward him with her head. "Like you."

Leonardo forced out a laugh, shaking his head.

"You're not lying. You're right." He looked her over again, putting the pieces together. "You're a bounty hunter?"

"Bein' anything other would make me a hypocrite."

"I see." He clicked his tongue. "Bad time to get into the business, no?"

"I'm not in it for the money, Muerto. I was always in it for *you*."

He nodded as he realized what was unfolding before him, thinking of any way he could get out of it.

"This is exactly what he wanted, you know. You, here, killing me, publicly. He wanted to make me a spectacle for all to see, for the papers to report." He sighed, feigning empathy. "What you're doing won't change anything. It won't help anyone. If anything, the moment you kill me, the moment the people see me dead, see what I have become, their spirits will be crushed. Their faith will be destroyed. If I had not killed him, the only difference would be that he would have done all this himself."

"Don't act like you give a damn about these people, and do yourself a favor in understanding that you cannot and *will not* manipulate me. The bottom line is that my father, the one you call 'Icarus,' had a choice just the same as you. Those choices had consequences, just like yours will. You took matters into your own hands. You didn't need to kill him... that's the dumbest part. I saw the soldier. He would have done it just fine, but you *wanted* to. You robbed him of his purpose, and you did it because you wanted to." She shook her head, scoffing again. "You never learn, do you? You have no concept of consequence. You are a loose cannon, armed with revolvers that don't even belong to you, that you didn't *earn*. You live a lie, just as you always have... It's time people know the truth. *That's* what they deserve."

Leonardo smiled out of his right cheek, shaking his head and looking down at the table before him.

"You got nothin' to say for yourself?" She asked.

"No," Leonardo replied.

Lily halfway smiled, almost sorry for Leonardo. He had become the very thing he hated, the very enemy he preached against, all by his own hand. She rose to her feet, revealing Icarus's gun belt around her waist, his gun held firm and in her right hand. He looked up and down the barrel, only this time he saw that it was loaded. He also saw the burn scars on the inside of her palm, detailing what seemed to be the outline of heated metal from the weapon. She slowly dropped the gun to her hip so as not to draw too much attention, as Leonardo looked to the right side of the gun belt and saw a burnt, browned sheepskin that was attached to her holster. "You ready?" She asked. "Yeah... I'm ready," he answered.

He stood slowly as she walked around behind him. "Stand up and walk forward, straight to the front. You reach for that gun, you'll have six bullets in you before it ever leaves its holster," she threatened. Leonardo continued his walk outside, the bottle of brandy being his last remnant on the table. Lily switched the revolver to her left hand so that the two dozen people inside the building would not react to the threatening scene, alerting Rosa and Bozco, who shared an exchange as they saw the stranger being forced outside at gunpoint.

Leonardo walked out the front door of Hotel Emilda, Lily closely behind him, ensuring that every once in a while, he felt the barrel poke the center of his back. "Go to the street. Dead center," she ordered, distancing herself from him. He did as he was told, the Aland Theatre's luminescent lighting the right side of his face in its familiar orange color. He looked it over, then followed it down to one particular, familiar area: it was the corner of the street just before the theatre, where a soapbox he had once stood upon was still there, just in view, as it had been many years prior. *They left it for me,* he thought. *I can't believe they left it for me.*

It was then he thought about his brothers and the people of his hometown. He saw their faces, or what little he could remember of them. Oddly, it was comforting. This was new for him, and it came with a feeling of closeness to them that he had never had before.

He thought about what Lily had said regarding the healing that would occur once the people knew the truth. Leonardo felt it was somewhat unorthodox how this healing would happen, but if there were no longer lies to plague the people, then they could finally seek the truth—the one that he claimed to represent, though he never really believed he did. They could finally have that hope, that relationship with the Lord, being led by someone far more capable than him. *Perhaps,* he thought, *there was some validity in exposing the fraudulent preacher, for if proving that some men of God were not as they claimed meant the people could be better than they were, then it was worth the price that needed to be paid.* Leonardo knew that after a death like his, there would be no more hiding for men like him; there would be no more wolves in sheep's clothing, at least here. Instead, the people would see what happens to the one who walks as a roaring lion, though not the actual one, so they might never draw near to it again. Instead, they would draw near to the authentic voice of the Lord, not men such as himself, who would sooner pay for his deception with this one final charge than be paid millions by deciding. With a hopeful thought, he figured this would be an undeniable act of good: setting the people free from his illusion.

"Preacher," Lily called out.

He looked at her.

"I gotta ask," she continued, "was it worth it, bein' a soap-box deceiver, and all?"

He was silent for a moment. "No. It wasn't," he answered honestly.

Lily almost pitied him, not because she thought he was redeemable, but because it was tragically ironic that he had finally learned his lesson at the end of his life. Because of this pity, she decided to give him the choice as to how he wanted to die, in a way she had heard the soldier do before her. "Would you rather die a man, or die a monster?" She inquired.

He looked at Icarus's revolver, thinking about the question he was asked as it aimed at his chest. "I would rather die a man," he replied.

Lily looked at his hands and saw them rest at his sides; the rest of his body relaxed as well, and his tension left him. She nodded her head as she raised her revolver, pointing it forward, fully extending her arm, and turning her body sideways. "So be it," she finished.

Icarus's revolver flashed brightly in the night, the crack of the gunshot echoing through the streets of Little York, alerting all in the vicinity. The bullet tore through his chest, throwing him backward with a violent thrust, then slamming him back-first onto the street. Pain shot through his right lung as he stared at the stars above him, noting their beauty in all their vastness, as the taste of blood crept up his throat and into his mouth. Lily marched over to him quickly as the people within the streets and Hotel Emilda watched in fear. She arrived, stood above him, and looked down, as Leonardo looked past her, continuing to take in the wonders of the heavens and those who waited within. She clicked the hammer again, pointed the gun at his head, and as she did, Leonardo thought of the one he once loved, seemingly seeing her in the stars.

He thought of Sophia.

Lily fired Icarus's revolver, blasting a hole into Leonardo's forehead, forcing his body to jerk and go limp suddenly. Blood formed behind his head as his eyes lifelessly stared into the sky, while Lily backed away and readied herself for the coming maelstrom. The people screamed, prompting the members of the Hotel Emilda to rush to the window and look at what had happened, noting the dead body. Lily quickly reached into her back pocket with her left hand and dropped the revolver in her right, leaving it to clink against the brick in the street as she unfolded the papers she pulled out. Whistles blared from the Sheriff's Office as the sheriff came rushing forward, rifle in hand, with eight men behind him. *"Get on your knees!"* The sheriff ordered. She raised both of her arms and surrendered immediately, the unfolded papers in the air, then slowly got to her knees as she continued to keep the wanted poster held high. The officers arrived.

"My name is Lily Barnesworth. The man lying dead before me is known as Leonardo Del Muerto, or the Dead Man. The wanted poster in my left hand is complete with the warrant for his arrest or execution," She quickly informed.

The sheriff slowed down in front of Lily as the people murmured, for each one knew, in some capacity, who Leonardo was. He walked over to Leonardo's body, recognizing the young man underneath the beard and the change of attire. He looked at him in horror as the people waited to hear the confirmation, for each was unwilling to believe the accusations Lily had made.

"It would do us all some good if you would make a quick call to the town known as Poachers Creek. Ask for Sheriff Hopper. He'll know who I am and who Mr. Muerto is. They'll be able to back up every word I've said," she advised, noticing the sheriff was frozen.

He walked over to Lily and ripped the papers from her hand, quickly reading each one to determine if what she said was true. As he read, his eyes slowly widened as he realized Lily had not lied "Murder? Robbery? Arson?" He asked, looking over to Lily. She slowly stood to her feet, one boot at a time. She dropped her arms in surrender and gently walked closer to him. "Sheriff, before we continue, can you please tell your men to drop the aim of their weapons? I see no need for more people to die, especially by accident."

He looked from Lily to the papers, then raised his hands to his men. "Put your guns away, gentlemen." He looked at her. "The woman speaks true."

The deputies dropped the aim of their rifles as the audience around murmured further, getting on their toes and bobbing their heads to look at Leonardo's body.

"Apologies for the scare, Ms. Barnseworth... you'll have to understand, this town has had a history with extreme violence... these days we can't help but assume the worst," the sheriff apologized.

"It's quite all right, Sheriff. I understand." She looked at Leonardo's body. "Some-times there's far more curses than blessings." She looked back. "But rest assured in knowin' your curses have been lifted."

"I certainly hope so."

He looked down at the body as well and shook his head, his eyes dropping with sadness. "I feel it's only fair to warn you, the press will want to hear about this. They've been following Leo far longer than you."

"I'm aware, and that's just fine," she assured. "I have statements prepared."

"Well... isn't that swell," he sighed. "I would've never expected something like this from him."

"We rarely suspect the Devil when he takes the form of an angel, sir," she said, looking down at Leonardo's body as well.

The people watched, witnessing the preacher's final sermon: one that was to be heeded by all who would lend an ear. To them, it was one for all generations to understand and remember forevermore. And they would, hearing this preaching sound further than Leonardo had ever rung, swifter than any of his messages from before. It was one he exem-plified louder than he ever roared.

And it was simple, *so* simple: that vengeance, oh, bloody vengeance, was in the hands of the Lord.

BOOKS BY JOHN ANDERSON

POETRY

Parable
Song of Cedar *(coming soon)*
Curtains
Lights *(coming soon)*

FICTION

The Price of Salvation: An American Legend
The Price of Retribution: An American Tragedy
The Price of Revelation: An American End (coming soon)

RELIGION, SPIRITUALITY, AND PHILOSOPHY

American Made: Volume I
American Made: Volume II (coming soon)

John Anderson is an award-winning poet, songwriter, playwright, novelist, and a Christian, as well as an escapee from the Message cult of personality. He lives in North Carolina, enjoys nature, is a cinephile, loves cats, and his wife. For his ministry, he seeks to lead people to Christ through biblical practice, providing nuance and realism to the average person's walk with God through mixed media. Currently, he's working on expanding into acting, delving deeper into theatrical writing, and contributing to the ongoing effort to combat Christian cultism in America, with a particular current focus on the Message.

Above all, he remains a storyteller.

VISIT JOHN ANDERSON ONLINE

linktr.ee/johnandersonbookworks

OnWithJohn

johnandersonauthor 📷 ♪

HOW TO FEED AN AUTHOR

Dearest Readers,

Thank you for taking the time to read this text and for your support. This is the fourth of many independently published texts I will be doing, and your support, though singular, is not in the least minuscule or devalued. To that end, I again come to you with another plea: to write a review of this book. Reviews are essential to this book's success and a game-changer in any small author's career. I'd greatly appreciate it if you wrote an honest review on the website where you purchased this text, especially on Amazon and Goodreads. Even if you didn't buy it there, please head over and write one. It matters and means a lot.

You can also share this book on social media, recommend it to friends and family, engage with the content online, subscribe to and follow the YouTube channel and other social media, create fan content, participate in discussions at your local book club, forum, or online discussion boards, and, of course, gift it as a recommendation to your local library or book club.

Once again, thank you all so much for your support, and may God bless you.

—John

QUESTIONS FOR DISCUSSION

1. The author's "Warning from the Author" describes the journey as "dark, graphic, violent, and scary," a "story of desolation and darkness," in contrast to a previous novel of "hope and light". How does this explicit thematic framing influence your philosophical engagement with the narrative, particularly concerning the necessity of "mature elements" to convey "crucial message and themes it explores"?

2. Michelangelo embodies the "Saint of Retribution," believing himself "the wrath of God come to pass judgment upon monsters." Discuss the philosophical tension between personal vengeance and objective justice as portrayed through Michelangelo's actions and internal conflicts. How does his journey, particularly his interactions with William and Rosa, challenge or solidify his understanding of what constitutes a "just" act?

3. The text grapples with the definition of "man" versus "monster." Characters like William Davidson struggle with this identity, claiming "I'm not a monster," while Michelangelo concludes "these days they're all the same." Analyze how Icarus's self-identification as "the wolf who killed the sheep" and his actions at Guarida Del León further complicate this distinction. Does the narrative ultimately offer a clear line between humanity and monstrousness?

4. Icarus presents a philosophy of free will within a predetermined universe, stating, "We are all believers and disbelievers in a universe ruled by God. We are like His ink spots on a page written before the dawn of time. All pre-planned. Predestinated." How does this view of fate and choice shape Icarus's mission to "challenge God" and his interactions with Leonardo, who initially struggles with God's "sovereign will" versus his own desire for control?

5. Leonardo DelMuerto, initially confident in his role as "the last remaining bible of the West", faces a profound crisis of faith when Icarus critiques his evangelism as "never legitimate." How does Icarus's method of exposing perceived hypocrisy among believers, and Leonardo's subsequent disillusionment and desire for "blood for blood," challenge the philosophical foundations of faith and spiritual leadership in a chaotic world?

6. The concept of legacy and remembrance is central to many characters. Caine Kingsley asserts his "legacy provides for thousands" and rejects the idea of being "forgotten memories." In contrast, Michelangelo contemplates his own "legend" and his eventual desire to be "forgotten." Discuss how these contrasting perspectives on lasting impact motivate or torment these characters, particularly after events like "The Little York Massacre."

7. The narrative explicitly portrays a breakdown of established law and order, with Michelangelo stating that "the law allowed for monsters to massacre." Explore the philosophical implications of this societal collapse. How do characters like William, who defends "law and order" as that "which separates the men from the monsters", and Captain Mathews, who acknowledges governmental inaction, reflect differing views on the role and efficacy of institutions in combating evil?

8. The story delves into the purpose of suffering and sacrifice. Sophia Rivera denounces her faith to Icarus to save Leonardo from being alone, stating, "I did it for you, so you wouldn't be alone." How does this act of personal sacrifice, alongside Leonardo's internal struggles with the suffering of his people, contribute to the text's philosophical exploration of love, loss, and the potential for meaning or futility in adversity?

9. William Davidson's journey highlights the struggle for redemption and self-for-giveness. Despite his past betrayals, including setting up Thomas for the bounty, William seeks to "make right my wrongs" and save Michelangelo, seeing it as a path to absolution. How does Michelangelo's initial skepticism about William's change reflect a broader philosophical question about the possibility of funda-mental change and the nature of forgiveness in a brutal world?

10. The text raises the question, "Is it better to live in a realm of brutal reality, or to be fine with our justified illusions?" How do various characters—including Leonardo after his confrontation with Icarus, Michelangelo with his "willful ignorance" regarding William, and Caine Kingsley with his "visionary" justifica-tion of his actions—navigate the tension between harsh truths and comforting deceptions? What philosophical message does this convey about human coping mechanisms in times of tragedy?

"Beloved, never avenge yourselves, but leave it to the wrath of God, for it is written, 'Vengeance is mine, I will repay, says the Lord.' "

— Romans 12:19

ANDERSON BOOKWORKS